PRAISE FOR
STELLA ATRIUM

"Stella Atrium's writing is fluid and her superior storytelling skills leave a spell on readers, forcing them to keep on turning the pages… Peppered with stunning commentaries and drama, it sure packs a punch for fans of science fiction with resonant themes."

– The Book Commentary

"…having spent my own entire childhood in a third-world country, I know what living under martial law looks like. I know what the refugee experience feels like. I know what it means to be viewed in a foreign land as 'other' and 'less than'…and Stella Atrium nails it."

– Asher Syed for Readers' Favorites

"Addressing fears of recreating oppressive traditions on other worlds, this space colonization novel is far more than standard sci-fi, the series is a femme-led examination of our societal ills, and a celebration of the strength found through open-mindedness and sisterhood."

– Self-Publishing Review

HOME RULE

BOOK III OF THE TRIBAL WARS

STELLA ATRIUM

Stella Atrium Writes
3023 N Clark Street
Suite 762
Chicago, IL 60657

Ordering Information:

Quantity sales. Special discounts are available on quantity purchases by corporations, associations, and others. For details, contact the publisher at the address above.

Orders by U.S. trade bookstores and wholesalers. Please contact Stella Atrium Writes: ADMIN@STELLAATRIUM.COM

Printed in the United States of America

ISBN (paperback): 978-1-958959-07-7

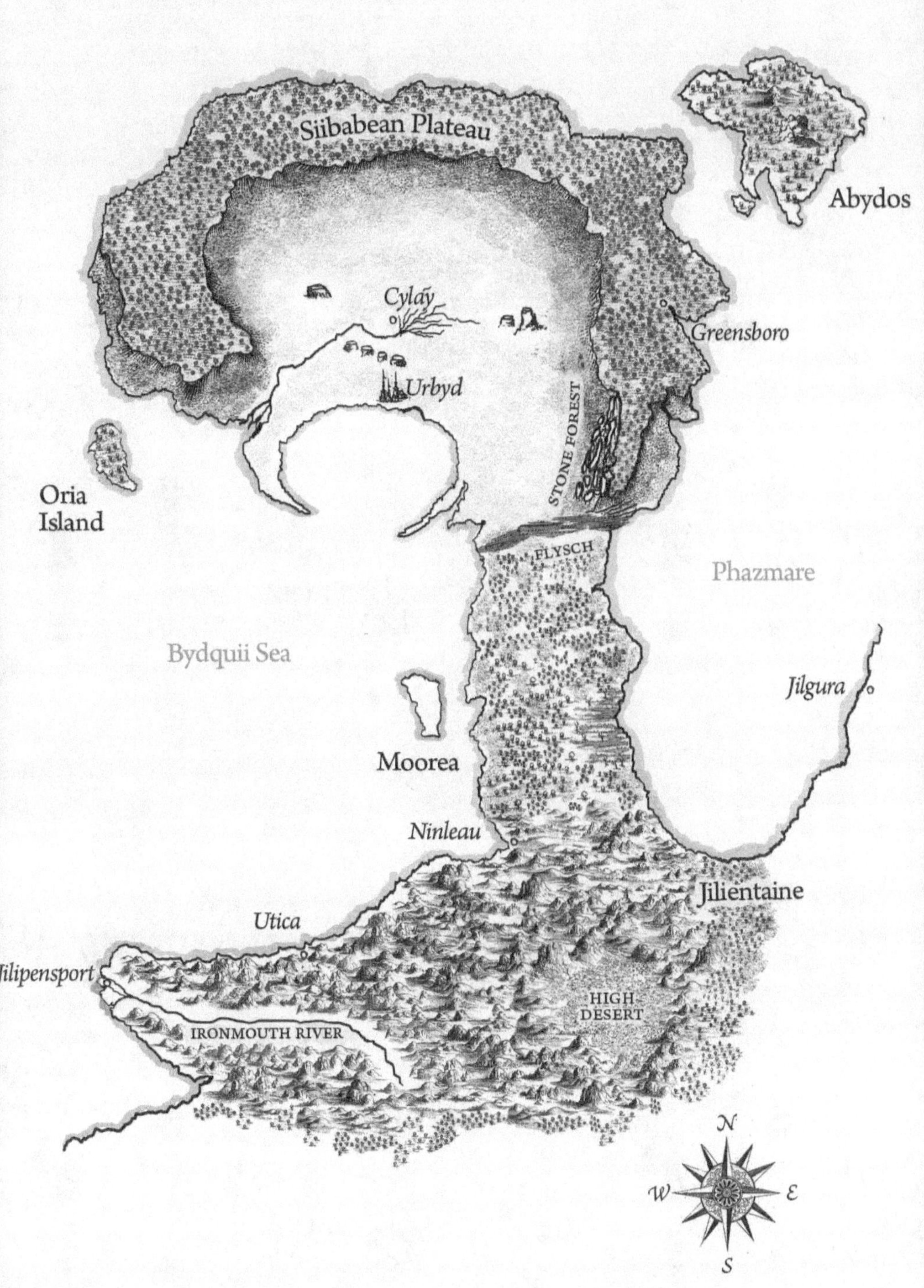

Siibabean Plateau
Abydos
Cylay
Greensboro
Urbyd
STONE FOREST
Oria
Island
FLYSCH
Phazmare
Bydquii Sea
Jilgura
Moorea
Ninleau
Jilientaine
Utica
Jilipensport
HIGH
DESERT
IRONMOUTH RIVER
N
W   E
S

For the reader's convenience, a glossary of character names with relationships, and a separate glossary of locations and terms, are found at the end of this book.

BOOKS BY STELLA ATRIUM

Seven Beyond

The Bush Clinic: Book I of The Tribal Wars
The Body Politic: Book II of The Tribal Wars
Home Rule: Book III of The Tribal Wars
Brittany Mill: A Dolvia Origins Story

PART ONE

Festival fire dying in the dawn
Embers shift, a spray of sparks
Unrecounted ancestors linger
Impatient for quickening
A warrior this time; never an unblessed one

Dolvia slumbers, blanketed by netta
Her contours known, and her familiars
Forces never stirring, a warrior alone
With lazy Nettki and ascendant Nettom
Forever and anon, Mekucoo need only the land

Our time like a breath on the wind
More erratic than Tunanin
Unspoken words like stones on the heart
What gesture in the presence of ancestors?
What words say more than a lingering glance?
Halting moments weave into the textured past

– Kelly Osborn

PROLOGUE

from Kelly Osborn

I MUST GIVE MY CONFESSION HERE. NOT FOR ME SO MUCH, OR for the record: more so young people know the reasons for our actions. I'm Kelly Osborn and I was part of the battle of Iamida shores. Arrivi won the river conflict but with heavy losses. I was nineteen and assigned to stay with the children of those in leadership since there was no time to evacuate. As the betrothed of Rufus, I was to watch over Colonel Sector's girls and the other children in the village schoolroom.

Our station was overrun by Borabean warriors of the Gora clan. We heard them outside our hiding place; running footsteps and bursts of gunfire, the sound so different from a karkar's report. My heartbeat was in my ears, and I felt 12-year-old Millie trembling next to me, not knowing if we would be dragged onto the street for rape or hacking off our arms. Tears marked Millie's face while she huddled with her sister Anna.

The door was flung open. A bearded man in galabia and boots stood with lowered gun and a bloodied knife. In my memory, the blinding sun behind him was tinged blood red. His dark eyes surveyed us, assessing what treasure he had found. Children whimpered and hugged the walls. A knot formed in my throat. Sweat moistened the hair at my temples.

The Gora man slung the weapon's strap over his shoulder and reached for Millie and her sister. He cuffed Millie by the neck of her tunic and dragged them outside, clinging to each other and limp against his rough gestures.

"Kelly, Kelly," Millie cried. "Help us!"

I bolted after him. I had a large kitchen knife and nothing else. But it was wrong what he was doing, just plain wrong. Before he was aware of my move, I sliced across his liver from behind. His back arched and he blindly reached behind, but I jumped away. I jabbed under his ribs with my graceless knife where he was exposed due to his own gesture. Thrust in-and-up as we had learned from Omiibuk. His brow furled while he stared at me. He looked down at his galabia quickly soaking with blood.

He still grasped Millie's tunic when his knees buckled and he collapsed in the doorway. The girls were pulled down on top of him, but they screamed and scrambled away. I wasn't actually thinking; I mean, forming thoughts. I remember kneeling beside the body before I balanced his automatic across his round shoulder, and the girls gathered behind me. I pulled off my glasses smeared with blood and worked the trigger many times sending a spray of bullets.

Millie grabbed plastic ammo clips from the fallen and handed them to me to fit into the weapon. Tat-tat-tat-tat. I saw bearded men fall and did not care that I wounded them from behind; I was uncaring about that.

Finally the gun was empty, the long barrel hot and smoking.

I remember that Omiibuk, wife to Karlyhi, came to my side amid the battle with praise for my first knife kill and how I had saved the next generation. She dipped her thumb in Gora blood and decorated my forehead with the mark of arisen Rularim. "Twice baptized in blood, Kelly Osborn," she said because I also saw the massacred village of Kyros Kenoma. My chest throbbed with self-hatred, and I heard a ringing in my ears. I searched the ground for my glasses while Omiibuk kicked sand over my shameful vomit.

Rufus was in the yard. He stopped in his tracks, his face stony, and glanced around to assess our exposure. His hair was loose on his shoulders. His arms were bloody up to the elbows, and spray from Gora wounds speckled his uniform. I caught an odor like burning tree bark. He nodded to Omiibuk and resumed his work amid the fighting warriors.

Omiibuk later lauded my 'great deed' to the others, and spoke to Rufus who said nothing. I felt ashamed and dirty. Much later on his return from the battle, Colonel Sector hugged Millie and her sister with tears watering his blue eyes. He stood and shook my hand in the Softcheeks manner, a high honor for me. Millie and I never spoke of that day.

Aegiv the lawgiver was killed in the melee. Madquii fighters were despondent until the second son Aeolis accepted Aegiv's mantle of leadership. Aeolis called for a time of fertility to replace the fallen.

Arrivi fighters assented to the custom, and many women laid down weapons for a season, their babies to harbor recounted souls.

And we knew a long season of netta. The parched savannah watered only with tribal blood supported few hyacinth vines or shoots of oleastra. Arrivi herds left the veld, migrating in clutches to the north grazeland. Brianna Miller sat for long hours with Karlyhi and Dacupitte in the village north of Mayschool where we slept sometimes. I still served but there were no lessons, no afternoons spent giggling over idle stories about a fabled robe of blue feathers. Brianna's heart was stone, her jaw rigidly set.

Campfire chants about Brianna as Rularim Arisen were numerous, the hero of the uprising. Militia members from all tribes sported the forehead mark made with gray ash or red paint, like the symbol for finding a square root of something.

Finally, Brianna noticed me. It was at one communal meeting or another; we tolerated many among the far-flung villages. She had cut her hair to cling to her temples only, claiming she had no time to care for its length. She wore the mottled militia uniform of the clutch of Murd and lightweight boots, along with a necklace of silicide and tektite beads. There was no animation in Brianna's face, just lines of care and the determined jaw.

"Kelly, you are now attached to the clutch of Kenru and may sleep near Dulcinea's place." I had envied others who were trained at Dulcinea's table. Now I felt rejected, pushed out of the leadership circle due to my shameful acts during the battle of Iamida shores.

With her hands on my shoulders, Brianna turned me toward her. "I will join you in a few days," she said. "We can have a nice talk like we used to." I forced a smile, but I knew karsci had done its work on all of us. Our friendship could never be like it was before.

ONE

from Hershel Henry

DKAR WAS MY LANDLORD IN CYLAY. A PUTUKI MAN WITH BULGING eyes that judged everything, he owned a converted warehouse eight blocks from the governor's house, if you can call them blocks. I paid rent for two rooms above the storefront where Cylahi-constructed furniture was sold to the newly rich residents of the Putuki city section. People on the street did not bother me much, sometimes to beg alms. My rooms were tossed and robbed, however, whenever I left to pursue a news story.

Aging and maimed warriors lingered in Cylay; desperate women with toddlers, free-roaming fowl and pigs. Electricity came on for two hours a day and the faucets never worked. Rabbenu Ely and the Putuki bazaari still held authority in Cylay, but rabbenu provided few services to the people. Unblessed ones, as poor residents were called, understood little of where the city funds originated and why foreign aid arrived at the governor's mansion.

I was in Dkar's office to lodge a complaint about being robbed again. Dkar sat in a squeaky chair behind a desk scrounged from an abandoned hotel. "The thefts are friendliness, Hershel Henry," he said. "Their way of saying that you are useful to them."

"Look, if you refuse to take my complaint seriously—"

"I like you, Softcheeks," he interrupted. "You can feel safe here. Safe as long as you allow the activity. If you should bother Putuki police about the theft, well . . . that's different, huh?"

"Is that a threat? Are you making a threat?"

"I want to help you, Henry. I'm helping here. Tomorrow we go to the bazaar, and there we find your solution." Dkar leaned forward with a grin, showing the absence of two teeth on the left side. "Trust me."

I had washed the insect repellent from my hair and beard, now a silvery blond against tan skin. I wore the dungarees and shirt of the clutch of Kenru, provided to me when I first visited Uburu land. I had a field vest with notepad and light meter. And I constantly wore the sheathed beltknife that was a gift, more for show against the hungry eyes of local beggars than for soldiering.

I was forced to keep my cameras and everything but a change of clothes at the hotel Press Club. John Milan and other journalists jeered at me for preferring to live among the people, and I was beginning to get the message.

"You got a woman, Henry?" Doug Endicott guessed when I was sharing drinks with John Milan and Regan Villines at the Press Club. Endicott was the network dog who parceled out paychecks.

I squinted at his smirk. "Just closer to events."

"You stink of that slum," Endicott complained. "You bring their diseases in here."

"I'll try not to infect the tribes with your attitude."

"Why did you even come to Westend?" Endicott demanded. "What was it, Henry? The lure of exotic locales, or running away from a broken heart?"

"Where I come from, everything is broken. The savannah tribes have a purpose."

Endicott shook his head slightly. "So . . . it's the romance thing. Your tour will end six months early. Mark my words. You'll shake with malaria chills for a decade."

"Maybe not. Australian pioneer stock."

"An urban pioneer?" Endicott realized his drink was empty and stepped to the bar for a refill.

The comtech over the bar had the volume turned down, but the news clip replayed Rabbenu Ely announcing a new business in Cylay for an upstart stock exchange. The rotund rabbenu wore a dark suit and blue silk sash to designate his office. Ely made a stately stroll down a gilded hallway to step up to the podium and face reporters. Three suited Putuki men and General Sector in a starched uniform, head of Consortium peace-keeping troops in Cylay, crowded behind Ely.

"Ely has gained weight," Regan said derisively. "And he chose blue for that sash."

"Why blue?" I asked.

"Blue is forbidden on the savannah," Regan said, seated shoulder-to-shoulder with me. "In honor of the blue macaw, the god-agent of Rularim."

"What's a god-agent?" I asked.

"You have much to learn about the tribes, Henry." John Milan said. "It's like a witch has a black cat, but some animals can share dream images with favorites."

"With you?" I asked him.

John made a snorting noise and looked around for the waiter. He sighed and went to the bar to order, lingering with Endicott.

"Why does General Sector lend himself to this charade?" Regan asked as she watched the comtech news. "That's the real question."

We saw Ely encourage a shorter man in a blue suit to step up to the podium, further crowding the ministers.

"Manenowski! Can you believe it?" Regan said. Her weathered face and khaki clothes tagged her as a veteran reporter. "He was promoted to captain under General Sector," she added. "He resigned his commission for this new position as a stock trader. And Sector just stands there, like that turncoat act was nothing at all. Man, this job will make you cynical."

John returned with drinks for him and Regan but not for me. I took the hint. I headed out from the Press Club, just catching Regan's comment as she speculated to John Milan, "How much different from Henry's station in Australia is that slum alleyway?"

It was four days and two thefts later when Dkar knocked on my door. I laughed and shook my head. The doorjamb was splintered where the most recent thief had gained entry after I had bars installed on the windows.

"Come along then," he said without preamble.

The Cylay local bazaar was long established—a narrow walkway where vehicles found no purchase. We walked past six-by-six kiosks with stacked shelves. Unlicensed, I was thinking, and each with a souk who mostly lived there. I saw second-hand goods near the walkway, also some aging and bruised vegetables. We had to step across a couple of vendors to get to another kiosk with better goods. We struggled through a narrow section where herbalists sold amulets, talismans, and magic poteens. Finally, Dkar stopped at one counter that I could never find again from trying. I was instructed to buy blue macaw tail feathers.

I squinted. "Bird feathers?"

"Trust me," Dkar said with that slimy grin.

The feathers were expensive.

We returned to my rooms where Dkar tied the feathers over my doorjamb with string.

"A new temptation for theft," I complained. "They'll be gone in an hour."

"A good message you send with these," Dkar said. "Your power is greater than theirs."

"My power to be robbed again?"

"For you, the mark of Rularim is not needed," Dkar said. "You wear Brian Miller's beltknife." Brian Miller had fallen in the tribal wars long before I came to Dolvia. "But your house is not covered," Dkar added, "only your person. And Rularim's mark over the door-jamb? Well, everybody tries that. Her mantel does not extend to Cylay."

"Blue tail feathers are a deterrent?" I asked.

"A taboo color. The blue macaw lives at the fortress, maybe longer than Rularim lives there. These unblessed ones maybe see a spiritual risk, frightful dreams or a sour stomach later. Only a discarded gualarep toenail is better. Do you have one?"

"I'm afraid not."

"Ah, too bad."

And I was not robbed again after that. I brought clothes and equipment to my small space. Later I set up an EAM connection complete with a coolant unit and battery pack.

Kids brought water in buckets in exchange for kam, the Arrivi penny that was a circular plug of copper. Cylahi warriors traded tool-and-dye services for twists made from precious metals. The oblu was their twist equivalent to the silver quarter. Rabbenu Ely had paper money printed with his face on the front, but the denominations were too high for most street commerce.

Dressed only in cotton shorts, many with rust-colored hair and stunted by malnutrition, the kids gambled on the kam lottery. On any street corner, a kam-man loitered continuously. Nothing was written down so he needed to know customers for collection and payoffs. Our local kam-man was a Cylahi warrior who spoke Arrivi. White splotches showed on his arms and shoulders, the result of old burns where the pigment was gone. He was known as Blanc. Over time I had won Blanc's trust, and he agreed to bring any news. If a broadcast segment or article developed where I was the first reporter on the scene, he received a small gratuity; that was our deal. I learned about recent deaths at the hands of the brutal Putuki police and where the abortion clinic operated. Later I learned that Blanc knew some English, but why show his cards, huh? I told Blanc that I sought political news—what Rabbenu Ely was doing for the people.

"Not anything," Blanc said with a shrug. "Ely does nothing for these unblessed ones."

The rainy season was getting underway. The unmanaged sewage that was so offensive in the unrelenting heat, during the rains became a disease-carrying soup in the alleyway outside my window. I had a rubdown at the Press Club to relieve aching muscles and considered getting the flu shot distributed in Cylay by Consortium officers. Tribespeople stood in line at police stations and academies, at long tables under the Consortium flag—a backward C tangent to a P, powder blue, on a sky-blue background. Children cried after an injection in the arm and took sugary treats from officers who wore powder-blue tams that designated them as peacekeeping.

At the Press Club, I booted the EAM to catch up with correspondence. "Herschel Henry, hiki," the screen blinked, using the Arrivi greeting.

On the news channel, an announcer with china-doll makeup and a crisp English accent introduced an event showing Rabbenu Ely at the podium, facing reporters again. John Milan sat in the front row and was asking a long-winded question of the embattled leader. Did Ely support the order of impunity that protected Consortium officers from local laws, or did Ely support Karlyhi's famous tribal logic? Was Ely content with the presence of peacekeepers who weren't subject to tribal law? Was Ely content with the continued presence of a circle of elites like Carl Hartley who disregarded tribal law?

The stormy look on Ely's active face was all the answer I needed.

I called up old news footage of the immolation of Kyle Rula in the Cylay plaza. I had watched the clip a thousand times. I remembered when I had first viewed the orange conflagration that had devoured her. I was sitting in an over-lit lobby of a lawyer's office in Perth, waiting to settle my stepmother's estate. My half-brother Trevor Scott sat across from me in a row of chairs against the wall. He was twelve years younger and two inches shorter. His mouth was screwed into an ugly smirk.

"It all comes to me, you know," Trevor said. "Mine by right."

"The two properties and the stock certificates are yours. We are agreed."

"What do you care?" he asked hotly. "You're headed to the other side of the galaxy."

I had looked away from his smirk and watched the Perth news on the overhead comtech with the volume turned down. A segment was showing a woman sitting cross-legged in the middle of Cylay's plaza. She struck a match and dropped it onto her broad skirt. The fire was instant and harsh, maybe fueled by gasoline. Bystanders screamed or backed away, not understanding the purpose. I remembered I was unable to breathe that day in Perth, and coughed slightly to draw in the harsh air. It was the surprise that impacted me, especially from a muted comtech. Why would a person do that? What drove her to such a dreadful act?

Trevor had only squinted at the images on the news. "And you're so eager to report their troubles? People in Westend are just like us. No better than us."

I had signed the estate documents, barely listening as the lawyer explained that my father's assets had been placed in trust for my return from Westend, and Trevor Scott received what his mother's will had stipulated. I had walked out with Trevor still loudly complaining.

"Go ahead, run away!" he shouted from behind me. "That's what you always do."

Now seated at the Cylay Press Club, I called up footage of three more self-torchings. Little about Westend events made Earth's global news stations, but these immolations had been broadcast. While I was in Indonesia, boarding a flight for Beijing, Marcy's self-torching was replayed on the Earth news channels. I had nearly missed my connection because I watched the footage. Marcy was the former wife of Rabbenu Ely and had chosen Ely's day of triumph when he signed a treaty with Borabean. The plaza was full of off-world photographers eager to capture close-up footage. The angry fire on her skin and clothes looked blue-yellow in the harsh sunlight and quickly died out over her blackened form. Ely's elation at his treaty success was not reported; instead, the China-doll announcers speculated on why Marcy had acted on that day.

I was waiting at Stargate Junction when the third woman, Karima Le, had entered the rabbenu plaza for a similar act. She was obese and crippled, an older woman whose husband had died in that same season. The flash fire had left a charred skeleton with the fingers curled in anguish. Several women under burkas shuffled forward to collect the remains.

I had sighed heavily and heard some travelers around me sigh. News announcers began to support a narrative of empathy for tribal women rather than protest against the repressive rule of Rabbenu Ely.

I met Karen once, the fourth woman to sacrifice herself in the Cylay plaza. A divorcee and mother to Kelly Osborn, Karen was not destitute or grieving. She had kids and the promise of grandkids. Was living under the burka a burden too great?

I took the first opportunity I found to learn their motivations. At the Cylay barrack in the Consortium blue zone, I talked to Hakulupe Le who was the tribal wife of General Sector. "Did you know the women who torched themselves in the plaza?"

"All cousins to me," she had said. As an officer's wife, she wore no burka, and the forest green eyes flashed. "Kyle Rula was sister to Karima Le, and Karen was my cousin by marriage."

"And the other one? Marcy?" I asked.

"Marcy was one of Lucy's kids and thus a cousin to us all."

I didn't know what that phrase meant—Lucy's kid—but I had a few questions to ask. "I'm sorry," I'd said. "I didn't mean to pry."

"You may ask," Hakulupe Le had said in English. "Their public actions were meant to prompt Softcheeks like you to ask questions." Softcheeks was their word for adventurers from Earth like me.

"Yah, sure," I'd said. "What did the women hope to accomplish with death-by-fire?"

"We want Rabbenu Ely to step down." She extended one finger after another. "The end of the crony system. No more foreign aid. Free elections, and home rule."

"And when you get free elections, who will be the next rabbenu?"

"Pete, of course. You know him as Dacupitte."

I smiled, hoping to keep her talking. "But Ely passed a law that only a tribal person may be elected as rabbenu."

"Ely has passed many laws that must be adjusted," Hakulupe Le said with humor in those bright eyes. "Pete is Scots-Irish by blood; that part is true. Pete is ground-born and raised by Kecouroo."

"And you're certain he's the next rabbenu?"

"It is seen."

I had nodded and wondered what that phrase meant. It wasn't that the tribespeople were secretive so much, but rather that I had not found the right questions to ask.

Recently, a new ordinance was imposed to regulate the use of a household fire for cooking or some workshop activity. Each head of household must queue up at the governor's mansion to pay the fee and receive a home-and-hearth certificate that souks called the ely. They knew the paper was worthless. Ministers who were Rabbenu Ely's cronies claimed that the risk of spread from cooking fires dictated the regulation. The Cylay police selectively enforced restrictions on residents who managed to compete with Putuki. Souks were being regulated out of commerce.

The only residents who stood up to the brutal police were teenagers in street gangs, already carrying long rifles called karkars. They disabled a waiting lorry or taunted officers to lead them on a merry chase through the alleyways. The souks sometimes hid the kids and supported them with food and goods, but the defiance failed to change the balance.

In the recessed doorway across from my building lived a Cylahi woman named Genki who cared for three children—three that I could identify among the throng. She lived continuously under the burka, a grimy black cloth that was her only shelter. She owned an iron pot and daily fried beans over a self-contained stove; beans she had secured on credit. She sold the beans on a patty to day laborers, fed the kids, and had a little something for herself. Each day this intricate commerce was undertaken for a kam's worth of beans. Her location in the doorway was a prized spot, shady in the morning while dayworkers passed and purchased beans. She endured two hours of sunlight around noon, before the area was shady again during the airless siesta hour. Other workers shuffled up and down the alley to avoid the scorching sun, but Genki remained rooted in her vendor's spot.

I bought beans from Genki some mornings and handed the patty to any beggar I found two blocks away, if you can call them blocks. Said that already, did I? I had heartstone for her and came to understand how my feelings of being violated by theft were a luxury.

One day her pot was stolen. The desperate ruckus Genki raised there in the doorway that went on for hours. But she could not leave with her compact stove to report the theft, fearful of being displaced by another souk. And she had never obtained the ely, the household permit. The building manager was trying to evict Genki from his doorstep when I returned with a new pot, a second-hand iron skillet purchased at the bazaar.

Their argument ended abruptly.

Genki turned her blotchy face to me; red-rimmed eyes glaring through the gauzy facial panel of her burka. She received the pot from my hand but seemed to reject it. "Too shallow," she said.

I was about to get insulted and snatch away the pot, when I saw her rub the inside with her grimy sleeve. Her livelihood resided there, as did the survival of three tribal kids. I left to spare Genki a difficult moment of gratitude.

But I was accepted, even adopted. Teenagers in the street gangs liked to count coup on me, but that was just a demand for attention. Aging warriors nodded when I passed; women blessed me and rubbed ashes on my forehead in the mark of Rularim. Kids clamored to have their photos taken or brought a message that I should be in the bazaar at sunset or at the corner in twenty minutes. Each time I went to the appointed corner, an unblessed one offered secrets for kam or just that I should know.

Genki brought forward a young Cylahi girl who looked fourteen but was probably seventeen. She was shy and desperate with rust-colored nappy hair, but clean. "Didn't I want this girl?" Genki asked. "Wasn't she worthy? A daughter of Dacupitte, worthy enough. Or should I prefer a boy?"

I had to claim that I had a sexual disease to get rid of them.

And my dreams were vivid—from Edwina's dreamscape, I was guessing. She was the matriarch of the gualareps and lived on the flats of Arim that had bubbling hot springs and sudden geysers in this season. Brianna Miller, known as Rularim, sometimes appeared in my dreams viewed from knee level while she stood talking with Karlyhi or General Sector. From Edwina's point of view. When Brianna walked with me in those dreams, my heart beat faster.

Other days, I dreamed that I basked in the sun with my jaws open. In my rooms I often woke after siesta with my jaw distended and aching, like I was a gualarep napping in the sun. I told nobody about my restless dreams.

In my humid rooms, the kam-man Blanc brought around a rotund Putuki man named Voki Manuki, a highly placed official who had six daughters. I recognized him from when Manuki stood behind Ely during press conferences. Cronyism had its own logic that seemed plausible on the upside. A bazaari could reason that graft money goes to somebody, so why not to him? The people had always been poor, too many to save with services.

"Rabbenu Ely has made plans for himself," Voki said, sweating profusely in his dark business suit. "For when his tenure ends. I was just at the academy where my daughters endured the hypo shot for the Softcheeks' runny nose." He wiped his nose with two knuckles to demonstrate. "So, I was thinking: maybe the sor'shum can help my girls. Maybe there's a place for them in your world." His eyelids drooped.

"I have always tried to be fair," he added with a hand out. His palm was a lighter color. "My wife helps the poor every day. But the people don't want charity now. Soon will be the time of retribution. My daughters—"

"What do you want from me?" I asked.

"If you could find some excuse for my little ones to visit the transport or Stargate Junction. Else, it's service to some Cicero matron for the older girls, maybe farmed out separately." His eyes watered, the moisture joining the streams of sweat on his fat face. "Can you help me, Henry?"

"What you ask is not within my power." I shrugged.

His shoulders slumped.

Voki Manuki left, and I saw Genki working under the burka in her regular vendor's spot. She adjusted the facial veil and spat in the street behind his retreating steps.

Cylay schoolchildren who had been inoculated against the flu grew feverish and coughing, so a makeshift isolation clinic was established a couple blocks down from my place, if you can call them blocks. I received an EAM message: Doug Endicott was assigning me to find the truth of the spread of the Softcheeks' runny nose, since I lived among the tribespeople and maybe was not vulnerable to sickness with my urban pioneer self.

I brushed insect repellent at my temples; it made my hair stiff. I threaded my belt through the sheath of the beltknife. I gathered my cameras and flak jacket with the pockets filled with photo equipment, and left without locking the door. The blue macaw feathers were all the covering I needed, it seemed.

In the dusty warehouse, I photographed the women known as the daughters of Deborah, a hospice group who moved among the cots offering water and comfort, but the nurses were helpless against the reaction to the flu shot. Stories circulated while parents sat with suffering kids; some adults were coughing as well. For comfort, mothers spun tales about Sheeks-Cylom who slept with dragons, and about the second Rularim to whom Dolvia whispered each morning at sunrise, and about Kyle Rula whose ghost flew over the savannah on murmurey wings. A favorite folk tale was about the ghost of Spindel who became an angry ketiwhelp when challenged.

I tried to stick to the facts of the outbreak, to developments I could verify in fact. Blame was placed on the Consortium that had imported the vaccine. The death rate seemed targeted on Cylahi kids, already weakened by malnutrition and poor hygiene. Other kids survived but their limbs curled and their cognition vanished, called autistic.

I saw General Sector bring in Michael Peter, his youngest, and lay him on a cot next to a slum kid whom Genki had fed on occasion. The toddler breathed with difficulty; a sheen of sweat covered his features. General Sector saw me when he pulled the blue tam from his head. It didn't feel right soliciting a quote when Sector was so clearly stressed. He lingered among his men for a time and listened to the nurse, but he was called away to quell demonstrations in the plaza.

"Big man," someone said behind me.

I focused on a teenager who ran one of the street gangs, a thin Cylahi with sandy hair chopped around his ears. He wore rags and bits of jewelry. Trophies from successful raids perhaps?

"Milo-pilo's kids can get sick just like us, huh?" he said. "Just like unblessed ones." Milo-pilo was the native handle for General Sector.

I had seen this teenager at the warehouse clinic before, visiting his sister where his mother wept and little help was offered. "What's your name?" I asked.

"Will you print my words, huh? Along with my image?" He sneered and turned on his heel to join three others about his age and with rust-colored hair who waited in the alley.

"He's Stuben," a worker said. "His sister will not recover."

I glanced at her, dressed as a daughter of Deborah in a brown shift with a white bib apron. "What do you see here?" I asked quickly. "What outcomes?"

She showed a world-weary face. "The Putuki want the officers arrested—the ones who provided the vaccine. Protestors shout slogans in the plaza. Death to Hamilcar, like he brought the flu here. It's all for show."

"Hamilcar is not to blame?" I asked. She meant General Hartley who led the Consortium forces on Stargate Junction. Hamilcar was his native handle.

"We trusted the sor'shum," the nurse said. "Officers trusted the vaccine maker. Karlyhi is right. The tribes should look only to ourselves for help."

"May I quote you?" I asked quickly. I raised the camera. "You're Uburu, right? What's your name?"

She pulled off soiled plastic gloves, discarded them in the metal bin, and reached for a fresh pair. "I'm Imogene, and I have no tribe or family." She passed me in the resigned trudge of those who served the dying.

I saw Voki Manuki, the bazaari with six daughters, sitting with his back to me on a low stool between two cots and weeping, his shoulders shaking with sobs. One girl had a sheet pulled over her face. The other girl jerked under the soiled sheet, the palsy that came with autism. Imogene touched Manuki's shoulder but he waved away her hand, covering his face with a big handkerchief.

I filed story after story with the Company news channel, my paragraphs laced with outrage at Consortium negligence. I watched the comtechs for several days to catch my story. Little about the vaccine incident was mentioned by the female announcer with her China-doll makeup and crisp English accent. She seemed more focused on volatility for the upstart stock exchange. I found two online articles that had used my images, but the tone was muted, emphasizing the pathos of rampant disease more than seeking to place blame on the vaccine provider. Within weeks, the dying stopped and no new cases were reported, but 27 children were impaired—fewer than one percent of those treated with the vaccine.

Hakulupe Le was at the warehouse that day, talking quietly with some workers while the general collected their son, now a cripple who would need constant care and remedial education to learn even rudimentary actions. Lupe spoke with Imogene about the geysers that had come early on the flats of Arim, as if that event carried weight. Lupe turned to me and held her palm high in greeting.

"Hiki, Hershel Henry, the agent of karsci." The label meant that I was often present when trouble started.

"Melinga, Hakulupe Le."

"So tragic," she told me, gesturing to indicate the room. "And now blame is attached to Hamilcar."

"Were the officers arrested? The ones who gave kids the shots?"

She shook her head, lowering bright green eyes. "The officers were reassigned to the transport. There's no clear path for placing blame."

"And Michael Peter?"

She touched my shoulder. "We'll manage. You should get some rest. You look awful." Hakulupe Le went to board the jeep and took Michael Peter into her arms.

The general walked around to the driver's side just as Voki Manuki rushed him. "The sor'shum did this," Manuki shouted. "The sor'shum is to blame. What help now for these unblessed ones? How will we manage?"

General Sector strong-armed him. I saw loss and guilt on his face. The soldiers who traveled with the general formed a barrier while Manuki tried to push past them with his calls for answers. Sector got into the jeep, his jaw rigidly set, and left while the soldiers hurried to the back of a nearby lorry. When they drove off, Voki Manuki stood alone in the alley, his hand held out in supplication and his chin trembling with despair.

I captured several images before I decided my job here was done and I needed to nap.

TWO

I FOUND A MESSAGE ON THE EAM THAT I SHOULD BE AT THE
officer barracks later that day and carry a pack for three days and cameras for a ride-along event. I thought about alerting Doug Endicott at the Press Club, in case there was a break in the standoff with Goras, but somehow I didn't send that message. Gora forces had cut off inland trade to the seaside palace and were fighting in the outskirts of Urbyd, but they were finding that Khalif Ananke was more resourceful than they had assumed.

I came up late to the barracks and was directed to a sleek stinger that was already loaded and the engine warming up. I flew to Beecham Place in the company of Dacupitte and Kenru, the leaders of the Uburu; both were dressed in militia fatigues. They were silent in the noisy compartment, so I stared at the dry savannah lit with amber and orange by the long sunset.

Dacupitte was tall with ruddy skin like only the Scots have. He wore his orange hair in long dreadlocks and daily smeared aloe on his arms and legs. He was the warrior of legend and the father or grandfather of the tribal kids with rust-colored hair. He showed me watchful blue eyes and a dry smirk.

We landed just before dark at Beecham Place, my first visit there. The white hospital buildings were grouped on a squat mesa overlooking the floodplain. In an unkempt yard behind the buildings, a communal celebration was underway around a big center fire. We were folded into the event and seated near Kecouroo, who was seated below the tribal leader Cara, blind and gaunt with white hair and milky white eyes.

Kelly Osborn was there but silent while the chanting and clucking held steady. Apparitions of firelight glinted on the round lenses of her glasses. Kelly and I had clashed more than once, and her impatience with this Softcheeks reporter was worn on her sleeve. She was dressed in a militia uniform just as though she had fought alongside the warriors. Her hair was secured in a tight tail, and she was kilos slimmer than I remembered.

I looked around for Rufus, her betrothed, but did not see him.

The commotion quieted a little. The smoky fire made me cough, and I was certain my clothes would later smell of wood smoke. Cara offered a chant in Mekucoo that I understood somewhat. His story was about a great ruler in the past who had distributed goods on a feast day. Cara's lanky frame was hunched where he sat cross-legged in the place of honor, and his knees were like the knobs of a thorn tree branch. The good looks of his youth when he had served as second to Cyrus were a distant memory, but his word was strong. In the chant Cara described the ancient feast in detail. The best food went to men and their families who had served this ruler's ambitions, but less was given to each successive group until an orphan girl stepped forward last of all, but received nothing from the depleted largesse. She was later found, having hanged herself in the ruler's fields. She was soon forgotten.

Cara's chant told how an unrelenting famine overcame the people, and holy women were petitioned to determine what act might bring an end to suffering. The ruler was required to hold another feast day wherein goods were distributed with a more even hand so that the last and poorest guests received the same portion as the first. The girl's bones were also to be found for a funeral pyre.

When the chanting ended and guests began to depart, Kelly brought Kecouroo to me. "Hershel Henry, the agent of karsci," Kelly said. She was civil for once, but maybe because the senior Mekucoo woman was present.

Kecouroo nodded twice and fingered tektite stones in a coarse necklace. She was tall and trim, garbed in a finely tooled suede garment but with nappy hair and bare feet. She was a teacher at the Mayschool academy but also a leader among the women. "Cara has made the calling," Kecouroo said in Arrivi. "All must be accomplished as he has said. Return the bones of Cyrus from Siibabean land. Cara named those honored for this duty as Dacupitte, Lynus and his Madquii wife Alaise, and the brothers of Omiibuk who are Siize and Siiloba. Also, Dulcinea and Kenru from the Uburu tribe. And Hershel Henry must go along." She stopped, looking at me expectantly.

I wasn't sure how to respond. "Why are so many people needed to bring back seven pounds of bones?" I asked.

Kecouroo blinked. She looked at Kelly's face and back at my face. She turned on her heel and walked in long strides toward the group of honor.

"You're an idiot," Kelly told me and left to follow the older woman.

"Hey, Henry," Lynus said from behind me. He came forward with an arm around the shoulders of his unveiled wife Alaise. Lynus had been my keeper when I had first disembarked and trudged across Madquii dunes to reach the savannah.

"Ready for another long walk?" he asked.

I also greeted the brothers of Omiibuk who I knew—Siize and Siiloba—tall, black-skinned warriors in militia uniforms. I realized suddenly what I was witnessing. The city with the governor's mansion was not the center of tribal society. Cylay was where those with no purpose waited for services that were not offered. The wellspring of militia strength, during gatherings like this event, was what uplifted leaders and reassured followers. Journalists who reported on events in Cylay, and in Urbyd for that matter, were providing no analysis of real events, only conjecture constructed in a power vacuum. The back of my skull ached from how my view of the world was turned around.

Although she wasn't on the list of names provided by Cara, Kelly Osborn joined our trek at dawn and used the hours of walking to learn Borabean words from Alaise. Kelly wore an Arrivi skirt today and carried a burka as a shawl. Alaise, dressed similarly, controlled her gestures and spoke only when addressed, but she was a patient tutor, with dark hair and dark eyes rimmed with kohl.

Alaise was saying that Abydian sons in Urbyd were educated in Cochin, an oceanside nation that was considered developed. Borabean executives jumped back to Earth for industry tours in China and the Middle East. And she had met Carl Hartley, one of the Junction Boys. "From what I know," Alaise said, "Carl has little contact with savannah tribes. I wondered if he even realizes that my husband Lynus is Arrivi."

Alaise related a legend of a great Borabean warrior of our own time, named Asmach, who performed wondrous feats and was fearless in battle. Now somewhat past his prime, Asmach sold stories of his prowess for drinks at inns up and down the Iamida River that meandered among the Uburu mesas on its journey to the ocean.

We set out from Beecham Place that was closer to Siibabean land than the other Arrivi centers. The men walked ahead to scout safe passage, with the women trailing and carrying food in their packs. I was folded in with Lynus and the Siibabean brothers who asked many questions about life on Earth and especially the wonders of Paris.

We approached the escarpment wall, a sheer cliff partly concealed by dry forest ash and tamarind. A heavy mist hovered at the cliff top as if unwilling to plunge to the suffering savannah. During the rainy season, waterfalls decorated the wall for several weeks while runoff from the lush Siibabean forest filled the billabongs below.

We took a break, preparing to climb a steep grade in a well-worn fissure in the cliff wall. Kelly sat with Alaise, gently drawing out the young wife about her origins. Dulcinea sat with them, without a head covering so that her remarkable looks were available to any warrior who wanted to see. She had a diplomat's manner, deflecting the interest of warriors to spend the day with the women.

Dacupitte came up from his brief scouting to find the women bent over their lessons, giggling together. "You must stop this now," Dacupitte said with irritation. "It serves no purpose."

The lenses of Kelly's wireframe glasses glinted in the sun. "For the future."

Dacupitte scowled and walked away with Kenru.

"Morta chi," Alaise whispered, and the women softly giggled.

A signal came from Kenru, so we stood to start the climb. The incline was not grueling and the day was cool. The hilly area on top overlooked the savannah, and a fine breeze came up while we regrouped. The afternoon was waning by the time we reached the old-growth trees on Siibabean land where troops of ring-tailed lemurs chattered at us from the safety of high branches. Siibabean did not cultivate the acreage, nor herd erriv, nor use their timber to build fine, roomy houses. Mekucoo land was on the right, and the cliff of the escarpment wall was left. Our western view looked down on the vast golden savannah.

General Mike Shaw was in the forest somewhere, I knew, forging a new route to the ocean. He had resigned his commission before his pension kicked in, but Siibabean accepted him. We heard stories of the creatures his group had encountered, described after similar ones on Earth since we had no encyclopedia for forest denizen. There were addax and hyrax and wild boar and leggy antelopes that sported manes like a lion. Moths were said to be as big as a Mekucoo cloak and their wings like leather. Glow-in-the-dark insects and giant snakes that feasted on pulpy fruit high in the trees. The keti-whelps were oversized and full of cunning.

And lemurs of all varieties; big and scary or small and cuddly. Endless packs of them in the daytime, and others, dubbed howlers, that filled the night with mating calls. Lemurs were apparently a bigger problem to camp security than were the ketiwhelps.

Siize and Siiloba led our group on a twenty-minute walk into the trails of the forest to an exposed knoll. Long ago an uncle had buried Cyrus there after Cyrus was slain in defense of evacuating Arrivi families. Lynus and Dacupitte set about digging for the bones, while Kenru somberly waited with Siize and Siiloba. The women clustered in a whispering group. I only shook my head; all these people to stand around and watch.

Kenru spoke to Lynus who was standing near me. "Siize just realized your father Cyrus killed his father and uncle," Kenru said. "There is a possible grudge."

Lynus stood tall, glancing at the dark stares from the brothers. "An honorable battle death from a conflict long ago. And Cyrus is dead as well."

Kenru shrugged. "Just the same. This ritual honors Arrivi dead but says nothing about Siibabean who fell in that same skirmish."

"That's for their elders to arrange."

The bones of Cyrus were gathered by Dulcinea who was chosen to wrap them, a great honor for her tribe. I snapped several photos using the powerful flash in the cloudy afternoon. Dacupitte signi-fied on Siize and Siiloba. Lynus also showed the open palm gesture, but Siize turned away. We filled the grave, smoothed the earth, and retraced our steps—a much easier hike downhill to Beecham Place.

My legs ached, and I stifled a yawn. The waiting funeral pyre seemed somber and private compared to the chants of the previous night. I sat heavily on a wood bench, rubbing grit from my neck.

Edna came up to nudge my leg demanding flank rubs. She was twelve stones maybe, with bowed legs and a forked tongue. Edna had helped me before with warnings of danger, and her chortle was familiar. She often shared dreams. I slid off the bench to sit cross-legged on the ground. Her warm marbled hide was a course texture against my chest while she tested my nerve to tolerate her second brush across my lap.

"Where were you today when we were climbing the cliff wall?" I asked her out loud.

"Ka!" she articulated. She explored my face with the wet tongue. Edna's breath smelled like she had been eating kariom. Her long side scar was obvious—a discolored stroke just behind her front leg, gained from an engagement with a stressed erriv bull.

"Just up from the billabong?" I asked. I used my sleeve to wipe saliva from my chin.

"She shares her thoughts with you?" Lynus asked from behind me.

I craned my neck and nodded. "When she's so inclined. I cannot reach out to her."

"Lucky bastard," he muttered.

It had not occurred to me that Edna had excluded him. I struggled to sit on the bench again, and Edna lumbered off to greet other favorites.

Lynus joined me. "My wife is Madquii. Edna shut me out. The sudden absence in my head made me suicidal for a time, like the world held no color."

"I had no idea."

"They can be unforgiving."

We drank from a flask of Kiam gin that Lynus was hoarding. We watched the crowd gather in anticipation. "So many pregnant women," I said.

"It's the call to fertility to replace fallen warriors."

"I thought that was for after the siege at Urbyd was broken."

"Ah, you see, Henry," Lynus said, maybe a bit tipsy from our elixir. "That's how little you understand the tribes. The call to fertility is for one time and for the warrior who gets there first."

"No second round for—"

Lynus chuckled and drank again. "Only a crafty warrior sees the faces of his grandchildren before the desert takes him."

Soon enough, Kecouroo joined Cara on the dais. Dacupitte brought forth the package and laid it on the pyre. Arrivi and Mekucoo gathered for the somber event.

I whispered to Lynus, "Cyrus was your father, but the honor goes to Dacupitte?"

Lynus grinned in his disarming way. "We don't decide family matters the same as Softcheeks." Lynus shrugged. "The birth mother sometimes passes a newborn to a cousin in a more secure village, or to one who lost her men in the conflict. To ensure that more children reach warrior age."

The fire was lit with a sudden whoosh, and cheering and clucking broke out. I had taken many photos during the outing, mostly of village life and Kecouroo standing with Cara or with Dacupitte. I now used the small camcorder that was too often confused by the firelight. My sense of this event was anticipation of the passing of Cara by paying reverence to ancestors who he would soon join, especially Cyrus who had been his leader in battle. My plan was to use the images in later stories as deep background for when the leadership structure was more public.

I dreamed that night of returning to the knoll where we had recovered the bones of Cyrus, traveling close to the ground. My eyes were wetted by dew in the grass, and my hide was stroked by low-hanging branches. I waited in Nettom's light and flashed my forked tongue as I stepped over the freshly turned earth, the empty gravesite. I held high my weighty head and allowed the breeze to overflow my green and marbled hide. I was at rest, the deed accomplished.

In the morning I wondered if Cara had dreamed the same.

A junket took the phalanx of Company reporters to Urbyd for the wedding of Akana, the second son of Khalif Ananke. Carrying my small pack and my camera bags, I arrived late at the hotel in the Royal Square, delivered by the brown and red mail-run chopper. None in our group of fourteen reporters ventured past Urbyd's Royal Square, even with a guide who had enough English to interpret. Some reporters understood and spoke Arrivi, but few had bothered to learn Borabean, me among them.

I had checked in and changed into a dark suit. I found John Milan and Regan Villines loitering in the Rendezvous Bar. They were dressed formally for a change. Regan wore a long decorated skirt with embroidered blouse and a contrasting colorful scarf that must have been two meters long. Without the layers of jewelry that were common among native women, though, she looked underdressed.

I had scraped my face free of whiskers for the occasion, so that my chin was a lighter color than my cheekbones. "I thought this city was under siege," I said.

"This is for show," John said. "Bloody but unbowed, and all that."

"Do you think we'll get close to Khalif Ananke or Aristides?" I asked. Aristides was the First Minister in Urbyd and the power behind the throne.

John snorted and downed his drink, hungrily licking the ice. "Abydian know how to channel traffic. You'll need the telephoto lens."

I was made to leave my cameras at the hotel desk. We were escorted across the square by guards in dress uniforms who carried ceremonial weapons only, a scimitar or a useless riding crop. The three-acre public square was dressed for the reception, but one didn't have to look far to find the scars of siege. "This display is meant to thumb their noses at Anaxagoras," John Milan claimed as we were hurried along. "Supplies are from Striiduc. Security is a stranglehold."

Inside a temple with decorations from a distant past, we were herded to a raised section well back from the dais to take assigned seats. The crowd was just beginning to file into the domed sanctuary, with its many fat pillars that obscured the view. Borabean were seated with men on the right and women on the left. "Why aren't you made to sit with the women?" I asked Regan. She punched my shoulder.

John leaned over her to whisper, "They disdain us and don't bother to impose their rules."

Regan rolled her eyes and bobbed her chin.

The reporter guests in the front row of our section were each offered a warm cloth in a shallow bowl to refresh our hands and faces. Junior reporters behind us only smirked. The female attendant, with her hair covered and a delicate chain across her cheek fastened to her ear and the ring in her nose, waited for the used cloths before she bowed and backed away.

Across from us was another raised section for gathered officials from other city-states. "That's Khalif Olpul, who you may have met at Stargate Junction," Regan whispered, resisting the urge to point. "And on the end, seated with his First Minister, is Otieno who hates Khalif Olpul. See how they're seated in separate rows."

Sorry to say, they looked alike to me: cousins with hooked noses and black eyes. Khalif Olpul was older with a long gray beard under his kaffiyeh and looking rather like a wizard in a child's fairytale. For Arrivi dignitaries, only Dacupitte and Kenru were seated together in blue business suits. Dacupitte's dreads were bound with a leather strap, and his coloring didn't stand out as much as it did on the savannah. Aeolis tapped his shoulder from the row above, seated with several Madquii, identified as a group by their stark white kaffiyehs. Dacupitte and Aeolis talked cordially for a few minutes.

I had been to Madquii camps in the desert dunes and had even met Aegiv the lawgiver before he was lost is a skirmish. Aeolis was the second of Aegiv's three sons and wore as his sigil the three-headed snake that was prominent on his agal, the binding cord to his kaffiyeh.

"Where are the Gora?" I asked Regan, only a little kidding.

John looked my way with an arched eyebrow.

Regan threw a thumb over her left shoulder. "Allowed to stand behind the wife's family, maybe ten in all. Relatives to Apetu's first wife who is Gora. Already resident in the palace when Anaxagoras started his march to Urbyd."

"The sidebar position is an insult?"

"What do you think?"

Weddings I had attended were about the bride's entrance and the groom's discomfort. Except the Abydian were different. The foreign bride waited, seated on a low cushion, as circus performers came down the aisle in colorful groups doing acrobatic tricks. Each bevy of performers exited close to the dais without taking a seat to view the proceedings.

I envied them.

King Ananke was seated by a spiritual leader and looked bloated and disinterested.

John snorted with his face twisted. "He barely knows that priest. Ananke prefers the Cochin circus women and the striisnia drug they give him."

Aristides entered silently and alone, sporting a tan kaffiyeh with an elaborate agal, and stood behind Ananke. Aristides was a cousin or uncle of Ananke and probably had paid the bills for the wedding ceremonies.

Akana and his nine brothers promenaded down a center aisle, wearing finely made clothes of subdued colors but no kaffiyehs, a turn from tradition. Akana walked with Apetu, the oldest, with the others following in rank of age. Akana was tall, his long limbs seeming princely and his beard was oiled and gleaming.

"He was educated abroad?" I whispered. "In Cochin?"

Regan nodded. "Two others were sent to the same school as the Junction Boys, but none became financial wizards."

"Today is probably the first time in their adult lives that all ten brothers are gathered in the same building," John added.

The ceremony was long and boring. The wedding couple mostly had their backs to the audience. I kept staring at the many sons of Ananke. How did Aristides find work for them all? The standing army that resisted Anaxagoras had absorbed four sons as officers. Urbyd was a port but maintained no fleet of ships for export. Silicide hoards were to be mined by foreign interests with their expertise, if at all.

Maybe three brothers could manage the palace guard or act as treasurer, I was thinking, but those duties came under the influence of Aristides. What did the remaining brothers have to do? Linger in the library and learn the genus and species of beetle types?

Eventually, the wedding was pronounced completed and the couple walked up the aisle followed by nine brothers rather than bridesmaids.

We were allowed to file out into the moist evening air smelling of the sea. "So different than the desert air of Cylay," I said, turning with my arms held wide.

"Why seek a reporter's post in Cylay when you can set up shop here?" John asked.

"And displace you?" I shrugged.

He gave me a long stare. John Milan had been in Westend for seasons before I came here. He was my corporate senior but envious of my connections with Arrivi. He and Regan were a couple now, but that was a long time coming too.

The Royal Square was dressed with tables and strings of lights for the wedding feast—regular folk only. Abydian stayed together in the palace with the exits guarded. "Where are the Chinese?" Milan asked. "They used to infest the square like June bugs."

"Gun shy, maybe," Regan chuckled. "And Rabbenu Ely is more besieged in his governor's mansion than Khalif Ananke is here."

John pushed past me and the other reporters to talk with some official about gaining palace entry. Regan and I sat at a round table and were served rich pastries with nuts on thin plates with disposable forks. We drank from mock-crystal plastic glasses. I sat back in the pleasant evening and stretched my elbows behind me.

I stood when Carl Hartley approached with Patrick Osborn and two younger men. Carl wore Junction clothes, with his razor-cut hair combed to hang over one eye. Broad-shouldered like his father the general, he seemed stressed with his shoulders hunched. His companions glanced around with boredom.

We shook hands.

"You know Patrick, of course," Carl said.

Patrick and I shook hands too.

"So, Rabbenu Ely didn't risk leaving the mansion for this event," Carl postulated. "We have a betting pool on how long Ely will remain in office. What's your guess?"

"Um, I'm new here. I couldn't venture—"

"Not very sporting, Henry," Carl said with an edge to his voice. "You didn't ask about my sister."

I cleared my throat. "How's Jesse? How is she liking Paris?"

"Don't know. She never reaches back to us. To the little people." His look was meant to convey meaning, but I wasn't sure what. "We're over here," Carl added. "Drop by and we'll throw some dice."

"I'll be by," I said heartily but had no intention of complying. They walked away with their two companions. Patrick looked back like his head was on a swivel stick.

I retreated to a seat next to Regan Villines.

"Stay away from them," Regan whispered with her hand in front of her mouth. "Guilt by association."

"The rumors are true? About taking street kids?"

She shrugged without interest. "I'm off to Cylay in the morning."

"Abydian don't grant interviews to women?" I asked.

She smirked with a knowing look, her weathered face lined with blue tones from the festival lighting.

"So . . . you and John Milan, huh?" I probed. "How long?"

Regan ducked her head, rather like a little girl. It was a charming gesture. "Romances that start in the field," she said, "never survive the field. Just enjoy it for today."

"Good plan." Pleasantly buzzed on cheap champagne, I watched the placid crowd. We were attended by solicitous servers who met our every need, so there was no line at the bar or buffet. "I could tolerate a posting at Urbyd," I said.

"Get in line," she laughed. "And stay in the square tomorrow. You heard the fate of that Frenchman who was found in the stream."

I had heard the story, though it was not reported on the comtech that carried Company news. The way it went was: a newbie reporter from France had disembarked from the shuttle in Urbyd but wasn't met by his people. Some locals had offered to carry his cases to the hotel. They had remarked on his shoes and offered to stop to purchase sandals that were more practical. They were most solicitous and offered a meal and a smoke. The newbie had no caution due to his sense of entitlement and allowed the service. He soon fell asleep from the striisnia smoke and was found three days later, naked and bloated, floating in a stream that led to the Iamida river. Urbyd residents were more upset that his body had polluted the stream than with the crimes against Softcheeks. When his company lodged a complaint with Aristides, they were slapped with additional regulations about disembarkment.

Regan pointed left to where the nine sons of Ananke, with their identical business suits, had come down the palace steps and were fanning out into the crowd to share well-wishes with wedding guests. They were immediately greeted by sycophants who offered bows and gifts. The sons touched the gifts to be polite, and attendants walking behind collected the packages in big sacks. The crowd by us thinned considerably while many rushed forward for a moment spent with Abydian. I grabbed more drinks for me and Regan.

My drink was mostly drained when the youngest son, Analli, approached our table with Aeolis the Madquii and Steve Swanweil. Analli was no more than twenty, with his features unformed and his beard just coming in. I knew Swanweil from Stargate Junction where he acted as a broker for hard-to-secure goods. Aeolis was taller and bore a look of disgust highlighted by the white kaffiyeh. I had met him too, but I doubted that he remembered. Swanweil made the introductions.

Analli briefly placed fingertips on his chest. "Do you have all that you need?" he asked. "Can we bring you something more?"

"Ah, we're fine." I slurred my words on purpose.

Swanweil's face was active from stimulants, and sweat stood on his brow. "Abydian can refuse nothing on the wedding night. What do you desire?"

"Can you make it rain?" Regan asked. Swanweil ducked his chin for a silly giggle. Aeolis only squinted.

Swanweil used crimped gestures to take snuff from a silver snapbox. "Don't worry," he giggled. "It's only snuff, not striisnia that builds stamina." Swanweil leaned over the table, almost spilling our drink glasses. "Be adventuresome. Anything you want."

He looked back at Analli. "What if I said that I wanted to fuck her?"

Analli and Aeolis looked away, but I stood quickly to face him off. "What if I said that I wanted to fuck you?"

Swanweil moved his shoulders in an odd rhythm. "Well, alright. But I get to go first."

I rounded on Regan, pulling her to her feet and guiding her by the elbow into the crowd. "I was just fooling with you," Swanweil called from behind us.

"Just like Abydian," Regan complained through her teeth. "All repression on the outside and seething indulgence underneath."

Somebody was roughly shaking my shoulder. "Hershel Henry! Henry! Wake up now! Are you awake?" General Sector stood over the cot. Two officers waited by the door, looking down the corridor in a defensive posture. I was back in Cylay, hung-over and dehydrated.

"I had a devil of a time finding you," Sector said. "Get up! Your services are needed."

I yawned. "I'll just grab my cameras."

"Not those services. Come along." He stalked out of my rented rooms above the furniture store. I grabbed my camera bag anyhow.

In the harsh sunlight, we four piled into a waiting jeep. Genki and the others must have thought I was being arrested. They just stared. While we bounced along in the rutted alley, I noticed that General Sector's features were drawn, and the mustache freshly trimmed. "Why live here, Henry?" he asked. "They steal everything."

"Theft is friendliness. It means I'm accepted."

He considered that, his salt-and-pepper mustache twitching under cynical blue eyes. "And what do they call assassination?"

"My presence here boosts the economy of this whole section. Why kill me?"

"Is that why they call you Blancom?"

"What?"

"Your kam-man is Blanc, so you have been dubbed Blancom, the last blonde."

"Yah, sure." The dry air made my tongue feel raspy. "Would you have a short bracer for—" I saw his look and shut up.

In the plaza, we drove to the municipal building across from the governor's house. The building was recently completed, with seven stories and a real escalator in the lobby. We parked in the back to avoid demonstrators who tended to flock to Sector when they saw his jeep with a truckload of soldiers trailing it. We crowded into a service elevator with his two silent officers and rode to the fifth floor. We walked along the front corridor where panels of glass overlooked the plaza with its non-working fountain. We entered a section containing offices for local officials, a notary public and the like, as well as a visitor's counter, its sharp edges gleaming with cleanliness. I was slapped with the acrid smell of soap, several types, in the halls and from adjoining rooms—cleanser and wood polish and hand sanitizer and perfume—each troubled my nostrils in turn.

I stopped at a public water fountain and drank deeply, wiping my chin with my sleeve. We arrived at a narrow trading room intended to seat three traders only with an overhead comtech, EAM monitors, and a ticker board that ran along the table's edge.

An Arrivi man and veiled woman waited there. The woman held her palm high. "Hiki, Hershel Henry," Hakulupe Le said. Her forest green eyes held my attention, even through the facial panel. "May I present our new trader, Len rabbe Murd, youngest son to Orin rabbe Murd?"

The big man, tan and muscled, wore pantaloons and broad sandals; probably just called in from herding erriv.

General Sector's officers waited in the hall as we four crowded into the seating area. I was made to sit in the chair in front of the screens while Hakulupe Le removed her voluminous burka. I stowed my camera bag under the table.

"We have a small crisis here," Lupe said. "Our trader is unavailable today and gum arabic is publicly offered for the first time. You know about trading stocks, yes?"

"I had some experience on Earth," I replied. "What standard?"

"The same," General Sector answered, towering over me. "The yuan equivalent is the Cicero romark. We have several accounts opened and want sizable sell-offers. Do you need more account numbers?"

"That depends. What volume?"

"Seventeen tons." Hakulupe Le said.

I stared, my mouth gaping. That volume represented several seasons, maybe a full cycle of netta, of patient collection and storage of the natural tree sap.

"The Bryant cartel," she calmly continued, "may purchase whatever is released. They may have unlimited funds for now. Then we anticipate a sell-off initiated by them. We must watch for that move and labor to keep the price stable." She showed me a sheet of account numbers, five on top and several more listed below. "These are for selling; these for buying small quantities, along with other commodities. Do you understand?"

"You want to offer gum arabic, then quietly buy it back when the price dips to build trader and consumer confidence."

"Precisely," she said, nailing me with those green-green eyes.

"And where is your trader today?"

"On the savannah. Billie Manenowski is honored with a ritual death."

"Listen, if failure means death, then I'm not—"

She actually smiled. "We know you will keep faith with us. It is seen."

"Because of Edwina?" Lupe's favorite gualarep liked me for some reason.

"That too." She waved a hand dismissively.

General Sector was called away by other concerns. He left with the officers who always attended him. "How do you feel about the captain's death?" I asked Lupe.

"A man with no purpose in his life is taken by the desert." Her ready answer meant that the question was settled earlier within committee.

"I'm so sorry for what happened to Michael Peter," I quietly said.

Hakulupe Le searched my face with her bright eyes and then turned to instruct Len rabbe Murd. We worked in front of the monitors for several hours. Whatever product we offered on the market was immediately traded higher. It was thrilling, really, this instant success. By way of continual group reasoning, we three considered when to make the next sell offer and how to assess who had responded. Len was quiet, absorbing the details of his new occupation. He seemed bright and a team player.

"Ananke's trading accounts are hardly in use here," I said to Lupe. "Perhaps the Borabean ruler is distracted by military concerns."

"You have heard of the Junction Boys, surely," she said. "Operating from New Shanghai on Cicero, but with Ananke's funds. Also, we know about the Bryant cartel. We know who has warehouses and licenses. We are not naïve."

"I did not mean to imply—"

"Our academy graduates are equal to them. The Junction Boys have no surprises."

"A sell-off may not soon start," I said. "I cannot spend the hours."

"Your service today is a blessing," she said in softer tones. "I feel I should warn you, Blancom, about sharing chi so easily like when you mentioned my son." I leaned in to better hear her words. "The afflicted children on the savannah," she said, "most of them are gone now. The fathers take care of it."

My chest constricted, and I had to remember to breathe. "As part of tribal logic?"

She nodded, perhaps misunderstanding my tone. "It's considered indulgent to keep the child, because the needed care draws time from, um, farm chores. Also if there's an attack, a mother or sister could be lost while trying to save this one. The afflicted child must be allowed to join our ancestors, to be remembered as he once was."

I breathed in finally, the hot air noisily passing my nostrils. "Michael Peter too?"

She waited a long moment. "Mrs. Shaw will find a place for my son with her at Two Forks on Cicero. To keep the peace in our house. It's different for Hardhands, I guess, but my son mustn't stay here as an affront to families who did the right thing. You can see that, can't you?"

"I'm so sorry. I won't mention him again."

Before she could say more, there was a shuffling noise in the hall, and we three stood to see what trouble was coming our way. Brianna Miller came to the doorway wearing a business suit with a calf-length skirt and peridot jewelry. She carried a burka over one arm like an inconvenient shawl. Siize and Siiloba flanked her, silhouetted by the bright windows, standing escort duty to this tribal leader. Four tense Consortium officers looked up and down the corridor, their blue tams looking Old World and out of place.

"Hiki, Len rabbe Murd," Brianna said, taking the initiative. "We are honored by your service today."

Len showed an open palm at elbow height. "Hiki, Brianna Miller, the betrothed of Dacupitte."

She held an upturned palm at elbow height. "Melinga. The geysers came early this season, so the harvest will be meager."

"The Murd family have some storage to share with the women of the savannah, if need be."

She nodded and glanced into the trading room. "I would speak with this Softcheeks for a moment, if you can spare his presence."

Len's eyes skirted from her face to mine. "Melinga," he said and turned back to his new duties. Brianna touched the arm of Hakulupe Le, and she also returned to her seat at the trading table. Brianna indicated that I join her in the corridor where she stood with her back to the windows, surrounded by guards who she ignored. "We are pleased with your service to the tribes, Hershel Henry, and your discretion with broadcasts on the comtech."

I frowned and nodded. Her eyes were hazel, not the arresting green of her cousin Hakulupe Le. Brianna's hair was short and her skin was golden as though tanned by the sun. How was that possible?

"I come today," she added, "with a request that you join an ambassador mission to Urbyd. These two warriors will go along, also Dulcinea the Uburu and her uncle Kenru. You would be, um . . . I believe the Softcheeks term is 'embedded.' A reporter embedded with our group."

"With you?"

"Yes, me too."

"You would be a great prize for the Abydian to capture."

"That's why we need a high profile group with our own reporter."

I nodded slowly. I may have been staring with my mouth open. Siize and Siiloba looked at each other over her head.

"We leave in two days," Brianna prompted. "Who do I need to approach at the network to gain permission for you to join us?"

"I'll take care of it."

"Good; that's good," she said, perhaps accustomed to people who go tongue-tied in her presence. "General Sector's men will ferry you into Uburu land. Travel light but bring the cameras." She offered her hand to shake. "I will see you soon."

Shaking her hand, I managed to say, "Yah, sure."

Siize and Siiloba flanked her steps going up the corridor with the peacekeepers closing access from behind. I returned to my seat in the trading room.

Len rabbe Murd and Hakulupe Le stared at the screens following the trading numbers. After a moment, Len leaned forward to look past Lupe at me, his eyes appraising and with deep laugh lines showing on his cheeks.

I abruptly left the trading room in the afternoon, carrying my camera bag, to cross the plaza to the hotel and catch my boss Doug Endicott before he closed the office and repaired to the Press Club bar. He was at the editor's desk, although the secretary had apparently left already. I knocked lightly on the open office door.

Endicott looked up from a file. "Henry," he said and held up a photo. "Do you know this guy?"

"Ah, that's Aeolis, the second son of Aegiv the lawgiver."

"You know his dad?"

"I met Aegiv one time, before he was lost at the battle of Iamida shores."

"Yeah, yeah. Can you get Aeolis to come into the studio for an interview?"

I chuckled softly. "Tribal leaders are not impressed with stories that serve the Company."

Endicott tossed the photo on the desk and leaned back in his chair. "If the leaders come for interviews, their voices can be heard."

"If my stories or John Milan's stories were reported honestly, maybe the tribes would begin to trust reporters."

Endicott smirked. "If you want to broadcast every word, then open a blog. Of course, you'll have no audience. Company news is the only news." He took in my barrio looks as I hovered at the threshold with my weighted camera bag. I was suddenly aware that my sandals were dirty and my hair uncut.

I glanced at the framed photos behind his desk of military buddies in field uniforms.

"What do you want, Henry?"

I leaned against the doorjamb. "I had an offer to accompany Brianna Miller on a diplomatic trip to Urbyd."

"Into Urbyd? How will you get past the Goras?"

"By river, I imagine."

He squinted. "You're close to the tribes, huh? I heard you talked with, um, with Kelly Osborn. Is she important to the conflict?"

"Kelly Osborn compiles native chants printed in seasonal pamphlets. About the warriors as heroes, mostly. It's like an oral history, but published."

"Uh-huh," Endicott said. "Can you get an interview with Wan Su in Urbyd? The Chinese executive?"

"Uh, I doubt it. The Chinese are gun shy. John Milan cannot get the interview?"

Endicott sighed and rubbed his face all over. He began stowing the items on his desk drawers to close up shop. "Milan had started asking questions about tribal logic. The Chinese executives don't return his calls anymore. Take a lesson here. Could happen to you."

I shrugged slightly. "I can poke around while I'm in Urbyd. Count heads and lay some groundwork. Will my report get printed this time?"

"That depends on what you report. When do you leave?"

"In a couple of days."

"Well, take the malaria meds and stay in touch."

I left quickly to avoid getting roped into a drinking bout that could last all night.

The following day, news of Captain Billie Manenowski's death was reported by Regan Villines and the China-doll announcer. Villines had been led by Arrivi women to discover the body, and she was provided evidence about how the captain had sold inside information for Cylahi gold. I suspected Regan's exclusive report had been arranged by tribal leaders just as my reports sometimes were. It felt odd to hear Regan's point of view delivered in crisp tones by the Chinese woman in stark makeup. Unfortunately, the term "inside information" meant little to the local audience since the securities exchange was a new addition to their economy.

For days, we heard on the comtechs and EAMs an orchestrated outcry from bazaari in Cylay and Urbyd over the ritual death of Manenowski. Unemployed Putuki men raised their voices in the square and burned a Consortium flag, maybe one stolen from a vaccine table. The order of impunity intended to keep Consortium executives safe had been violated, they claimed. Hamilcar had removed the officers who had vaccinated the children, invoking the order for that action, but had provided no protection for Captain Manenowski against Karlyhi's tribal logic.

On the comtechs, Captain Manenowski's military record was publicly examined. He had served under Milo Sector and lived in married officer quarters in Cylay with his wife Vera, an accountant for Somule Gems. All the women worked for Somule Gems in some capacity, but Vera was counted as a friend of Brianna Miller and helpmate to Hakulupe Le. She had been crippled when held captive by the Bryant cartel seasons ago.

Protestors ignored the positive bio and claimed that Hamilcar must punish his officers who gave the poisoned vaccine to children. What protection can bazaari and souks expect from the Consortium general who ignored the ritual death of his own officer?

Death to Hamilcar! Death to the sor'shum!

Pipe bombs went off in the Cylay bazaar. I never understood why protestors destroyed their own stuff. Fresh-faced reporters rushed to the scene and faced the cameras with commentary to connect dots that didn't exist.

I saw Voki Manuki's angry face on the comtechs behind a blithe reporter, and Dkar was in the crowd but seemed to avoid the cameras. The idle workers were frustrated without control over their lives, and they responded to what they saw on the comtechs and heard at the dinner table. And I noticed the backlash didn't include General Sector, often called Milo-pilo, who had overseen the flu vaccine effort. He was a closer officer, married to a native teacher and with his own son afflicted. He was not a straw man for protest.

Even Carline Bryant joined the fray, appearing on a comtech news segment opposite Mrs. Shaw, both residents on Cicero. Carline Bryant's face seemed blanched on the comtech screen. Her suit was too tight, and her hair was trained in a stiff upsweep. She asked with her lip curled, "How can the tribes hope to attract new business to the savannah if Consortium officers are subject to the arbitrary acts of tribal logic?"

Mrs. Shaw used no nervous gestures, rock steady before the cameras. She had been a bush doctor who had developed vaccines for native diseases. She was wife to General Shaw, although they lived separately. "Manenowski was caught profiteering," she said in even tones. "It's not the same as peacekeepers who were helping with the vaccine process."

"Karl Wyley caught him?" Carline shot back using the Company name for Karlyhi. "Karl Wyley doesn't know what insider information means," she said to the interviewer, a Cicero professional in a dark suit, not a Chinese woman speaking English. That's how far removed the arguing women were from Dolviet news.

"There were no charges, no arraignment, and no trial," Carline articulated in practiced tones. "The captain was a Consortium officer. Where is the complaint from General Hartley about his unlawful death? Hamilcar is to blame here."

The two women argued loudly, and Carline shook a finger at Mrs. Shaw who only shook her head.

THREE

I RODE IN A CONSORTIUM HELICOPTER THAT LANDED NEAR A wood frame home in a gorge protected by Uburu mesas, the gorge where forces were often mustered to face the Borabean. Siize and Siiloba greeted me in the pasture that served as a landing pad and hurried me to a military tent where a heated discussion was underway. In the tent with the flaps pulled down, the air was close and smelled of sun-warmed canvas and the mineral oil used to clean weapons. General Hartley was seated, wearing a blue uniform with many medals. General Sector in camouflage fatigues paced behind him. An embarrassment of riches I felt was here with both senior men present, and I was eager to get their statements on the ritual killing of Captain Manenowski.

"You cannot go!" General Hartley insisted. "We refuse to provide protection."

I leaned forward to look past Siize who had picked up a ceremonial shield, and I saw Brianna Miller seated alone far from the tent flap.

"A truce is negotiated for the mission," she countered quietly. "Too easily, maybe. Ananke may be seeking an exit from the palace ahead of Anaxagoras's assault."

"You're too exposed," the general said. "There's no reason to trust Ananke or Aristides."

"You have dinner with Aristides whenever he visits the transport."

I chuckled softly. General Hartley was renowned for his tolerance. He had allowed the child labor trade but also allowed Consortium officers broad latitude in local conflicts. Hartley seldom took a public stance on any issue; instead, he worked behind the scenes to maintain the balance.

"Goras set off pipe bombs in the Urbyd plaza," General Milo Sector said to Brianna Miller. "You may become a random victim. Not even the target."

"They want to process the silicide," Hartley said in a quieter voice. "That's your real goal, isn't it? To spy on their industry? They have more silicide than you have. Abydian will always have more silicide than you have."

Brianna shrugged and avoided his look. "If the palace falls, the storage silos are at risk. Are they empty? Are they guarded? What does your man Jessup Chandliss say?"

Hartley sighed, like a horse blowing air from his nostrils. "He's gone missing."

"I'll be sure to ask after him in Urbyd."

"You may well join him in a shallow grave."

Her tone was measured as though she repeated a rote lesson. "Not if I have Consortium backing for the ambassador mission. The order of impunity would apply here."

General Sector controlled his smile and looked at the seated senior man. Hartley only shook his head. I remembered thinking there was stuff going on with him and Brianna. A scent in the air; a glee at the exchange between equals—these two had history.

The Siibabean brothers stepped back when the general stood suddenly to leave the tent. Hartley was big and square shouldered, but he carried extra weight at his middle. He looked out of place in his blue Consortium uniform.

I touched his arm as he brushed past. "Sir, if I could have a few moments. What is the troop strength among the Uburu mesas? How many—"

"Another time, Henry."

General Sector was hot on his heels, so I turned to him. "General, what is your reaction to the ritual death of Captain Mane—"

He pushed past me. "Not now, Henry."

Brianna Miller joined me at the tent entrance, wearing the Arrivi gown with a blue shawl. I noticed that she dressed differently for each audience, sometimes taking the role of western business-woman extending her hand to shake, and sometimes posing as Rularim or a simple Arrivi souk. She played them off, showing the face that secured the most leverage.

"Why is the question of silicide storage part of the ambassa-dor mission?" I asked quickly. "Are you seeking an alliance with Ananke or Anaxagoras?"

"Always asking the good questions, huh, Blancom?" Humor lin-gered in her voice. "These warriors will show you where to stow your gear. We leave in two hours."

"And the generals?"

"They're leaving now. You were tardy." She pushed past me, walking with some extra bounce in her step. Dulcinea joined her and they walked down to the boats.

Borabean long-tail boats waited for us at a stream that flowed into the Iamida river. I carried my small pack and cameras, wearing the uniform of the clutch of Kenru so our group looked cohesive at first glance. Siize and Siiloba had set aside the ceremonial shields, apparently needed only to impress visiting generals, and were dressed in identical uniforms the same cut as mine.

Kelly Osborn was there but just to help with the loading. Rufus and his men came to the sloping bank with bundles of trade goods wrapped in canvas and three heavy cases of munitions that we were delivering to the Madquii clan. Rufus was brother to my friend Lynus but showed none of his friendliness. A young warrior just coming into leadership, he still minded the voices of the women with status.

"You must speak with Kelly," Dulcinea told Rufus as the others labored. Rufus squinted. Dulcinea spoke again. "Just share with Kelly the journey's purpose."

"Kelly's purpose is to serve Dacupitte's woman." He meant Brianna, not Dulcinea.

Dulcinea was silent, but her stance spoke volumes.

Reluctantly, Rufus stepped to where Kelly struggled with Brianna's shoulder case, trying to load it into the wide and decorated boat. Rufus took the case from Kelly's hand and untangled the strap from the auburn tresses cascading over her shoulder.

Kelly pushed her glasses up on her nose. She reached for the case but Rufus held the leather binding from her grasp, an awkward moment of uncertainty.

"You are blessed by Dolvia," Rufus said through clenched teeth.

Kelly's expression froze and her eyes skirted to where Dulcinea stood with me. The laboring Mekucoo who served Rufus turned their backs to hide the humor in their faces.

"You have honor among the tribes," Rufus added, "as a woman of the savannah."

Kelly hesitantly nodded and pushed at her glasses again.

Rufus glanced at Dulcinea, perhaps wondering if the terms of her demand were satisfied. How much more must be said? He shortly sighed. "Many among the tribes note your good work," he added to Kelly.

Not understanding a bit of this, Kelly held a palm high in the traditional manner. "Melinga, Rufus."

Rufus touched Kelly's elbow and guided her onto the dry bank, shooting a hateful look in our direction. I kept recklessly eyeballing them, ignoring Dulcinea's squint.

Kelly's hair glowed coppery in the sunlight. As Rufus lingered, the river breeze fanned curly strands across her features. My bones ached to know what more transpired between them, maybe Kelly's comeuppance. That hope was too great, though.

Rufus walked away. Tongues of fire seemed to ignite with each of his steps, as the battlefield clung about him, the aroused aura of Cyrus. Warriors were suddenly busy with their labor.

Dulcinea chuckled and I twisted quickly to catch a glimpse of her smile. "Dolvia blesses this mission of diplomacy, Blancom."

"Yah, sure," I mumbled.

We boarded the boats and shoved off into the stream's current. Siize managed Dulcinea and Kenru's boat, as Siiloba guided ours. In the stern, Lynus served as lookout for the roomy highbrow boat, with Alaise, Brianna, and me nestled in its belly. It came to me suddenly that this group was the same as that tasked with bringing down the bones of Cyrus, without Dacupitte but with Brianna. That coincidence meant nothing, really, but the symmetry was delicious.

Once we had cleared the shadow of the mesa, I sat back to enjoy the swift current and passing view. Beyond the narrow fields and the mida trees, sand dunes rolled toward us. Streams of mauve sand blew over each crest, threatening our water-needy existence with timeless indifference.

Speaking in Borabean, a language I understood a little by then, Alaise gave reverence to the river. "Iamida was raised on violets in another age and fed honey by snakes. He is the grandfather spirit who brings seasons of plenty when the people are deserving. He resides within the river's chi, and we partake of his generosity. It's said that Iamida's song of the river is the same as Bydquii's song of the ocean. Any person who can hear kariom singing can also hear the sea serpent's trumpet and the water's own song."

"Can you hear this song?" I asked.

Alaise showed a sly look in profile. "It's said that gualareps hear the water's song, and that's how they mastered talking. It's said that the gualareps' song is the same one heard in the oceanside city of Utica."

"Can the gualareps hear sea serpents?" I asked Brianna. "Are they part of the beastmaster ability?"

"If only—" she said. "Who can get Edwina to sing?"

I reached for my notebook and pen, ready to jot down impressions to develop into an article later. "So, Brianna, what do you hope to accomplish with this ambassador mission?"

Brianna gently pulled the book away from me. "No questions for today. Enjoy the adventure." She sighed and stretched her shoulders, pushing the mat of short hair off her forehead.

The river's motion grabbed my energy, dazzling me with the sparkle of sunlight on the current. The motor's gentle sputtering was a comfort. I stirred, shaking off laziness like brushing sweat from my brow. "Alaise, do you also know about the Striiduc sailors? Do many visit Urbyd?"

"Abydian say that some Striiduc women are hedge witches who can make you fall in love with a stranger or sell all your goods for kam."

Brianna chuckled, so I turned to her. "You don't believe in witches?" I asked.

"Arrivi had a healer named Quentin in the days of Cyrus. His gift was real."

"Have you met any Striiduc women?" I asked.

Alaise shook her head no. "The smaller clans were scattered during a pogrom, but not allowed to disembark at Urbyd. Striiduc women are said to be trained fighters and tireless lovers."

I raised my eyebrows pretending to be grateful. "Witches and warriors and sailors; that's quite a combination." I had no use for the inflamed gossip of port traffic.

Alaise shrugged. "Less worthy than the privileges of Dacupitte?"

I saw the cold steel in Brianna's eyes as she tolerated the slur on her betrothed.

"How do you reconcile the interest of Hamilcar," I probed, "and your obligation to Dacupitte?"

"There is no obligation."

"Not even for the call to fertility?" Alaise asked. "Dacupitte has rights."

"He has fathered 300 kids. I owe him nothing."

"But now is the time of—"

"Enough!" Brianna said as she stood. Standing to pace was her first response when irritated, I was thinking. The boat rocked, but there was no place for her to go. She sat again.

In the bow, Lynus twisted with question on his face.

Later we came to a trading pier, and Siiloba steered us out of the current. We tied up at the simple landing place for interior clans who followed the river carrying trade goods. Unsteady patches of shade were provided by three or more spears planted in the dune, with erriv hides stretched across their heads. Two low huts were for public storage against the blowing sand. Lynus and Alaise shouldered their small packs, ready to complete the Madquii homecoming on foot, and we offloaded the cases of munitions to make low stacks.

"Where are your helpers?" I asked.

Lynus showed that disarming grin. "They'll be along."

We began to re-enter the motorboats, but a noise on the side made the warriors turn. With karkars poised they surrounded the storage hut. Siize reappeared with a curt gesture.

Brianna and I peered inside the pen expecting the worst. But it was the Softcheeks scuba diver, Jessup somebody, seated in the shadows, gaunt and shaking with malaria chills.

"Siiloba was poised to kill him," Lynus said, "but he showed this. He said it was a gift from you."

Brianna glanced at the peridot earbob, a quality gem formed as a single teardrop pendant. "Give it back to him. There may be another day when the token is useful."

"We'll take him with us to the Madquii dunes," Lynus said. "But he has information you should know."

Brianna nodded and knelt to chat with the stressed Softcheeks man. "Jessup Chandliss, you are a puzzle. Always on the wrong side of events."

Exhaustion rode his face, and the red-rimmed eyes watered. "Gora warriors are drifting back to the dunes," he said in a rasping voice. "They expect the Arrivi will not mount an attack in support of Ananke when Urbyd falls. They expect that Anaxagoras will take the palace this week. Your mission is ill-timed."

"Expectations seldom work out as hoped," Brianna said.

"What's in Urbyd that you need so badly?" the suffering man asked.

"What has forced you out of Urbyd?" she returned with an arched eyebrow.

Jessup's sunken eyes looked at me and at the warriors. "You think I'm a plant," he guessed, "sent here to misdirect you. I barely escaped with my life. Anaxagoras has a taste for blood."

Brianna was quiet for a long moment. "We appreciate your concern. Alaise has some medicine for you." She turned to go, and I followed her to the low threshold.

"I saw your boys, the kenoma captives," Jessup Chandliss said to our backs. Brianna turned, listening tolerantly. "Not three days ago in a Gora camp," he added. "They are made to work with the livestock and punished for . . . everything."

Kristos and Karry were sons to Kyros and had been captured in a Gora raid. Infrequent stories about their treatment at the hands of Gora wranglers were harrowing.

Brianna's face was hard, revealing only her lack of trust. "Tell Lynus about the camp's location. If we can rescue kenoma captives, then I'm in your debt."

We went back to the long-tail boats that Siize and Siiloba managed. Dulcinea and Alaise shared hugs. Brianna spoke quietly with Lynus and Kenru for a moment before Kenru helped her into the boat next to me. Kenru entered the lighter boat with Dulcinea. We waved goodbye and pushed out into the current.

The river widened, growing shallow and muddy to shape a delta with shipping lanes and lazy eddies near the ragged bank. Siize sought the center channel where a meandering current made the surface frothy. He and Siiloba steered using the tillers, and we glided several kilometers in the afternoon sun.

I stretched my legs and allowed my thoughts to drift. I felt jealous, a little, of the Siibabean brothers who shared everything like they were twins. I had brothers once, but not a confidant. Prankish older brothers, and later, a young fellow who claimed he was my half-brother, sallow and hesitant. I had felt no blood connection when I met Trevor Scott on occasion, even when this boy took over man-agement of his mother's few possessions: some land and a stack of stock certificates. My wormhole number was active by then, so what did I care?

Urbyd was visible finally through the rising thermals, white against a yellow sky. Plumes of smoke from two fires, from the street fighting in surrounding communities, marred the view of a squat skyline. The city was not large and had few tall buildings looming over gilded temple domes.

"Chi cylay," Brianna said to me. "Gora rule here."

"You didn't believe a word that Jessup Chandliss said, did you?"

Her look was sharp and knowing. "So convenient, to happen upon the one man from Urbyd who I might listen to, don't you think?" After a moment, she added, "Did you hear the news about Mike Shaw?"

I shook my head no.

She looked out at the expanse of water, showing a wistful expression so different from her militia commander pose. "They think they found a route through the forest. Each attempt before had led to a cliff or gorge that was impassible."

"Mike Shaw and the gualareps?"

"And some Siibabean friends. Clans there are isolated from even the next village, but their stories consistently tell of an oceanside temple overlooking a fishing ground. The family groups have tools and metalwork that can only be Striiduc. We're guessing some exiles, forced out for using magic or worshipping a different god, have made a community on that side of the peninsula. You knew we live on a peninsula, right?"

"I had heard that."

We reached a flat delta that seemed to go on forever, where barges ready to steam upriver were tied up and vacant. Family jukungs bobbed in the water, several lashed together to form a floating vegetable bazaar. Each flotilla carried an armed Gora warrior sporting the triskelion emblem that resembled a three-legged octopus, his stance shifting as he watched us pass in the current. The riverbanks were lined with family businesses that included free-roaming fowl and goats tied in the back, and behind them were oleastra and Borabean willows, their long streamers sweeping the breeze.

Closer to the city, we tied up at a jutting wooden pier, one among many. An Abydian man—tall with a long beard under his kaffiyeh—stood there with his hands folded before his galabia. My traveling companions climbed out and waited in a group. Brianna struggled with the ceremonial burka but got the facial panel in place, and we finally reached the dock made of planks.

"Hiki, Brianna Miller of Arim, granddaughter of Kyros, the beloved of our great mullah Abyd who built the city palace." The minister spoke English, touching the fingertips of one hand to his chest. "I am Aristides el Abydian, come to greet you."

I knew the story of the earlier Kyros, of course, from the chapbooks of compiled tribal chants. She had traveled to Urbyd two generations ago to meet the king who was building the palace. She returned to the savannah carrying his child who became Cyrus, the father of Rufus and Lynus. They were all related, even though reputation was gained by killing each other.

Brianna bowed with one hand held high, palm up. "We are honored that King Ananke sends his favorite minister to greet our poor band." Her English was superior to his, but she flubbed a few syllables to be gracious.

"I am a simple scholar," he said. "Come this way."

I knew better. I had seen Aristides at Stargate Junction where he negotiated with Striiduc sailors who wanted the labor contracts for asteroid mining. And I had met him again as minister to Khalif Ananke.

We walked in procession through a riverside bazaar where squads of Abydian soldiers stood in tense readiness, creating a safe zone for trade. Souks stopped their whispered conversations and stared, mostly at the blue-black Siibabean brothers with their decorated shields and prominent beltknives, the ever-present karkars slung over their shoulders.

Aristides barely noted the warriors or the traders. During this conflict, many bazaari had destroyed their own market goods so Anaxagoras could not grab the bounty. Their beasts of burden, which were oversized centipedes called sigpywa, had been slaughtered in droves as hostile forces had retreated. Piles of sigpywa were burned in the corrals making a smoky fire, tan and billowing, so full of oil were their wormy bodies under the plates. I glimpsed a smoky fire in the near distance. The odor was daunting.

"Just so there's no confusion," Brianna said to Aristides as we walked along the lane of the bazaar. "Kyros, the mother of Cyrus, was no blood relation to me. My aunt Kyle Rula of Arim was a second wife to Cyrus."

"But you are Rularim Arisen."

"So it is chanted. A simple confusion of the facts."

He nodded slightly, barely turning her way. "Women of your kind are said to offer riddles."

Brianna acknowledged his interest. "The one Kyros in her day posed riddles. These were provided by Mekucoo advisors, and taken from ancient stories."

"We also have ancient stories."

Brianna spoke quickly, taking the initiative. "But your interest is for today's riddle."

"How do you know that? Perhaps from second sight?"

"I wish I did have second sight. I have curiosity and memory."

"Memory is a throng of women with voices like squeaking bats," Aristides recited, "intent on tasting the black blood of the dead."

"Within our tradition, memory honors lost ancestors and connects us with Dolvia."

"A word to the wise," he said through his disdain. "Don't blaspheme by extolling the virtues of Dolvia."

"She guides each of my steps," Brianna retorted from under the veil.

We were escorted to the city proper where paved streets, mostly deserted, had no population of beggars. Armed soldiers were at rooftop stations and occupied some storefronts for defense. The bazaar was shuttered, and few civilians were in the plaza that fronted the palace. The atmosphere of siege was so different from my memory of the evening of the wedding feast.

We were quartered in a spacious apartment in the east wing of Ananke's palace. Under the ceiling arch inlaid with mosaic tile, tall doors opened onto a limestone balcony overlooking the gentle surf of the cove. Images of beetles, the emblem of the ruling Abydian clan, were carved into the limestone and wooden doorjambs. We were not officially greeted, however, nor were we invited to a meal for diplomats as reporters often were. Brianna and Dulcinea did not receive an offer to greet women of the royal family.

The following morning, as we prepared to investigate the city, the apartment door abruptly opened. Siize and Siiloba stepped forward with hands on their beltknives.

"Nu delaya," Brianna said, and they waited. Two Borabean guards entered and took up stations by the door. Aristides entered and stood with his back to the wall, somewhat distant from the door and windows, and folded his hands before his chest.

Our women wore no burkas and didn't reach for them. "It's a pleasure to greet the spirit in your face," Brianna said with Arrivi gestures.

He spoke to her only, using English. "There has been some talk. These who serve are of different tribes. And this one," he said indicating me, "is Softcheeks?"

"I am the betrothed of Dacupitte," Brianna said, "who Borabean call morta chi. Kenru is Uburu, and recently attended the wedding of Akana in the Royal Square. This is his niece Dulcinea, a business associate through StrikeStone. Our enterprises, as you know, hold export licenses for wormhole trade. And the journalist Hershel Henry is embedded with our ambassador mission to record our talks with Khalif Ananke." She didn't introduce the Siibabean, perhaps because Aristides would not care who served as guards.

Aristides disdainfully snorted. "Why do you travel with Softcheeks and former enemies?"

"These are my chosen attendants," Brianna said, "and that ends the question."

Aristides snorted again and walked in long strides toward the doorway. I watched his arched spine as the armed escort followed him out.

"That went well," Brianna said to Kenru who grinned. She turned to Dulcinea. "I am sorry to request this. Today we will be seen in Urbyd by those of many factions. You must show your face—in the company of Kenru, of course."

"Whatever is needed," the Uburu beauty said.

Brianna passed around throw-away cameras she had ordered from the transport, the kind that made a whirring sound and rolled each print out from the casing front. "Be aware of your surroundings. Pipe bombs in the bazaar are the greatest threat to our mission."

I instructed Dulcinea and Kenru on the functions of the cameras.

"Photograph the children and offer the prints to parents," Brianna added. "With humility. Take no photos of Chinese, if you see some. It's considered insulting."

I pulled from the baggage my most lethal weapon, the Earth-made digital camcorder complete with self-adjusting telephoto lens. It rested easily in the palm of my hand.

The palace occupied four blocks of the city center; its gleaming white limestone walls banked on three sides by street commerce. Abydian warriors stood in tight groups, heavily armed for a possible assault on the palace. Livestock pens, now empty of erriv and sigpywa, were maintained near the fourth and western gate where deliveries were once made. The receiving docks were now torched and barricaded. Produce markets were deserted, except for a few souks selling strange pulpy fruits imported from beyond the ocean. To my surprise, some Arrivi goods were for sale, especially olive oil and over-garments made of Mekucoo leather.

The harbor that Ananke controlled, with three steel ships anchored there, was west of the river delta and west of the cove. Another ship was steaming in from the choppy ocean. Commerce thrived in this isolated port, and I called Brianna's attention to what we could see of the activity, maybe pointing too obviously. The telephoto lens did capture images of some guests with Chinese faces aboard the steamers.

We requested to stroll the cove beach along the palace grounds where surf lapped the gleaming sand, but we were denied access.

"I went surfing there when I had first disembarked," I told Brianna. "The waves hissed as they approached shore, like they were talking to me."

"The ocean's song?" she asked with disdain.

We promenaded in the square facing the temple. Brianna wore a blue burka as a shawl and was flanked by Siize and Siiloba. Dulcinea wore a brightly patterned sarong and matching headdress, and Kenru was in a simple baktu and sandals. Many stared at the handsome and armed Siibabean, but Dulcinea was the main object of wonder, especially for Borabean men due to her looks that relaxed the eyes, as it was said. She sighed shortly and tolerated their lascivious glances.

"Men are so simple," Brianna muttered within my hearing.

From the square looking east, we could see the storage silos for silicide with their square refrigeration units and long fat pipes for circulating cold air. Behind them and not so clearly visible in the seaside air, were the furnaces built to refine the silicide for use in industry, but they now stood idle with no smoke belching from the stacks. I captured short videos from many angles using the long-distance lens.

We approached the boarding school next to the airy religious building. One section was scarred from a recent pipe-bombing of a souk's kiosk. Kenru and Dulcinea employed their insta-print cameras to the delight of staring children just released from the classroom. Borabean kids drew back at the whirring sound before they inched forward to see the prints. Dulcinea bowed and offered the photos to parents from her open palm. Rotund and hairy Borabean women in their flowing desert clothes were brusque in the company of gehenna, but they could not resist the bright faces of sons and daughters. They grudgingly received the prints and took the youngsters home.

Soon the afternoon rains were approaching, so we returned to our palace quarters.

Aristides sent a message that very afternoon. In the future he would act as our guide, and would Brianna care to visit the apiary?

Brianna sent back a message claiming her primary purpose was to gain an audience with Khalif Ananke. Was Aristides empowered to facilitate this request, or was there some other Borabean man who she must approach?

"His arrogance won't stand for that," Brianna said. "This shouldn't take long."

My dreams that night were vivid and troubled. I saw a warrior with red dreadlocks riding a desert horse like a fisher king in Earth folklore, and I knew it was Dacupitte. My view was from ground level so he took on heroic proportions. He was joined by Asmach the Borabean seated on his over-sized black stallion. Waiting quietly, waiting and spying, they and two more warriors bolted for a sudden rush into a Gora camp. Barking, nipping at horse legs, I gave a defensive slap from my muscled tail. Shots were fired; warriors were suddenly on the ground. Horses squealed. *Must free those two. Where are they? Where to find?*

Dacupitte stood among the Borabean with karkar fire all around. He slashed them with his beltknife, left then right. Exposed, suddenly exposed. His chest was pelted with bullets. I saw a spray of flesh like big raindrops landing on the parched desert. *Ka, ka, ka, ka, ka.* Where were they? They must escape with kenoma captives. *Ka! Run! This way, run!*

I woke suddenly and sat upright, blinking in the deep night, wondering where I was. Limestone with beetle effigies . . . oh, yeah . . . that's right.

When Aristides arrived the following morning to accompany us to an audience with Khalif Ananke, his armed guards squared off with Siize and Siiloba.

"I have decided," Brianna casually told the bearded scholar, "Siibabean time is best spent in the company of Dulcinea. Mr. Henry will be my escort and to make the record. Perhaps Dulcinea, meanwhile, can visit the palace library? Or greet the women of the royal family?"

Aristides barely blinked. He nodded to a tall guard and gestured that I should walk out ahead of him. My throat constricted. This was all too easy. At Brianna's side, I stepped into Aristides's trap.

Brianna and I were led the long way into the palace grounds, where a circular racetrack included a single set of viewing stands near the finish line. The sky was overcast, and big clouds heavy with moisture rolled in from the east promising to water the savannah. The stables, with many empty stalls, were at the left, all made of wood like a temporary structure. John Milan had reported that the horses were slaughtered during a raid, or after one. Anaxagoras had them killed for blood, so the story went; the corpses strewn in the grazing pasture on the outskirts of Urbyd, and now the stables were empty.

Ananke the Usurper stood with his entourage on a rise near some empty corrals. He was darkly handsome but soft under his decorated galabia. His kaffiyeh was white silk, and the agal included a beetle sigil. A hooded harpie clung to a leather binding on his extended forearm. Waiting at his elbow and wearing an embroidered vest and loose trousers was a fierce looking sailor who I knew as Otieno; he had attended the recent royal wedding. Otieno was of a different cut, balanced and alert. Him I did not want to cross.

I stepped back and raised the camcorder. Its slight whirring noise brought a sharp look from Ananke.

Aristides led Brianna forward and bowed low. "Master, our Arrivi guest."

Brianna held an open palm high before glancing at the other man.

"Perhaps you have met our neighbor during your travels?" Aristides added. "Otieno of the city-state Striiduc in the Cochin nation. He claims to be an offworld traveler."

"Consortium travel channels together people of many philosophies," she said in Borabean.

Otieno's weathered face did not change.

Ananke removed the harpy's hood and strongly pushed his arm upward so that the sea-eagle took wing. All watched as the bird circled our position, but I turned the lens toward the stables where Wan Su, wearing a Company suit with a panda logo on the breast pocket, stood waiting his turn for an audience. I noticed him because we had seen few Chinese faces in Urbyd. Chinese executives had supported Ananke's rule in the past but were less accommodating with the siege.

The big bird keened sharply and returned to Ananke's arm to receive a sliver of meat from the ruler's hand, obedient from dependence. "Isn't she a beauty?" Ananke asked in a self-satisfied way.

"Barn-raised?" Brianna asked.

I hid my smile and shifted position to steal another glance toward the stables. Wan Su was no longer visible from my position.

Ananke's look toward Brianna Miller was cold and evil. I suddenly understood the purpose of the staged wedding during a time of siege. A first-generation ruler dwelling in the palace of a more famous man, Khalif Ananke must flex raw power to rekindle his belief in its existence. Bolstered by Otieno, this ruler would not escape in the middle of the night. He would order his soldiers and civilians to fight to the end, sacrificing ten sons and the best warriors of his clan, if need be.

Khalif Ananke glanced more than once at Brianna's blue shawl. Otieno made no gestures to discern the interest in Ananke's eyes as we talked. He did not care to compete with others for Ananke's time, I was thinking. I learned much during our barnyard encounter.

Soon Brianna and I were returning to the palace through the bazaar. We were met on the street by desert emirs with tense shoulders and hot eyes. Aristides stepped aside to hear a messenger's words.

One emir approached me. "You will come," he said in Arrivi, a jarring phrase in a foreign land.

I glanced around. Lynus stood with the emir's group and calmly nodded. I looked back, finally recognizing the bolder man as Aensilus, whom I knew. Aensilus had been my guide, along with Lynus, when I had trekked across the Madquii dunes to meet Aegiv the lawgiver.

"Of course," Brianna said. "Whatever is correct."

A pipe bomb went off in a nearby business, a small explosion meant to harm patrons and disrupt commerce. In the confusion of screams and smoke, Brianna and I were separated from Aristides, spirited through the bazaar, and guided down a crooked alleyway. Her burka was taken, and we each were given an old kaffiyeh to cover our heads. Mine smelled of cooking oil.

We were crowded into a low kitchen where we waited in silence for perhaps twenty minutes. With the impending rain the room was humid with brooding shadows. We climbed a pole ladder and scurried along several rooftops before we dropped onto a hay mound near an empty sigpywa pen. We awaited a signal, crouched alongside two jittery goats that were staked in the pen.

Aensilus shifted his position; his look sought Brianna's eyes. Then he grabbed my attention and nodded, further indicating we would next move left toward some commotion there. We waited in a crouching position until my knees ached.

Brianna strained to see over the kneeling Borabean who were our escort. "A cook wagon," she whispered to me in English.

"That bomb was a convenient distraction," I whispered. Two men showed us hot stares, and we fell silent.

We were forced to mount the wagon back. Lynus sat on the driver's bench seat and showed his face for reassurance before he slapped the reins over the backs of two erriv. At the last minute, Aensilus jumped in with us. With his karkar poised, he crouched against the tailgate and watched the receding crowd. The wagon rolled through a winding closed bazaar and away from the city center. The rains came suddenly in blowing sheets, and the few pedestrians scurried into doorways. We had traversed several intersections by the time Aensilus relaxed his watchful vigil. He sat back and broke a small kari stem to chew.

Brianna relaxed some and stretched her legs. "Aeolis honors us by sending his father's favorite."

Aensilus smirked. "My brother cares nothing for your mission. This is to make it known we are not the ones."

"The ones what?" I asked.

He considered me with disdain. "Madquii do not send our pregnant women into the enemy camp."

My eyes went round as saucers and my mouth dropped open. "You're pregnant?" I said to Brianna. "That's why the mission had to happen now, no matter the political danger. You would not be able later."

"Everything is political," she complained bitterly. "My whole life is political."

Aensilus looked away.

Brianna worked her jaw and met my look. "I carry Dacupitte's son as part of the call to fertility. Not for broadcasting on the comtech, though."

Aensilus made a snorting sound and looked out the tailgate while the rain eased and the wagon cover dripped noisily. I took a chance with my questions, but asking questions was how I made my living. "Have you met the Striiduc sailors?" I asked him. "Do you know Otieno?"

Aensilus hesitated, possibly wondering how much to share. He shrugged and offered, "Softcheeks weapons and steel ships mean fewer Striiduc men find work as soldiers or sailors. Otieno seeks work for them at Stargate Junction."

"But you don't agree?"

"Abydian lose themselves," he said with a shrug. "Ananke's sons want houses in Ninleau or Moorea to make dance videos with their friends and go water skiing. A big mess."

"The sons are no longer in Urbyd?" Brianna asked.

"Ananke indulges them, maybe because he has so many."

We arrived at the terminal for transport shuttles. Three airbuses were parked at the entrance, idle and rusting since the offworld shuttle no longer made stops at the besieged city. A big Consortium helicopter buzzed overhead, just taking off. I hoped that wasn't our travel connection that we missed. The wagon halted near a landing pad, a freight site far from the passenger terminal.

General Sector reached into the wagon to help Brianna step down.

"Milo?" she said.

"Quiet!" he returned in a harsh voice.

Brianna and I scrambled from the wagon and crossed to board a waiting Consortium helicopter. The wide-bodied vehicle had two sets of rotary blades, one to lift the ample cargo bay. Both sets were humming and slightly circling, sending thin streams of rainwater in all directions.

A Borabean handed something to Dulcinea who was waiting there. Her shoulders slumped as if she had received bad news. Then he joined us.

"This is Aeolis, heir to Mullah Aegiv," Aensilus said.

The tall and bearded man touched fingertips to his chest while Brianna and I did the same. "We're sorry for your trouble," Aeolis said with furrowed brow.

"What trouble?" I asked.

Without more words, the Borabean escort regrouped by the wagon.

General Sector hustled us toward the chopper's hatch, but Brianna pulled back. "I'm not ready to leave," she said. "I have work here."

"We told you the timing was wrong," the general said. "Now you make us mount a rescue and put these Madquii allies at risk."

"So dramatic," she smirked and entered the chopper cargo bay.

At the last moment, I glanced back at Aensilus. Erriv heifers drew the cart forward while the Madquii brothers walked along the muddy track as though heading out to barter market goods.

I scrambled inside and saw Dulcinea in tears; Kelly was seated behind her. Dulcinea patted a folded burka. Brianna's face fell, and she shifted to a seat next to her business partner. "Not the house in the grove of mida trees?"

Dulcinea's chin trembled as she tried to muster a brave face. Tears streamed down her hot cheeks. Brianna sighed heavily. "Not injury to our friends," she said in the same tone.

The chopper jerked heavily before it lifted and banked left. With a thump I sat on some piled tarps. Dulcinea straightened her shoulders, her eyes seeking Brianna's face. "Your fight is my fight now. There is no forgiving."

General Sector spoke from the copilot's seat. "There's more. Warriors mounted a raid last night to rescue the kenoma captives. Dacupitte was sacrificed."

Brianna stood suddenly. "What a bonehead move. I said to not challenge Gora, just locate them. What coordination?" There was no room for pacing, but her back was arched as she stood staring out the round window.

"They were on reconnoiter," Sector said. "They came up on the Gora camp too quickly, a kilometer from where they expected to find it."

"How many?" I asked.

The general showed a weary face, his untrimmed mustache twitching. "Dacupitte and Asmach, with two others on mounts. The kenoma captives escaped, though Asmach took several bullet wounds. Pete's body was . . . well . . ."

"Edwina was with them?" I asked.

"She brought the captives to safety and alerted the sentries. Why?"

"Where is she now?" I asked. Edwina was often in my dreamscape, but I couldn't feel her presence now.

"What do you mean?" Kelly asked.

"Brianna, can you feel Edwina?"

Brianna made a furtive gesture with her back still turned. Her words were measured. "Edwina may have banned remote viewing, from anger. This has happened before." She turned to General Sector. "The Goras will not take Urbyd. Ananke has help from Striiduc. Gora warriors are retreating, or deserting. They destroy whatever's in their wake from spite. I knew this yesterday. Why didn't Dacupitte wait to hear from us? If he had just waited for—"

Dulcinea placed a hand on Brianna's forearm and encouraged her to sit. She placed a palm on Brianna's tummy for emphasis. "This is the last son of Dacupitte. What you choose next must be for his security. Borabean fate belongs to the Borabean."

"Our plans for the silicide don't include—"

"Silicide production can wait for this new leader to get born."

Brianna stood again, even though there was no room for pacing. "I'm not reconciled to this. Aeolis will make peace with Ananke, and the Striiduc will start silicide extraction. Arrivi will have gained nothing! Nothing but death and, and—"

General Sector turned his attention to me. "What did you see in Urbyd?"

"Brianna speaks the truth." I shrugged. "King Ananke no longer listens to Company men. His port is full of metal ships and more streaming in. Goras could not have taken the palace without taking the port first. And why were you so conveniently in Urbyd today?"

"Two choppers that we sold to the shuttle service are missing," Sector said. "I came to secure Consortium equipment from pilfering by either side. Aeolis sent a warrior who claimed that I should wait for Blancom and two pregnant women."

My mouth fell open. "Two pregnant women? Both by Dacupitte?"

Kelly smirked from her place behind Dulcinea. "You're an idiot. She carries the son of Aeolis. Why do you think the Madquii helped you today?"

I showed Kelly a sour face, wondering why she traveled with the general on this inventory errand.

"Kenru and the Siibabean brothers?" Brianna asked the general.

"They're in the other chopper, already airborne. All is secure." He turned at a signal from the pilot, donning a helmet with a low-fic mic.

Brianna finally sat, drained of outrage. "So . . ." she said to Kelly, "this is the workings of prophecy. Pete will not lead after Ely. I will not be his bride."

Kelly smiled sadly. "Dacupitte has led these many cycles. Nobody acts on Ely's word. You have been his true mate since you were younger than me. Second sight holds true."

"Or so you will write in your chants?"

General Sector looked back into the compartment. "We're changing course, headed for the savannah convent. The news is . . . there was a raid."

"A Gora raid?" I asked quickly.

Sector tapped his headgear but shook his head. "I have no other details."

We settled in for the longer flight. Sector remained in the copilot's seat. Brianna stared blankly. While she calculated the next moves for militia strategy, I was thinking. Kelly comforted Dulcinea, who seemed the only one who grieved. I checked the battery charge on my cameras, just in case the convent location held more surprises.

The wet weather in Urbyd had not traveled inland. The parched savannah suffered under an extended season of netta. Sad acacia trees and low oleastra bushes were the only green against tan and red chaparral lands. I squinted against the harsh light and spied a lone female minister walking under a burka, her long strides measured to endure the distance between villages. A companion gualarep lumbered at her side.

Arrivi buildings on the savannah were mostly adobe or red brick. Little wood was available for campfires or construction of outbuildings, so the tracks of Gora marauders were not easily spotted from the air by way of plumes of smoke from destroyed villages. As we approached the savannah convent, though, two bright smoke columns were illuminated by the harsh sun. They were rose-colored, with a flickering red interior—a sure sign of combustible fuel. Our chopper circled near a dusty road banked by oleastra, the disturbance from our blades troubling the billows of smoke. Peering out the round windows, we could see the burning helicopters and dead Gora warriors nearby.

"We found your missing choppers," Brianna called to General Sector.

Soldiers wearing uniforms of the clutch of Kenru were heading back to the convent wall; two of them were limping. One waved us in for landing near the arched entryway. As our chopper approached the convent, we saw that the area was scarred. Bodies of dead erriv were strewn along a southern route, and a few women stood over them, probably convent residents. But wait—not all slaughtered animals were erriv. Some were gualareps. How did the Gora get the drop on gualareps? Where were the scouts, or the ministers, or the network of gualareps in communion with convent residents? Where was Edwina now? Or Edna? I could feel no connection with either of them.

I looked at Kelly's worried face. "Can you feel the gualareps?"

Her glasses misted with unshed tears. "I don't know. I just don't know."

Brianna was pulling the hatch open even before the chopper touched down. She jumped out and hurried to the unveiled women who were hurrying to her—one tall and plain-looking and the other shorter and plump. "Sarah! Cymarta!" Brianna called. "You were spared. I was so worried. How many are lost?"

General Sector was greeted by militia leaders, but I followed Dulcinea with Kelly to catch up with Brianna and Sarah in a tight gaggle. Sarah's eyes were rimmed with red, and her face showed dirt and tear tracks. "Goras came to slaughter the gualareps. Gora warriors walked right past the women. Only three are lost."

We all gasped.

"But why?" Dulcinea asked.

"Tactics," Brianna said in a hard voice. "We had an edge because of the gualareps' song."

Sarah led Brianna past the high brick wall, and Cymarta signaled we should follow. "Prepare yourself," she whispered when we reached the arch. In the convent yard, I saw Brianna's stricken face and followed her gaze left. Several gualarep bodies, maybe twelve altogether, were stacked like cordwood, all missing heads and front feet, the bloody sinews of their necks drying and buzzing with insects. Some were all black on the marbled hides, meaning they were fighting when killed.

Brianna turned away and retched onto the yard.

I sighed and lifted the camera to make the record of Gora spite. Cymarta spoke behind us. "The heads are taken for bounty. The feet can be sold, fashioned into ashtrays for Company officers."

I moved around the pile, but sneaked candid shots of the gathered women, angling to capture each with her face exposed to the sun, her eyes bitter and set with vengeance. Dulcinea never lifted her eyes from the ground, so I could capture no sure shot of her anger.

"Where are the warriors?" Brianna asked.

Cymarta again. "Kenru's clutch pursued the Goras. We don't expect prisoners."

Brianna sighed. "Are the kenoma captives here?"

Sarah shook her head no. "Waiting past the gate. Karlyhi's stinger will take them to Somule. It's bad, what happened to them."

"Where's Edwina?"

"Nobody knows," Cymarta said. "She left earlier, we think to grieve for the loss of Dacupitte, so Edwina was already absent when . . . when Goras came here."

I was moving around the pile. Only one gualarep was missing a tail, its bloody stump visible near the bottom of the stacked bodies. Perhaps tails were too time-consuming to disarticulate. Some hides were fading in color, but the black seemed vibrant still. One guala-rep that was missing a head and feet, partly visible under hacked bodies, also bore a long scar behind a leg and shoulder, identifying her as Edna. I lowered the camera and touched the hide where the tan scar was obvious. Edna had robbed the desert of one.

Kelly was at my shoulder and caught her breath in painful gasps. I met her look of horror before she ran into the convent wailing in a loud voice. Dulcinea and several women followed her.

More women poured through the gates carrying a weighted litter that held a warrior under a bloody sheet. I heard the motors of two helicopters so I assumed bodies were arriving from nearby fight-ing. More bustle was on the left where women rushed from kitchen to infirmary. We were held in place, though, by the horror of the courtyard sight.

Brianna stepped forward, peering at the scarred side of Edna as if for confirmation. Sarah and Cymarta waited. Brianna sighed, her bitter look beyond anger and beyond vengeance. The weight of leadership rested on her like a warrior's aura. She needed to make decisions for them all, and her choices must fit the situation. There was no luxury to indulge the personal.

Her voice was too calm. "General Sector will take you back to Cylay now, Blancom. Report everything, except the pregnancies of course. Those will be obvious soon enough."

"Do you have a quote for me?" I asked quickly, acting on instinct.

"You know that I have no confirmation that Aeolis will make peace with Ananke. You know I have not consulted with Karlyhi about the loss of Dacupitte."

"From today's point of view, what words from Rularim Arisen may I print?"

Her features barely moved, but her eyes softened. "A warrior expects to be lost on any day. Our treasured gualareps were in service, trained by warriors, even though gualareps hated the killings. This quiet time of mourning does not mean we have lowered our guard against the Gora. Any Gora warriors we find on the savannah will die."

"Are you ordering their deaths?"

"I know Karlyhi's mind," she said barely above a whisper. "Anaxagoras has lost his bid to rule in Urbyd or anywhere on Dolvia. Go back to Cylay now, Blancom. I must spend time with these women of the savannah."

"I appreciate your trust."

"Dolvia has provided. Go along before the general leaves without you. This is not a good time for a long walk in the desert."

I hurried out of the convent gate and ran to the chopper, holding the heavy cameras close. Two stingers had also landed, and both were missing the mounted missiles that were used in skirmishes. Four women stood on the side near stacked crates of supplies. General Sector saw me sprinting to him and held out a hand of warning that I must wait. I joined him near a group of warriors that included Karlyhi and Kyros Kenoma who was seated on two stacked crates.

Karlyhi was an imposing man for Cylahi, olive-skinned and lanky, as though his skeleton was too big for his skin. His face was grim like he was waiting for battle even though the skirmish had ended. He had fresh bleeding marks on his bare chest and blood on his dungarees.

The rescued sons of Kyros were there, ragged and starved with hard faces that showed only hatred. Kyros stood and reached to embrace them. Karlyhi encouraged them to step into Kyros's arms and the younger one complied, stiff and unloving. The older one named Kristos stepped back, looking at Kyros with the fathomless eyes of betrayed trust. Kristos motioned to the brother—I was thinking that his name was Karry—and they followed Karlyhi to the stinger.

Kyros rabbe Sudl, known as kenoma, put a hand on his chin to control a show of emotion while he watched his sons leave with the warrior. The helicopter lifted, and Kyros sagged. He sat again with both hands over his face and his shoulders shaking with sobs. We waited several minutes before General Sector led Kyros to a second stinger where a pilot was already seated. General Sector spoke as he worked the shoulder strap for the distressed man, and then signaled the pilot who touched the controls so they lifted and banked left, heading in a different direction.

General Sector bent against the disturbance and walked to my side. "Too much heartstone," he said. "Kyros didn't rescue his sons. He couldn't protect them from abuse. They may never reconcile."

"Karlyhi will only feed their hatred."

Milo Sector nodded. "We're leaving Asmach here at the convent. The women will manage his recovery, if he recovers. Why didn't

Dacupitte wait for warriors to reinforce his position? After all this time. After he came through every skirmish unbloodied. Why now?"

I shrugged and stared at the ground.

"Let's get mounted." General Sector saluted the women who didn't acknowledge him.

We climbed into the transport chopper, and I got the hatch closed just as the machine lifted. The general went to the copilot seat, and I sat on some piled tarps, staring through the round window at the red sands of the savannah.

FOUR

THE FUNERAL PYRE OF DACUPITTE WAS HELD AT KECOUROO'S village above Mayschool. There was no body to burn, but his few possessions were located there. He had lived as Rufus lived with little more than the respect of warriors and the company of ancestors. I was not invited to this tribal event, but the city of Cylay was suddenly empty of his descendants with rust-colored hair. Many younger ones filtered back within a couple days, but I had the feeling that warrior ranks were suddenly swollen with new recruits.

I often saw Mark, an older Cylahi with a sparse gray beard and a pronounced limp; many residents solicited him for news. Wicked and fresh cuts, maybe self-inflicted, were obvious on his arms and bare chest. He chatted with Genki and set up shop next to her in the shaded doorway. Blanc lingered with them some mornings before he took up his kam-man station.

Mark enjoined a quick enterprise fashioning arm amulets for those who mourned Dacupitte: a binding strap with a garnet or reddish topaz secured with gum arabic. Mark wet his fingers on his tongue and then dipped them into a pouch of resin. He lined the leather with the paste and quickly bound the stone a client had selected. The package was passed over Genki's cooking fire until heat set the resin, and then traded for kari root stems or a sprig of cumin. I was thinking the red stone was popular to display in remembrance of Dacupitte.

I saw Mark prepare a talisman for Stuben, the street gang leader, but refuse payment. Stuben had not left Cylay for the funeral so Mark's gesture seemed strange. Maybe they were related, though, both being Cylahi.

Nobody spoke of the kenoma captives. Their rescue was a private matter, much like the removal of General Sector's son was private.

I slept heavily and without dreams. The gualarep song was silent, and I missed the images sent by Edwina or shared by Edna. They were the first residents on Dolvia who had made me feel welcome. One night, as I lay awake with my worries, and I heard Mark outside the window offering a chant for the local audience. It translates poorly to English, and I am no poet. I recorded here what parts I thought to reconstruct.

> In the days when General Sector led,
> Known to all as Milo-pilo
> Kyros was kenoma, Ely in Cylay
> And all minds turned to Dacupitte
> During this endless season of netta.

Ely raised a hand against Rularim,
Saying "Whore! Whore of the Company!"
Dacupitte stayed his hand
And let the switch fall on Ely's back.
Finished then, his words vanished in time.

Brianna's heart was thus won,
Where before she had only frowned.
Her adoptive brother a lover became,
She to deliver his last son.
He who carries the mark of the furled brow.

Aeolis the Borabean gestures
Toward peace and restoration.
For rights to sire more to replace those lost
He and his men from the fight retire.
Send Dulcinea for the season of fertility.

Brianna claimed no second sight,
And Kat has not spoken.
Karlyhi reinforced Aeolis,
All men can destroy, only some inspire.
Kenoma souls cry out for new breath.

Aeton and Asmach sallied forth,
To free kenoma children.
Dacupitte with valor fought
The daily victory to transpire.
But this father of so many sacrificed.

Brianna found Karlyhi at the pyre,
Mourning his lost brother.
"He was generous, kind and no liar,"
Were her words of honor.
"Also he had a fine singing voice."

"He was too good for us," Karl stated.
She added, "He was too good for them."
"A fine funeral we have piled," said Karl,
"For Dacupitte our brother,
Then of this one, a warrior we can raise."

"Perhaps to ban the warrior way,"
Claimed Rularim, "And make the peace anon."
Karlyhi breathed out to settle his ire.
"Then who in your armies will serve?"
And those raised by Sheeks-Cylom now lead.

John Milan had secured the cushy reporter's station in Urbyd. My teeth ached with jealousy. His reports were rerun every twenty minutes on the comtechs and were full of developing events. Gora officers, with no expertise for managing industry but with polished automatics, recklessly rode in trucks through the Company refinery yards on the outskirts of Urbyd. The Chinese panda logo proudly displayed on silo walls was mutilated with bullet spray and splattered paint. Unused refinery equipment, most of it still in shipping crates, was dragged from refinery buildings and trashed before the media cameras. Wan Su and Tuang Cho retreated to the orbiting transport, a common Company maneuver.

Between Karlyhi and Aeolis—and with no help from Ananke who didn't rouse himself to save his tribesmen—the siege of Urbyd was broken and Goras retreated to remote dunes. Aeolis emerged as the voice of reason, a bridge between Ananke's craftiness and Karlyhi's hot vengeance. Aeolis was seen on comtechs while his sigpywa-riding warriors delivered relief rations to Urbyd. Before the cameras, Aeolis shook hands with Ananke and Otieno from Striiduc, seated together in ornate chairs in some ceremonial room of the palace. Karlyhi, ever camera-shy, was not present, nor the Consortium officers.

I saw it all on the comtechs, each event introduced by the China-doll announcer.

Anaxagoras had escaped the site of the siege but was spotted on Gora dunes with his loyal warriors protecting his flank from internal strife. They trashed Borabean villages to cover their retreat. Women and children were stripped of resources. Uncles and cousins were held in pens or conscripted for future conflicts. Stories surfaced of ritual rape and mutilation. These atrocities were against his own people or against families residing on his own lands—people Anaxagoras ruled over.

My armchair advice was sometimes broadcast on the comtechs, tacked onto the war news by the China-doll announcer. "Meanwhile, back in the capital of Cylay, our correspondent, Hershel Henry—"

I mostly spoke to the issue that there was nothing to report, nothing new; except I reveled in the news that the commodities market fluctuated wildly. The Cicero romark was devalued by twelve percent.

Within the turmoil, leadership in Cylay was under pressure. Rabbenu Ely was not liked by Aeolis or Ananke and had no positive relation with Karlyhi. Increasingly isolated, even though he still received Softcheeks foreign aid, Rabbenu Ely granted an interview with Regan Villines who was seated in an opulent room of the Cylay mansion. I watched the political theater from the bar in the hotel Press Club. Junior reporters were seated at the bar's table, drinking and voicing minority opinions. On the overhead screen, Ely wore a western suit and spoke in crisp English.

"What Mekucoo owns a suit?" one fresh-faced reporter asked. "It's like he's making his case to Softcheeks."

"Will you hold free elections?" Regan Villines asked on screen.

"Of course," Ely answered smoothly, "after certain conditions are met. We need to take a fresh a census first, so savannah tribes are counted for voting rights. Credentials must be established for who may sit on a judge's bench. The militia must lay down arms to prevent riots at the voting booth. Security comes first, after all."

"All those are delaying tactics," the reporter at the table insisted. "Ely only exposes his weakness."

I glanced over my shoulder at him. That newbie won't last long with Doug Endicott, I was thinking. I avoided engaging in the discourse, though. I collected my kari root cigarettes and lighter and left the bar.

I stopped by comtech offices at the hotel and sought out the network dog again. Doug Endicott was packing to leave; a document box held sports trophies and framed photos. "Be quick, Henry," he said. "I have a plane to catch."

"Rotated already? On to New Shanghai?"

"Actually, I had an offer from a news enterprise in Cochin. You heard of them?"

"Yah, sure. Developed nation, friends with Striiduc."

"They have a cellphone system with their own satellites," Endicott said. "They want to expand to include Urbyd and the whole savannah here. Cellphones for Cylahi. Think of it. Cochin execs are hiring for an upstart network that reports non-Company news. You should be interested, given your complaints."

"No safety net?"

He smiled tightly. "When I step out of the Company sphere, when I leave this building, I'm cut off from salary from any Earth corporation."

"Going native, are you?"

He took a moment to write something on a slip of paper. "Did you know the Chinese Company uses child labor on the freighters? Brought here from Earth."

"Everybody knows."

He showed me a hard look. "And that's not a story to you?"

"I have to report what's in front of me. The Company keeps the traffic under wraps."

"And what did you learn in Urbyd?"

I shrugged slightly. "My report is filed. Gora are retreating and slaughtered the gualareps at the convent."

He squinted. "Yes, yes. But what about the Company? Why just withdraw? They must have some other route to riches."

"The Company is already rich from managing Junction traffic."

"They brought some big space ships," Endicott said. He waved one item before putting it in the box. "Through the wormhole.

Smelting ships for asteroid mining. Why import minerals they can mine here, huh?"

"Smelting ships? Those are too big for the wormhole."

"Stripped down and then re-tooled in Westend. And they brought slave labor. That's the big story. Forcing workers into press-gangs for the smelting ships. It's own kind of hell."

"To get the proof," I said, "you would have to travel with the press-gang and then find a route back. No guarantees. Better to focus on—"

"The siege at Urbyd will soon end," Endicott said. He finished his packing. "The slaughter of some gualareps is small potatoes."

Easy for him to shrug off, I was thinking. "And you're leaving to pursue the child labor story?" I asked, trying to remove the tone of disdain.

Endicott stopped and breathed out heavily. "Look, you were right, Henry. The Company news network is self-serving with these rabbenu wars. The rosy gloss-overs while the real stories are quashed; it turns my stomach. These self-torchings are only the surface." He meant the four tribal women who had died in front of Ely's mansion, the story that I had wanted to pursue.

"And the order of impunity?" he added with a down-turned mouth. "I must be a romantic, always cheering for the underdog."

I didn't bother to remove the skeptical tone from my voice. "So, you're moving to Ninleau in Cochin in support of home rule on the savannah?"

"I'm doing it for the money." He grabbed his half-filled box and headed for the door. "Oh, you wanted something. What was it?"

"Doesn't matter now."

He handed me the slip of paper. "These are my EAM codes. When you decide to make the jump to real news, you'll find me in Ninleau."

"I hope it works out for you. Melinga." I watched him walk down the decorated hall of the hotel like a mirage, a phantom presence not resident long enough to leave an impression. And yet I admired his courage. Hadn't we all come adventuring to Westend to make our fortunes?

I went down to the bar and found Regan Villines, dressed in khaki and seated among the loitering junior reporters, searching through her notes for some lost fact. She looked up with irritation before her features cleared. "Henry, I just completed an interview with Ely. He's full of excuses, huh? Did you see my piece on Captain Manenowski? Karl Wyley took him out on the desert and—"

"I covered the slaughter of gualareps. The vaccine deaths too," I said, feeling defensive. "The incidents didn't surface on the broadcast news. Not even a ripple."

She showed the hard features of a veteran reporter. "Kids die here every day. What you need is a real story."

I shifted my weight from foot to foot, unwilling to sit with her. "Like child labor on Company freighters?"

Her mouth twisted in a smirk. "You talked to Endicott. Suddenly, he's a great crusader. He'll abandon that story; just his excuse for leaving early. Listen, can you secure an interview with General Sector about the new stock exchange and the futures on gum arabic?"

"Ah, yah, sure. They have a new trader: an erriv herder named Len rabbe Murd."

"A threat to the Junction Boys, is he?" She shook her head. "Like chaff in the wind, these Arrivi. They understand nothing of the real world."

I only nodded. "You keep reporting that," I said. "You'll find true success reporting that." I moved to the bar to drown my worries in a bottle of Kiam gin.

To fill the hours some days later, I was culling some files of photos at the EAM in my rooms. Dkar knocked at my door and said I should join General Sector, who was waiting outside. I ended my connection with the orbiting transport, closed the coolant cover on the EAM, and grabbed the camera bag.

General Sector was not the one who waited for me. I was driven by militia officers in a—well, like a dune-buggy called a bobcat—to the public square in front of the governor's mansion. They pushed me out and sped ahead to a more secure location, barely avoiding a sigpywa that lumbered along the lane, led on halter by a couple of convent residents. That seemed strange. Sigpywa were bred in groups and mostly by Borabean.

The standard cache of protestors, allies of Rabbenu Ely who often burned blue tams when a cameraman was in the plaza, nudged each other and started my way. I never reinforced their rhetoric with images or quotes, so I wasn't one of their favorite reporters. Putuki bazaari stood nearby, also several academy workers under burkas. Voki Manuki in a dark business suit tried to send the women away, shouting with big gestures. "Go home! Go back to your work. Nothing to see here; just another business day."

The veiled women shuffled out of his way but regrouped to stand vigil.

My throat was tight. My camcorder was making that whirring noise as it captured the movements of four unveiled women who stepped forward from the crowd. They were lashed together with common twine and wore long skirts drenched with gasoline, obvious from the smell of accelerant. Their leader on the far left limped markedly.

Voki Manuki pressured them, but they only shuffled left. He shouted at the leader, leaning into her space, demanding that she obey him. She dropped a lit match and was immediately consumed. Manuki scrambled away as Vera's loose hair rose with the updraft in delicate strings of fire. The orange burst whooshed across the group eating their clothes and flesh. And that smell. Two women flailed their arms and twisted in pain, maybe in regret. Their knees buckled, first Vera who pulled the others down. Gasoline burned hot but not for long, only charring the blackened bodies. Below the rolling black smoke, twisted skeletons were discernable under the seared skin.

I captured it all on the camcorder. And I resolved that this was the last time. No more.

Please, no more.

Voki Manuki stood defeated on the side. His eyes were dull, and his skin glistened with sweat in the humid air. He was thinking the same as me. Please, no more.

I focused the camcorder on Manuki who was too well-informed. The bazaari spoke into the lens. "The leader was Vera, the wife of Captain Manenowski. She was shamed by his death, shamed that he had sold Arrivi secrets to Borabean. These others had afflicted children with the poison vaccine. They sacrificed themselves so Hakulupe Le would not. Four unblessed ones in the place of one. These self-torchings must stop. Find some other way."

"What were the women protesting today?" I asked from behind the camcorder. "Are they calling for home rule?"

He balled his fists, and his face twisted. The cache of protestors appeared behind him; all Putuki, all angry. "The sor'shum is to blame," Manuki said. "Hamilcar and the sor'shum protect their own. Nothing for us! Nothing for the tribes."

Behind him, the protestors gathered and took up the chant. "Death to the sor'shum. Death to Hamilcar."

"Wait! Wait!" I called. "What about home rule and solidarity with Karlyhi?"

"Hamilcar must die!" one called, looking into the lens. "Death to the sor'shum."

I lowered the camcorder and shook my head. This was the wrong message from the wrong messengers. I wanted no complicity with spreading Ely's excuses. The Arrivi women had sacrificed themselves in silence, but now the message was muddied.

It started raining followed by a healthy downpour. The crowd dispersed. Residents of the nearby academy wearing matching burkas came forward to manage the remains.

I was at the network office that same afternoon, submitting the footage along with my background report on Vera's place among the tribes. In the Press Club, I watched the evening Consortium news for the segment, but my second report was excluded. The China-doll announcer mentioned that Vera had despaired after the ritual death of her husband at the hands of Karl Wyley. Vera was cast as a victim of the tribal conflict, a veiled and illiterate woman with no understanding of events that swirled around her.

I shook my head. The slaughter of the gualareps was unreported, and these martyrs had torched themselves without gaining the attention of Westend or even the tribes. My reports were silenced, filed away because reporting the Arrivi narrative upset the smooth balance that the news organization filtered so the Chinese Company could polish its brand.

Over the next couple of days, I endured a round of interviews. Voki Manuki was also on the talk shows trying to act as an intermediary, trying to save his own ass. "A forum is needed," he postulated, "for the people to voice their complaints. Putuki can see that need now. The bazaari are ready to lend our support." His cutting glance skirted left then right. "A public debate is needed, a town hall meeting perhaps. I can lead here."

No Arrivi applauded when he spoke. Rabbenu Ely made no public statement.

My heartstone showed on the comtechs. My answers were cynical. "How many more Arrivi must sacrifice themselves before Rabbenu Ely sees the handwriting on the wall?" I asked the Chinese interviewer. My Softcheeks idiom was lost on the tribal audience.

I also sat with Regan Villines for an interview with her byline, providing background about political dynamics and what to anticipate in Cylay. We got the real news out for any who watched the segment. Regan's piece included footage of earlier self-torchings by tribal women, and we presented their motivations from the angle of tribal logic. When the segment was completed, I asked if Regan had interviewed any of the women who had torched themselves.

"I met Karen in passing," Regan said, "as the mother of Kelly Osborn and keeping the old ways. There was no indication Karen was political. Did you know them?"

"The earlier deaths all happened before I disembarked. Have you interviewed Kelly Osborn about the protest?"

Regan showed me her veteran's face. "We asked to talk with her and with Hakulupe Le, but they always refer us to Mrs. Shaw. And she lives on Cicero."

I made the rounds to the hourly talk shows, each with its own armchair expert serving as anchor, and I even completed an editorial segment opposite Mrs. Shaw, by video of course. Our conversation was broadcast to Cicero cities and on Stargate Junction. Mrs. Shaw sat in the studio with the Cicero interviewer and claimed the deaths-by-fire were an accepted means of protest.

"What were Vera and the others protesting with this act?" the commentator asked.

"Rabbenu Ely must step down," Mrs. Shaw insisted. "The message behind each death-by-fire is the same. Kyle Rula was first, then Marcy who was rabbenu's first wife, followed by Karima Le of the land of Murd. Kelly Osborn's mother Karen was next and now this group who died together. All tribes want a change of government in Cylay for this whole region."

"Do you agree?" the commentator asked me. My image hovered on a big screen behind them.

"As I have said previously," I replied, "I knew none of these women personally. The four deaths focus attention on tribal voices and their demands for home rule."

"A democratic election is needed," Mrs. Shaw added, ticking off their demands. "A forum for debate among governmental parties, including welfare ministers from the savannah convent. The end to cronyism, and a new accountability among decision-makers for the use of funds from offworld aid."

After the segment was taped, Mrs. Shaw chatted with me trunk-to-trunk. "Your voice was strong today, Henry, with words of iron like sacrifice and home rule."

I blushed. "I have been talking about this death of Vera Manen-owski for days now. I didn't even know her or her husband. But tell me, you're the Sheeks-Cylom that tribespeople claim sleeps with dragons. Isn't that right?"

She smirked, apparently aware of the tale. "The commentators call me acerbic."

"Yes, ma'am."

"Just because I can see," she continued. "Just because I can visualize the logical end of a problem. I'm supposed to keep quiet and wait for them to catch up. And when I say something, anything at all, that's acerbic. Ha! They cannot accept the truth from a woman. Acerbic is a pecking order question and nothing more."

"Yes, ma'am," I repeated.

She abruptly ended the call.

Later at the hotel, I picked up a paycheck and asked to speak to the administrator. A new network dog sat in Endicott's seat, Paul somebody. He had puffy cheeks and a jutting chin. I was guessing he came from business news and not from military reporting like Doug Endicott.

"I want to buy out my contract," I said.

He wrinkled his nose as though detecting a bad smell. "I read your file, Henry. It's seems my predecessor didn't care for you so much."

"The camera equipment is mine," I doggedly continued, "and I'll buy the EAM equipment, on installments of course."

"You would sacrifice the right to jump back?" he asked incredulously.

"There's more than one channel for wormhole travel."

"You mean through Somule Gems? Brianna Miller is at the fortress and, uh, in a family way. Did you knock her up?" I slightly shook my head no. "The other one is also pregnant and has returned to an Uburu mesa where her father is dying. We figure Jessup Chandliss for her lover. He trudges up the mesa side with supplies."

I decided to stick to today's topic. "I need new EAM codes, but I can go through the Consortium for that. Anything else?"

He smiled dryly. "I spoke with Milo Sector, by way of verifying some facts." He opened a desk drawer and stacked several small packages on the scarred desk. "You can have these doses of mefloquine to fight the malaria, Henry. You can keep your locker key." He held up one page from the thick file he had pretended to peruse. "This form needs my signature to exclude you from the Press Club. Somehow it got lost." He dropped the page into a trashcan. I stood and stuffed the drug samples into my camera bag, and reached to shake hands. "I didn't catch your last name."

"Spurlin. Paul Spurlin. I wish we had met earlier."

"We are often through events before we understand their meaning in our lives."

I ran into Regan Villines as I was leaving. "Come into the bar," she said. "We can drink Kiam gin and swap lies about how we earned the Pulitzer."

"I have an appointment." I shrugged.

"Yeah?" Her eyes were hot with curiosity. "Kelly Osborn is feeding you tomorrow's scoop, huh? Something more for me, do you think? Something about buying shares of gum arabic?"

I shrugged her off and headed for the exit. Regan followed me into the light rain. "What does Kelly know about the stock exchange?" She grabbed my arm and turned me toward her, her hair hanging heavily with moisture. "What's wrong with you? We accomplished this! Do you think peace in Cylay is possible without reporters? Do you think Ely would lose power except for the media cameras? We did this."

"Do you think offworld aid would serve Ely's greed without our reports?" I lost my temper, hot and itchy despite the rain in my eyes. "We had a hand in Dolvia's fate; you're right about that. But not the truth, nothing close to the truth."

"We're needed here," she insisted. "Regime change without spilling blood."

"They die of our diseases, don't they? They're robbed on our stock exchange, aren't they? Ely was made by us and bolstered by us."

Regan wiped the rain from her eyes. "Just come inside. We can talk this through."

"The talk means nothing. Talk only makes it worse."

"What do you want?"

"Tribal logic." I walked into the street and looked back with drenched eyes. I saw Regan apparently in slow motion, shimmering in the blowing rain with her arm waving in a circle. Come in; come in. Join our ghoulish company.

I went thirsting after tribal logic; solid and clean and intolerant.

I walked home in the rain, glad to punish myself with the drenching as I tried to make sense of it all. People in the neighborhood did not believe Rabbenu Ely could be unseated. He had always lived in the governor's house. Putuki bazaari had always cheated their way to fortune while tribal children had no schools and soldiers had no boots.

Mark and Genki hugged the door in the shaded station where she lived while sheets of rain obscured my view of them. I only waved and beat it into my place.

The unblessed ones knew only what they heard among themselves, wrapped in chants of romance and heroism. Mark was chanting to entertain himself until the rains stopped. I heard his words through my open window as I changed clothes.

> Rularim was arisen and fought
> In battles long and gritty.
> Against Anaxagoras a worthy enemy,
> With Karl and Kenru and Orin she won
> Honor beyond Dacupitte, the supposed husband.

Of battles many she grew weary and sought
A word from her cousin Kat.
"Lay down arms, begin anew,
Dolvia will deliver your enemy
And also you into the arms of Dacupitte."

That night, I dreamed of hunting on the savannah, moving with ease through tall grasses. Ketiwhelp ran alongside, yapping and drooling with hunt-fever. I reached the low bank and glided into a swift current leaving the ketiwhelp frustrated on the mucky side. Schooling kariom joined me in joyful singing. But there was more, an additional voice. The river provided a deep-throated hum. It had always been there, Iamida's timeless song. I felt the thrilling rush of recognition of a soul more ancient than mine, a soul long dwelling on the body of Dolvia.

PART TWO

Eggs are pecked and wet, hatchlings coo
Breathe in their scent, tangy and new
Down to the bank, splash in the water
Life and song and brother
What could be better, anon?

FIVE

from Kelly Osborn

EDNA WAS GONE. NO MORE DREAMS OF SWIMMING IN THE grotto or egg tending or basking near the billabong. I pushed strands of coppery hair from my face and blew my nose before I put on the wire-rimmed glasses. I remembered Edna's joy at greeting Brianna at the Uburu digs. I remembered Edna's pranks on Blancom and how she lulled her tongue to show disapproval. I remembered walking and waiting with her, the calming sensation she shared, so generous. *Kelly, ka, ka, ka, ka.* But now the song was absent . . . ended, silent.

Edna was found in the pile of carnage, not singular, not honored. A two-day funeral pyre consumed the gualarep bodies. Two pyres, actually, one outside the convent walls where we also burned the erriv corpses.

Corpse. Edna was a mutilated corpse, missing her head and feet. The head taken for bounty to show Gora officers or Khalif Ananke or Company paymasters. Count the heads, pull the teeth, preserve the hide. I hated the violators, the bile of spite tasting like cilantro.

I felt small, shrunken, an empty husk. No vista across the savannah in my dreams, no amber sunset over a Mekucoo knoll, no song rising in celebration of life and sunlight and cool water. No adoration from my mentor or loyalty or strength or . . . love. I was missing the better part of my soul, as though I was suddenly deaf while attending a festival, unable to make sense of actions. I looked up expecting to see Edna waddle past the door, waiting for my step, waiting with her heart of forgiveness. I checked at the threshold; but no, only a passing resident.

Edna was gone.

I was not alone in my grieving. Sarah shuffled along the convent halls, dispirited and with bent shoulders like a patient who had essential organs removed. Her face was grey; her eyes were dull. Sarah knew them all. She was present at the hatchings, the first Dolviet graced with the birth songs. Sarah blamed herself for not protecting them. She blamed herself for training them for militia duty, for risking them where trust was absolute. And now she was excluded from the song.

Cymarta had stepped up to manage daily convent events. She hovered over me some days while I sat here in the patch of sunlight that violated my room that held a padded chair, a writing desk, and a narrow cot. I was a burden, I knew, while I searched the droning silence for the song, a refrain, a sign that I was remembered. I didn't expect forgiveness, just a touch.

Cymarta was here again with a tray of food. She handed me tea in a pewter mug. The tips of my fingers registered heat from the tea mug. "Come out now, Kelly. Can't you walk in the garden today?"

I saw Cymarta and heard her, a whisper from out there.

"And General Shaw has reached the Siibabean shore on the other side of the forest," she was saying. "They found a fishing village there. Isn't that great news? A reason to celebrate."

I had no response, no reason to speak. I sipped the bitter tea.

I watched the sun pass over the convent garden, left to right. Gentle morning light, strong midday sun to nurture oleastra bushes, the afternoon rains, followed by long shadows as the day waned and the blessed night cooled the walls and muted my senses.

I should write.

Maybe tomorrow.

I moved with no ambition from the chair to the cot, turning my face to the wall. I had no need to pray for dreamless sleep; the blanks hours were my punishment.

Sunlight on my eyelids made them flutter. I sat up and craned my neck to peer past the windowsill. Eight young girls were in the garden below my window, seated in a half-circle and looking down. No gestures, no laughing, no jostling. Two lifted their bald heads to feel sunlight on their faces. Rescued convicts; I knew the story. They had labored on the transport that orbited Dolvia, or another Chinese ship where they were devalued as cargo. They had no connection with the tribes and no hope for a better future.

A couple of convent residents, maybe age fourteen, joined them with touches and smiles and offering treats of fruit and sweetbread. The bald girls dressed in shifts watched without expression. From the side came a chant.

"Dacupitte can have any
woman except the two he covets.
Dulcinea is afraid of
the other called his beloved."

Giggles and shuffling. Dacupitte had been lost in a skirmish, his funeral pyre not a cycle of Nettom past. Why so blatantly chiding?

"Brianna visited the stars with Sheeks-Cylom and Mike
Then onto Earth and the land of Nordhagen.
From Paris she was fetched by Kyros and Rufus.
She returns to us as though arisen and despite
Dacupitte's promise to get even her pregnant."

More giggles and the girls joined the circle of bald girls and chanted again. "Dacupitte can have any . . ."

Cymarta entered my room carrying a tray with tea and fruit. She looked up sharply when I spoke. "Who are those naughty girls? Disrespect for Dacupitte so soon after he's gone?"

Cymarta stretched to see out the small window. "New conscripts—"

"No, the naughty girls in green," I demanded. "Where are the chants of honor?"

"Perhaps you can teach them some new chants."

Shame washed over me. Cymarta had so many cares but had complained not once and took all barbs without anger. Shame sat on my grief like a baby marmoset on its mother's shoulder.

"Kelly, do you remember Denise Datong?" Cymarta asked without looking at me.

"Ah, sure. One of the Softcheeks trainees that Brianna Miller brought back from France. Teenagers mostly and called the clutch of Cleo."

"Oh, I'm so glad you remember her. I don't, not a whit."

"Bernice left early. She took a trainee position with Somule Gems on the transport."

"Well, she's at Stargate Junction now," Cymarta said, "and running the show, apparently. That's the thing. Somule Gems is for all of us. We all participate, right?"

"It's a cooperative for profits that supports the convent here."

"And we're grateful, but we do our part," She showed a palm to indicate the convent. "And we just went through . . . And we just had . . ."

"What's the problem?"

"Bernice used Somule Gems funds to purchase these convicts," Cymarta said, close to complaining. "In the garden. Bernice expects us to mind their needs. Just like that, she's giving orders."

"Rather they should beg on the streets in Cylay?" I asked.

Cymarta ducked her head with a turned down mouth. She brushed dust from the desktop. "I wonder if you have a moment today, Kelly. Asmach will not recover from his wounds. He has lingered these many days, but his last hours are soon. Warriors are fighting among the mesas, pursuing Goras who are deserters. There is no time for Asmach, no vigil of honor while the residents are stressed with, um, other duties. Could you . . . a trip to the infirmary as the betrothed of Rufus, just to mark a warrior's passing."

"We can go now."

Cymarta showed her round face with expressive eyebrows. "Really? I'll help you stand."

"I can stand and walk and . . . and be impatient. Thank you, Cymarta."

We walked up the corridor and I noted the cloying scent of oleastra, of wet razor grass, and the acrid tang of jasmine blossoms from the brace that climbed the wall. The tall and curving convent wall was warmed by sunlight and looking more orange than brick red. I breathed in the sense of urgency during work hours, with clanking bowls in the kitchen and raised voices in the classrooms and the scrape of utensils from gardeners who minded the many rows of oleastra. I heard a low pounding and knew the press was operating. Duty and the daily tasks drew me into the tumbling moments of time.

"Is Sarah well?" I asked.

"She feels sick in the mornings, but spends afternoon hours with her account books."

"Morning sickness?"

"For the call to fertility," Cymarta said with melody. "A son for Kyros Kenoma."

"From when he was just here?"

"Kyros Kenoma is a neighbor who often brings supplies. Sarah provided a moment's comfort. This was before . . . before the rescue of Dulcinea in Urbyd."

"Are you . . . Did you . . . ?"

Cymarta grinned, sunny and lighthearted. "Oh, no. I want a husband who stays."

"Can the gualareps recover?"

She shook her head no, looking down. "The males have a season of musk. None are old enough yet."

I didn't ask if she had lost a gualarep companion. It was still too soon for personal questions. We entered the infirmary where two nurses chatted, heads together. Cots lined the wall that led back to a cool interior with mosquito netting pulled back over each one. In the shadows was a raised platform with candles burning, a place for reverence for those too weak to walk to the chapel. The convent had been established for the Softcheeks protestant religion, after all. One nurse wore a brown shift with a white bib apron, the common dress of the daughters of Deborah. She led us to a private room, not large but bright and clean. I saw a high bed with flickering lights on monitors and a medicine drip on the side. I heard regular, wet breathing.

I stepped to the bedside and looked at the old warrior, the subject of many fireside chants. Asmach who was friend of Aegiv and had fought alongside Dacupitte; now his face was ashen and sagging. Behind me Cymarta gave instructions in a whisper. The curtains were drawn and the lights lowered. It was no longer hospital-like, more a hospice for the dying. I drew a book of chants from my skirt pocket. I chose from the old stories, those no longer painful due to the distance of time.

> Cyrus and Cara on Arrivi land set foot
> To kill the erriv mutilator.
> Upon the faces of four sisters they looked,
> The daughters to Len rabbe Arim,
> And forgot Mekucoo wives wedded to the land.
>
> The youngest, a feral child, did please
> The warrior who had sired Kecouroo

Second sight told Kyle Le
This man and she were connected
Together within the body politic.

Cyrus defended Len rabbe Arim
And suffered three beatings in prison.
Cara showered the barracks with snakes
And easily strolled in to release him.
One stripe, one snake became the legend.

Against the Company Mula led the fight,
And Cyrus was healed by Arim waters
While with Kyle Le he often griped
Few kind words to grace the goulep's heart.
Her gift and her will she must submit.

Tao Chek's heart within his chest still beats
Not granted the death of an honored enemy.
Netta settles on the savannah and all retreat
To Mekucoo land for a season.
Until kari comes again.

Two sons Kyle Rula gave to Cyrus,
Plus the service of her gift.
With Kecouroo and in the village
These ones were raised anon.
Rufus and Lynus the Borabean.

Siibabean, tall and black,
Came against fleeing refugees.
Cyrus called and they turned back
So Arrivi were saved that day.
And his bones interred at the grassy knoll.

I read more chants from the chapbook; those composed by Mark that named warriors who maybe were present around a nightly campfire. And chants from Cara whose memory was long, and more chants from the clans that ringed the savannah with their own heroes and brave acts. Asmach was mentioned often among them. My voice was warm and lilting, but then felt hoarse. Asmach had not stirred beyond a break in his breathing for a shallow cough.

I wondered about the rescued conscripts in the convent garden and what they must have endured. I had visited the transport more than once and even Stargate Junction. Conscripts were kept out of the common areas there so we saw little of the traffic, but I heard frightening stories about the Chinese armies who had nor-ma-lized satellite countries on Earth and taken workers for press-gangs. Families were separated and the women sterilized. Children learned the guttural freightate language of overseers and worked every day of their short lives. Their shaved heads easily kept them isolated from other transport residents.

The outrage of conscript treatment was not reported on the com-techs or EAMs, the news more focused on the upstart stock exchange. I doubted that Herschel Henry even knew about the conscripts.

The nurses entered and opened windows after the heat of the day. The gauzy curtain was active with fresh air streaming in. One checked the comfort of Asmach and took his pulse, shaking her head sadly. The other changed the lamp to a stronger setting and replaced the water pitcher before they left.

I flipped through the pages to verses I had written before I was part of the song, but had never offered for public consumption. I read aloud "The Ballad of Kelly Osborn."

It was in the days of Arisen Rularim
Kelly was granddaughter to Heather
Mulatto with one-half Arrivi blood.
With black-rimmed glasses and auburn hair,
She made the record, wrote it all down there.

Kelly's works were noted by the tribes,
Her service to Brianna Miller.
A place was open by Kecouroo's side,
A pole hut, a garment, a token.
For her with glasses and auburn hair.

Travel with Patrick, take some classes,
Live on the transport and with money.
Forget the journals, trash her glasses,
Attend a ball and maybe marry.
To what appeal the daily toil?

Dolvia's law is meant to constrain
The criminal acts of men.
Women by laws more ancient are trained.
The deeds of men for history only,
Culture breathes by the deeds of women.

I heard whispering from under the window, followed by a voice repeating.

"Women by laws more ancient are trained.
Culture breathes by the deeds of women."

"What does it mean?" another asked.

"It doesn't rhyme," claimed a critic.

"It's not supposed to, you dolt," the first claimed.

I turned to the older chapbook, the one I had often explored for inspiration. I kept my voice, hoarse from vocalizing, slow while I articulated clearly:

Festival fire dying in the dawn
Embers shift, a spray of sparks
Unrecounted ancestors linger
Impatience for quickening.
A warrior this time, never an unblessed one.

Our time is a breath on the wind
More erratic than Tunanin.
Unspoken words like stones on the heart
What words say more than a lingering glance?
Halting moments weave into an untextured past.

There was silence; perhaps they had left their eavesdropping from boredom. I heard a shuffling sound and a sniffling from one with a runny nose.

"Stones on the heart," one repeated.

I heard them moving away.

"Like a stone on the heart!" she shouted down the quiet walkway.

The following day, I attended morning prayers in the high sanctuary amid whispers behind my back. I was returning to my vigil with the dying warrior when I saw a new arrival greeted at the gate by Sarah and Cymarta. Kecouroo slid from the back of a sigpywa that she rode alone. The sigpywa was long and armored with rows of horns on her many plates over feathery feet, resembling a mammoth horned centipede.

"The geysers came early this season," Kecouroo said to Cymarta, handing her a small package. "We share our cumin with our sisters on the savannah."

I joined them with a face of question, and Kecouroo flashed a wicked grin. She wore a form-fitting suede garment with a tektite necklace and no other adornment, and she was barefoot. "What do you think of my new friend, Kelly? She guided me here from the Uburu mesas. I believe she can smell the convent's pool of old water."

"The sigpywa can throw her thoughts?"

"The poor dear is simple," Kecouroo said gently while she placed a hand between the head pincers. "And lonely. Halter trained, though, and rescued from the fighting. She only wonders, 'Where are more of her kind?'"

A couple of older residents led the sigpywa to a corral outside the convent wall.

Kecouroo entered the cool interior, walking with Sarah while Cymarta and I trailed behind. "Where is Asmach?" she asked. "I came for the honored farewell and his funeral pyre."

I breathed a sigh of relief. I was poor company for the moment of passing. Kecouroo knew his lineage and his great deeds in battle. She had lived in the time of Asmach, the companion to Aegiv the lawgiver.

"I talked to Rufus earlier," Kecouroo called back. "Rufus is on the land."

I glanced at the sudden cheer in Cymarta's face before I cut back to hurry to the gate. I hovered just inside its shadow and peered at the dry yard under unrelieved sunlight. I strained to see down the way, left and right or around the tall acacias. Nothing, no movement. No chatter of parrots or the plaintive cry of the murmurey. I squinted at the harsh heat rising in thermals. My lungs were suddenly tight from the heated stillness, so I ducked back inside.

Kecouroo greeted Sarah and they went in for a long talk. I wandered back to my room. Seated at the narrow window and counting my breaths, I hugged myself and rocked slightly, moving out of the patch of sunlight into cool shadow. I remembered Edna and how one day she had pranced in the convent garden, rocking on one front leg and one back leg, only to switch legs in a dance and jerk around so her tail toppled the chair. *Ka, ka, ka, ka, ka.*

I remembered greeting her on the savannah one day while I traveled with Jesse Hartley, my friend from a visit to the orbiting transport. Jesse was on the savannah for the first time and had been frightened by the presence of the big gualarep. Edna, with her generous heart, had thought Jesse might accept her if they went to the grotto. Who could refuse swimming in the grotto?

I remembered Edna at the village of Kecouroo during a communal dinner, spreading goodwill and rocking her head at the chanting dance. I remembered Edna. I knew I was trying the song, sending out refrains, searching for a response. I couldn't stop; the memories fresh and funny and treasured. Who will join in my song? Who will celebrate Edna's passing by sharing memories with me?

Someone shouted in the garden. "Nomay be's wanting dat name!" My window was open to the cooling afternoon, and I heard raised voices drift in with the dusty breeze. "Memay be's called Bernice, same as her. Vymay demands a name, so Bernice be's for me!"

I concealed myself at the edge of the window's light and cocked my head sideways so I could glimpse the trouble. Kecouroo and Sarah stood over the row of bald girls assembled in the garden. They were the same group I had seen before, maybe less gaunt. One held her chin out, with the corners of her mouth pulled down, the universal gesture of defiance.

I padded down the hall to the colonnade where I joined Cymarta waiting on the side. "What's the problem?" I asked.

She showed me a round face of concern. "Sarah decided to give them tribal names, so they feel planted here. But the first one asked for the name Bernice, which is not tribal. Then another piped up saying that was her choice too. Now they all want to be called Bernice, after the one who rescued them from slavery."

"After Bernice Datong?" I asked. Brianna Miller had disliked Bernice and pushed her to take a position in the care of Mildred on the staff of General Hartley. Plain and dumpy, Bernice who had the mark of kant; she was the savior who the conscripts wanted to emulate?

"These ones cannot read or make decisions," Cymarta said. "We offer them choices for what color ribbon for your sleeve or what food from the platter. And names: what name do you want? But they all want the same. They don't understand that each must be different."

"That each one is unique in the world," I added.

"Yes, yes. How can we call them all the same?"

I stepped into the yard, and the conscripts settled briskly with eyes lowered and hands in their laps, a gesture meant to deflect attention that brought punishment.

Kecouroo turned with a smile for me. I had known her as a strict and unbending teacher. Why was she grinning now? "Kelly," she called, "come meet the new residents for the convent. We are choosing names to honor the lost women from the village of Kyros Kenoma. Say hiki to Loranice."

The bald girls remained seated. They would have to step up to Arrivi manners soon.

Teaching by example was Kecouroo's method, so I held my hand high. "Hiki, Loranice. It's good to see the spirit in your face."

Her eyes were green with brown flecks, but her features were active with questions that she would not have considered in the conscript quarters.

"May I present Caronice, who disembarked not four days ago?" Kecouroo said.

"Hiki, Caronice," I said with a hand held high. "I'm so glad to find you within Dolvia's embrace."

Her eyes were frightened and bitter, perhaps a resentment that would trouble her for many cycles of Nettom.

As we moved down the row, greeting each individual with her new name, one nudged her bench mate. "Like a stone on the heart," she whispered.

"And what is your name?" I asked her.

"Kellanice," she said with a look of challenge.

I only smiled turning to Sarah. "We can name the next group after lost gualareps perhaps, like Ednanice. The pain is too sharp today, though."

Sarah was silent, deferring to the actions of her Mekucoo superior. I tried again to engage Sarah. "These seem older than the first group. Are all the younger conscripts gathered?"

Sarah slightly shook her head no. "Except for the actions of Bernice Datong, these were marked for asteroid mining."

My eyes grew big, and I crossed my arms to control my gestures. Asteroid mining meant no return for conscripts. I was slapped with a wave of guilt. I had wallowed here in self-pity while these ones faced slavery and slow death without even a unique name.

Behind me Kecouroo pinched my arm above the elbow. I jerked slightly. "Chi cylay," Kecouroo said with that familiar sternness in her voice. "Kelly, the betrothed of Rufus, let's continue our vigil of the honored warrior in the infirmary. His last hours are soon."

We showed palms at elbow height to the group and walked left Sarah with them, passing Cymarta with her round worried face.

Our footsteps sounded as we walked with long strides in sync toward the infirmary. "You will read some chants from the chapbooks," Kecouroo said without looking at me. "You brought them?"

I nodded and kept my eyes forward.

"Cymarta has ordered the pyre," she continued, "constructed from fallen acacia branches. Rufus will attend. Later you and I will take the sigpywa to Cylay to visit Hakulupe Le, isn't that right?"

I nodded and swallowed hard. I had not managed my heartstone enough to note the suffering of others. Maybe that simple realization was a step onto a path to recovery.

"We heard from the Siibabean," Kecouroo added, "that General Shaw is making friends with the forest clans. They like Edwina and the promise of new hatchlings, I'm told."

"Hatchlings? But the males are too young."

"You have heard of the feral gualarep named for Cyrus?" She grinned, more cordial than I had ever known her. "Soon, road-building will provide work for warriors, now that the siege of Urbyd is ending."

We entered the darkened hospital room and took up the station of vigil. Not forty minutes later, Asmach slipped away in his sleep.

Kecouroo sighed. "I wish there was more time for celebration."

"Asmach celebrated often, I was told."

"With so many dead, each passing carries less weight."

"He went without a murmur," I said. "Without a home or family members to mark his passing. Maybe I will be the same, with nobody waiting to collect my ashes."

"Stop with these comparisons, Kelly," Kecouroo said in her stern teacher's voice. "You always count yourself as less, or cheated, or not promoted. You have three homes—the house in Somule that was Karen's, a place open for you in the village above Mayschool, and a reserved room here at the convent. And more: connections with Carline Bryant and Jesse Hartley."

She added under her breath, "And with the Sheeks-Cylom."

We grinned together. The women of the savannah mostly avoided service to Mrs. Shaw despite her native reputation as Sheeks-Cylom. "You must step up now," Kecouroo added. "Embrace what Dolvia has gathered for you."

"I only wish we had the song." As soon as the words left my mouth, I regretted them. Kecouroo had not reached the song, try as she might. "I'm sorry."

"Stop being sorry. Be Kelly, the betrothed of Rufus." I noticed that Kecouroo wasn't wearing the necklace of tektite stones that she had so treasured.

At dusk, we held the funeral pyre. I was surprised at the number of convent residents who gathered. Aensilus the Madquii arrived late and stood with Rufus, across the way from the row of women in leadership—Kecouroo, Sarah, Cymarta, and me. I knew Aensilus by reputation. He was the younger brother of Aeolis, who led the militia against Gora forces around Urbyd. I was embarrassed that Rufus had friends that I didn't know. The realization made me feel small. What did I bring to the betrothal? Unpublished poems?

Rufus and Aensilus wore amulets of mourning on the round muscles of their right arms, and Rufus had fresh cuts that bled freely. Somebody was chanting softly.

> Trained in the old ways, tempered by battle
> Friend and foe to Abydian, well nigh of respect
> Asmach made the gold mine truce
> Bringing peace to the mesas of Uburu
> His family lost, his soldiers sacrificed

> He fought nonetheless, clinging to tradition
> And forged a name worthy of this evening's
> Song and a warrior's emulation, anon.

My tears flowed for Asmach who I barely knew, and for the loss of Dacupitte who had been Edwina's favorite. I remembered how she had joined the dancing in Kecouroo's village one time, jerking and switching her tail, facing Dacupitte in the undulating line and in competition with Dulcinea. I remembered trips to the grotto with Edwina, and walking the trail to find a patch of sun for warming our blood after a chilly swim. I remembered Edwina standing with Rufus in the long shadows of sunrise as the chopper I rode left the Feast of Oria and headed for Cylay. Edwina, the littermate to Edna. I remembered Edna. I knew I was attempting the song, seeking an answering refrain. My stream of memories was solo, though.

As part of the ceremony, Rufus led forward the warrior's horse that had belonged to Asmach. It was black and saddled with a harness that included gold emblems of his clan, the three-headed snake. Horses were another Softcheeks import, but most had been slaughtered by Anaxagoras, so this black was a treasure. Rufus made a great show of handing the reins to Aensilus, who had inherited the spirited animal. I had never seen Aensilus ride a horse or a sigpywa, and he did not make the attempt in front of the company, only leading the horse away from the pyre.

As the fire waned, Rufus touched my elbow to indicate I should walk left. I glanced back at Kecouroo and Sarah, but they carefully averted their eyes. I heard low clucking and chanting and knew that later there would be dancing. This celebration for a lost warrior was oddly female, with high voices and tight circles of giggling girls. I felt older, like I was the grownup here.

I stood with Rufus under the acacia trees with insects raising a chorus of chirping. The rains were little in this season of netta, barely enough to keep acacias green. Parrots and other transient birds were few and the billabongs already receding. "I'm concerned about your coming trip to Cylay," Rufus said. "Even traveling with Kecouroo, you are exposed on the savannah."

I stared at him, surprised that he knew.

"Gora marauders still trouble the villages," he continued. "I would prefer—"

"It is as Dolvia would have it," I murmured. "My place at Kecouroo's side."

The edges of his mouth turned up slightly.

I took that as approval.

"Events in Cylay are fluid," he continued. "Rabbenu Ely has arrested Carl Hartley for abusing a Cylahi boy, several actually. Your brother Patrick is included in the accusation."

"But . . . but . . ."

"Simon Sumuki delivered Carl to Ely," Rufus said. "To gain favor."

I didn't know who Simon Sumuki was, but I was silent.

"Ely uses this arrest to pressure Hamilcar," Rufus added. "Ely's rule is ending. He seeks an escape offworld."

"Maybe Ely can live on Cicero next to Aunt Carline." I heard the bitterness in my voice. My heart pulled down in my chest, and I worried suddenly that Rufus found me ungracious, not worthy as the betrothed of a Mekucoo warrior.

Rufus raised his eyebrows, taking my words seriously. "Ely has moved some wealth to New Shanghai. Planning ahead, I guess."

I had stumbled upon some truth, and I appeared knowledgeable. I was willing to allow that assumption to stand. "So Ely will step down?" I asked.

"When the jour-na-lists focus cameras on you, when you are in Cylay with Kecouroo maybe. Speak to how women of the savannah want home rule. Speak of purchasing stocks for gum arabic in faith with home rule."

"Shares cost more than a woman can afford."

"A few shares as part of solidarity."

"But the price will fall. The women will lose out."

Rufus exhaled to show his patience. "If you speak in public soon, when you reach Cylay maybe, then the principle is the same now as after the price falls. Women can continue to buy, high or low."

"And spending the food money on stocks is a better protest than death-by-fire?"

Rufus looked sharply at my face, thinking I was stupid, stupid—I was sure. "Arrivi women will remember," he articuled slowly, "that Kelly Osborn called for home rule and for this act of solidarity. To buy shares of gum arabic. You understand?"

I understood that I was receiving instruction, but not the reasons for promoting stock purchases by women who could barely feed their children.

Rufus turned me to him, an intimate gesture that made me feel suddenly flushed, overheated in the cooling night. "I wanted you to have this before you leave with Kecouroo." He held an engagement bracelet made of gold acacia leaves joined side to side, the most difficult workmanship.

I drew a quick gasp. "But that belongs to Brianna Miller."

"Actually, this bracelet was given to my mother by my father, and later gifted to Brianna Miller by Dacupitte. There's a necklace for the correct day."

My head was spinning. The engagement bracelet that Kyle Rula had worn, and Brianna Miller wore after her.

"Don't fight me on this," he whispered.

I blinked several times and raised my arm. He spent more than a moment working the delicate clasp, but got it fastened finally. He quickly wiped his upper lip and stepped back a fraction, perhaps feeling overheated the same as me.

"It's lovely," I whispered without looking up.

We heard giggling from the dry bushes. Rufus stiffened, touching my elbow to guide me back to the convent archway. "Aensilus and I leave in the morning," he instructed, "and you will travel with Kecouroo. Always know that your place is secure."

"Melinga, Rufus."

We heard more giggling and shuffling of feet.

Rufus sighed shortly, and the sides of his mouth turned down. "Melinga." He turned on his heel and walked from the scene of the funeral pyre of Asmach the warrior. I had my token and my marching orders, like a green recruit taking instructions from her captain. We're all counting on you; don't fail me. Duty was all.

In the morning, I found that ritual must be satisfied before I could leave riding the sigpywa. The women and girls inspected my bracelet, and each mentioned how she coveted one just the same from her future beloved. I carried gifts for Brianna Miller and Hakulupe Le, and personal messages for the clutch of Cleo from convent residents. Finally getting beyond the arched gate, I joined Kecouroo waiting by the sigpywa, stroking the bony plates between the faceted eyes.

"Does it bite?" I asked.

"This one is from across the ocean and her training includes, uh, how to say? She has manners, I guess, more than the ones roughly trained by wranglers." The creature rose at the shoulders and flayed its many feathered feet in pleasure. "She remembers parades where her plates were painted bright colors and her horns were hung with many chains of gold. Flowers littered her path to the temple while music played and her rider was honored."

"Does she have a name?"

"Yes, but I cannot pronounce it. I call her Desert Belle. What do you think?"

"Very romantic."

We wore the uniforms of the clutch of Kenru, as was our right. I lashed my small pack to the middle horns for easy carrying. We sat single file on her back, and I grasped two horns for balance while the swaying body carried us to Cylay, a journey of six hours, much shorter than on foot. Twice, we saw a black stinger buzz overhead, and we looked around for the troops it must be escorting.

"Rufus monitors your progress so no harm comes to us," Kecouroo speculated.

"I'm sure it's just on patrol."

"So the daily log will record."

Birds were nesting near billabongs, probably more successful breeders without the gualareps troubling the banks. Egrets drifted in on thermals, while black globs of kiki bobbed and dipped after swarms of insects. Herons of dark blue walked the shallows on their stilt legs, huddled in a tight dance, each touching two others. Gray parrots with yellow tipped wings, red ones, and a few rare blue parrots, flew overhead, along with the sand grouse that was more comfortable when the water was less.

The sigpywa follow the road a bit before Kecouroo tugged the reins and turned off. I tapped Kecouroo's shoulder, but she waved a hand dismissively.

"I know a shortcut," she called back.

We came to a seasonal stream that was sure to feed into the Iamida river that passed Cylay. The sigpywa hesitated before she sidled up to the water, easily stepping over the stones on the bank.

"Hold on!" Kecouroo called out to me when the creature slid into the sluggish water, buoyant and drifting, her backside racing ahead so we rotated in the current. We pulled our legs up to keep our sandals dry, but her broad back served as a dry raft.

Kecouroo laughed and laughed.

"Did you know she would do that?" I asked.

"Desert Belle likes the water. There had to be a reason."

A blue stinger buzzed overhead and hovered for several moments, facing us as though it would fire the mounted missiles, before turning back on its correct path.

"He's a bit of a nag, huh?" Kecouroo whispered, just as though the helmeted pilot could hear us.

I didn't know that it was Rufus; it could have been anybody.

We drifted a good long while. The water was deep but not fast moving. I saw erriv on the side that lifted their heads with dripping snouts and flicked their ears as they watched us drift by. I hoped to pass someone I knew, so I could wave and point, but that didn't happen. I could see the warehouse buildings of Cylay when we came onshore and dismounted, allowing the sigpywa to lift the front of her body, as much as the plates allowed, and shake herself before she groomed her pincers and antennae. I checked my pack and shared kariom on patties with Kecouroo.

"We have a task for you, Kelly," Kecouroo said as she picked at the food.

"Rufus mentioned I should be ready to speak before the cameras."

"A good encouragement, but there's something more. We want you to travel to Stargate Junction with the clutch of Cleo, the ones who will jump back."

"Jumping back is not my—"

"You felt rejected after the battle of Iamida shores, I know. Rufus said that you must not be exposed again."

"Rufus said?"

"The killing fields don't serve a poet," she added. "Instead, you will travel with the clutch and return to Cylay in time for, um . . ."

"In time for what?"

She grinned suddenly, being evasive. "In time to witness the stepping-down of Rabbenu Ely. A happy day, huh?"

I wadded the paper from my patty and stowed it in my pack. "There's no guarantee. And now Ely holds my brother with Carl Hartley."

Kecouroo stood and brushed the back of her dungarees. "General Sector is working on getting them released. Rabbenu Ely won't deport them. He no longer has that power."

"I cannot travel offworld today. I brought no traveling clothes."

"You have the right papers and the right inoculations. Ready to go."

"But Rufus didn't say anything."

"What did I say about your constant complaining?" she impatiently said. "This matter with the clutch of Cleo is decided among the women."

"I haven't seen them for several turns of Nettom." I wondered about their training as Somule Gems managers. The two boys had been sacrificed in the massacre at the village of Kyros Kenoma. Cleo and Camille lived on the savannah now and trained with the holy woman. The four remaining girls had met Somule Gems managers to learn about the products we hoped to market along the route back to Paris.

Kecouroo looked around as if to check the time by the sun's position. "Well, we should get there soon. Let's mount up."

Desert Belle carried us into Cylay where we received many open-mouthed stares. Of course, we wore no burkas. Traffic buzzed around us with many honking horns, and pedestrians stopped their work to stare and whisper.

Kecouroo called to people with big greetings, twisting and waving. I had to laugh.

We stopped at the wide plaza just outside the governor's mansion and dismounted. Two academy residents waited there and took the reins to guide Desert Belle past the gate. Kecouroo patted the creature's bony skull, sad to see her go. Another veiled woman offered us burkas to wear. Kecouroo snapped the ends of one so it fluttered in the air, and turned so the length of cloth settled over my head. She straightened the facial panel, and I could see her face through the gauze, tanned and smiling.

Kecouroo refused when the academy resident used insistent gestures to offer the second burka. She looked up at the punishing sunlight, and glanced left to the acacias that overhung the wall to the academy, the leaves rattling loudly in a breeze.

There were many people in the plaza, and some Putuki protestors in a tight group loitered outside the gate of the governor's mansion. I saw Blancom there with his camcorder, photographing anything that moved and talking with a Putuki man. Four women under burkas stepped forward, lashed together with simple twine. They had their backs to us facing the ornate gate. Henry pushed some bystanders aside while he monkeyed about to get the best angle of light.

A sudden flash of bright flames rose from the woman on the right and spread quickly across her companions. The crowd stepped back instinctively, except for a few veiled women in vigil, and Blancom of course. The odor made me gag, and the rolling smoke covered us for a moment. No danger to us, just the smell of gasoline and burning flesh. I coughed as my eyes watered. When I lifted my gaze again, it was all over. Four discernable skeletons were covered with the goo of burned flesh and cloth. Blackened and crumpled, and the skulls seemingly in a death grimace.

Stunned tribespeople stared and whispered. Blancom knelt closer with his camcorder recording the last of the flames. He stood and looked straight at us from across the way. I threw back my shoulders, ready to face the camera with my message of solidarity. He turned to a Putuki man, though, focusing the camera lens on that face and asking rapid-fire questions. Protestors gathered in a tight group to shout into the camera. Typical.

Who was I, though, wearing the burka of another?

So much despair and lack of song. Kecouroo led me to the academy gate where we entered without ceremony. Later we learned that Vera was the leader; Vera whose husband had been honored with a ritual death on the savannah. Vera and three academy residents had torched themselves, it was said, so Hakulupe Le was spared. How did that story get started?

There was a din of voices and giggles and rushing footsteps in the corridor. I entered a room with Brianna Miller and some of the clutch of Cleo who were packing several rucksacks.

"You won't need those sandals in Paris," Leah said. "In fact, set them outside for a good airing."

"We can take the jewelry? It's mine now?" Rosalyn asked Brianna, while the girls handled well-made peridot necklaces. "And the earbobs too?" They were spoiled and coddled, hand-picked by Brianna Miller, loyal only to the clutch.

I bobbed my head and rolled my eyes.

Brianna noticed me finally. She was more than plump, standing tall to manage her pregnancy burden under the Arrivi gown. "Ah, there you are, Kelly."

The girls from the clutch dropped their labor and gathered around. Rosalyn grabbed my arm and stroked the engagement bracelet. "Let's see it. Let me touch it."

"Oh, so beautiful," Claire said. She was a head taller than when she had arrived, and her face had stretched long-ways with a jutting jaw. "And from Rufus, no less."

"Okay, back to your own treasures," Brianna said. "Kelly and I must talk." She led me to the windows while the girls packed their belongings and shot glances our way. "Kelly, I want you to accompany the clutch to Stargate Junction. Leave today on the shuttle."

"Must I?"

Her eyebrows went up in surprise. Brianna seldom heard the word no. "You're already inoculated," she crisply said, "with the right papers. You must talk to Bernice Datong."

"I saw conscripts at the convent."

Brianna shook a finger in my direction. "A pricey business, that. Don't get any ideas." She guided me a few extra steps away from the clutch. "I want you to speak to Otieno, the ambassador from Strii-duc. You remember him? Tall, weathered face, embroidered clothes. Learn his intentions with this courtship of Bernice."

I just stared. Courtship?

"You know all the players," Brianna said. "The girls in the clutch, the Striiduc group, Mildred and General Hartley."

"Why is the general involved?"

Her voice remained crisp, the tone used for instruction. "There's no need for this drain on the general's time when you are there to manage the negotiations."

I forced a smile. She talked as though I had not been excluded from the leadership circle. She talked as though I had not spent my time of mourning at the convent refusing EAM activity. She talked as though I understood strategy and big concepts like ne-go-shee-a-shun.

She was still talking. "You must learn if Otieno is trying to buy Bernice. Not buy, exactly. His tribe has the custom of bride price. Just find out what are his honorable intentions."

"But he's a generation older."

She nodded. "He brought his favorite nephew, he claimed, to meet Bernice. The nephew refused, so now Otieno has offered himself. What advantage does he seek here?"

"Maybe he loves her."

Brianna squinted and allowed several moments to pass. "Here's what I know so far," she continued. "Otieno saw Bernice at a dinner held by General Hartley where it was common to invite the agents of Somule Gems in the absence of Jesse."

She saw my smirk and abandoned her story. "Two women of Otieno's family will be at the Junction," she said. "We asked that Bernice learn something of their customs, maybe a few phrases, so she gets along better in public situations."

"I heard Striiduc women practice hedge magic."

"That kind of talk is silly. I told Otieno: no trickery."

"You told him?"

She barely reacted to my question. "I need to finish our travel arrangements for the clutch. Only these four have completed their training, but I suppose that's expected, what with massacres and demands of the holy woman."

I smirked tasting sage. Brianna always managed to stir my feelings of spite.

"And here, I brought you something." She handed me a package.

I troubled the brown paper wrapping to see the edge of a blue Arrivi veil.

"Your other burka shows some wear," she said, always on top of the practical concerns. "I'm sorry these arrangements are rushed, but Carl and Patrick may take the next shuttle offworld, and you must not board alongside them. Too much explaining is involved."

"Patrick?"

"General Sector is negotiating a release from Rabbenu Ely. It's complicated."

"But my brother is not indicted?" I asked. "He's not implicated in the abuse?"

"Guilt by association is all we can ascertain. Accused to get him to turn on Carl Hartley, most likely." Brianna glanced at my blank stare. "Our arrangements are rushed, but you're needed here. Go down the hall, second door I think. Hakulupe Le wants to say farewell." She stepped back to the noisy girls without a thought that I might refuse this task, or have other plans for my time, or not perform as instructed.

I found Hakulupe Le standing head-to-head with Kecouroo, talking quietly. She turned at my entrance. "Those girls are ungrateful," she said right off. "With four martyrs to cremate, all they can think about are . . . are . . ."

"Peridot earbobs," I finished for her.

Anger flashed in the lambent eyes. "If Kecouroo had not brought the sigpywa, you would have missed the shuttle and Brianna's plans would be delayed. But all events conspire to facilitate her needs. Arisen Rularim. When I think of the amount of time I spent with the clutch of Cleo . . ."

Kecouroo's voice was calm next to Lupe's ire. "A fresh adventure for the clutch. Why spoil the moment?"

Hakulupe Le thumbed through the chapbook taken from my pack that Kecouroo handled. "Let's see what we have here." She pretended to examine the notebook with big gestures and read aloud:

> "I record here with this pen
> tales of the recounted Dead.
> Those Dolvia holds in waiting.
> Acts more of lore than fiction,
> And offer mine over group opinions."

She looked up. "What does this mean, the recounted dead?"

"Souls of ancestors." I shrugged. "Those who will return with the call to fertility, counted again by Dolvia."

"Ah, the re-counted dead. And what purpose for this writing?"

"I don't know." I reached for my pack. "I mean, so many losses from battles and death-by-fire. How to bear it? Dolvia cradles the warriors and returns them in another form. What actually is lost? The absence of their presence for a time."

Lupe placed the notebook on top of my package from Brianna. "And, at least you have the courtesy to—"

The doorway was suddenly darkened by the girls in the clutch, quiet and contrite.

Leah stepped forward. "We're leaving soon. We wanted to say, um—" She looked back and shrugged.

"We'll never forget you, Lupe," Claire offered from the group. "We'll miss you mightily." Dominic sniffled, and they entered the room then, without Brianna of course. Brianna hated goodbyes. I realized that's why she had offered a gift, to avoid the other parts of goodbye.

"We wanted to give you something," Leah added, "but all that we have comes from you and your caring."

Lupe held out her arms. The girls rushed forward in a gaggle and hugged her and cried, and hugged me, and even hugged Kecouroo with promises of EAM notes every day.

I was crowded with the clutch into an ECCAV and driven to the shuttle launch pad. I still wore the uniform of the clutch of Kenru and carried my pack and the new burka in its simple wrapping. We were rushed through the security checks and hustled onboard. We strapped on our seatbelts and waited only moments before I felt the push of the boosters that would hurtle us into the sky, a common event that no longer attracted journalists to follow the traffic with questions for dignitaries about home rule or solidarity.

I swallowed hard and tasted sage, the flavor of my spite. I would miss the funeral pyre of Vera and three others. This sending off was typical of Brianna, I thought. Her tasks must be completed ahead of all other concerns.

SIX

THE CLUTCH OF CLEO PASSED THROUGH CUSTOMS ON THE ORBIT-ing transport. The special Company stamp on their passports still carried weight. In midship Bernice waited to greet us. She wore an Arrivi gown with her hair coiled at her neck, but looked dumpy and provincial. I resolved that the clutch should dress in business suits. Maybe I would too.

Dr. Spinelli stepped out of the crowd in the cramped concourse that smelled of stale recycled air. He was Softcheeks and had tolerated a doctor's rotation at Beecham Place. I had once visited the Uburu digs where the research doctors were logging the valuable finds from an ancient shrine. "Workers were forced from the digs by the warriors chasing Gora deserters," Dr. Spinelli now announced, "so I'm just waiting for the shuttle to Stargate Junction."

I held my palm high. "I'm so glad to see you. We're headed that way too."

Dr. Spinelli grinned and his bushy eyebrows went up and down. "Brianna Miller said you might need an extra hand guiding the clutch. Is this all of them?"

"Four only will jump back. What do you think, Dr. Spinelli? Should they dress in business suits now that they have finished with the savannah? I think I'll purchase some clothes for their new lives, not the life they just exited."

High spirits from the girls in the clutch worked on my nerves, even while I spent Brianna's money re-outfitting them. Dr. Spinelli avoided this particular errand, and I spent sparingly at the transport shops since there was little selection. What need did midshippers have for business suits? There was a dust-up at the shoe store when I suggested choosing closed-toed shoes with low heels. Leah lingered at the display window where a glittering pair of impossible high heels scintillated under the lights. Among the clutch members, Leah was considered the pretty one.

We had difficulty finding an appropriate style for Bernice, and the suit jacket sat wrong on her round shoulders. I made a point that Bernice should wear a different color or an added sash to designate her as the Stargate Junction agent of Somule Gems. "I work in an office with no windows," she said, "alongside several women who are staff for the general. Nobody will notice me."

"Somebody has noticed you," I said.

Bernice was immediately defensive. "That ambassador complained to you? What is with him?"

"Otieno spoke to you?"

"The servant cut her hand, that was all," Bernice complained. "I removed the glass shard and pushed her hand under the water faucet. Why is that wrong?"

"Otieno didn't say you got it wrong."

Bernice fretted, rubbing the palm of one hand with three fingers of the other. Stroke, stroke, dig, stroke. "He brought his nephew around, you know," she said. "An object lesson, I guess, about how I had touched a servant. You'd think I was beating her or something."

"I'm sure he didn't mean—"

Stroke, stroke, dig. "I'm banished now from dinner at General Hartley's table. And for what?"

I grinned, trying to reach out to her. "Bernice, you misunderstand. Otieno has made overtures for marriage."

"To that simpy nephew? He has a hare-lip, you know."

"Bernice, Otieno wants you as his wife. His own wife."

Her eyes went wide and she stepped back. "Oh, he'll think I'm stupid. He'll hate me, so clumsy and . . . and . . ."

My heartstone for Bernice was immediate. I knew just how she felt with a suitor who was beyond her station. I also knew that I could help her.

For the shuttle ride to Stargate Junction, the clutch settled in quickly, their luggage stowed separately. They were accomplished travelers, after all. I was seated next to Dr. Spinelli.

"How goes the fighting?" he asked. "Does Rufus still serve with Kenru's clutch?"

"I have little news about the conflict. I'm kept separate from events."

"You're pregnant?"

"Ah, no . . . but thanks for asking."

"I mean, Omiibuk fights unless . . ."

I smiled to be cordial. "I know about the call to fertility. It's a great honor, but I'm not one of them."

"Why risk making Rufus angry, huh?"

"Rufus does not decide for me." I shifted in the seat, struggling against an itch between my shoulder blades. "I was at the savannah convent after the loss of our gualareps."

"You saw Asmach's funeral pyre? I regret that I could not save him."

"You were his doctor?"

Dr. Spinelli nodded absently, handling his pipe. "We were at the Uburu digs. Several pottery fragments were on the table there, some tagged and pieced together. Karlyhi entered the building with three warriors from his clutch; he just walked in like the laboratory belonged to him. 'You're a doctor? You will come,' was all he said.

"Gutierrez told him that we're scientists," the doctor continued, "not doing medical rotation. I had a sudden fear that Karlyhi would drag us out, so I reached for the acrylic boxes. We needed to stow the specimens first. Karlyhi swept them from the table with a strong-arm gesture. A whole season we had spent with sifting and tagging, and the specimens were trashed with one stroke."

He absently fingered his unlit pipe. "I told him I needed my doctor's bag, but Karlyhi drew his beltknife. From the side Omiibuk called nu delaya, the only one who talks back to Karlyhi. Did he fight without weapons? she asked. So, then, could we save lives without scalpels? And Karlyhi deferred to her; he just turned on his heel and left. We were marched down to a lean-to in the gorge where Asmach was in a fever."

"I didn't realize it was you who helped him," I said.

He shrugged with an open palm gesture. "My help was clumsy. I saw nothing of Dacupitte. Apparently, his body was the focus of Gora rage. I did examine the rescued kenoma captives, those two boys. Their scars are grievous from many seasons of abuse. The older one especially is . . . um, I don't know."

"Karlyhi took them for initiation as warriors," I said. "He will make Kristos into an assassin."

"How do you know this? By second sight?"

I shook my head. "A natural fit for him."

We talked quietly until I yawned, unable to suppress the urge. Dr. Spinelli took the hint and was quiet for a long time.

I couldn't nap, though. I shifted my position trying to stretch my spine. I saw him glance up from the book that he held but wasn't reading. "Is Stargate Junction much changed?" I asked to be polite.

"The Striiduc who follow Otieno have opened many shops."

"Do they sell wards and potions?" I heard the snide tone in my own voice and knew I was being peevish.

"They claim to see the souls of lost conscripts."

"A trick to create interest in contacting the dead."

Dr. Spinelli lowered the book. "I'm surprised at your disbelief. You write about recounted souls on the savannah. Didn't you ever wonder? When a person dies in space, what happens to the soul?"

I snuggled deeper in my seat, turning away from him. "You know, I never wondered about that." What a silly question. Just something to fill the idle time.

Stargate Junction had seen many travelers pass through customs. In the face of the chatter from the clutch of Cleo, employees in Consortium uniforms sought infractions of the rules to exert authority. I stood with Dr. Spinelli and waved shortly to Mildred waiting for the moment of greeting.

I saw Ambassador Otieno in the long concourse. I wondered if he sought a moment with me, or maybe with Bernice. He didn't seem the naive suitor type, though, in his embroidered vest over an open shirt and roomy pantaloons tucked into wide boots. He greeted two women of his culture who were released from customs, and I realized these must be the ones brought to instruct Bernice, should she agree to the union. The women had traveled on the same shuttle as the clutch of Cleo, channeled together in Company comfort. The older woman had dark eyes and hair like Otieno and a hooked nose. The younger one was most likely my age.

The ambassador saw me staring and nodded briefly before he led them away.

Mildred was the chief of staff for General Hartley. She had held that position for a season of om, it seemed. Mildred greeted Dr. Spinelli and had porters ready to manage the clutch with rucksacks and packages of new clothes.

"Where did you get this great business suit?" I asked Mildred.

"I know a tailor," she said, ever the professional. "I'll introduce you."

The presence of so many young girls created a stir in the concourse leading to the wider promenade. I saw young journalists loitering there, probably with no permit for ground duty, and prepared myself by silently rehearsing the phrases from my message of solidarity.

The reporters looked right past me, though, and pushed microphones under Dr. Spinelli's chin. "What about the drop in price for gum arabic on the securities exchange?" one asked.

Another jumped in with, "Will Rabbenu Ely allow the release of Carl Hartley, do you think?"

Mildred patiently waited, her back stiff and her chin held high.

"I have little connection with Dolviet politics," Dr. Spinelli said, pushing his way forward. "Kelly Osborn here is the betrothed of Rufus. She could answer—"

"Will the tribespeople honor the law of impunity?"

"The tribes have laws they esta—" I began.

The three journalists barely glanced at me. "What can Arrivi expect for investment if Ely doesn't comply with the order?" one asked Dr. Spinelli.

I tried again. "We believe the women of the savannah should buy—"

Another spoke into her handheld mic. "Who would agree to open a business there?"

She thrust the mic under Dr. Spinelli's chin again.

"You seem to answer your own questions." He grabbed my arm above the elbow and we walked out of their circle. So much for broadcasting my message of solidarity.

Mildred also directed her remarks to Dr. Spinelli. "The general invites you to dinner tonight at seven, common standard time, along with Kelly Osborn. He hopes you are not too tired from traveling."

"We are honored by the general's request."

"I'll send someone around with the tailor's card," she told me and headed in the opposite direction as the porters.

We were assigned rooms along a blank corridor. Mine had a cot and desk, about half the size of my space at the savannah convent and with no uplifting view. There was a tight bathroom with a basin and air bath. I yawned and removed my glasses, considering a nap before the dinner with the general. I answered a knock at the door and was surprised to see Mildred. "The need for a tailor is not that pressing," I said.

"Ambassador Otieno requests a meeting, if you don't mind."

"I should get Dr.—"

"I will accompany you."

"Well, then. Let's jump right in on the negotiations." I grabbed my glasses and room key and pulled the door closed behind me. While I followed her up the corridor, I added, "I talked briefly with Bernice. You probably know more about this situation than I do."

"The ambassador has noticed her other, um, mission. He's most well-informed."

"I met the conscript girls, but I don't—"

Mildred turned down another corridor, walking fast, with me trailing her steps. "Bernice had some funds from the treasure of Kyle Rula. I had shown her already about the securities exchange. It turns out that Bernice is good with numbers and nearly doubled the amount she could expend for, um, securing these girls. She pays more for the secret, you know, than for the individuals."

"I didn't know."

"Well, Otieno takes some conscript boys, quietly," Mildred added over her shoulder. "We never asked why. Business here is discreet and has few public gestures. You could mention that to the Soft-cheeks girls."

"Yes, ma'am." I was breathless from trotting after her long stride. "And what about the women of Striiduc? Have you met many?"

Mildred didn't break her stride. "Some have shops here, and they don't like to be crossed. They apply curses to make you blind or your hair falls out. Silly stuff. None of that is tolerated in the concourse."

"And how would you know if—"

"Tricks are quickly exposed and punished."

"So, they do have this power with curses? Or is it really with wards?"

She had led me to the main promenade that included consumer shops and teahouses. There was a bustle of people in many styles of dress, mostly businessmen or soldiers, Stargate Junction being primarily a waiting area for jumping back.

"A word of caution," Mildred said, in her stiff manner. "Otieno resents negotiating with a woman. I believe he thought this effort was simple. Just buy the girl and remove her."

"You're sorry to see Bernice leave?"

Mildred surveyed the promenade noise, her face still. "Her training was nearly finished. A loss of man-hours that must be repeated for the next candidate."

She led me into a shop that was downscale, I would say, where she walked straight through the consumer area and stepped into a back room. An inventory table was there, along with some loose merchandise and an old EAM12. I had not seen one of those since I was a student in Hakulupe Le's classroom. Ambassador Otieno waited on the side and bowed slightly with the fingers of one hand touching his chest.

Mildred stepped forward offering her hand to shake. His features didn't move, but he squared his shoulders before he reached to shake her hand. "May I present Kelly Osborn, the betrothed of Rufus?" Mildred said. She turned to me. "Ambassador Otieno of the Striiduc nation."

I held my hand high with palm up, an instinctive response in the presence of a new acquaintance. "Hiki, Ambassador Otieno. You honor me."

"Melinga," he said, as his eyes moved over my face and form. I was glad I had worn the business suit rather than my uniform from the clutch of Kenru.

Mildred indicated we should sit, so we attempted that in the cheap molded chairs at the rickety table.

"As the betrothed of Rufus," Otieno said, "you are being present at the funeral pyre of Asmach the companion of Aegiv?" His voice was deep, but without the edge of disdain I was expecting.

"You knew Asmach?" I asked.

He blinked twice behind the hooked nose. "To be a second officer just off the boat. To see my first horse then."

"His black stallion is a beauty."

He glanced at us as though gauging how much was needed for this encounter. "The black horse is recent; his third, I think. One is being shot out from under him during the offensive to win back the gold mines." His use of present tense verbs for past events was peculiar to Striiduc.

"Another horse is stumbling during a raid into Siibabean land. To be attached to that creature is Asmach, so I am made to step up to, um, shoot it. No choice with a fractured leg, a mercy even. The black is being a gift from Khalif Ananke."

"So you fought alongside Kenru . . . and maybe with Dacupitte?"

"Too young for the gold mine conflict in those days, but brave enough." He looked at Mildred with a cold stare.

I followed the sign and asked, "Mildred, I know little about the promenade. Is it possible to have refreshments delivered here? Tea and some softbread?"

She blinked at me twice, nonplussed, before she quickly rose and left.

"Women of your culture are said to pose riddles," Otieno said when we were alone.

I smiled. "No riddles today, just logistics. The clutch of Cleo will jump back with the next opportunity. Bernice was counted among them and must be allowed the honorable goodbye."

"In twelve watches?"

"Uh, yes, if that's when the Company yacht leaves."

"My sister and daughter are here as requested, although I don't see the need."

"We just want to ensure that Bernice Datong understands her future duties," I said. "Maybe learns some phrases from Striiduc, so there are fewer embarrassing moments."

"Why would she need to know Striiduc?"

"For the . . . For the . . ." I sighed shortly, squirming in the uncomfortable chair. "I need to ask: what do you see for Bernice? Say, in a few seasons. Do you have a house in a port city? Do you have other wives, or daughters?"

"I have four daughters, all grown. Two sons are lost to the fighting, I'm afraid."

"If this is difficult—"

"In my culture we don't, um . . ." He set a stack of platinum chips on the table. "I am thinking 6,000 romarks, but now that I see the interest of Arrivi leaders, I know that my price is too low."

I avoided looking at the cache of wealth casually stacked on the table. "Let's not get ahead of ourselves. In fact, I want Bernice to know . . . except, um . . . May she bring a friend as a guard against loneliness while living in Striiduc? What kind of house—"

He squinted. "Why would I take her there?"

"Pardon?"

He squinted, his eyes piercing behind the hooked nose. "Bernice has a position with Somule Gems," he said flatly. "The four women who jump back must report to her, isn't that so? Why make her weak?"

Just then Mildred was at the threshold with a waiter who carried a tray. I indicated the stack of platinum chips, and Otieno quickly removed them. I signaled Mildred to leave as the servant set the tray on the table and began arranging the wares. There were three cups and three dishes. The waiter left and I reinforced my message of dismissal with, "Thank you, Mildred, for this service. We won't be long."

She showed me the professional secretary face and left.

I turned back to the ambassador. "Marriage would make Bernice Datong weak?"

His eyes bored through me. I did not move while the question hung between us. Finally, he looked down at the teacup. "My wife from before is being a beautiful woman from a good family. My older son is lost at sea. When our younger son is also killed, the light vanishes from her eyes. To fade from this life and quickly. Do I want to repeat that, do you think?"

"I appreciate your generosity to share something of your life." I reached to pour tea into two cups. "So you feel that Bernice should stay at Stargate Junction?"

He ignored the tea. "I will provide a suite that my sister and daughter are decorating."

"Bernice can keep her position and her salary?"

"And her other activities as well."

"Was the rescue of conscripts what attracted you?" I showed him a smile and sipped from the teacup.

He moved three fingers along his jawline and chin for a moment. "As a young sailor, I am being captured by a pirate group to be abused and chained to the cargo hatch. Nobody is trying to ransom me. To escape, I am diving overboard after killing my jailer. The pirates are placing bets on whether the barracuda get me before I can swim ashore."

I returned the teacup to the tray. "Tomorrow we can meet your sister and daughter at a teahouse in the promenade. Say, ten in the morning, common standard time? I can bring Bernice and a second, maybe Dr. Spinelli."

"Will she think me too old?"

At that moment I loved him myself. I lowered my eyes to hide my reaction. "Bernice will think you're an honorable man with much to share with a young wife." I stood and held my palm high. "Melinga."

"One moment," he said. "My sister offers tokens of friendship, if you will pass them along." He held out a colorful scarf tied in a knot.

"Tokens only?" I asked to be certain. "Nothing of great value?"

He shrugged.

"And does custom dictate that Bernice offer tokens to the women of your family?"

"I'm certain my sister expects it."

I nodded and took the scarf. "We shall see you tomorrow then."

After I left the ambassador, I entered a teahouse and found an EAM that was turned away from the entrance. I placed a trunk call to Brianna Miller and tapped my finger on the table until her image came on the screen.

"Kelly!" she said. "No trouble at Stargate Junction, I hope."

"I need your permission to establish an office for Somule Gems." Her image waivered for a moment, making her face look broad and squat. "On the second floor of the promenade," I added, "and Bernice should have a staff to serve her, a minimum of three."

"The negotiations fell apart already?"

"May I rent the suite today? We could keep the clutch occupied choosing decorations while they wait for the jumping back moment." I barely paused to grab my breath. "Somule Gems has outgrown what Mildred can offer."

"And what of Bernice?"

"I suspect this is not a marriage of convenience. The ambassador is in love." I waited two beats for Brianna to absorb that news.

She was grinning. "Establish a line of credit through the export licenses. Don't go overboard."

"We need an upscale office with Bernice as the primary agent. Dr. Spinelli is a good neutral presence, but perhaps Mrs. Shaw could visit on the next shuttle?"

"To get a better bride price?"

"You know that lesson you repeated so often about living large. I believe it applies here. Can Sarah from the convent visit and bring a couple of residents to serve as staff?"

"Oh, I would have to get papers for them, and inoculations."

"I'm certain you can pull something together. Sarah should arrive before the clutch jumps back. Um, please?"

Brianna smirked and looked right; she was probably thinking through the needed steps and who to approach.

"Oh, and one more thing," I added. "I will contact Petra Mitterand in Paris. The clutch should consult with her about fashion and what to avoid in Beijing. The trunk call is expensive, so—"

Brianna was grinning again. "Do what you think is best. I trust you, Kelly."

"Thank you. Osborn endit."

Brianna Miller had spent time with Petra Mitterand when she had jumped back in another season. Petra was an older woman and niece to Pierre Mitterand who had grown rich after his tour as a savannah doctor. The clutch would travel until they reached Paris, France and reported to Petra Mitterand. Why not reach out now to make the journey smoother?

My next stop was gathering the clutch members with Bernice in a concourse teahouse. The Chinese red trim and mandarin yellow walls with bamboo hangings that depicted long-extinct animals were a nice distraction. I sat with Bernice and the four girls in the mostly vacant teahouse with a row of EAMs for rent near the kitchen. I needed to persuade Rosalyn, who was the unofficial accountant of the clutch of Cleo.

Rosalyn's suit jacket was open to show a white business shirt. Her peridot ear-bobs the girls so prized looked wrong with a tight suit. I noticed the valuable matching necklace at her throat. I explained the need for a Somule Gems business suite and would Rosalyn spearhead the gathering of equipment? "There's an empty space on the second floor," I said. "I want quiet colors, very corporate but upscale and feminine. Secure what you can at the retail shops."

"Don't buy retail," Rosalyn said. "I can get a better price from the partners with export licenses."

"That's a good principle in general," I said patiently. "We cannot wait for delivery from off-station warehouses. Bernice should make friends among the shop owners here. Let's use restraint; buy the floor samples maybe. We can swap out some lower quality pieces over time."

Leah turned to the others. "Oh, and we can paint the suite ourselves."

"Hire the workmen so they receive wages," I countered. "You are management now, no longer seeking day work."

Dominic whispered to Bernice, "I think grey and rose should be your colors."

I held up a finger of caution. "Why not place a call to Petra Mitterand in Paris? Maybe she has some Softcheeks magazines you can glance through to get some ideas."

"Oh, may we?" Claire asked. They looked to Bernice, who was frozen with fear and dismay.

Bernice stood stiffly and drew me away from the clutch. "Mildred has been so kind," she whispered with lowered eyes. "Why can't I just stay where I am? I have all that I need there."

"You have a higher profile now. You haven't told the clutch about your suitor?"

She shook her head no.

"Are you ashamed?" I asked.

Bernice fretted again, rubbing the palm of one hand with three fingers of the other. Stroke, stroke, dig, stroke. "You told me just yesterday. I thought maybe I heard wrong."

"Would you like to come with me to dinner at General Hartley's?"

She shook her head no. "If I may, there are only a few watches before the clutch jumps back. I, um, I don't want them to outfit the new office with pink and more pink."

"Bernice, I need to speak to the clutch soon and ask a favor of them. Ambassador Otieno offers this from the women of his family. They expect a return token." I gave her the knotted scarf. She backed out of sight of the clutch who were gathered around the teahouse EAM waiting for the connection with Paris. Bernice untied the knot and looked at the contents, a filigree oval on a chain designed to hold a token like a lock of hair; a stickpin in the shape of a squid with its tentacles splayed; and a dainty kerchief that was little more than a doily and its use undetermined.

She looked at me with trepidation. "Is this the bride price?"

"Not likely," I said. "That amount will be breathtaking." I handled the filigree bauble and placed the chain over her head. There came a tingling in my fingertips, and a grayness passed over Bernice's face. I drew in my breath at the bold assumption. "Take it off."

"But . . . but—"

"May I tell the clutch about your suitor?"

Her hands were busy again with stroke, dig, stroke. "What will they think?"

"They will be pea-green with jealousy. Take this off now."

Dominic broke from the group and joined us. "Come talk with Petra before the call ends," she pleaded with Bernice.

"Dominic, advise me here," I said. "I'm trying to choose a gift for Mildred. Put this on while I have a look." I took the necklace from Bernice and placed it in Dominic's hand.

"Very unusual," Dominic said. "Are the edges sharp? They feel sharp."

"Go ahead."

"Um, maybe . . . If you want me to." Dominic put the chain over her head and looked at me with question. She brushed the back of her ear, as if flicking an insect. "I don't like it," she stated flatly. She removed the bauble, handing it to Bernice, and retreated quickly to the clutch.

"What does that mean?" Bernice asked.

"May I hold onto this chain? In fact, all of these tokens are suspect. We'll ask the women of Striiduc when we have tea with them in the morning." I led her to the clutch and allowed the trunk call to end before I mentioned a suitor and that Bernice need not agree.

"Who is Otieno?" Dominic asked.

The girls glanced at each other, while I reinforced a lesson for how to handle clients who take the suitor's stance to gain favor in business. Bernice had anxious hands wringing out her stress. "We need a token," I added to the clutch, "for each of the women of Striiduc following their customs. Unfortunately, this token must be from Dolvia and not purchased in the shops here at Stargate Junction. I need your peridot necklaces for the sister and daughter of Ambassador Otieno."

The four girls hesitated and looked at each other for agreement. "Which ones?" Rosalyn asked.

"All four of them," I said.

"Oh, that's different." They all removed the necklaces that Brianna had gifted them not three days ago: graduated strands of bluish gems in platinum settings. In my hand they looked like a treasure.

"Oh, you cannot sacrifice these," Bernice objected. "Too valuable."

"Equally sacrificed," Rosalyn said. "Then we're still the same."

I had to chuckle. The appeal to group solidarity was so like them. "Two will go to the sister and daughter of Otieno," I said. "The two others Bernice will wear tomorrow as a double strand."

The girls all nodded. "We're so happy for you," Claire said. "I hope my station beyond the wormhole is just the same."

Bernice nodded with that look of fear lingering behind her eyes. Stroke, stroke, dig.

They went back to planning the business suite. I left to prepare for dinner with the general. There was much to teach Bernice Datong before I could return to the savannah.

Our meal was casual in the general's quarters with its long dining table. Cold dishes were displayed in a row, obviously catered. Dr. Spinelli and I filled our plates, and we sat together where the salt and pepper were set out.

"Will your son arrive soon?" Dr. Spinelli asked the general as though the question was common.

General Hartley squinted and set down his fork. His hair was severely combed back from the receding hairline. He had shed his uniform coat with the red tooling and many medals. His shirt carried insignia that showed his rank. He was never not the general. "These self-torchings in the square." He shook his head. "Four women torched together in protest of Ely's rule. Ely has dug in his heels."

"He won't release Carl and Patrick?" Dr. Spinelli asked.

"Ely has tied the release to my announcement that his continued tenure is legitimate."

"Are the prisoners abused?" I asked breathlessly.

"I'm concerned for your brother, Kelly," the general said. "The charges against him. Little proof has been offered, even with leaks about Carl's habits. The accusations from Simon Sumuki were shaky at best."

"I have heard the name."

"Ely inflames residents of Cylay," the general explained patiently, "to show his own authority for imposing the law of impunity. If my son and by implication Patrick are not criminals, then Ely's actions cannot provoke a response from a general."

I force a smile. "Unblessed ones believe little of what Ely says."

He nodded to show he took my words seriously. "The story doesn't have to be true to be accepted, or reported by the upstart news network in the city-states of Cochin. People see this tawdry story as their first impression of the savannah tribes."

I had heard about the news channel that developed their own reports, mostly about events in Moorea and Ninleau. News segments were on the EAM if the viewer subscribed, and a print version each week was for sale in Cylay for consumers who read English.

"Where will Carl go when he's released?" Dr. Spinelli asked.

The general kept his look neutral. "He can visit his sisters in Paris: Heather and Jesse. Speaking of the future, I had a visit today from Ambassador Otieno. Kelly, have you been talking to him?"

I glanced at each of them. "Uh, we had the meet-and-greet today. I have a question, though."

"You know he has offered a proposal about Somule Gems and the bride price?"

I squinted. "Offered to whom?"

He held up one hand, showing me the palm. "Not to me." He and the doctor smiled together, so I guessed my face had betrayed me.

Hartley had consumed little from his plate, and now he pushed it aside and sat back. "His idea is ingenious, really. Otieno wants to front an investment for Somule Gems in his fleet of refurbished freighters. Let's say, 14,000 romarks assigned as capital investment from Brianna Miller. A similar amount then gets earmarked in the treasure of Kyle Rula for the purchase of conscript girls."

I knew about the treasure of Kyle Rula that had underwritten the Somule Gems company as a co-op, but I was surprised General Hartley still used that old term.

"Because the treasure can have a stake in the freighters without a cash outlay," the general said, "then the treasure has more resources available to Bernice Datong."

"But that's a fortune," I said. "Far more than Bernice needs for buying conscript kids without attracting Company attention."

"I believe Otieno means for Bernice to use the funds over time, and maybe invest the bulk like she did once before. This move positions Bernice as the lynchpin to a partnership that is risky, I grant, but that could yield dividends later depending on the success of asteroid mining. Do you see the tracks of his reasoning?"

"The freighters themselves," Dr. Spinelli added, "with freedom from the Company traffic lanes, may prove more profitable than any mining venture."

The general nodded. "Otieno was careful to separate his contracts for mining ore. His offer is for the freighters only, a sweetheart deal meant to befriend Brianna Miller and Somule Gems."

I shook my head, wondering again at Brianna's easy agreement that I should spend her money to establish the office suite for Bernice. Always showing the expected face, that one, and keeping secrets all day long. "Did the ambassador mention this deal before today?"

"He's been buying used or salvaged freighters for a good long while. He has engineers and mechanics here working around the clock at his own docking bay. This is the first time, though, that Otieno has offered to share anything."

I nodded. "May I show you something?" I put the colored scarf on the table and undid the knot. "This was intended as a token from the women of Otieno's family to Bernice. As required by custom, he told me. What do you see?"

The general and doctor looked at the pieces without touching; another difference from the girls of the clutch, who could not resist handling and admiring jewelry. Dr. Spinelli shrugged, so I held up the filigree bauble on a chain. "Handle it," I said.

Spinelli touched the filigree and pulled his hand away immediately.

"A ward?" the general asked.

I placed the item back on the scarf. "I believe this bauble is meant to make Bernice appear unattractive to Otieno. My question is, why does Otieno push so hard with sweetheart deals while the women of his culture make this move?"

Both men sat back for a long moment of silence.

"Striiduc women have no voice in business," the general said. "Otieno probably didn't glance at the tokens tied up in a scarf."

"He has only daughters now," Dr. Spinelli added. "He may dote on a new son."

I put both elbows on the table and cupped my hands. "Here's my idea. I believe the ambassador is in love. This is not a marriage of convenience. I want to confront Otieno at tea while his sister and daughter are there, and see who acts guilty. Watch for who he tries to punish."

"Kelly, there's more riding on this match now," the general said.

"If he's in love, his reputation will feel bruised. If he's not in love, then the deal has to be structured differently so Bernice is not risking her life." I pointed with my index finger. "I believe the first is true."

"What does Bernice believe?"

"I haven't told her. I want to make this play first, just to know."

The general grinned. "You have grown, Kelly, since the days of the debutante ball." I remembered my poor showing at the coming-out ball so many seasons ago, but I allowed the goodwill to warm my smile.

Later I went to my blank room to grab some hours of sleep. I thought about Edna and Edwina and about floating down the stream on the back of sigpywa in the company of Kecouroo. I thought of Dacupitte who was Edwina's favorite, and about Rufus who was mine. It wasn't long before I was softly snoring.

Bernice and I met the ambassador in the teahouse at a discreet table. The Striiduc women wore more jewelry and scarves than on display at a concourse kiosk, but I tried not to stare. Their names were Otolay and Olola. "Everybody calls me Olly," the younger one said. At my signal, Bernice placed two gift boxes on the table.

"As a token," Bernice said, "in hopes that we share many years as friends."

The women of Otieno's family opened the gift boxes and seemed pleased with the peridot necklaces, except I couldn't tell if they were acting. Olly glanced at Bernice's double strand necklace, noting that the gifts were similar and from Dolvia. The ambassador glanced at Bernice who blushed a lovely color of pink.

"I feel I must speak frankly, Ambassador." I placed the knotted scarf on the table. "We are returning these tokens offered yesterday. Perhaps you were unaware, the filigree has a ward that we find, um, unpleasant." Otolay was suddenly still, and I knew I had my culprit. I offered her an easy escape, though. "The gifts are most unique," I added. "Perhaps where you bought them, you didn't know a ward was added."

Otolay stood with her chair making a scraping noise and snatched the scarf. "It's wrong to return tokens of friendship." She walked out of the teahouse. Olly's shoulders sagged and her face was pained. She looked at Bernice and at Otieno. He jerked his head indicating that she should leave.

Bernice watched Olly rush out before she turned at me with eyes of accusation, ready to burst into tears—just the reaction I was hoping for.

I set my face. "Ambassador, we should discuss the suite you claim the women of your culture decorated. I'm a little uneasy—"

"Kelly," Bernice said in a whine. "What are you saying?"

I gave Otieno a level stare. His features didn't move, but I imagined the gears working in his mind: blood ties, progeny, loyalty, guilt, business, reputation. "Bernice may choose her own space," he said evenly, "if we come to an agreement. My sister and daughter are leaving on today's shuttle." He glanced at Bernice's pained expression, her pleading eyes ready to drip tears. His eyes returned to my face.

"I'll be in contact later today." He stood, bowed slightly with fingertips of one hand on his chest, and walked out in long strides.

"Kelly!" Bernice immediately cried. "You make it too hard for him. In public and everything." She also stood with gestures that were too strong with anger. "He won't try again. You ruined it."

After she stomped out, I fingered the teacup and falsely smiled at a staring patron.

I walked up to the new Somule Gems suite where a bevy of workmen wearing painter's pants labored with brushes and poles. Claire and Dominic had silent questions in their eyes so I knew that Bernice had arrived already.

"Did you order an area rug for reception?" I casually asked.

From the other room Bernice shouted, "Do nothing she tells you! Kelly ruins everything."

We glanced at the workmen who had stopped to stare. We went to the next room joining Bernice, Leah, and Rosalyn who closed the door. "He won't try again," Bernice wailed with a blotchy face and streaming tears. Her fretful gestures now included stroking her hair at her neck; stroke, stroke, pull. "Go away. Everything is wrong now. All ruined!"

"What happened?" Rosalyn asked.

"Today's event went according to plan," I said.

"Aaaaahh, I hate you. I hate you."

I took three steps toward her. "Then you should know the worst of it, Bernice. Your response was genuine. Otieno has no doubt that I found the ward and I was offended. Not you, but me."

She sobbed and hiccupped as she considered what I said. "But why did you have to return them in public? Why not just—"

"I had to call out the culprit while Otieno was sitting there. His response was also genuine, I believe. He's sending them home."

"Nnooooo," Bernice cried. Stroke, stroke, pull. "Everybody's leaving. You separated me from Mildred. The clutch is jumping back. I'll have no friends at all."

There was a soft knock at the door and it opened part way. "Hello?" we heard before Mrs. Shaw entered wearing a business suit and with her short hair in a perfect coif. "I'm seeking the clutch of Cleo? Am I . . . Oh, it's Kelly. I'm in the right place then."

"Don't accept any favors from Kelly," Bernice called from her wailing place. "She'll ruin your life."

Mrs. Shaw looked at me and blinked twice. "Making new friends, I see."

The clutch gathered around Mrs. Shaw who played the visiting celebrity with compliments for each girl, more valuable than peridot, and easy reinforcements for their décor ideas. She took them off my hands, including Bernice, to visit Mildred's tailor. I sighed and walked back to my blank room, thinking to nap.

I turned a corner and fairly slammed into Ambassador Otieno. I straightened my glasses hoping they weren't smudged. "Pardon me, sir. I should watch where I'm going."

"Does she refuse me?" he asked without preamble. His face was set in that hawk look that was his signature, so I could find no place for hedging.

I squared my shoulders. "Bernice is angry with me, not you."

"What must I do?"

"Just wait for the clutch to jump back. The air will clear nicely."

"You are Kelly Osborn from Somule, right? Your brother is Patrick Osborn, held by Rabbenu Ely for ransom, I think."

I tried not to gasp. "General Hartley is working on a release," I said evenly.

"I can have Ely eliminated, so you don't need to—"

I showed my palm in a gesture of caution. "Nu delaya. No, no, not needed. The Arrivi must find their own route for regime change."

"I will make the bride price 22,000 romarks, if we agree—"

I shook the hand of caution slightly. "I feel you misunderstand. These moments are full of misdirection and high emotion. Let's take our time here."

"She's different, you know," he said, suddenly chatty. "The women of my clan cultivate talents to improve on nature: wards and spells and carromancy. Bernice has no agenda but meets each day to face that day's problems. Do you see her nature too?"

I slowly nodded. "The mark of kant, we call it. Her spirit is untroubled. Ah, no scheming."

"Untroubled: the same today as tomorrow." The ghost of a smile passed over his features. "I offer 28,000 romarks, the equivalent in platinum chips, to be routed through Somule Gems as suggested by Rularim. I want to meet the girl again."

"Your offer is most generous," I said, "and I'm certain that, um, Rularim is agreeable. Let's say tomorrow for tea at ten o'clock. Perhaps Mrs. Shaw may join us and we'll tour the military section of Stargate Junction. She likes to report to General Shaw about upgrades."

His eyes went wide for a moment. He bowed to me and stepped away. I wondered what new error I had just made.

I spent the next several minutes rearranging in my mind the hierarchy of leaders among the women I knew on Dolvia. Those with a personal agenda fell to last, concerned with manipulating events for advancement, while those who met each day squarely rose in my estimation, Sarah and Kecouroo. Time was truly a loop.

SEVEN

THE NEXT MORNING IN THE TEAHOUSE THAT HAD BECOME OUR meeting place, I waited at a smallish round table with Mrs. Shaw. She wore a loose-fitting suit and sensible shoes with quiet jewelry. Her hair was in a wide coif. I didn't know how she maintained the same hairstyle as yesterday. I thought about how my long braid marked me as a savannah resident just as surely as conscripts had bald heads.

Six of Otieno's engineers sat in a row with their backs against the wall and each refused service in turn. I felt sorry for the confused waiter who went to his boss with a big shrug. Two engineers talked on small cellphones, I assumed through the local system and to workers on Stargate Junction.

We stood when the ambassador led forward the tallest engineer from the row. "May I present my smogen, Onetel, who runs the engineering crew in our docking bay?"

Onetel showed Mrs. Shaw and me a stiff bow with the fingertips of one hand on his chest. Mrs. Shaw bowed to the same depth, and I held my palm high, still bound by Arrivi customs.

Onetel glanced at his superior and sighed shortly. "My daughter Onela has some English and attends the Consortium school; very pro-gres-sive. May she greet the agent of Somule Gems to share ideas for a new living space?"

Mrs. Shaw smiled widely. "We are charmed that the friends of Ambassador Otieno want to meet Bernice Datong. We are glad to greet Onela when she's ready."

The smogen looked at his superior to be certain the demand was met before he returned to stoically sit with the others.

We waited long moments, so I leaned in to whisper into the ear of Mrs. Shaw. "What did I do now?"

"Brianna wants to find work for you as a marriage broker," she whispered just as General Hartley entered with Bernice, who joined Mrs. Shaw and me.

The general pulled at his uniform collar and approached Ambassador Otieno. "We have a conference room set aside for today in the military section, if you are agreeable."

The ambassador nodded, and we all shaped a loose parade to the security doors that had excluded Striiduc personnel until now. Our group gathered in the cool Consortium corridors with directional icons and smelling of vanilla. We turned left and crowded into a conference room just down from Operations, the smogens again sitting in a silent row with their backs against the wall.

"There's an EAM here," Mrs. Shaw said to me. "Why don't we log on and chat with Brianna Miller? Bernice, you know the codes, don't you?"

Bernice made a sour face, anxiously stroking the palm of her hand, but sat before the monitor and entered her code.

Mrs. Shaw nodded to General Hartley, and he suggested to the ambassador that the Striiduc smogens follow him for the tour of Ops. Their eyes were suddenly bright, craning their necks to absorb details of this tour of a restricted area.

Otieno joined Mrs. Shaw, hanging back from the group. Just as the last engineer exited, a teenage girl entered alone, pushed forward by Mildred who seemed to disappear in a flash.

All this I saw watching over Bernice's shoulder as she sat at the EAM. "Bernice, I believe you should join Mrs. Shaw now," I said. "I'll keep the call open. Go on." I sat in the chair and described a blow-by-blow to Brianna Miller, whose face loomed on the screen.

Meanwhile, Mrs. Shaw acted as host for the introduction of Bernice to Onela. They were of a similar age and groped for words in a shared language. Bernice giggled and a ripple ran across the room, a break in the tension. Mrs. Shaw shepherded them to the table, where Bernice sat with the ambassador and this other— well, she was a girl—looking so young next to the severe bearing of the ambassador. They admired each other's jewelry and looked to Otieno to help with unknown words and chatted without guile.

Mrs. Shaw came to my side and grinned into the monitor screen at Brianna Miller. "Youth is wasted on the young," she said. "If only they knew what we know."

"By the way," Brianna said on the screen. "How did you arrive at Stargate Junction so quickly? The shuttle isn't expected for several hours."

"I came with the mail run," Mrs. Shaw said. "How do you think we remove the conscripts?"

"I had wondered," Brianna returned. "Kelly, how did you raise the bride price so high? By ignoring the first offers?"

"I have a theory about that," I said. "When men negotiate a marriage, they are really making a pact among men. Nobody is concerned with the bride's future comfort. The father is basically discarding her. When I asked questions about where Bernice will live and the language barrier and so on, the ambassador had no response for issues he had not considered. I seemed to grab the upper hand just because I cared."

"You caring serves you in many situations," Brianna's image claimed over the EAM. "So there's one lingering question. How did Kelly recognize the ward when nobody else was sensitive?"

I looked from one to the other. "I just, um . . . I felt a tingling sensation and saw a shadow on Bernice."

Brianna was grinning on the screen. "When Sarah arrives, she'll bring girls for Bernice's staff. Kelly should take Bybiis shopping in the concourse. Bybiis has some skill. See what you can uncover for recognizing wards and such. A great service to the general that would be." She looked left at something off screen "Ah, I have company. Miller endit."

The screen went to vivid blue, and I looked at Mrs. Shaw. "Brianna just loves to give orders."

Mrs. Shaw chuckled. "She looks plump with the pregnancy. Is she healthy?"

"She's been living on the flats of Arim surrounded by helpers. Sarah's pregnant too, as part of the call to fertility, but she's half a season behind the others."

"It's good that you called in reinforcements, Kelly." She glanced at the three trying to communicate at the table. "When the clutch jumps back, you and Brianna are the only real family Bernice has. Make a good show for the ambassador."

"If we don't agree soon, he'll buy Stargate Junction as a wedding gift."

We fooled around on the EAM, calling up email and chatting with Cymarta at the savannah convent. She reminded us to meet Sarah in customs. I chatted with Mrs. Shaw about Cicero and Two Forks, and how the twins were doing in school. She showed me several photos of them that she carried; actual physical photos, not on the EAM. The boys looked like their father, and one was missing a front tooth.

"They were rough-housing one day," she said with a shrug. "No hard feelings, though."

I asked where General Shaw was now, and she told a story about an immense forest on Siibabean land. "I'm to meet a biologist and a pair of botanists when the Company yacht arrives. We cannot keep naming animals and plants after the amalgam they resemble from Earth creatures. A fox with a flat tail is a platyfox, or a spoon-bill turkey vulture. They misnamed oversized rosehips as a type of pomegranate. We must find the real connections in the genus and species chains, the Dolviet evolutionary lines."

I thought that was a monumental task, the forest teeming with plants and strange creatures. "And Edwina is with General Shaw?"

"Some reptile yearlings scout for my husband, and the Siibabean accept them. No, um, roasting the flank there." I was certain she referred to the fate of Ralph who had been Mike Shaw's gualarep.

Our talk ran down as the girls entertained the ambassador. We began to get bored, but we couldn't desert our chaperon duties. We glanced often at the group of three who talked or sat quietly or used gestures to get through awkward moments.

"I think we've tortured them enough, don't you?" Mrs. Shaw asked. "I'll manage the ambassador, and you walk the girls home."

"Thanks for coming to my rescue. I was messing this up badly."

"You were doing fine, Kelly. We just needed to make a louder noise, that's all."

Mildred waited in the common area, and returned Onela to her studies at the Consortium school. I walked with Bernice back to the new business suite.

"Onela is sweet, don't you think?" Bernice asked. "She liked my suit. We may visit the tailor together later. Before I . . . you know."

"Bernice, you don't have to agree to the marriage," I said quietly as we walked. "Except maybe now you do, so that Otieno doesn't lose face in front of his smogens."

"It's alright," Bernice said, showing bright eyes for the first time. "If this deal depended on just me, you know, if I smiled or flirted or served at table just right, then we are lost. But my role is part of something larger, not about pouting my lips or tolerating a touch. I can handle some business, and I know my place there."

We had stumbled onto a role where Bernice saw a future for herself.

In the new suite, I sat with the clutch who were choosing credenza styles for Bernice's office. I was still giving instructions when Mrs. Shaw entered with Sarah, Mildred, and two others. She must have waited to meet the shuttle docking without me. I was doubly glad this adventure didn't depend on my wits alone.

Mildred seemed chummy with Sarah. They stood together with Mrs. Shaw, while Bernice met the convent residents who would be her staff: Sallmus Le and Bybiis who was dark-skinned with a broad stance and broad nose.

I joined the older group and Sarah said, "Bybiis called Mrs. Shaw a dragon sleeper."

Mrs. Shaw rolled her eyes. "Don't I have enough names?"

"Dragon sleeper?" I asked.

"A simple misunderstanding of the facts." She shrugged. "From when Edna and Edwina were hatchlings."

"Bybiis may have a gift of Dolvia," Sarah said. "You remember that Brianna asked that you go with Bybiis into the concourse."

"But she's not Arrivi," I objected. "She cannot have a gift."

"It is as Dolvia would have it," Sarah said, in even tones. She was taller than the others, her pregnancy burden just beginning to show. "Bybiis was gotten from rape, so she's part Borabean," Sarah added. "It was Cymarta who noticed that Bybiis avoids conflicts, seeming to know what's coming. Bybiis sounded the alarm before the Gora raid at the convent and saved the lives of many."

I made a sour face. I always seemed to spoil progress with my knee-jerk spite.

"The ambassador's smogens," Mrs. Shaw said with humor, "asked about you. I was forced to explain that you are betrothed to Rufus."

"Anyone they meet is an object of speculation," I said.

"All sailors are the same," Mildred added.

Sarah and Mrs. Shaw grinned again, stifling a laugh. "You know that the space above this suite is available too," Mildred added dryly, "and zoned for residential. We could put in a false wall and a simple lift so Bernice could come and go privately." She and Sarah walked left to join the clutch and staff.

Mrs. Shaw lingered with me. "Carline Bryant was on the mail-run with me. She asked for you."

"Aunt Carline? Here?"

"I'm slated to tape a news segment with her tomorrow about who can replace Rabbenu Ely. You should come to the taping, just as audience with Dr. Spinelli, if you want. It's scheduled for just before you settle the bride price with Otieno."

"But you should be the one—"

"This whole adventure centers on you, Kelly. Address his fears tomorrow."

Onela came into the new Somule Gems suite after her school hours had passed, bringing three Striiduc students who were daughters of the mechanics who refurbished damaged freighters. I excused myself from the gaggle of girls and went with Bybiis to the concourse, trying to complete some assigned errands before the dinner hour. Our excuse we told ourselves was to select a gift for Mildred in honor of her good service to Bernice and Somule Gems.

I stopped suddenly outside the row of conference rooms where regional leaders often met. Khalif Olpul of Utica was talking with

Apetu from Urbyd, their heads close together. The khalif's kaffiyeh obscured his features. Neither had ever spoken to me, even as the betrothed of Rufus. Bybiis looked around, not recognizing them. She waited with question on her face.

I sighed in resignation and signaled that we should continue. We passed several shops and entered a couple to finger the goods and wave away the solicitous shopkeepers. Anything we chose could easily be purchased by Mildred for herself, so the errand seemed silly to me.

We entered a lane I had seldom walked through and found a Strii-duc shop with scarves and jewelry and sundries galore. Bybiis stood stock still in the aisle, but I didn't know her, so I didn't know what that meant. Her color was high when she turned to me with forehead wrinkled in anguish. I touched her arm above the elbow, the Arrivi gesture for calm. I nodded to the shopkeeper, a dark-haired woman with a hooked nose, and walked Bybiis out and down the lane. We were ten paces away when she finally exhaled.

"What was it?" I said.

"Her necklace has power, but no stronger than the tektite Kecouroo wears. The entrance to the back room had a ward similar to one we found on a Borabean cart abandoned on the savannah. She doesn't like you, though, and makes no effort to guard her feelings. The women of Striiduc want their men for themselves."

"And the girls who came in with Onela?"

Bybiis shrugged, looking down to avoid my stare. "They're jealous of Bernice. They love their fathers, but want more freedom than . . . than mothers allow."

Since Bybiis had accepted a position as staff to Bernice Datong, I realized that the needed covering had arrived. I was eager to finish with matchmaking and return to the quiet of the savannah. "Anything else?" I asked.

"I keep seeing a woman's face as though she stares at me through water. The Striiduc may have a carromancist. I read about the magic in our library, the one at the convent, in restricted books. Don't tell Sarah. She'll be mad at me."

I nodded three times to show that I took her words seriously. "A carromancist? Who views events by staring at hot wax poured into water? That may be why Otieno is so well-informed."

We were nearly back at the suite. "Guard what you say to Bernice," I instructed, very auntie-like. "Develop a system of small gestures for coming danger or fresh lies. Work it out with her in private with the lights down and your voices low, maybe with some music playing." Bybiis nodded as though these instructions were the same as what jewelry to wear to greet the Striiduc. She glanced up at the ceiling several times.

"What is it?" I asked.

"The Striiduc ward in the shop. It was against spirits; the souls of lost conscripts."

I stopped and squinted. "Really?"

Bybiis ducked her head, a defense against my disbelief maybe. "Many have died here," she whispered. "Violently, without hope, without ceremony. Apparently, Striiduc women are troubled by a disturbance. Hence the ward."

"And you can see these souls?"

"Like bubbles skirting the surface of a billabong during a warm rain." She reached to touch my arm but hesitated. "Do you want to see?"

I leaned back a fraction and brushed my upper arm with my other hand. "We should get back." I walked ahead with resolute strides. I had troubles enough for today.

We entered the concourse where a small crowd was gathered watching a sideshow. A single performer in bright motley was performing tricks for the children and parents. He held a ball of blue flame in one hand and directed fire toward a model ship made of string that ignited suddenly and burned evenly to ashes. We paused to watch for a moment.

"His hand is warded for protection," Bybiis whispered. "The fireball is from chemicals. See how it's blue and not hot."

The jongleur doused the fire and threw up a screen of fine graphite particles that hovered in the air. He passed his hand in front of it and the gray pieces gathered in a replica of his own face, smiling when he smiled and frowning with him. He stuck out his tongue at it and the kids giggled. The mimic graphite looked insulted before the face pulled back in a raucous laugh.

"A simple trick done with magnetism," Bybiis whispered.

Both the jongleur and the mimic screen noticed Bybiis, gesturing that she should step forward, and the screen changed into a facsimile of her face. The children giggled and parents scowled as Bybiis stepped a couple feet closer through the crowd. The graphite face stuck its tongue out at her.

"The only face you have mastered?" Bybiis poked a finger into the nose and the graphite collapsed into a long stream of weighted dust that fell to the floor. The jongleur twirled suddenly with his motleys swirling in a blend of color and seemed to disappear. He reappeared on the other side of the stage, and displayed a deep bow amid applause and cheers from the crowd.

Bybiis signified on him with her palm in the air and joined me to walk away. "The first two are magician's tricks," she whispered. "The last one takes talent with making a glamour for misdirection. We are watching the motleys swirl, but he has already moved to the other spot."

"Can you do that?" I asked incredulously.

Bybiis shook her head no. "But I know how to disrupt his talent. I mean, I read how to disrupt a glamour. Did you see his lute?"

The jongleur had carried a clear acrylic pouch that contained a three-pipe wind instrument that he probably used to entertain the crowd, maybe his prize possession since he kept it close to his person. "It made of chime coral, very rare. And the lute had three tubes!" Before we entered the new suite, Bybiis added. "Edwina says hi."

My mouth fell ajar. "The song is back? You can hear the song?"

"Not really, but some strains are heard. Edwina liked that you remembered Edna, maybe with a chant of her own."

"You can hear Edwina now?"

Bybiis shook her head no, again averting her eyes. "Edwina will return to the savannah for your wedding to Rufus. She looks forward to the wedding."

"Thank you so much."

The wedding, I thought, while we rejoined the chattering girls. My wedding that nobody discussed, or asked to set a date, or angled to be a witness. My status was betrothed, my web of friends unraveling. I was as much an orphan as Bernice Datong with no family to make bridal arrangements. My parents were both dead, Karen by her own hand. Kecouroo was engaged with walkabout, and Brianna Miller viewed me as somebody to give orders to. Hakulupe Le was my former teacher, but my needs were not hers. Omiibuk would agree to help, but only during a lull in the fighting when she spent time with her kids. Mrs. Shaw lived on Cicero and knew me as Jesse's friend. Jesse had jumped back to live in Paris. I had nobody to stand up with me; I shared Bernice's feelings of being abandoned.

I dreamed that night of racing through the tall grasses of Siibabean land, with other gualareps running beside me. My tongue flicked to taste the air, and I scooted left following a trail. We reached the rushing stream filled with tree debris where we trapped bush pigs against an outcropping, squealing and terrified. I allowed the younger reps to make the kill, tearing bloody pieces from the hoary hide and tossing the flesh in the air to better slide down their throats. *Soon we can return to the grotto. These hatchlings will like swimming in the grotto.*

It was too early for me. I yawned while I waited for Dr. Spinelli outside the audience section of the comtech studio. I was glad I saw them before they saw me, because Dr. Spinelli was accompanied by Dr. Richardson from the New Shanghai hospital. Seasons ago, before the battle of Iamida shores, I had known him when I had completed an internship at the hospital that Aunt Carline had arranged. Dr. Richardson was paunchy and pasty white, I suspected from his long-term drug habit. Wasn't he under indictment for distributing the vaccine that poisoned Cylahi kids in Cylay?

Dr. Spinelli easily shared chi with Dr. Richardson. The scientist was always talking about his potsherd specimens and would I like to see them, so the same was maybe true here. I composed my face, showing what they expected when they stepped my way.

"Kelly, you remember Dr. Richardson surely, from the New Shanghai hospital?"

"Kelly? Sure, I remember." He began to reach to shake my hand, but stopped mid-gesture when I raised my palm high in the Arrivi greeting.

"Hiki, Dr. Richardson. Melinga."

He nodded with a vague smile before he turned to the seating area. I suspected he didn't remember me.

I was seated with them in the audience area. Mrs. Shaw and Carline Bryant sat across from a Cicero interviewer whose name I couldn't remember. I scrunched in my seat to avoid contact and ignored the two men engaged in collegial chatter. I yawned, missing my sleep rhythm and wondering how many minutes before I must again sit with Ambassador Otieno to settle the bride price. At least all parties were calling the Striiduc custom the same thing now, since he had raised the amount so high. Mildred was enlisted to draw up a formal contract. The amount and the signatures were all that remained to complete my part of matchmaking.

In the Consortium office where she worked, I had gifted Mildred with the burka given to me by Brianna, still in its plain wrapper. I mentioned that the burka was from a cache found in the fortress and was once owned by Kyle Rula. Mildred had seemed especially touched. "And it's blue," she said. I offered to show her how to fold the material as a shawl, but she pulled the package close. "I have seen them," she said coldly.

Before I had left, though, she was sneaking a peek at the material. That moment had made my heart soar more than any at Stargate Junction. These surprising moments should have a native term like strikestone, more than a failed enterprise to secure the silicide.

At the news studio, the interview had not yet started, but the brilliant lights made my eyes sting. Dr. Richardson talked on his cellphone, and Dr. Spinelli whispered harshly to me. "You could be more cordial. Recruiting isn't easy, you know. Dr. Ingram was massacred and Mitterand had a native disease. Dr. Gutierrez at Beecham Place is appalled at the prevalence of hepatitis and river blindness, both curable diseases."

"Dr. Richardson will serve at Beecham Place?"

He squinted at me, his bushy eyebrows pulling together. "Richardson has agreed to serve at the hospital in Urbyd. Fewer homeless patients riddled with worms and hemorrhoids."

I could not remember when Dr. Spinelli had ever been so angry with me.

When the event finally started, I turned a cold shoulder to Dr. Spinelli. Mrs. Shaw was rock steady under the lights with her chin jutting out. Aunt Carline was her same aggressive self with layers of controlled rage wafting from her. I wondered how Bybiis viewed my aunt who didn't bother to guard her feelings. While the interviewer spoke into the camera to introduce today's issue, I thought again about my wedding: maybe at Kecouroo's village with Cara presiding, with dancing and feasting and new chants. Edwina and Dulcinea and Omiibuk with her brothers would be there.

Dr. Spinelli nudged me and I sat up straight, stifling a yawn. Carline was talking, her heavy features projected on two monitors mounted high behind them, left and right. That was more of her face than I needed to see. "The order of impunity covers the Junction Boys and any who are on the savannah with skills to serve the tribes," she was saying.

"On Cicero, Carline," Mrs. Shaw asked, "are the Putuki and Cylahi refugees exempt from the local laws? No, because they aren't an overclass who can rape the girls and confiscate property without consequence."

"There is no theft here," Carline said. "Rabbenu Ely is holding my nephew and the general's son for their own protection."

My shoulders sagged. I was so tired of this argument. We all knew why Patrick was in custody. He should have found new friends long ago. My mind wandered again, this time to my months with Aunt Carline in New Shanghai and how she had waited for off-hand approval from Carl Hartley while she shunted me off the local hospital so I could learn 'a valuable skill.' I decided to not invite Carline to my wedding. That was just desserts.

"How can we be certain the next rabbenu will be an improvement on Ely's rule?" the interviewer said. "Who should be a candidate?"

"Several are qualified," Mrs. Shaw said. "Orin rabbe Murd who has ties with the securities exchange, or Kenru of the Uburu tribe, or Kyros Kenoma who negotiates with the Goras for a truce in the fighting."

"You didn't mention Karl Wyley," he returned.

"He's not qualified," Carline objected. "Karl Wyley never fin-
ished school. The one person who really worries tribal leaders is
Brianna Miller. The Putuki won't follow her, and a truce with the
Goras will fall apart."

"Is a woman eligible to run for office?" the commentator asked.

"With the treasure of Rularim backing her," Carline said,
"Brianna Miller is a force in the elections."

Mrs. Shaw shook her head. "The treasure is managed by several
women and has never been used for politics, only to serve the
people."

"Maybe Brianna thinks," Carline said, "that her election is
serving the people."

"This is speculation for the cameras," Mrs. Shaw said in measured
tones. "You don't realize the trouble you're making for Brianna."

"I'm making trouble? Me? I'm making trouble?" Carline's face
was ruddy in the harsh light. "She pushed us out of Cylay."

"Brianna Miller was a child when you left Dolvia," Mrs. Shaw
said evenly. "And she jumped back for more than a decade. How
can she be responsible for your displacement to Cicero?"

Dr. Spinelli whispered, "They really go at it, don't they? And this
show is live."

"What is live?" I asked in a whisper.

"The audience sees the discussion in real time. They cannot delete
the statements that don't fit today's question, like Brianna as a candidate."

I blinked at him. "She would make a great rabbenu."

"General Hartley hates this idea, especially with an infant at her
breast. Too risky."

I nodded, trying to be amicable. I didn't mention that Brianna Miller had no intention of raising Dacupitte's last son herself. The men never got it right, always assuming they decide for us. What man in leadership made decisions for Kecouroo or for Brianna Miller?

After the taping ended, I greeted Aunt Carline, braced for her disapproval. "Hiki—"

"Don't start that Arrivi jargon with me," she said. "They say you keep the old ways, whatever that means. You're not pregnant?"

"Ah, no."

"Well, there's that. You should clean your glasses sometimes. I can see the smudges. Let's see it." She worked her hand in an impatient gesture, and I realized that she meant the engagement bracelet. I held up my arm, and she looked askance at the gold leaves strung side-to-side. "And where will you live as a newlywed? Not in some hut in the bush, I hope."

"Maybe in Somule. I still own Karen's house."

She squinted, making her eyes look even closer together. "You mean Joey's house. My brother's house. Patrick has asked about it. He may want to live there."

"Um, of course, but I thought . . . I mean—"

"Oh, you aren't concerned about Patrick. Don't play false with me." Her lip curled just as I remembered it when I had stayed at her house in New Shanghai. "Only your Arrivi friends count for you. You could try to help your family sometimes."

"Help you?"

"The ambassador from Striiduc has been seen with you in public," she said, "talking about investments and shipping channels. But you never think to ask Patrick's advice, or to involve the Bryants in this new venture. Only for your Dolviet friends, huh? All for them."

I just stared. I thought of how rude Patrick had been to me at the governor's mansion one time, pushing me into a cab. I thought of how rude he was to Karen at the debutante ball, refusing to be my escort. I remembered how Carline had once spoken so rudely to General Hartley at dinner after her third drink. I was glad for my choices.

"General Hartley is negotiating the release of Patrick along with his own son," I said, trying to keep my remarks in safe territory.

"That's what you know," Carline said. "There is no release. Carl and Patrick will run Ely's securities exchange until Ely reinforces the alliance with Khalif Ananke."

"But Ely is stepping down."

"That's wishful thinking from your Dolviet friends. Just wishful thinking."

"But with the news segment, you just said—"

"Comments are calibrated," Carline said. "Don't be so naïve. Why do you think I'm invited back time and again, huh? The network paid for my trip here, although they didn't know I came to catch up with you."

I stretched my face into a smile, but I was shocked that her worldview was so different from the narrative about home rule and investing in gum arabic, not that I had reinforced that sentiment during my travels. I was eager to ask the general which vision was true, since no truth was found on the comtechs or subscription news.

She signaled an audience member and, to my surprise, Steve Swanweil came forward. "Steve, you remember my niece Kelly Osborn, sister to Patrick?"

"Of course." He offered his hand to shake. I had raised mine in the instinctive Arrivi gesture, though. "Melinga, Kelly. It's good to see the spirit in your face."

"Kelly has been talking with Otieno about a new deal with Somule Gems for trade routes," Aunt Carline said. My brow wrinkled and I stared at her. "It's no secret," she added. "There are no secrets on Stargate Junction."

I rolled my eyes, searching the ceiling for hidden cameras.

"Otieno's new openness," Swanweil said, "may bring jobs for some who live here. Don't you agree?"

"I know nothing about his business."

"Well, Striiduc bazaari don't involve the women." He put an arm around my shoulder, guiding me a few steps forward. "Perhaps you can introduce us, just for a greeting? I can take it from there. When do you meet with him again?"

I shrugged him off. "Um, I'm not comfortable using . . . I mean, my purpose is—"

"We understand." Swanweil shrugged. "A marriage alliance is not with Bernice alone, but with her whole family."

"Bernice has no family."

"You are her family. Therefore, we are her family."

I slowly shook my head. "I'll not help you with this. Don't ask me again."

Swanweil's dark hair was brushed back and stiff, gleaming under the lights. "I understand your loyalty to Rularim," he said. "You keep the old ways, as it's said. But we live in a new season now, the season of kari."

The words of honor were jarring from his lips. I stepped back. "You cannot claim kari as yours."

Swanweil showed that indulgent smile one gives a stubborn child. "Let's keep a channel open, shall we?" When he left with Aunt Carline and the two doctors, I left with Mrs. Shaw. That action told any bystander all there was to know about loyalty.

We went to the new suite to prepare for the appointment with Ambassador Otieno. The clutch was busy showing Sallmus Le and Bybiis access codes on the EAM. As a demonstration, I called up chime coral in the Junction's library. The images were surprising: old drawings of fishing boats that had salvaged sizeable nodes of coral with bundles of long pipes like a pipe-organ cactus. The encyclopedia entry claimed that the hollow pipes were made of secretions from tubeworms that used them for housing. Strong and fibrous, the tubes became brittle in the dry climate. The tubeworms were extinct and chime coral rare but mostly used for arcane wind instruments.

"Chime coral can be made to sing," Bybiis said over my shoulder, maybe trying to impress the clutch members. "Or I read they could, using a tuning fork. But I never saw one before yesterday."

Mrs. Shaw drew me away from the girls and to a sitting area. "Let's talk, Kelly." I sighed and stretched my back. The burden of match-making was more than I wanted. "The title dragon sleeper isn't from Arrivi or Borabean," she started. "Bybiis said it was in her dreams about a woman in water."

"You mean, not our words." I looked at her with blurry eyes, my elbow on the chair arm and my chin resting in my palm. "A carromancist maybe," I murmured. "The Striiduc may be spying on Somule Gems." I had promoted this idea before, but my concerns had fallen on deaf ears.

"Good, I don't have to explain this to you," Mrs. Shaw said quickly. "There's more, though. Just a theory I've been chewing on. Maybe the gualarep girls could always throw their thoughts, even as yearlings at my bush clinic. They weren't trained to target a favorite, so they perhaps broadcast widely. Arrivi who travel have reported receiving dreams from Edwina or Edna while on the transport and even on Stargate Junction, like you. So it's possible that we drew attention to ourselves through many cycles of netta when a carromancist in Striiduc also participated in the song."

I sat back in the wide chair and stared at her, trying to digest the idea. "But, wouldn't we have . . . I mean, did Edwina ever—"

"They were untrained. We didn't know about, um, spillover."

"But the carromancist would have tried to answer back, surely."

"Depending on motive."

I blinked; the suite lights were too bright. I watched the clutch for a moment while I sorted what I knew about the song. "I mentioned to Bybiis that she should develop a secret code with Bernice, maybe hand signals for actions like run, lies, agree, and step back. And they should talk about this private code only in whispers and in the dark."

"That's good advice."

"What is the motive, besides learning our secrets?"

"I suspect their motives changed after Otieno met Bernice. There may be a struggle among the Cochin city-states."

I felt an itch along my back and moved my shoulder to rub against the seatback. "How can one participate in the song without the presence of a gualarep?"

"We don't know," Mrs. Shaw said. "All these possibilities we are considering during Edwina's ban on remote viewing. I wanted you to know. My husband says that Edwina is sorry that you feel rejected."

My irritation vanished. I had felt unworthy, rejected by Edwina. The ban was a precaution, not for me only, but for all members of the song until we knew more. I looked down, blinking back sudden tears. The lights were definitely too bright in the suite. I needed to adjust them and impose a rule.

Mrs. Shaw placed a hand on my wrist over the engagement bracelet. "You'll keep this quiet, of course."

"Bybiis knows?"

"Bybiis first suggested to Sarah that strangers could hear the song."

"How could one hear the song and not join in, not make herself known to us? What kind of discipline does that take?"

Mrs. Shaw scrunched her face. "We know little of the history. Apparently, there was a tribe living near Striiduc gifted with spiritual powers. Some were persecuted with beheadings, burnings, and drownings. They fled to the mountains or became sailors, but some interbred with other tribes. So the spiritual talents can appear anywhere along the coast, or on the savannah like Quentin the healer. We call the exiled families Stroenuk, but as it turns out, that's a Striiduc word for outcast." She pronounced the word strew-knock.

"Bybiis could have this Stroenuk blood?"

"Bybiis never knew her father, so we don't know. I wanted to tell you all this in person. We have to be careful now with the EAM and, um, everywhere."

"Let me ask," I whispered, leaning closer. "The souls of dead conscripts. Here at the Junction. Can you see them?"

She chuckled. "One of Dr. Spinelli's favorite topics for dinner talk. What happens to the souls of those who die in space?" She saw me nodding and added, "Cleo could see them drifting near the ceiling, I was told. Do you?"

I shook my head no and sat back. I felt limited. "Bybiis and the Striiduc women can see them, I think." Mrs. Shaw patted my hand and stood to end our talk. A sudden thought came to me; so many concerns. "Oh! Don't trust Dr. Richardson. Don't trust anything he says or does."

Mrs. Shaw grinned again, showing her teeth. "Why do you think we're sending him to the Borabean city of Urbyd?"

The teahouse where we had so often met was overflowing, and the harried waiter had enlisted two Chinese-descent women to deliver entrees to the tables. He was short-tempered with them and spoiled the service experience for many Striiduc smogens who waited at the tables. I saw my mistake that we should have catered this event.

With Sarah as their chaperon, Bernice sat with the clutch of Cleo, Bybiis, and Sallmus Le, who were staff to her, and several female Striiduc students. Striiduc boys sat with fathers, and the women of their culture were absent. Mrs. Shaw and I sat across the table from Otieno and Onetel with the agreement papers between us. Patrons at all tables, and pedestrians in the promenade even, craned their necks to better view our gestures. The jongleur in his motleys began a performance—never waste an audience—but few turned his way. He noticed Khalif Olpul and Apetu, oldest son of Khalif Ananke in Urbyd, waiting in the back. The jongleur deserted his performance space and withdrew to the shadows. What was that all about?

"I am hearing," Ambassador Otieno said at the table, "that the peridot necklaces are intended for the clutch of Cleo."

I pulled my attention to the immediate and pasted a smile on my face.

"Since two necklaces are sacrificed to appease the women of my family," Otieno continued, "I want to replace them with jewelry of equal value." Onetel placed five boxes on top of the agreement papers waiting on the tiny round table between us.

I glanced at Bybiis, signaling her to bring Bernice forward. I turned back to the ambassador. "May I glance at one?"

Otieno made an accommodating gesture, so I snapped open one velvety box. The necklace was a string of fiery opals, mostly pale blue, with cabochon settings in perfectly graduated sizes. Far greater in value than peridot.

Bernice caught her breath as she stood at my shoulder. I glanced back at Bybiis, seeking the signal that no hedge magic was present. "Bybiis, would you ask the clutch of Cleo to join us?"

I replaced the box on the table. "Truly, Ambassador, you must stop with these extravagant gifts. We cannot hope to match your generosity." I felt Bernice's light punch on my shoulder, a genuine reaction not lost on the men.

The girls in the clutch crowded around, so we all stood. The four girls held hands high with palms upward, murmuring hiki. Bybiis had hung back with Sallmus Le since they weren't scheduled to jump back.

"These are Bernice who you know, Leah Datong, Rosalyn Datong, Claire, and Dominic." Both Striiduc men bowed with fingertips of one hand on his chest. The ambassador gestured to the boxes, saying, "To replace the peridot." I stepped back with Mrs. Shaw and watched the squealing and giggling and melingas all around, as the girls helped each other to wear the necklaces there in a public place.

I took the opportunity to fill in the bride amount on the contract. I settled on 22,000 romarks, probably appearing weak, before I signaled Bernice to affix her signature. The noise subsided immediately, and they all stared at me.

"You will be responsible," I said, "so we should add your signature, not mine."

She glanced at the bridegroom and signed the paper with a flourish.

I turned her to the full company and positioned him at her side before I announced, "May I present Bernice Datong, agent of Somule Gems at Stargate Junction and the betrothed of Ambassador Otieno of the Striiduc nation?"

There was general applause that caught me by surprise, along with clucking from Bybiis and Sallmus Le while the men queued up to congratulate their boss. Even Dr. Spinelli took a turn. I retreated to my stance next to Mrs. Shaw and glanced around the teahouse, where many were talking eagerly, even the haughty waiter. A few bystanders used space phones as a camera to capture an image of the new couple.

Mrs. Shaw held out her cellphone to snap an image. "For the general." She shrugged.

"You were right," I said to Mrs. Shaw. "Youth is wasted on the young."

She chuckled. "The girls in the clutch are not two seasons younger than you, Kelly."

The clutch still had the jumping-back moment to endure. I must start lessons with Bybiis and Sallmus Le about detecting wards, and discussions with General Hartley about carromancy. Mrs. Shaw patted my arm. "You did well, Kelly. Asking Bernice to sign in your place was a nice touch."

"We should have catered this event, not in public like this."

"Again, your instincts serve a larger purpose," Mrs. Shaw said. "Bernice cannot be dislodged by underhanded tricks with impunity."

"I hate that word—impunity. It only means disregarding the law, like we're outlaws or something."

We looked up at a sudden commotion at the crowded entrance of the teahouse, and I saw the promenade was full of people who huddled in tight groups and looked up at comtech screens. Mildred and Aunt Carline entered and quickly came to Mrs. Shaw and me.

"There was an attempt on Brianna's life," Aunt Carline said, ignoring Mildred's stare at her intrusion on the news. "Brianna and the fetus are fine, but two are dead and Rufus is wounded."

"But how do you know?" I asked.

"It's on the comtechs, breaking news."

In the promenade, people watched the overhead comtech, their faces all canted at the same angle. Dr. Richardson and Steve Swanweil had cellphones out and were searching options, only to glance up and compare the two news sources. In the teahouse, Carline described more of the event in Cylay, but I knew only that Rufus was wounded. Colors were brighter to me, and I felt I was breathing toxic fumes.

Mrs. Shaw touched my arm above the elbow. "Kelly, you must leave with Mildred now. General Hartley is waiting. We'll send your things along."

"But . . . but—"

"This is why we attend events in groups," Mrs. Shaw said with her rock-steady assurance. "If one must see to other duties, there's no loss. You did well; now go."

Sarah had joined Mrs. Shaw as her second. The girls stood in a tight gaggle around Bernice. In a daze I followed Mildred out and across the promenade, not even stopping to say goodbye. I caught a glimpse of Khalif Olpul and Apetu retreating to the business area. I looked back to where Aunt Carline was greeting Ambassador Otieno and introducing Swanweil and Richardson. I wanted to intervene, to stop her insinuating ways that traded on my name, but my need to reach Rufus had more purpose.

With a buzzing in my head, I trailed Mildred's long strides as we passed through the doors of the military section and down the corridor toward Ops.

We hovered at the doorway. General Hartley with a red face was shouting at an EAM screen. "You will release them without conditions, or I will come to the governor's house and throttle you myself!" He punched on the keyboard to end the call and cursed with vigor. "By the lashes of Cyrus. The pig-headed, weaseling—"

John Milan was there with him, standing with hands on hips. "Another reason to broadcast this footage, Eugene. The death of Anaxagoras cements the armistice with Aeolis. But if people know how he died—" I hadn't realized John Milan was on Stargate Junction. Maybe he had arrived on the same shuttle as Aunt Carline and Dr. Richardson.

"The Company has already turned you down," the general guessed to John Milan, unaware of Mildred and me in the corridor.

"I know!" Milan said in disbelief. "But you can broadcast the story through Consortium channels, to show that their news is not true events."

The general squinted at him. "The Company news where you have reputation? On the comtechs?"

John Milan tapped the package on the desk. "But this is the truth, actual footage. Anaxagoras was executed on the dunes after his men surrendered. There was no . . . no . . ."

The general shook his head slightly. "Try selling the clip to Endicott at the Cochin network."

"The story abuses their good relations with Abydian, Endicott claims, even though it was Karl Wyley and those captive boys who did the deed."

"It's gruesome to watch?"

"The oldest boy, Kristos," John said, "had this tub of blood, I guess, taken from Gora officers. He cut the throats of two so they bled into the tub. Then he and his brother grabbed Anaxagoras and forced him on his knees. Kristos started to drown him in the tub, but allowed Anaxagoras to catch his breath twice. Only twice. Finally, Kristos just turned Anaxagoras toward my camcorder, all wet and dripping blood, and sliced his throat. Bloodier than Karl Wyley that boy has become."

"I cannot release that image. What will people think?"

John Milan held his arms wide, not believing the resistance. "The truth has to come out somewhere."

"The tribes need to settle," the general said, "not find a new reason for an uprising."

John Milan dejectedly sat in a chair. "All this time . . . The first real news I captured. And I cannot even give it away."

General Hartley noticed me finally. "Oh, there you are, Kelly. Let's set you on your way." He left John Milan, who was shaking his head and staring at the Ops officers in disbelief. "Thank you, Mildred," the general said softly, and he guided me left with a hand on my arm above the elbow.

Milan shouted from behind us. "But what about my story?"

General Hartley and I made a couple of quick turns down narrow hallways and came into a mechanic's area where several smaller craft rested in service bays. The odors of heated metal and new wood troubled my senses, along with rank air heavy with rot and bad water, so different from the oxygen-rich public areas.

"Where are we going?" I asked breathlessly.

"You'll want to get back to Dolvia, I'm sure. We'll just send you with the mail."

"Is Rufus dying?"

"Siize and Siiloba are lost, and Rufus took the Tzu beam meant to destroy Brianna's child. The stuff of new chants, huh?"

"Siize and Siiloba? Really?" The general seemed not worried for Brianna who he had invited to live on the transport. Was this more of his diplomat's manner for my benefit?

He stopped short and I almost crashed into him. "Let's see; it's this one, I think."

"Where are we? Do you know this place?"

"There are sections of Stargate Junction I have never visited. But I know the mail run well enough." General Hartley looked around the next corner, and approached a bullet-shaped speeder that looked battered and refurbished. "Judell, there you are. All fueled up?"

Judell was a scrawny man and missing his eyetooth and two others on the right side. His blue eyes looked like he was crying, and I immediately suspected cataracts. He stood with a hunched back on bandy legs and gestured toward the hatch of the rocket.

"This is the mail run?" I asked.

"A special non-stop run we make on occasion to Dolvia, or sometimes to Cicero. But no worries. Judell has been successful many times."

"And others have not?" I asked.

"You pregnant?" Judell asked.

I pulled back with surprise. I must be getting fat with so many people interested in my health.

Judell shrugged. "Nomay be's taking one that's pregnant 'cause 'a the cold."

The general showed me a bright smile, so I said, "You're being dishonest."

His face fell, and his energy settled. "There's a reason," he began more calmly, "that we keep a transport in orbit around Dolvia. The distance from Stargate Junction to Dolvia is at the far end of our fuel capacity. We found that if we lower the temperature of the whole ship, like a speeder, we have less friction in space and can cruise better. I wouldn't send you, though, if I didn't trust Judell. Precious cargo."

I squinted at the little man's face. He raised an eyebrow and shrugged.

"You do want to see Rufus," the general added, "before he's evacuated to Beecham Place. Here are letters for General Sector and remembrances for Brianna. We'll send along your luggage with the shuttle. Oh, and put this on."

He showed me an insulated parka with a fur-lined hood. "For the cold." After two beats, he added, "Please."

I stepped into the parka's weight and pulled my arms through the long sleeves that had mittens attached. I stowed the small items in the parka pockets.

Judell was drinking from a container and offered me one of the same type. "Vumay be taking liquids now," he said and finished his portion.

I sniffed the sugar water before I drank, and then stepped through the hatch. Only two crates were secured in the netting of the cargo area that had two empty seats. I caught the odors of old rope and stale air. I moved to the copilot seat that was padded with insulation under fur and also had big boots ready to provide additional protection. Ready lights were on and I could feel the engine idling. The hatch snapped closed, and I was suddenly deaf to the engine noise of the larger ship.

I had not performed the honorable goodbye with the busy general.

Judell handed me a hood and some goggles. "Nomay be's needing your glasses. Goggles be's real tight 'cause 'a your eyes are being sensitive to the cold. Vumay be gettin' the mittens on real snug too."

Judell worked the straps on my too-warm seat before he strapped himself into a similar contraption. He affixed a hood and goggles on his head, and looked my way like a swimmer intent on winning a match race. "Here we go," he said and eased the big double lever forward. The engine engaged and we slipped out of the docking bay.

I knew we were free by the sudden drop in the pit of my stomach. I felt strangely calm, light-headed and drifting. "How many hours?" I asked.

"Less than a day, but nomay be's feeling it."

"Ah, you're joking! A sedative in the drink?"

"Best I be's giving you the right one," he said with his partially toothless grin. "Else I'll be dozing and vumay be's sending out distress signals."

And I had worried about the Striiduc men. Ha! General Hartley was craftier than them by half. I was passed out before Judell engaged turbo speed.

EIGHT

I WOKE UP RETCHING. SOMEONE HELD A PAN FOR ME ANTICIPAT-ing my move. A bad taste lingered in my mouth, metallic and organic. Somebody wiped my chin, but I couldn't focus beyond the halos on the room lights.

"Your vision will clear in a moment." It was Hakulupe Le's voice. I was in Cylay on Dolvia.

I struggled to sit up, but she pushed my shoulder back. "Just relax. You'll be dizzy for a while."

I blinked and blinked, finally discerning a second bed where Judell sat slumped like an old man with his legs dangling over the side. "That run from the Junction ages you, huh?"

He squinted to focus on me, and moved his jaw to relieve the tension. "Three months' pay." His lassitude was dissipating. "Re-entry be's the bumpy part, but vumay slept like a newborn."

"How do you get off planet now?"

"Ah, plays at piggyback on the shuttle 'til we be's breaking gravity, then she be's in her element right enough."

"Thanks for your care."

"Vumay be's feeling morose awhile, maybe from the cold. Some pilots be's nursing bad thoughts, but that's a choice, in'a it?"

I lifted my chin. "I'm free to choose how to respond. Thanks again."

"Weren't much trouble." He looked up at a nurse's entrance. "My turn under the lights." He grinned, showing the absence of three teeth, and moved to the wheelchair she offered.

I turned my head to consider Hakulupe Le who looked older by a season of netta. "How bad?"

Her lambent eyes were hooded. "Rufus took the laser fire from the Tzu that was meant for Brianna. He stepped in front of the flash, just like that. The lazer missed his lungs, though. He'll have a scar down his back on the left." She attempted a smile. "He uses his right arm for the whip and pistol."

So, it was bad. "Are you wounded?"

"Kelly, Kelly, always worried for others," she said sadly. "Siize saved my life, and Siiloba saved Kecouroo. Ely's hired assassins were trying to destroy the last son of Dacupitte, we believe. We were wearing veils, so I guess they thought to murder us all to ensure they destroyed Karisma. That's the name Kecouroo chose. Karisma. Do you like it?"

"How soon is Brianna due?"

"Not for half a cycle of Nettom, but maybe sooner. This child is strong and wants to be about his business."

"Don't set expectations for him that he cannot reach. Our stories that we tell each other . . . they may not fit real events." I thought about Carline's definition of reality, and the offer from Otieno to remove Rabbenu Ely, and why I had refused it. I thought of John Milan's frustration with his new narrative, and no avenue to get a real story on the news. "Otieno may have a carromancist at Stargate Junction," I informed Lupe. "Or she's in Striiduc and Otieno pays for her insights. Otieno speaks against hedge magic but seems too well informed." I moved in the bed, aware that I was dressed differently and my hair was brushed down. My vision was better, except for the halo effect around the lights.

"I have remembrances for Brianna and—"

"We found them. Just relax."

I attempted to sit up, and was immediately nauseated, falling back on the pillow.

"Give it a few minutes," Lupe repeated.

"Why attempt this mail run, if recovery takes as long as the shuttle would take?"

"The shuttle won't arrive for three more days," she said.

I must have dozed, and I woke again when a nurse brought a tray of food. The smell made my throat tight, but I didn't retch.

"You must eat something to settle your stomach," she said.

Under her stare I nibbled the edge of a patty, and my stomach growled so I tried another sliver. I rubbed my nose that was tingling.

"Your nose itches," she noted. "That means the feeling is returning." She checked the water container on the nightstand, and left with the soles of her shoes squeaking on the tiles.

I put on my glasses, taking them from the nightstand. That helped with my vision issues. I swung my legs off the bed and tried standing. The cool tiles sent tingling sensations through my bare feet and up my ankles, but it wasn't really pain. I breathed in gasps and walked to the window, moving my jaw to relieve tension as I had seen Judell do.

Judell, what a sweet guy. I wondered about his origins and what had brought him to Westend. All these resources mustered to facilitate my return, after more had been mustered to get me to Stargate Junction. I was blessed with friends. Except that the best of them were gone. Edna and Dacupitte, my parents Karen and Joey, Siize and Siiloba, Asmach, Vera. How I wanted to greet them again, to send them a song of thanks and . . . and I don't know. I knew I mustn't attempt the song after the general had worked so hard to return me secretly to Dolvia.

I sighed, choosing to push away remorse. On impulse, I grabbed the robe on the chair, pulling my loose hair free to hang past my shoulders. I opened the door to peer down the corridor. Two warriors with ceremonial shields stood sentry at one room, so I figured that was where I would find Rufus. I padded down the tiled floor on my tingling feet, probably not in a straight line. I was panting when I reached the Cylahi sentries who moved shields to block my way.

"I belong with Rufus. I just risked my life to get here, and you will let me pass." I felt a pressure on my lungs and my breath came shortly again.

The door opened and Kecouroo stood there with her nappy hair backlit by the sunlight from the windows. "Nu delaya," she said to the sentries, and caught me with a strong arm across my back just as my knees went weak. She walked me into the room and to a chair where I collapsed into a bundle of bones. The high bed was above my sightline, but I could hear the monitor beeping and see a form with his head pillowed.

"He's in a bad way," Kecouroo whispered. "We're trying to keep his fever down with this alcohol wash. We bathe his shoulders and face."

"Where is your necklace of tektite stones?"

She touched the front of her garment, and showed a sad smile. "Kelly, you notice everything. The necklace is at my village where you will find a cache of goods meant as keepsakes for you and, uh, family members. Sit awhile, and I'll send the others along."

"Help me to the bed," I said.

She reached for me again, and soon I was seated next to Rufus while his warm chest moved with each breath. She left quietly while I focused on him.

Sunlight streamed through the window and fell across the bedcovers. Rufus was pale, with many red scars gotten in battle. His dark hair was matted on the pillow, and bandages were wrapped around his midriff and one shoulder. His presence was . . . less present. I soaked a cloth in the pan and reached to place it on his exposed arm. His eyes opened and he caught my wrist, as if plucking a bird out of the air. I gasped.

He released my hand and his expression changed showing, uh, pleasure maybe. "Your hair is loose," he said in a hoarse voice.

"There was no time." I rested the cloth on his undressed arm so I could pull the weight of my hair over one shoulder, the better to make a braid. "Leave it," he said. "It catches the light."

"Can I get you something? A drink perhaps." I reached for a glass on the table and overturned the metal wash pan that spilled and clattered onto the floor. I wanted to kneel to set things straight, burning with embarrassment.

"Wait," Rufus said. "Don't go."

I turned back and pushed my glasses up on my nose. I waited with hands on my lap and eyes lowered, begging Dolvia for no more blunders. "Anaxagoras is dead," I offered as my report. "Ely won't release Carl and Patrick yet."

"I know," he said with a parched tongue. "A book on the stand. Read a little."

I picked out the chapbook from among the medical supplies on the stand. It was grimy and worn, like he had carried it through many battles. I turned it over and brushed the cover with my palm. My voice cracked when I said, "One of mine." The chapbook held chants I had compiled, adding some of mine, to be shared around the evening campfire.

His eyelids drooped and his breathing was shallow. I looked around, but felt confident nobody would disturb us for a time. I thumbed through the book and came to a dog-eared page with smudged text. I read out loud 'The Mark of Rularim' while Rufus closed his eyes and a faint smile crossed his mouth.

> Baptized with blood and kneeling
> Next to Bibi Le in the killing fields
> Of Southwest Arrivi, home to Kyros
> Her destiny known, her life not her own
> Brianna becomes Rularim renowned
> Given, sacrificed, spent, or troubled
> Living symbol of the struggle, anon

I looked at his face that seemed slack like he slept. "Rufus," I said in a whisper. "Rufus, I don't want to travel any more. I don't care about rabbenu or the clutch of Cleo or Somule Gems. I just want a home and hearth and the step of a husband by the door. Maybe at the village above Mayschool."

He turned his head slightly. "Mekucoo need only the land." He moved his arm to brush my arm. "And each other." His eyelids drooped heavily.

And that was my moment of commitment; strikestone as it were. No gifts of opals for attendants; no announcement in a public teahouse; no business colleagues on the side with congratulations. Just three words—and each other. All we needed was the land and each other. I read several more chants from the chapbook, naming heroes and events. I bathed the arm and forehead of Rufus with the cool cloth and moved to the chair where I may have dozed again.

I woke with a crick in my neck and my feet swollen and tingling. Somebody had put socks on my feet, cotton and ribbed. Hakulupe Le was seated in a chair next to me, one dragged in from the hallway. Reading glasses were perched on her nose while she looked over the chapbook. She glanced up over the reading glasses, her eyes flashing with humor. "Brianna Miller is saved by Rufus. A blessing from Dolvia."

I sat up and stretched my back, brushing the hair from my face to begin plaiting it over one shoulder. "A festival chant is needed."

Brianna was there too, and she moved from the window to Lupe's side. Her face was plump and her hair was short. She wore a blue Arrivi gown that barely reached her ankles over the pregnancy burden.

I held my palm high and ducked my head. "Hiki, Rularim."

"Melinga, Kelly, the betrothed of Rufus. Will you dress now and walk with Lupe?"

They helped me down the corridor to my own room, where clothes were laid out for me: a uniform from the clutch of Kenru and wide sandals for walking across the savannah. Hakulupe Le pulled my hair tighter and quickly added a braid while I yawned and blinked to clear the halos around the room lights.

"Wear this," Brianna said, showing me the dressy peridot necklace that had once belonged to Heather Osborn.

"It looks silly with a uniform," I objected.

"It's correct for today." She clasped it on my neck under my braid. "Do you know what I saw on the street just now?" she confided. "Before we entered here, huh? A funeral for a Putuki man, a cousin to Martina. A victim of a pipe bomb in the plaza. The coffin was held high, and some instruments played. The widow and grown children had bleeding cuts of grief. I saw orchids and hibiscus; that was something. And you know what I thought, huh? I thought, such an elaborate show for a single body. One corpse only, after all that you and I have seen, the day squandered on grief."

"What must I do?"

"Your voice has volume now, Kelly," Brianna said, "as the betrothed of Rufus."

"Brianna must stay out of sight," Hakulupe Le said. "We cannot risk another attempt on the life of her child. You will speak where needed. Come along."

She pulled me to the door, where I turned back to Brianna. "What should I say?"

"Speak out your message of solidarity and home rule. Go on. I'm safer here with Rufus and his guards."

Hakulupe Le seemed distracted while she hurried me through the barracks yard to a waiting lorry. We were in the Consortium compound near the quarters for married couples, and several blocks from the plaza in front of the governor's mansion. We crowded next to a driver I didn't know.

"Shouldn't we have veils?" I asked.

"Not today."

"General Hartley is livid with Rabbenu Ely," I reported. "He threatened to disembark and dislodge Ely himself. Dr. Spinelli said that the general wants Brianna to live offworld with the newborn where he can keep them safe."

"Did you feel safer at Stargate Junction?"

I had to smile at her question. "No."

We stepped down from the lorry into the plaza where the shrine to Kyle Rula was maintained. A non-working fountain of rabbenu limestone reflected the unforgiving sunlight, as big shadows from fat clouds passed left to right. The new municipal building was across the way, and to the left was a line of shops and EAM cafes with tables set out in the sun, devoid of patrons. We loitered a few minutes as soldiers and workers and souks came and went. A cache of Putuki protestors was alert, seeking media exposure for their rhetoric against Hamilcar. Facing them were several tribeswomen, without veils and from all tribes, each one sporting the dirty forehead mark.

"Rularim, Rularim," they chanted in unison.

Regan Villines was there with a cameraman, looking around to detect an event worthy of comtech reporting.

"What is this?" I asked Lupe. "Where are their burkas?"

"Chi cylay," Hakulupe Le whispered.

Kecouroo entered the square from the academy gate with her long stride and her gaze focused on the shrine. She was tall and stately, perhaps fifty years old, and her one-piece suede garment was drenched with some liquid. Gasoline, it must have been. She looked at nobody and said nothing, but she sported the mark of Rularim on her forehead. Before the shrine and facing the governor's house, she rested on her knees and toes.

"No!" I said. "No, no, no, no!"

Hakulupe Le pinched the soft part of my arm above the elbow. "This is Kecouroo's day, not your day." Lupe quickly stroked my forehead with her thumb, applying the same mark so my allegiance was obvious among the crowd of protestors.

Kecouroo had brought a small container of gasoline, just to be sure. She spilled it over her nappy hair and shoulders, and struck a utility match. I saw the flash of angry flames, yellow and orange in the sunlight, and rolling black smoke. I heard a short scream when she breathed in fire, and her mouth gaped open. I couldn't avoid the smell of burning flesh and spent fuel. Exposed arms and legs were eaten by the conflagration, and soon enough the blackened bones rested in a crumpled heap.

I felt a weight on my chest like my lungs wouldn't fill. I suddenly knew Kecouroo's mind, the tracks of decisions she had made from before she started with walkabout—a cache of heirlooms left in the village including the tektite necklace, honor to Asmach who was blood uncle to Dulcinea's newborn by Aeolis, the ride on sigpywa into Cylay, the naming of Brianna's unborn child, the final goodbye for Rufus with instructions for his betrothed; also her high spirits as she treasured those last days under the savannah sun. And this honorable end, in protest to the stubborn rule of Rabbenu Ely.

Putuki protestors were chanting their usual slogans. Women with the mark of Rularim positioned themselves between the Putuki and me. Regan Villines stepped into my line of sight and thrust a microphone under my chin. "What was Kecouroo saying with this act?"

I heard the whirr of a camcorder and knew the tears on my stricken face would be shown to the Westend audience, along with my peridot necklace and my uniform from the clutch of Kenru. I felt sunlight glint off my glasses as I looked into the camera lens. "Kecouroo is the ninth martyr to destroy herself by fire in protest to Ely's tenure as rabbenu. Arrivi struggles have become a Mekucoo fight. Ely will lose."

Time seemed to slow. The plaza was suddenly too bright as the rain clouds had rolled past. The Putuki protestors stopped chanting when convent residents, who I suspected indulged self-mutilation under their sleeves, stepped forward to gather Kecouroo's remains. I knew that chatter on the comtechs would increase within the hour, and Kecouroo's sacrifice would be weighed by all factions. Even Aunt Carline at Stargate Junction would offer an opinion, perhaps calling Kecouroo a victim of grief after the death of Dacupitte. I must make certain the news story was from a tribal source, the definition of events as we saw them unfold.

The women who wore no burkas arrayed themselves behind me. The mark of Rularim on my forehead showed the comtech audience my loyalty and those who supported me. I lifted my chin. "Ely's rule is corrupt. Arrivi tribes are united in our demand for new civil authority. Siibabean and Uburu are inspired by Kecouroo's wordless statement. We have a single message: Rabbenu Ely must step down. His cronies must be replaced by freely elected welfare ministers. We must have home rule."

"Will more women torch themselves in coming days?" Regan asked quickly.

"There are means of protest that don't include fire," I said, in measured tones. "I encourage women of all tribes to purchase gum arabic on the new stock exchange, whatever one can afford. Shares not for trading, but for having in solidarity with home rule. When we have a new leader, we will have a place at the table among nations."

"But the price for gum arabic may fall," Regan said. "Why encourage the risk?" She thrust the mic under my chin again.

"Tribal women can buy gum arabic stock," I repeated, "to show solidarity with free elections, where we establish our own laws that all residents of the savannah must follow."

"And who will be the next leader, do you think?"

"Dolviets will decide. Not you or me, but the people bound together in home rule."

Hakulupe Le drew me aside as I wiped the tears from under my glasses. Regan Villines turned to speak directly into the camera.

My duty was fulfilled. I had delivered the message of solidarity.

PART THREE

Kenoma in layers like the banks
Of red sandstone after the floods
Taken, abused, rescued, and lost
So Kristos in our memory lingers

Village burned, sisters and nan sacrificed
Brother saved, honor and work come late
This one of renown the deep pool has claimed
So Kristos in our memory lingers

His legacy complete in the person of Karry
Who stands here today, but feeling too late
How brave was the one the deep pool has claimed
So Kristos in our memory lingers

NINE

from Jessup Chandliss

I SUCKED AIR FROM THE EMPTY TANK, DRAWING HARD AND tasting dried limes. The muscles in my legs felt locked, and my arms moved like steel girders. I must breach the surface in a few seconds or die. Careful. Go slowly. Don't rise faster than the bubble stream, I thought. Don't exhale. Hold . . . hold . . . just hold for a moment longer. Another moment passed. My lungs screamed for air, and I was seeing stars. Then I felt air on my palm above me.

I broke the surface and tore off my diving mask, inhaling with great gasps that ripped through my lungs like raw tearing. I floated with my arms out and my legs vertical until the spin in my head slowed and my vision cleared. Alright . . . breathing now.

Water bubbles streamed from below me, and I knew what that meant. I reached down, feeling for any handhold to grab Karry

and pull him to the surface. His air hose was what I grabbed—
not a good indication. He was already drifting. I pulled with all
my might, tasting water as I submerged. I breathed out to flush my
nostrils and dunked to see his form underwater and get a better
hold. Up . . . up . . . just a moment more. We broke the surface, and
I pulled away his mask and hood. Karry's mouth was slack and his
eyes unfocused.

"Live, you bastard!" I shouted. I slapped him and pounded his
chest, my strokes weakened by the volume of water between us.
I put my mouth on his and breathed out, grabbing a breath and
forcing the air into his lungs.

Nothing. No response.

I grabbed him under the arm and paddled to the spit of sand that
edged the pool. Once on my knees, I discarded the air tanks on my
back and on his back and pulled off the hood of my wetsuit. I leaned
over Karry's form, checking for any movement. I pumped his chest
and breathed into his mouth. Pump, pump, breathe. And again.

Karry coughed, spitting water and bile into my face. He leaned
up and retched on the other side, mostly water from his lungs.

I sat back, unzipping my wetsuit to breathe deeply and hiccup-
ping against the pain.

Karry turned my way with tragic eyes. "We have to go back,
Jessup."

"We can collect the body, but with fresh tanks."

"Kristos is not dead. We didn't come this far together for a simple
accident."

"He cut the rope to save you. He's gone."

Karry's look was fierce, his eyes flashing determination under the exhaustion. "We don't know what's in that chamber. He could find air pockets or another opening."

I leaned back on an elbow, still catching my breath. "And will we find air pockets when we enter the aperture? He saved you. Be content with that."

"My brother has saved me many times," Karry said simply. "I won't let this go, Jessup. Besides, I still have the guide line." He showed me a reel at his waist with a line of waxed string that was mostly played out, taut and leading into the pool.

"Let's get fresh tanks then, and a longer rope," I said.

He tied the guideline to a stake we had there and slipped off his long flippers. He made for the opening while I kicked sand over the mess from his lungs and dragged the empty tanks forward.

After Karlyhi had brought them to me some weeks ago, I had trained Kristos and Karry with scuba equipment and the underwater cutting torch. Just kids, really, but made men from their experiences as Gora captives. They were sullen and silent under my instruction but learned the needed tasks well enough. They slept together by an open fire and kept themselves clean, so I focused on the work at hand, not troubling them with questions or therapy or pity.

Working with the three feed lines for the underwater cutting torch was difficult and dangerous, but the brothers seemed to orchestrate their movements with little instruction. They were helpmates who depended on each other only. We had brought up maybe eight bushels of rock crystal that was silicide, a rich find. We were guessing how much more was in the deep pool, and we had found an opening that led to an unexplored chamber. The current was swift where we worked, as the water slammed through the sluit to fill both pools evenly. Our reasoning was that if we could widen the aperture, the force of the water would lessen and we could swim into the dark and flooded chamber.

Kristos had forced a breach and switched off the torch. He had pulled at a section that was loose suddenly, and the rushing current had pulled him into the other volume with no handhold to stop his descent. We had watched him spin away and both grabbed the lifeline to steady him and pull him back. Kristos must have entered the flow of an underground river swollen from the rains. He seemed to swing left and right as we tugged at the lifeline with all the underwater strength we had. Our air was low, and so was the air in the tanks Kristos wore. We fell backward in the water when the lifeline went slack.

Immediately, Karry had made for the opening, ready to follow his brother. I admired his lack of hesitation. I detained him, though, indicating the air gauge on my wrist. We had to rise or die. He struggled with me but gave in after a few moments, and I guided him toward the entrance pool. Our air had run out, causing a deep sucking feeling and lightheadedness, and those last harrowing moments with bursting lungs.

Now when we poked our heads above ground, Yuri and Mica rushed forward. They were my former officers who had traveled with me through the wormhole. Karry walked to the spare tanks and began to assemble what he needed.

"You can't go back," Yuri said. "The tanks are only half full. The mix is wrong."

Karry looked around briefly. "I'll take two tanks and the spare blusterpack." He grabbed the equipment, packing his belt pouch next to the big knife, and headed back to the pool entrance.

I shrugged to Yuri, grabbing the other spare tank to follow. "Just refill these tanks, and quickly."

"You cannot dive twice more. The light's fading."

"We'll use a searchlight."

"This is madness," Yuri said.

"You wanted adventure on Dolvia." I shrugged. "You wanted to test yourself against the savannah, hey? Now we are."

Yuri turned to Mica shaking his head. I caught up with Karry.

"Even if you make it to the opening . . ." I said while we dropped into the pool entrance. "Even if you have enough air . . . even if you can follow the guideline through . . . two men cannot make it back on this much air."

"The second chamber," Karry insisted as he pulled on his flippers, "is more like a grotto maybe. We tested that. Kristos can reach air. Discard his tanks and is swimming freely all under the savannah."

"Then he doesn't need a rescue."

Karry barely grinned on one side of his face, the other side being stiff from a blow he received as a Gora captive. "Why should Kristos have all the fun?"

The boys were damaged. Any person could see that. The marks on their wrists were enough to make a sane person draw away. I had glimpsed Kristos's back more than once as he struggled out of his wetsuit. It was like the lashes of Cyrus, which I'd never seen but heard about in fireside chants. Kristos had a lively death wish that I spoke against often, talking about teamwork and how the other

diver depends on your will to live. I felt that Karry was more balanced, but his loyalty to his brother made him reckless and unreasonable. They were brave—nothing like it—but neither expected to
live to see another season of om. They'd just throw away their lives
on adventure and renown. They scared me, together and separately.

It was after dark when Karry and I sat in camp chairs by a fire that
was bigger than needed. The two moons were in the dark phase of
their cycles, so the night seemed close. We had attempted two more
dives searching for Kristos, even working after dark and disregarding the safety measures I had imposed for all divers. We came up
empty. When we could no longer depend on the guideline to search
the bigger aquifer, we stopped for the night. We were done.

I passed the bottle of Kiam gin to Karry. He was too young to
drink by Softcheeks standards. He was old enough to suffer loss,
time and again, so he was man enough for me.

When Karlyhi and his Cylahi followers had brought the brothers
to me, Kyros Kenoma was not with that clutch. Apparently, Kristos
could not forgive his father for failing to rescue them. Kristos chose
to follow Karlyhi, so the brothers were taken for warrior training.
When Anaxagoras was trapped and executed, Kyros had not been
among the warriors that day either. Kristos was allowed to deliver the
kill stroke; his actions caught on camera and his place made secure.

Kristos had wanted to reach out to Edwina, but the gualarep massacre happened on the same day as his confrontation with Kyros
Kenoma. Now Edwina was mourning Edna and the other gualareps

while she hunted on Siibabean land, or so I was told. I had become the surrogate caretaker. My quality guidance these past weeks had led to Kristos's death and Karry's current mood of despair. Bully for me.

"So, you were using the underwater torch well," I said to fill the silence. "I suppose you're good with erriv, too."

"I'm perfect, in fact," Karry said dryly. "I learned from Gora to be perfect at anything; the first time and every time." He shrugged at my questioning look. "The wranglers used us for entertainment. They assigned me some impossible task and when I failed, they began to beat me. Kristos always got between them and me. After they beat him down, they just turn back to force me into some other job I had no training for. Kristos would get up and get between them and me, and they . . ." He took a long drink. "So, I'm perfect. I perform perfectly with a rope, a whip, a knife, and even managing a halter-trained sigpywa."

I glanced at his head where the muscles were unresponsive. "She gave you that mark?"

"Gora wranglers mistreated the sigpywa even more than Kristos. A glancing blow from her pincers as she was dying. I was out cold for a full day. Some numbness in my left hand after, and I was told my pupils didn't match for a while." He passed the bottle to me. "But I was still made to perform. In any condition, with either hand, I performed perfectly the first time and every time because I had to."

My right eye wanted to close, a sure sign that I was plastered. I stretched my jaw in a yawn. I thought we needed a new chant to savor the sterling character of Kristos, but the pain was too fresh. Maybe compose a chant tomorrow.

We heard movement in the bush. Mica came out of the tent pulling on his suspenders and without boots. He grabbed the karkar from the rack and shouted, "Who goes there?"

I laughed at his militant stance. "Stand down, Mica. If they wanted to kill us, we'd be dead already."

Someone called from the dark. "You drunk, Chandliss?"

"Blotto."

"Where's the other boy?"

My shoulders sagged. "We lost him today to the aquifer."

I strained to hear in the long moment of silence before the voice came again. "Karry? Where is your brother?"

"He has robbed the desert of one."

Hershel Henry came out of the shadows, his karkar slung on his shoulder. He was flanked by Mark and some other Cylahi warrior. They entered the circle of firelight. Henry wore the uniform of the clutch of Kenru with his hand on the hilt of a big belt knife.

"And your job was . . ."

"Yeah, yeah," I grabbed the Kiam gin bottle from Karry. "You try cutting silicide underwater with no support and stolen equipment. See how far you get."

Henry relaxed, releasing his grip on the knife. "You got a signal fire to the Borabean going here. Maybe a death wish?"

I started laughing again. Henry looked at Yuri and Mica standing together, and Mica shrugged. Henry grabbed a bucket of water we had used for dinner dishes and dumped it onto the fire, dousing most of the flames and sending up a smelly plume of smoke.

"Now they can smell us out," I said and fell back into the camp chair.

"So, it's a pity party," Henry said. "Kristos wasn't your brother."

"He was my responsibility."

"Stow the weapons and make some hot tea," Henry instructed Mica. "I brought help."

"You're late," I said from my seat while Yuri and Mica did as they were told. "You're a whole day late."

Mark went to the fire and greeted Karry who stood. "Hai."

Karry recoiled like a blow was coming, probably drunker than he looked. Young people were like that. I knew Mark from other gatherings with his scraggly beard and marked limp. Mark was the composer of chants whose voice had warmed many encampments.

"What happened to Kristos?" Henry said in a different tone.

I sighed heavily, feeling a weight on my chest. "Through the sluit, into the current, and—gone. We searched for hours but found no trace. No debris, no tension on the guideline, not a trace."

"Stand up, man. Try to look like a leader." Henry grabbed my shoulder and dragged me to my feet. "I said I brought help. You must make the honorable greeting."

When he felt I could stand without falling, Henry motioned to the bush.

Dulcinea stepped into the light also wearing the uniform of the clutch of Kenru and shouldering a karkar. She gestured behind her to a gaggle of women, maybe ten altogether, wearing new work clothes with the package creases still showing, and carrying heavy packs.

Dulcinea looked at Henry and then at me. "Like a pair of mangy ketiwhelps."

I had spent several cycles of Nettom on the mesa while the Uburu beauty, her pregnancy just showing then, sat with her dying father. Dulcinea had negotiated with Brianna Miller via EAM for this venture for silicide diving. We had haggled over wages, and it felt good to engage an equal who knew the need for project authority. I had moved down here with Yuri and Mica to investigate the pool of old water known commonly as the butterfly pool.

Dulcinea wore an arm amulet as a sign of mourning for a lost loved one. Her pregnancy burden was gone, and I assumed the newborn was one of the many bundles the women handled. "Aeolis allows you to travel so soon?"

"Aeolis makes no decisions for me." She had not been added to his wives, but rather had responded to the call to fertility as part of the armistice with Borabean.

Yuri and Mica stepped forward to help with an ungainly trapezoid the women dragged. "Nu delaya," Dulcinea quickly said. "These are rescued brothel workers, and you are their enemy."

Yuri's eyes went big, and Mica stood tall, hitching his belt. He wore suspenders and a belt; I had often chided him for that.

My head was fuzzy and I suppressed a yawn. "What do you have here, Henry?"

"Blancom has his charm only," Dulcinea said. "I brought you this recovered diving equipment and these workers."

Henry showed a wide grin, and someone stifled a laugh.

"You will make the honorable greeting to Marna Le who was raised Uburu," Dulcinea ordered.

Arrivi greetings could take more than twenty minutes. Soon I was seated again with a big mug of tea and Marna Le's judging face across the table, underlit by a camp light. She was cousin to the Uburu beauty and had similar bone structure, but the combination was not relaxing to the eyes, as it was said. Karry had gone to his bedroll, lucky him, and Yuri and Mica watched openly from the mess area while the clutch of women set up their own camp tangent to ours.

Hershel Henry and Dulcinea joined us at the table. His hair was slicked back with some native paste to ward off insects and his skin was tan and freckled. "An agent for Somule Gems at Stargate Junction," Henry filled in, "noticed our wormhole orders went unfilled, so she checked the shipping channels. Turns out, Company customs officials were rifling through our shipments. They diverted mining equipment, machine parts for industry, and these diving supplies. Madquii warriors mounted a sortie into Abydian land to, um, re-requisition our supplies. Madquii found these women held in a brothel where Goras were camping. We're still sorting that out, what clans and what surviving families."

I must have been getting sober, because I thought I read a signal between Henry and Dulcinea about how much to share with this old Ukrainian scuba diver. "Where did you grab this stuff?" I asked.

"Next to the Urbyd silos in the building with smelting furnaces. It's wetsuits and tanks and something else I don't recognize. Some was still in shipping crates. So we decided to combine the rescue of workers and rescue of equipment, and reinforce your position here."

My mouth was dry and my eyelids drooped. "We aren't military. We aren't a clutch."

"You are now," Dulcinea said. "The clutch of Marna Le."

Seated next to Dulcinea, Marna Le was taller with short hair and fire shooting from her eyes. I blinked and rubbed my face all over with one hand. I looked again at her stare. No fire; just the power of suggestion. "What's their story?" I asked.

"We don't have it all," Dulcinea said. "Marna Le claims she was mistress of—or, rather, used by—one of Ananke's sons. The brothel was near a rear guard of the silo campus. So what was Ananke's kin doing there?"

"Ten sons," Henry said. "How to find positions of honor for them all?"

Dulcinea shrugged. "More travelers will arrive tomorrow for a funeral pyre."

"I suppose you want me to train these desert-born women for diving?" My tone carried the whine of self-pity. "With no common language and no experience with water."

"Actually," Dulcinea said, "you will train Marna Le only, and she will train the women. You mustn't touch them or even look at them while they are allowed to heal."

"What dialects does she speak? Any English?"

"Uburu and Borabean. Mostly she knows the language of humiliation, so that's the one you must avoid. And do try to keep them alive."

I gestured widely to include all our losses from today. "And that's what comes of adventuring through the wormhole."

"Let's get you to bed," Henry said, "before you collapse into the fire."

I exited the tent with a dry mouth and a blinding headache. "What is that pounding noise?" A latrine was already dug and covered by a tent with several flaps. They had disassembled the trapezoid, I assumed to use the wood for constructing an additional mess table.

Millie Sector approached me with a big mug and Arrivi gestures. "Hiki, Captain Chandliss." She was a little thing, less than five feet tall, wearing a traditional Arrivi skirt that came to her ankles and her hair coiled at her neck.

"Melinga, Millie. When did you come into camp?"

She showed me flirtatious blue eyes. "It's past noon, you know."

I took the tea from her hand and yawned again. I sat at the table and she soon returned with a big plate of food that smelled great. "Are those real eggs?"

She scurried away, and Kelly Osborn sat across from me. She was dressed in the uniform of Kenru's clutch, her coppery hair bound in a tight braid. She must have arrived in camp with the same group as Millie Sector. She wore an arm amulet—maybe for Kecouroo who had recently died from self-torching, or for another lost warrior. This state of mourning seemed continual among them.

Kelly's round glasses glinted in the sunlight. "Breakfast is at sunrise, and only then. You and I need to talk about training and wages."

I shoveled food into my mouth, fearful she would snatch the plate. "What wages?"

"For the silicide cutting. I was thinking piecework, like with artisan skills."

"That method doesn't build teamwork," I said with my mouth full. "Not all workers will use the tanks or the torch. Most will tote and carry."

"There's also the issue of modesty. You cannot train them."

I spoke between bites. "Yuri and Mica are soldiers, not divers. I'm your man."

"Listen to me," Kelly said. "You will train Marna Le. She will train the others."

"Leave them all untouched and untrained, for all I care."

The plate was clean. I rubbed my eyes with my fingers. When I looked up with all ten fingers on my cheeks, Marna Le stood at the table's edge, her hard face showing disgust. I imagined the fire shooting from her eyes again.

I dropped my hands and straightened my back. "So you want to be a diver? Alrighty, then. Let's go diving." I stood, knocking my chair over.

Marna Le stepped back as if bracing for a blow.

"This way." I walked past her and down to the pool entrance, where divers dropped down four feet to where we kept the ready tanks.

Henry was below on the sandy ledge we use for entrance into the water. He looked up with cynical eyes. "Water's cold."

I scooted down beside him. "Give us room to get into the wet-suits."

Marna Le and Kelly stared down at us from the ridge.

"Does she understand me?" I asked.

Kelly seemed to make a snap decision. "Millie will explain."

Kelly left my line of sight and two beats later, Henry was helping Millie drop onto our beach with question hovering on her face. Behind her, a spray of butterflies rose flapping toward the sunlight. She must have bumped against the shaded scrub where they gathered.

"Alrighty, then," I said. "This is the gear Marna Le needs for today. First, we suit up. Canna stay submerged more 'an ten minutes without the suit." I stepped into the legs of the rubbery body suit and stripped off my shirt before I put my arms into the sleeves. I looked back at them. "Let's get to it. Diving's not for slackers."

Henry handed the wetsuit to Millie, who turned it over and over. Marna Le looked at her own clothes before she grabbed the suit from Millie's hand and stepped into the legs. She turned her back and pulled her skirt and blouse over her head. Millie positioned herself for modesty and helped the big woman struggle into the sleeves. I was already working with the tanks.

"No diving after you eat," Henry said in a sanguine tone. "A rule you made. Clean the bile from the hose your own self."

"I'm not taking scornful looks from a woman who canna' face the beast. She follows me down or she leaves."

Marna Le shunted Millie aside and took a monkey-see-and-do approach. I had the tanks on my back, so she shouldered a set we kept at the ready.

"Today Mica can show you maintenance and safety checks," I explained. "For now the basics are the hood, the mask, air hose, and valve." I touched each item as I named them, and Millie's voice murmured in translation. I pulled on the hood and knelt to moisten the mask in the water. I positioned the mask over my eyes and nose. "Real tight. Do you see?"

Marna Le nodded, her hard face now full of curiosity and determination. She got her mask wet and placed it over the hood, turning to look around with no side vision. I pulled mine off and indicated she should also. I kept my distance and touched only my tank to explain the process. Lastly, I held the mouthpiece to my lips. "Breathe through your mouth only." I blew out a couple breaths to demonstrate. "When we rise, never swim faster than the bubble stream."

After Millie translated, Marna Le spoke a long stream of gibberish. Millie grinned and asked, "What is bubble stream?"

Henry was sitting back on his haunches, his elbows resting on his knees and his hands dangling. "You spent three days with the kenoma boys before you allowed them to get wet. What's with the rushed lesson?"

"Let's see what she's got."

Millie was still translating, so Marna Le glared at me after that remark.

"Besides fire-eyes," I added. I showed her the lights on a bar that we used, switching mine on and off. She nodded and tried her set.

"Do you intend to include the 'what if I'm drowning' lesson today?" Henry asked in an accusative tone.

I only sat and pulled on the long flippers. She sat heavily on the sand next to me and pulled on the other pair. I repeated the process with the mask, and she followed my gestures.

"Alrighty, then. Let's get wet."

Millie joined Henry disturbing the butterflies again so that they fluttered around her shoulders. I pushed off into the water.

Marna Le's stance was tense and her fists balled, but she followed me without a word of complaint.

I swam out to the glory hole, as we called it, which led to deeper water. When I turned, she was right at my shoulder. I positioned the mouthpiece and waited as she got hers into place and seemed to get the breathing rhythm right. I bent double and dove vertically so my flippers breached the surface. This was the deciding moment. Would Marna Le follow, or would she tread water at the surface waiting for help, waiting to decide to take the plunge?

I stroked once or twice with the flippers, diving deeper, and switched on the lights I carried. To my left, lights came on from her bar. She was keeping pace with me.

I swam to the silicide beds that Karry and Kristos had already exploited. I felt a sudden twinge as I remembered the good work Kristos had accomplished with little praise and less pay. My time invested in training was lost now; starting from scratch. I slowed and turned to indicate the nets and metal baskets we used. I showed Marna Le the underwater bell where we had stashed the cutting torch and its three lines to the torch head. She nodded with big gestures and patted her chest.

Mica would have to teach her the standard signals that divers used.

I gestured that we would travel left and moved with my lights toward the opening where Kristos had tumbled through. We were deep now, and the only sound was the rebreathing flow. The only illumination was from our lights. I moved slowly using legs only. She came up beside me like a real pro and looked mask to mask for instruction. I made the gesture for current, waving my forearm up and down with a flat palm, then held forearms crossed with my fists balled indicating danger.

I probably should have taught her those signals before the dive.

She mimicked the gesture for danger and nodded, so I led her to the aperture, swimming backward against the current. I illuminated the problem area with my lights, and she directed hers toward the sluit. I noted her competence in the wetsuit, a big woman with long legs and broad shoulders. She needed strength training and discipline, but she could stay.

I tapped the air gauge attached to the arm of my suit. She stared at mine, but then realized she wore one too, tapping it and nodding again. I removed my mouthpiece and waved it to show how the bubbles rose in the water. I forced the mouthpiece back in my mouth. I made the up gesture with my thumb before we began to swim back. She moved beside me, three feet apart, steady and confident and seeming to embrace the thrill.

My chest released some tension, maybe some I had not acknowledged with the loss of Kristos. We could recover. We could just get on with the job at hand.

People kept arriving all afternoon. Kyros Kenoma came in with four warriors wearing similar uniforms. Karry spoke to his father, brought forward by Mark. I watched their halting exchange with little by way of reconciliation. Kristos was gone. Kyros hadn't saved him, and neither could Karry with me assisting. Layers of kenoma, as it was said in the chants.

As the sunset grew more vibrant covering us with a fuzzy glaze, I sat with Hershel Henry smoking kari root stems. Kyros was sitting on the side with his chin in hand until Dulcinea joined him with a bundle in arms. Kyros stood for the greeting and accepted her empathetic gestures.

"So he's the one Dulcinea chose?" I whispered to Henry. "Out of all the warriors who were her suitors, Dacupitte or Aeolis. Kyros is the one?"

Henry gave me a long look. "I believe it started at the massacre of his village, or even earlier when the rice patties were destroyed, and before you took up residence on the mesa."

I chuckled softly. "Ah, I always knew she was too good for these old bones, but Kyros is not a war hero or . . . or—"

"He'll come home each night. He'll put her needs ahead of warrior service. Can Omiibuk claim the same about her man? Or Kelly?"

"What's with Kelly's attitude?"

Henry rolled his eyes. "Rufus was wounded, you know, while Brianna Miller was still pregnant. Rufus cannot lift his left arm past his shoulder, and his back is damaged too. He tried to release Kelly from the betrothal. Don't mention it or you'll get the treatment."

"And why is Millie here?"

"She's assigned to Kelly. That's how they raise up the next layer of women, by tagging along with the meanest ones they can find."

"Maybe Kelly's just mean to you."

"With this stain on her engagement, she spills her spite where she can."

As if we had conjured the devil, Kelly came to the table. Henry actually jerked away as if expecting a blow.

Kyros and Dulcinea also came forward. "Hershel Henry and Jessup Chandliss, may I present Karisma, the last son of Dacupitte?" The babe in close wrapping was blanched and with a fuzz of orange hair. Henry stood to admire the squished face. I squinted, trying to wrap my mind around events. Dulcinea had abandoned her own child born on Madquii land but would raise the newborn of Brianna Miller. Kelly and Millie had brought the newborn to this dry station to complete the switch up in relative privacy. What a curious system.

We heard a scream near the stacked pyre, and Millie came running like she was pursued by banshees. Yellow butterflies sprayed in all directions behind her. "The ghost . . . Kristos visits the pyre! I saw his ghost! White all over and naked, just standing at the pyre with tears for his own passing."

Karry came up from the side. "Stay back. Let me investigate."

We all peered into the gathering dusk past the campfires, as Karry stepped closer to the apparition standing with its back to us by the stacked kindling. It was apparently naked and covered with white lime, its short hair greasy and streaked with white.

"Kristos?"

The figure turned, staring at Karry, and wiped away a tear, exposing real skin on a real face. "Karry, you're not dead?"

"And you're still alive!" Karry said.

"I thought this pyre was for you," Kristos said through the white color. "That you didn't make it back from the pool."

"We searched for you but found nothing, not a trace."

Kristos place a hand on Karry's shoulder. "But you're alive!"

"And you're not dead!"

They hugged and stomped around with jubilation.

"So we don't need this pyre," Kristos said. He kicked it with a bare foot.

Karry shouldered the branches with an upward push. Kristos joined him and they forced the pyre sideways so the branches tumbled and crashed in the yard.

I hurried to Kristos with a big hug, smearing my shirt and trousers with the white lime. I felt the ridges of whip marks that decorated his back and sides.

"You look like a ghost!" I said. "What happened?"

"You know that stand of acacias where two lean at an angle?" He held up two fingers partly angled. "Well, one of them leans more now." He lowered one finger only.

Karry laughed and pounded his brother's shoulder. "I knew you were swimming all under the savannah. I knew it!"

"What's with the lime?" I asked.

"You cannot travel the dunes in a wetsuit," Kristos said through white lips, "so I cut off the legs and shirt. The sun was harsh, though, so I used a Borabean trick of digging up lime to cover my body for protection. I guess they taught us a few good tricks, huh?"

We laughed all around. Kristos's bravado was infectious, and Karry didn't flinch at the mention of his time as a captive.

We turned to the others who stood in a long line staring with gaping mouths.

"No need for the pyre! Take it away!" Karry said joyfully. We walked back to the table while Yuri and Mica slapped the shoulders of Kristos and shouted their relief.

So as it turned out, Kristos had cut the towline when the current caught him so he wouldn't drag Karry into the stream. He had struggled against the flow but had hit a wall and forced right, only to fall into a deeper chasm. That had saved him. The waterfall meant he could surface and breathe without the tanks. He struggled to an outcropping there and dragged himself up on a ledge.

"When I could focus," Kristos told the company, "I knew my escape was neither going back nor going forward. I tied off the guideline, though, so we can exploit the pool later. I lost the light bar, now resting at the bottom of the bigger pool. I searched the ceiling for an opening but saw no daylight. I used my beltlight and felt around until I came across acacia roots dangling down. I dug with the knife and with my hands until I had forced a hole to the surface. Amazingly, it was still daylight above. I felt like I had been there for days."

Kristos had spent an hour trying to find purchase for climbing onto the savannah, still wearing his wetsuit. "Then I had a new problem." He shrugged. "I couldn't walk back to camp in my wetsuit, and I wore no other clothes." So he had cut away the suit legs and top, fashioning shorts.

"I was turned around," Kristos claimed, "for how distant from camp I was. I found the trail, though, and knew the butterfly pool was west because I remembered a chant about Aensilus who had gotten lost the same as me."

Karry laughed. "I know that chant. Aensilus and the butterflies. Kecouroo found him at the pool."

At the mention of Kecouroo, recently dead by immolation, our spirits seemed to deflate. Kelly and Dulcinea with the babe turned away, walking back to the women's camp. Millie stood next to Henry, staring with her mouth open. Mark stood with Kyros who the boys had not yet acknowledged.

Kristos's face fell when he saw his father. "You must make the greeting," Karry said.

They stepped to him and Kristos held out a hand to shake, covering the awkward moment with a Softcheeks gesture. Kyros moved to hug him, and Kristos stiffly tolerated the touch. Kyros turned his son's shoulder to view the scars, his brow drawing up in anguish. Kristos shrugged off his touch and stepped back a fraction. Why spoil a moment of triumph with old news?

Kyros stood tall, acting as though he couldn't decide what to do with his hands. Henry went to Kyros's side and led him away, with Millie following.

So much suffering. So many fresh wounds.

The women gathered by the center fire, dragging the unneeded branches with them for a bonfire. Some were chanting quietly and slapping thighs. Millie brought Kristos a shallow bucket of fresh water to remove the streaks of lime. Kristos pulled on a tunic to hide his scars from curious stares. I went with Yuri and Mica to the camp table and opened a fresh bottle of Kiam gin.

"You have turned my sorrow into dancing," I quoted and drank.

Chanting from the rescued women grew to a higher pitch with rhythmic pounding and thigh slapping. I don't remember what hero they lauded. Mark took a central role, using an instrument that looked to be a hollow section of bamboo to control the beat. He chanted four lines, and they all joined in for the refrain. The young people segregated themselves, males on one side and females on the other, and they danced with abandon to celebrate the twice-recovered Kristos, as well as the birth of the last son of Dacupitte. They celebrated the rescue of sex slaves who had new work for wages bringing up silicide from the pool. Millie was drawn into the dance, her traditional Arrivi skirt looking provincial among the many uniforms and work trousers. She faced off with Kristos and Karry, learning the dance steps quickly enough. Dancers undulated back and forth from the fire, stomping in unison with knees and elbows rising to the beat.

Kelly came to the table again, wearing a scornful look that mirrored the one I often saw from Marna Le. "About the wages . . ." she said.

I sat up straight. "They can work as a clutch with regular bonuses for some who labor underwater. Call it hazardous duty pay. A bi-weekly draw for each woman, and more when a wagonload is tallied. The bonuses can be parceled out by fire-eyes. The clutch keeps their own mess, provides their own clothes, and manages their, um, women's business. If one decides to leave, she's cashed out for wages only. If a dispute cannot be settled among the clutch, both parties are cashed out for wages only. When training ends, Yuri, Mica, and I are paid from the enterprise called StrikeStone, and Marna Le can run the operation. Any problems with that? Too bad; it's all set."

Kelly smirked. "Kyros will establish a training ground here for militia troops, covering your work for defense. No Company officials need visit. When you're asked about the presence of so many women, just say it's a brothel to support the training camp."

"That's nothing to me, but word will get out."

"Hence the presence of the troops. Millie will serve Dulcinea. Mark can work as translator for a time. What other supplies do you need?"

"We're good here," I said. "Talk to fire-eyes about her needs."

Kelly went back to the women's camp. I made a face at her back. I won't be missing that viper when she leaves. I mean, sorry for her trouble with Rufus and all, but how was that my problem?

The bonfire collapsed suddenly, sending embers into the dance lines. The women squealed and pounded their clothes to prevent scorching while the men laughed and pointed. I saw Karry and Kristos talking together, as Kelly explained the new arrangement to Marna Le. It pleased me that the brothers still lived, that I didn't have to account to Brianna Miller for lost workers. I chuckled again over the spent pyre that each had assumed was built for the other brother. In my head, I was already setting tasks for these refugees: days of training to reinforce discipline among the women divers. A new season of kari was upon us, after all.

TEN

I PUT YURI TO DEMONSTRATING EXERCISES FOR STRENGTH TRAIN-ing, and Mark translated his instructions for the new clutch of divers. Mica shared mess supplies and lingered on the camp's perimeter, craning his neck to see how the women managed cooking fires. Kelly and Millie hovered near the new mother. Kyros had the men working some distance from us, making long troughs for baking clay bricks in the sun.

Their power structures kept all working in concert. Mekucoo warriors arrived with a couple of extra women, but no greeting ceremony was engaged. Henry had provided the hai and led them to the activity by Kyros. Warriors established scout positions, as Kyros set the regular soldiers to digging foundations to build barracks. They were here to stay.

Karry and Kristos had taken Marna Le diving, so I had a moment to myself. I broke open the crates of recovered supplies and found a 3D laser beam scanner with a battery pack. The second carton contained the sonar resounder I had been missing. I was glancing over the instructions, holding the page at arm's length, when I saw movement to my left. I caught her arm in midair, twisting to confront the little thief who had grabbed the closest shiny object.

Her mouth made a round pucker and her brown eyes were wide with surprise. "Oh, oh, oh."

"You're like a little wood owl, huh, feathering his nest by the labor of others." She jerked her arm to get free, but I held her firm. "Oh, oh, oh," I mimicked. I saw her friend hovering just out of reach staring with oriental eyes. "Ah, two culprits."

She moved to avoid my grasp, but I caught the nape of her Arrivi gown, turning her to mete out punishments.

"Nu delaya," Kelly called from the side as she rushed forward.

"Wood owl here could steal an essential piece," I complained "and we'll never get the resounder working."

Kelly stopped in her tracks, her startled eyes glancing at the slant-eyed girl and back to me. "You touched her?"

"Your rules against touching only work when you manage their thieving habits."

Behind Kelly, Dulcinea spoke. "It's because he's Softcheeks," she said while she passed the bundle of sleeping newborn into Millie's arm. "The same as with Henry. He can touch Cleo without feeling om."

Kelly nodded several times as if digesting this very important information. I looked at the wood owl. "Thieving is punished in this camp. You'll have extra duties today."

Kelly and Dulcinea chuckled, covering their mouths with their hands. Demure marriageable women weren't supposed to show their teeth, although they could spread spite easily enough.

I released the girls. "What?" I said, facing the viper.

Dulcinea took the initiative. "May I present Camille Datong and Cleo Datong who is touched by om? Her burden means she does no work alongside the divers or any workers."

I had no idea what she was talking about, and I didn't care. Arrivi drew too many lines for what was allowed. "Perhaps these naughty girls have more freedom than they can manage. The wood owl was caught red-handed."

"Others in their clutch are older," Dulcinea said, "and left already for wormhole travel." Dulcinea's brief hand signal sent the girls scurrying into the women's tent. A head tilt sent Kelly following. Dulcinea showed me a shy smile. I could commune with this betrothed woman due to our long business association.

"They all want nicknames, you know," she said. "Like beauty and fire-eyes. Kelly is aware that you call her a viper."

"I'm not feeling that creative today." I turned back to my unpacking.

"What do we have here?" She stepped closer.

I pulled the sonar resounder out of its cushioned wrappings. "Now maybe we can get some real work done. With the proper software, we can map the underwater chamber."

"You'll do better in the next cycle of Nettom when the water volume falls. The current should slow and the need for tanks is less."

"What do you know about it?"

"I was born on this planet."

We laughed together and my irritation eased. Dulcinea had that way about her, able to stroke away the tension. "We noticed that Blancom feels no trauma at Cleo's touch, and now you. What do you have in common? Both Softcheeks."

"From different continents with different languages."

"But not ground-born." She turned her back to enter the women's camp, and I was sorry for that. "Good to know," she said over her shoulder.

By afternoon I had the equipment assembled and the software working. I wore my reading glasses and watched the flickering screen as I focused the scanner on a nearby mound of packing materials, creating a graph to show the shape and mineral content which was minimal.

As if in competition, Kelly opened an EAM on the mess table in the women's area to talk with someone at Stargate Junction. She glanced my way often as if soliciting questions about her close work.

I ignored her and all the women as I had been instructed.

Henry came into camp while I was checking connections for the sonar resounder. He dropped a lizard carcass on the table next to me and used the big beltknife to open the hide. He shaped a long slit on the throat and down the soft tissue of the belly to the tail attachment. He dumped the guts into a bucket and stuck his bare arm into the body cavity to scrape out the residue, separating the heart and organs for separate stewing.

"Must you do that here?" I complained.

"Not enough wood to make a second table." He shrugged. "You can move the imaging machines down by the diving pool."

"Once I get it working." He fingered a clump of silicide I used as a paperweight, smooth and opaque with long striations on its crystal tower. "The Borabean call it clearstone, did you know?" he said. "But silicide is not clear at all. More opaque than amber."

"For industry use, it can amplify a clear signal."

"So call it signal stone."

"I'll mention that to Aristides when I see him next." I knew Aristides as Ananke's minister who managed the project to bring up the undersea silicide hoard.

Henry only smirked and slammed the carcass on my table. While we labored and talked, the wood owl and her oriental friend edged closer, maybe attracted by the idea of fresh meat for dinner. Henry removed the lizard head with a big slam of his knife and then brandished the head at the naughty girls. He stepped to our wash bucket and soaped his hands and arms to remove the slaughter gunk. The girls were crowding forward again with big eyes and active hands.

"Watch that little wood owl," I said. "She'll steal the gold caps from your teeth."

"Wood owl, huh?" He sat at the table and took the oriental girl onto his lap. "You're not the only one handing out nicknames. The kenoma boys are Tom Sawyer and Huck Finn now. You remember the story. Tom Sawyer attended his own funeral after he ran away."

I looked over my reading glasses at him. "American novels? Really?"

"Yah, sure," he grinned. "The Finn brothers. Get it? Diving, fish, fins. The Finn brothers."

The girls grinned without understanding, basking in his Softcheeks charm while he shared chi, as it was said.

"And Tom Sawyer," Henry added, "played that trick about whitewashing the fence, using lime in the mixture. Get it? Another connection through lime."

"What about you? Got any family?" I asked.

His mouth turned down. "Lost to me, like most Softcheeks who venture to Westend."

I tried to keep it casual. "Not all lost. The gypsy says you have a brother."

Henry kept his focus on the gypsy, walking his fingers up her arm like a spider. "I met my half-brother when he was brought forward with a claim to Da's estate. Younger than me by twelve years, and I was the youngest."

"No sisters?"

"Two sisters; older, married, free of Da."

"Your father was hard on you?"

He touched Cleo's nose to elicit a giggle. "I don't know. Define hard."

"You're making me drag it out of you."

He looked at me, finally, his mouth in a thin line. "They're scattered, gone. The boy studies chemistry for research."

"So . . . he's no longer a boy. You weren't your father's favorite?"

"I was nobody's favorite."

I ended my struggles with a dismissive gesture toward the sonar, removing my reading glasses with a jerk and sitting back. The wood owl brushed against me, silently asking for the same privileges her gypsy friend enjoyed with Henry. I drew her onto my leg without thinking. She weighed nothing at all, maybe eleven years old. "You're certain that's not a gualarep hatchling you butchered," I teased Henry.

"One method to break Edwina's silence, huh?" he grinned.

The soldiers were filtering back into camp, muddy and grumbling after their day making adobe bricks. Kyros left them and came to the table, indicating the lizard. "That's for dinner?"

Henry nodded, and a soldier scooped the fresh meat away in a flash.

"Mica can show them how to strip the hide," I said and received hard stares all around. "Or not," I back-pedaled. "I'm confident the soldiers know more—"

"What's this for?" Kyros interrupted.

"A 3D laser imager. Schedule some time with it in a stinger, flying back and forth, and we can assemble a chart for topography and mineral content of the surface."

"Will it finger the sufferstone?"

"He means uranium," Henry added.

"Ah, ah, no." I squinted. "Mostly uranium is found in volcanic rock and deep beneath the surface, probably closer to the gold mines. When I get the sonar resounder working, we can structure a three-dimensional map of the aquifer."

"Will the resounder detect u-ra-ni-um?" Kyros asked.

I shook my head no, not certain how many of my technical words Kyros was picking up. "You need a Geiger counter for that, and they don't work under water."

"In the season of netta then?"

I frowned. "I thought we were focused on silicide. Not dangerous to handle and needs little processing for industry."

"Sufferstone is like the ketiwhelp," Kyros said. "You don't want to bother it so much as know where it is and which way it's headed."

I looked at the wood owl's open face with her unblinking brown eyes, raising my eyebrows twice for effect. "Very prudent," I said. She hunched her shoulders and giggled with melody.

"Get along," Kyros said.

The two girls slipped off our laps and headed back to the women's camp.

A soldier brought up a straight-backed chair, and Kyros sat without acknowledging him. Kyros was the headman, his uniform spotless and with creases still showing along the pant leg over wide sandals. How did he manage that?

"You made Marna Le paymaster for the clutch?" Kyros demanded.

I only shrugged. His brusque manner was common among Arrivi men, even though the same tone from Kelly seemed spiteful.

"Marna Le went from being a sex slave with no rights," Henry explained, "to paymaster for a clutch that uses Softcheeks technology. Kelly took credit for raising her status, just like she took credit for other matchmaking—"

"Now wait a damn minute," I interrupted. "There's no match here. I was directed to work with fire-eyes only. There's no match-making."

The two men broke out with raucous laughter while many in camp looked our way. I grinned and looked around, mostly to avoid appearing to be the butt of their joke.

Kristos and Karry came up with Yuri and Mica from the other direction, shouldering the spare tanks and diving paraphernalia. Marna Le was behind them, looking grey and exhausted after a full day of working underwater. She would sleep well tonight. They all glanced our way, envious or hateful, before they went about evening duties.

"That reminds me," I said. "We'll need a steady diet of erriv meat for the divers and carriers. Exhausting work."

"Women who eat erriv get pregnant more easily," Kyros said.

"I have not touched her!" I insisted, only to hear more booming laughter.

Marna Le ducked into the women's tent, and we didn't see her again that night. Around the campfire that night, I told my tales about scuba diving and the undersea monsters off the coast of Urbyd; conveniently naming the creatures using Softcheeks words since I didn't know what Borabean or Striiduc called them. Kyros and the others heard about the treacherous tentacles of squid that could drown a three-mast sailboat. I described a scaly sea serpent with a raised ruff behind its gills. Yuri and Mica sat with Mark and his compatriots while I talked about sea turtles whose bite could snap an oar made of mida wood, or about swarms of glass shrimp that turned luminous when the water was churned, coloring the night waters like a searchlight.

Kyros didn't believe there were creatures in the water bigger than the palace at Urbyd and spouting water columns through a blow-hole that rose higher than a man. He resisted the idea of a starfish or the octopus that could change its color to blend with the coral. He laughed heartily when I described tuna that could fly, and how whole schools of them jumped into the boat as though eager to be captured. Henry only shook his head as the bottle of Kiam gin was emptied and others began to wander off to bed.

Our encampment grew daily. Kelly opened a manual sewing machine at the women's table and spent the hours assembling new clothes for Millie, Cleo, and Camille while they took turns managing the infant that could fuss for forty minutes at a time.

Rufus and Karlyhi arrived in a blue stinger. I was at the landing site in three seconds, poking my head into the pilot's compartment with all the instruments and blinking lights. Karlyhi wore an arm amulet with two stones dangling. He went to confer with the warriors who were our sentries. I noticed that Rufus favored his left side, with a truncated range of motion. He would forget for a moment and reach to open an air vent, only to moan lightly when he lowered his arm and accepted the pain. I never saw his wound from the Chinese Tzu, but I saw the results.

Rufus offered a joy ride and I nodded eagerly. We were strapped into the stinger's passenger seat in minutes for a tour of the surrounding dunes. Surprising to me how isolated was our activity from Arrivi and Madquii landmarks, a transit area only and denuded of tree cover or oleastra bushes. We saw flocks of birds heading both to and from the ocean, but only the stubborn sand grouse made her nest near our encampment, panting in the heat with her misshapen tongue stuck out. From the stinger I located the spindly stand of acacias where Kristos had reached the surface. It was more than two kilometers from the butterfly pool so the aquifer was extensive under this area.

After we returned and Rufus made the greeting with many Dolviets, lingering to acknowledge each one, the construction workers marched into camp with two wagons hitched to erriv. They took instruction from Karlyhi to assemble a rounded metal hangar for the stinger, Rufus's prized possession. First, they marked out a sizeable rectangle near the barracks foundations, ready to mix cement for the floor. We planned to move the technical equipment to the hangars as soon as we could. I cautioned that the underground fuel tank must be situated at a distance, maybe near a wadi of bedrock and far from the tunnels of the aquifer.

Discussions about mapping the aquifer quickly turned to military applications for the 3D laser imager. Karlyhi wanted to map the palace at Urbyd and peer into the corridors to locate defense stations. "The palace is only a shiny object," I instructed. "Better to map the adjacent port. If Madquii can capture the port, they can starve the palace."

Karlyhi and Rufus were silent, but their eyes shone with new ideas for defeating Borabean enemies should the armistice not hold when Rabbenu Ely stepped down. Karlyhi was ready for trouble, though, and liked to make trouble too.

The next day I worked with the divers in the early afternoon, glad to have the solitude of wet work, silent except for the rebreather and hand signals under the lights. We were coming toward camp with our empty tanks when we saw a fight circle where the women anxiously watched a confrontation between Karlyhi and Rufus. All in good fun, I assumed, since Karlyhi had his right arm tied to his side and was wielding a wooden dolrod for a weapon, shorter than a broom handle.

We dropped our gear and joined the circle that included the construction workers just in from making mud bricks. Kyros, Dulcinea, and Kelly were there, as was Marna Le and most in her clutch.

Karlyhi was lean and long-limbed, wearing cut-off dungarees only. Two stones in his arm amulets clacked together when he moved, and his leg scar was outlined with yellow paint. Rufus was smaller, soft from his time of healing, and his fire burned in the belly, as it was said. Rufus's hair was tied in a warrior's tail, and he wore the uniform of the clutch of Kenru; a maimed militia officer who must re-establish his right to lead.

The two combatants circled and challenged each other, Karlyhi laughing and Rufus serious in a fighter's crouch. Karlyhi used a round kick to the wounded shoulder to taunt him. Rufus dropped his side and his eyes crossed. The onlookers stopped laughing and concern entered their faces. Karlyhi's play could damage any warrior. Rufus protected himself from the next blow and managed a hit along Karlyhi's thigh. They circled again before Karlyhi executed a series of practiced gestures that Rufus parried like they were dancing. Rufus tripped the larger man, throwing him off balance, and landed a solid thwack on his arm and shoulder blade. As if he felt no pain, Karlyhi reached behind and grabbed Rufus's leg above the knee to throw him down, delivering another kick to the wounded side. Rufus writhed on the ground, and the women's group moaned in empathy.

Karlyhi stood over him, taking his time, grabbing an ankle and twisting Rufus's leg, distracting him from one pain to address another.

The women were loudly clucking.

Mark joined the fight circle, feinting toward Karlyhi to draw his attention. Karlyhi stepped back, allowing Rufus to gain his feet, as if eager to take on both maimed warriors in a test of tactics. He released the binding cord so he had use of both arms. As they repositioned themselves, I saw Hershel Henry come up with some construction workers who joined the fight circle. Henry shook his head and went to wash his hands and face near the mess table.

I heard a grunt followed by a satisfied laugh from Karlyhi. I turned back to see that he had Mark in a headlock and was turning steadily to face Rufus while Mark delivered weak kidney punches and attempted knee kicks. Rufus landed a couple of blows before Karlyhi tripped him. All three landed in the dirt, and Karlyhi got Rufus in a leg lock, still holding Mark firm, and seemed to enjoy inflicting pain as they both struggled against his grasp. Rufus cried out for the first time when Karlyhi twisted to awaken the pain of his earlier injury. Disapproving clucking was heard from many women.

Kelly joined the fight circle. "Stop it; stop it, you bully. Can't you see he's hurt?"

Karlyhi looked at her appraisingly and twisted again so that Rufus went limp from the pain in his damaged shoulder. Kelly kicked Karlyhi's side twice, hesitant blows that did nothing to weaken his lock on either man. Karlyhi released them both, opening his arms and legs wide to expose any vulnerable spot to wound. Both men scrambled away, leaving Karlyhi on the ground facing Kelly whose balled fists were held firmly at her side.

"Nu delaya," Kyros said from the side. He entered the circle and offered a hand to Karlyhi, who took it to rise in a single fluid motion. He was a beautiful man in his own way, lethal and cunning.

Rufus was bent over, panting and holding his side. Kelly stood between them facing Karlyhi with her chin stuck out but holding no weapon.

Karlyhi chuckled and went to Mark, delivering a brotherly shoulder punch. Mark mocked-punched Karlyhi in the chest. Rufus stood tall, walked around Kelly, and offered his arm of camaraderie. They shook hand-to-elbow, and Karlyhi reached forward for a brief hug that Rufus could not return due to his injury. The women turned away, and the workers went to wash up before a meal. Rufus drew Kelly away from the company.

Karlyhi saw me and Henry standing together and nodded briefly before he and Kyros left the group, followed by Karlyhi's personal guard of four men.

Karlyhi reappeared at dusk while we sat at the mess table; Kelly with Rufus, Dulcinea with Kyros, and both Mark and Marna Le standing at Kelly's shoulder. Karlyhi was dressed in the uniform of his clutch and shouldered a karkar, the same as his followers.

Karlyhi held the karkar over his head with both hands. "Hai!"

Rufus held the dolrod used for their fight in the air with one hand only. "Hai!"

Karlyhi nodded to Kyros who had remained seated. Karlyhi left, marching in tight quickstep with his warriors, to enjoy a night of crescent moons for campfire chants about past exploits. Rufus sat again, and Henry gave me a wry look.

You didn't have to speak the tribal dialect to know that Rufus now commanded this garrison—and who were his supporters.

ELEVEN

THE CONTEST WITH KARLYHI DIDN'T MEAN RUFUS WAS DONE WITH his struggles. There was trouble in camp the following morning between him and Kelly, boring to me except that the argument distracted Rufus from our efforts to mount the laser imager on the stinger. All the women seemed to take sides in the fight. Loud complaining erupted during the hot siesta hour, and in more than one dialect.

Kelly sat at the EAM with her faction gathered at her shoulders. "Unblessed ones have a right to know how an enemy died," she claimed.

Apparently, a camcorder video of the death of Anaxagoras was making a splash on social media, each viewer sending the gruesome footage to five friends. Kelly thought all who lived in the camp should view the scene where Kristos executed his greatest enemy, thus raising his profile. Rufus thought the images created unrest, stirring up the Gora.

Even when the men left for construction and Kelly worked at the sewing machine, the factions seemed to argue loudly. "These garments are worn by agents of Somule Gems on Stargate Junction. The same is proper for women of the savannah."

The women who supported the position Rufus had taken, something about modesty, spoke angrily from the mess table. Their refrain was "Mekucoo need only the land," although I couldn't tell what that had to do with the new clothes. I actually felt sorry for Rufus and the trouble he would have with Kelly. Why did he stick it out with so many savannah women in the camp?

While Marna Le's clutch worked by the diving pool, Kelly helped Millie try on the new clothes she had assembled. It was like, um, pedal-pushers I think they're called, with a sleeveless pullover. Added over those was a second garment with sleeves and buttons down the front. The waist was fitted and the mid-length skirt was split to show the wearer's knee and glimpses of thigh, sleek and practical. Modest enough with the slacks underneath, and less cumbersome than the Arrivi gown with its full skirt.

Kelly turned to the EAM and waved away butterflies that had settled there. She fumbled with the machine to use the built-in camera for a photo of Millie in her new clothes. Millie saw me watching her pleasure at receiving the new clothes and giggled before she moved so Kelly blocked my view. Kelly shot her finest scornful look my way, so I turned my back to their activity.

Rufus and Karlyhi were out with the stinger, teaching Mark the laser's functions and testing it on the dunes. Henry had taken the Finn brothers lizard hunting while Marna Le conducted breathing exercises with the divers in the entrance pool. Dulcinea, with the sleeping baby, came to sit at my table as I struggled with the sonar resounder. The gypsy and wood owl played a ball-and-jacks game in the dry yard at Dulcinea's feet, wearing new clothes similar to Millie's handmade outfit.

Dulcinea cooed at the baby, so I took the opportunity to ask the question that had bothered me for days. "Why the switch with the newborns? Don't you miss your own child?"

She graced me with a rueful look that rode her beauty like a bird skimming a bright pool. "His name is Aeocin, born with dark hair and black eyes. A sister of Aeolis who lost her husband to the fighting will raise him, the third son of Aeolis, thus keeping her place among the siblings."

"Will you see him ever?"

"I am free to visit when I can." She softly sighed. "If I was brave like Marna Le, I would have stayed with the Madquii and tolerated the harsh treatment from the women who were jealous. If I had purpose in my life like Rularim, I would start new enterprises in this season of kari. But I'm neither brave nor full of purpose. The small role that I can manage is nurturing this last son of Dacupitte. I knew him, you know."

"One of your suitors?"

"If you want to define it thus."

"And Kelly, does she have purpose in life?"

"Rufus is diminished by his wound," Dulcinea explained. "His aura is collapsed on one side. Only the presence of Kelly ignites vapors of Cyrus for him now. They must settle in together to become who they are."

I blinked at her over my reading glasses before I returned to my tinkering.

"You don't believe me," she said.

"This native mumbo-jumbo only gets in the way of real work." I finally got the connecting screw to come loose and removed the motherboard for inspection. "What will happen to your friends, the rescued women?"

"They will become daughters of Deborah, I imagine."

"Who? Some ancestor I missed in the chants?"

"Deborah was the first wife of my uncle Kenru but was rejected by him. She's Uburu and not a favorite subject in Arrivi chants. The story goes that his third lover, when rejected, sought out Deborah and they made a pact. Then more women were included around questions of hygiene, clean water, the early education of girls. Our Uburu men were lost to conflicts with Gora, and the women were victims of rape or mutilation. So now the title sticks, daughters of Deborah. They must find work and manage the children on their own."

"But they aren't rejected by the tribe?"

"Some daughters of Deborah joined a protest in Urbyd about birthing rights. Led by Abydian women who have the same struggles. A married woman must be the one who decides when she has children. But protesting in the city is a grim life with little income and less status in the public square. The remnants of Gora are crowded into a fishing village called Agora that's below the cliffs. They're given to setting pipe bombs in businesses that refuse to serve them. Several daughters of Deborah were victims of the bombings."

Dulcinea glanced down at the sleeping baby in her arms. "Protestors recently added," she continued, "the right for women to inherit a business, so an enterprise where she worked all her married life doesn't transfer to a distant male cousin. Aristides had several protest leaders imprisoned."

"Uburu and Abydian protesters?"

"Abydian women were sent to their husbands with a strong reprimand to keep silent. The daughters of Deborah have only their own voices, not covered by a man of any tribe."

"So they're imprisoned?"

"The ones who won't return to the mesas."

"And Kenru takes no care of them?"

"Kenru avoids them." Dulcinea shrugged as she rocked slightly. "From shame or confusion over the honor they afford him. My uncle is a brave man in battle, and the warriors follow him. But he cannot be a friend to a woman. Either she's a lover, or she's rejected while he organizes the clutch. She cannot remain after his, um, after—"

"After he sees a younger woman, you mean."

Dulcinea watched Cleo for a moment. Why she treasured the naughty girls and kept them close I could not fathom. "Captain Chandliss, you have said that creating a graphic with the laser is only half the battle. The user must also learn to read the images for mass and depth and detail, isn't that so?" She saw my suspicious look, but only continued, "So it is with spiritual gifts. I was wondering if you would help us. Cleo's training today is about targeting her gift, blocking some viewers while she reaches a specific person in a crowd. Since you are not flattened by her gift, we were hoping—"

"I'm your test subject?"

She flashed that smile that relaxed the eyes. I thought it was good that she was engaged to the headman. Any worker was vulnerable to her manner, even with a suckling babe in arms. "What is needed?" I asked.

"Allow a touch and be open."

Cleo came to my side and placed three fingers on my wrist like she was taking my pulse. I saw her suddenly as a burning bush, just like in the Bible illustrations. Dulcinea was a single shaft of blue light shooting up and unaffected by Cleo's glow. Camille, still seated on the ground, was riddled with holes like Swiss cheese, and muddy.

I softly chuckled and looked around. Kelly was sitting in front of the EAM at the table in the women's camp and focused on the monitor. She was like a big pustule with many tentacles of different lengths extending from all areas of her body. Eight tentacles hovered near her head, the ends like faces apparently focused on the EAM screen. Other streamers lazily searched tent flaps and open crates, only to curl out and explore the next likely object. The tentacles avoided the small pack that belonged to Rufus, dropped at her feet. The tips of four long tubes were positioned at the edge of the women's camp and pointed our way, gathered like parrots on a tree branch.

I heard Dulcinea's voice in my ear. "Kelly is bloated with potential, but has low self-esteem maybe. She seeks acceptance where she can find it. She had a recent success at Stargate Junction and contacts Bernice often to bask in the glow of their regard. She's interested in us while she rejects the very place where she must find her core."

"With Rufus."

"So we have defined what Cleo sees."

Dulcinea rested the babe on her knees. She made a fist with one hand. "Rufus is closed inside himself. With the overlay of Kelly who is into everybody's business . . ." She spread the fingers of her other hand tightly over the fist, then opened both hands outward. "Only together can they come into their own among the tribes."

I pulled my wrist away from Cleo. "Tell her to stop now." I turned to the sonar resounder and stretched my face to relieve tension and consider again at the problem at hand. Immediately, I saw the tracks of my efforts and knew where my mistake had occurred. The problem was easily fixed if I switched off the power source, reversed one connection, and rebooted. "Oriika's eyes!"

Camille giggled, the same melody I had heard before. Cleo returned to her companion and the ball-and-jacks game. "Is she still reading me?" I asked Dulcinea.

"Part of today's lesson is learning when and how to stop."

"Tell her to get out of my mind. Oh, and tell her thanks."

At a hand signal from Dulcinea, the girls went to the women's camp and stood at Kelly's side seeking EAM time. After watching the vapors of tentacles curl around them, I looked away. "I suspect that kind of viewing is addictive."

"I think so."

"You're not impacted, serene in your own, uh, glow. But the wood owl is eaten out by proximity. She'll age quickly. The gypsy will need a long sequence of assistants."

"We have something in the works now."

"Conscripts rescued from the space station," I guessed.

"Very perceptive. Not ground-born, the same as you." Dulcinea held the baby again, rocking her arms back and forth. "You define the images well with no, um, dross from your own needs."

"Just tell the gypsy to stay out of my head," I said while I tinkered with the connection. "I'm not interested in a shortened life of viewing the problems of others."

Ten minutes later, I got the sonar resounder working. I still had four hours of daylight so I carried the unit down to the entrance pool, eager to get started with instruction for use and maintenance.

Kristos and Karry were stacking the tanks and binding ropes. A wagon waited on the side loaded with bushel containers of raw silicide crystals that looked like big quartz.

"Hey," I called. "Back to the pool. I got the sonar working."

Aensilus came around the wagon and waited. I was surprised to see Madquii in our camp that I had assumed was secret from Borabean. "What?" I said.

Aensilus touched fingertips to his chest with the briefest bow. "These ones are reassigned."

"Aw, come on," I complained. "I just got them trained. You're wasting my time here." Aensilus only shrugged and turned back to harnessing two erriv geldings.

I turned to Mica. "Get beauty down here."

He left, and I turned to Kristos. "With this machine we can see the contours of the cavern. We can see the ceiling and the floor under water to finger the silicide. Don't you want to stay for that?" His face was hard, showing only bitter determination.

"Just think of the possibilities," I added to Karry, who nodded to be friendly.

Dulcinea arrived in her stately gait, just as her cousin came up from the pool, still wearing the wetsuit and carrying a mask and flippers. I saw them waiver like they were underwater together, almost an exchange of spirits. Marna Le was strengthened by her connection to Dulcinea, but the cousin was also made stronger. I shook my head to resist the vapors of being touched by om. I stomped over to the beauty, still toting the weighty unit.

"Is this your doing? This touched-by-om crap?"

She blinked twice. "The kenoma brothers are to be separated from Kyros to study in Cochin. They are now called the Finn brothers."

"They're trained for scuba diving. Kyros can leave."

"Their paths go a different way," she said mildly.

"Why? Who will dive with me?"

She indicated fire-eyes who was shooting flames my way. "The one you named."

"Are the Finn brothers really going to Cochin, or to some hidden pool to bring up silicide with stolen equipment?"

"To Cochin," she said, "but that's an interesting idea." She turned to Marna Le, unperturbed by my objections. "With the right equipment, we could work two teams." Fire-eyes spoke in her dialect and they began to chew on the idea, sharing chi, as it was said.

Kristos and Karry stepped to my side. "We are sorry to end this time with diving," Karry said. "You spoke to us as men and provided real work for wages. Melinga."

I sighed heavily, trying to accept the inevitable. My project was robbed of the best workers because some gypsy girl and her giggling wood owl friend saw images in om. Dolviets would be the end of me, I was confident of that.

"In Cochin we can learn sailing," Karry added eagerly, "and maybe a little magic."

I looked at Dulcinea. "We could have talked."

"It is as Dolvia would have it," she said vaguely and went with her cousin to look over the harvest of silicide ready for transport. They talked openly with Aensilus about wages and bonuses for the wagonload of silicide.

I looked again at the brothers. "When do you leave?"

"With this wagon."

"Did you intend to say goodbye, at least?"

Karry ducked his head. "We have few attachments. We didn't know how to—"

"Honesty would have worked just fine," I interrupted. "I'm, uh, glad for you. A new adventure. The language is difficult, though."

"I have a few words already," Kristos said with a brief shrug. "Cochin mechanics mixed with Gora, so we, uh . . ."

Karry showed his half smile with the immobile side of his face in shadow. "It's the sailing we want. We saw small boats when Gora were near the shores of Urbyd. The white sails on blue water cutting through the waves. Sailors are free, not ruled by any other."

"Not made to go diving into dark caverns?"

"We like diving," Karry said with his half smile. "The teaching you provided, um, helped us get past other, um, things. And now we have no fear of water."

"Very brave. The first thing I noticed about you was bravery." Then it came to me in a flash, this new path thrust upon them. "With

sailing and diving experience, you can work the deep water platform to bring up ocean silicide, maybe manage a crew there one
day." Kristos said nothing, but Karry raised his eyebrows in agreement, nodding several times.

"Brianna Miller surely can plan ahead," I added.

"They call it clearstone, you know, the Borabean," Karry said. "So
misleading. Most residents of Urbyd have never seen silicide, only
heard the promises of wealth. Abydian are focused on the future
promise, not on today's task."

We walked back to camp together, Karry carrying the sonar unit
and Kristos shouldering both empty diving tanks. I intended to
knock off for the day and open a fresh bottle of Kiam gin. Perhaps
I could drown my anger at Dulcinea and Cleo.

In the women's camp Marna Le was telling a story from her
culture, the one about how Ohunt had agreed to allow Ohero's
daughters to record the secrets of the carpenter guild. "The husband
of the eldest daughter," Marna Le related to the women who had
gathered, "learned the features of stone and warded tools to work
long hours without fatigue. The husband of the middle daughter was
sent to the forge, where he learned to manipulate metal into girders
and add wards for strength and appeal. The husband of the youngest daughter stayed in the woodshop, where he fashioned tools for
fine carving and learned to work wards into the wood for protection and warning, using silicide to energize the wards. This husband
was said to be the most talented, and he caused the houses in Utica
to glow together after dark and sing the city's song.

"So Ohunt approach Ohero one day," Marna Le continued. "I
have kept my part of the bargain, he claimed. I have trained the

husbands in the secrets of creating wards. Now you must show me the beastmaster talent."

"Two principles guide the beastmaster, Ohero told him," she continued in a raw voice. "The first is trust, spending the time to know the animal and share a needed task. The second principle is respect. Ask the beast to complete only those tasks that it performs in nature. If you are too tired to carry your helmet, ask the lemurs who carry their pups all day. If you cannot swim to the distant shore, ask the sea serpent to carry you, he who swims just under the surface without tiring.

"But Ohunt asked how to speak to the creatures. Ohero insisted the answer was trust, as he already explained. The words to speak were different for each creature. Find a meeting place and bring a token. Spend the time and show a needed task. From friendship, the creature will offer his help.

"Ohunt took offense that he had supplied so many instructions for the sons-in-law, but Ohero refused to demonstrate the beastmaster talent. Ohunt left Utica with the city half-finished, and the husbands had to labor without further instruction to complete the buildings. And that was how Ohero and Ohunt fell out after seasons of friendship."

"Do you know more stories of Ohero and Ohunt?" I asked Henry as he was cleaning his fingernails with the big knife he carried.

"Arrivi have a story," Henry said as he worked, "about how Ohero and Oria had hunted the giant ketiwhelp together. Arrivi follow the warrior way and turned away from forcing animals. A man lives with only the respect of warriors and the company of ancestors."

He stood and stretched. "I'm going down to the stinger. Maybe check on night vision and beg a ride." He sauntered off to find Karlyhi.

I was not but a fourth into the bottle when I decided to wander down to the wagon and speak to Aensilus about his return for the next shipment. Millie was there wearing her new clothes, looking like a modern young lady, like she had shed an old skin and emerged more grown up. A spray of yellow butterflies were on the wagon and wheel and bush, the most I had seen in a single place.

Millie spoke quietly with Kristos and offered a small notebook that was stained with dirt and blood. He pushed away her hand. "It was Bibi Le's," Millie said. "Brianna said you should have it to carry and remem—"

"I don't want it! I want nothing from the past!"

Kristos walked my way, leaving her to watch his retreat with her mouth open. The butterflies lifted and scattered, still active after dark. That was a wonder. I tried to catch the arm of Kristos seeking a private goodbye, but he jerked away and walked into the dark bush. When I turned back, I saw Aensilus speak to Millie and take the notebook from her hand.

"It's the truancy book," she said simply. "Brianna found it where Bibi Le was lost in the killing field of their village. Bibi Le carried it to the last. Tell Kristos that Brianna wanted, um, I don't know."

"I'll take care of it," Aensilus said.

He waved a hand at a fluttering butterfly near his head. A few had come to rest on the wagon's side. Tears misted Millie's blue eyes. She saw me approach and stepped away. She turned back slightly like she had more to say, but thought better of her move and walked toward the women's camp. Three yellow butterflies followed as if trained as protectors.

Aensilus was smiling. "I approve of the change of clothing style."

"Say that to Rufus before you go, huh? I'm so bored with the squabble in camp."

"He wouldn't want to hear that from Madquii," Aensilus grinned through the facial hair. "The new look only calls attention to her, so tiny and fresh."

"Where are you taking the wagonload?"

"Oh, there's a wadi south of here that the Goras never found. Stockpile some clearstone until furnaces can be built and defended, maybe here at the butterfly pool with the new militia station."

"I remember now; you're the one from the chant."

Aensilus showed a butterfly pendant that he wore. "When she found me dying from thirst, Kecouroo had claimed she often visited this pool on a known trail, but I doubt another could find it from trying. We named this place Chrysalis after the butterflies, you know. I don't know if Arrivi have adopted that name."

I nodded, not really listening. "Tell the Finn brothers I wish them all the best, will you, if I miss them before you leave?"

"They prospered with you. They knew a healing. We won't soon forget."

"Are they really going to Cochin?"

Aensilus shrugged. "So goes the story. Kristos has certain fame now, due to the video that's circulating about the execution of Anaxagoras. No loss there. The notoriety brings unwanted interest to your garrison, though. Kristos must leave so you are safe."

"Because of the execution? I thought the Goras were beaten."

He seemed to turn away, hunching one shoulder. "We're all cousins, you know. Goras are . . . some are absorbed into related clans. For Kristos, a student exchange was first suggested by Otieno on Stargate Junction. Otieno likes that Arrivi allow no conscripts on the savannah. He likes that you found work for recovered captives. He wants to work with the tribes."

"Because of the silicide, do you think?"

"Otieno?" Aensilus said shaking his head. "He wants to mine the asteroids using his own freighters, maybe go to the source of clearstone rather than seeking the remnants of an impact crater."

"Very forward looking." I tried not to roll my eyes so he could see.

I didn't secure the honorable goodbye from Kristos or Karry before the wagon left. The women's camp was quiet. I sat at my table with a drink glass, chewing on my finger and trying to puzzle out Arrivi motives. Rufus was working a second shift with the construction crew, in a hurry to provide shelter for his stinger, and maybe to avoid his betrothed. We heard the machinery buzz and saw camp lights. Karlyhi loitered in that section with his constant companions but was doing no work.

In our camp, Henry and Kyros joined me without ceremony, and Henry poured himself a drink. Kyros never imbibed, or no longer since his days as kenoma were in the past. "Cleo Datong is working the tallow bowl in the big tent," Henry said. "They are using tektite and om to sort out the past."

"That little gypsy and her wood owl friend? I pass."

"Not for you," Kyros said.

"Yeah, yeah. Everything's a secret. Aensilus is related to Gora, you know. He's stockpiling the silicide for you."

"He puts it where we direct him," Kyros said, "and he tells his friends what we want them to know."

"And you move the silicide?" I sat back and rubbed my face all over with one hand. "This whole encampment is a plant, isn't that right? Borabean think we are defending a valuable site, but the pool is nearly denuded of silicide. You'll move to the next grotto once the divers are trained. Leave Rufus stationed here so Borabean think the site is worth defending."

"Leave you here with your grumpy old self," Henry said. "Borabean will assume the pool is the center of the universe."

"Is any part of what you told me the truth?" I asked Kyros.

Kyros expelled air through his lips. "Ah, yeah. Parts of it."

Dulcinea approached with her cousin Marna Le. There must have been a seamstress among the women with more skill that Kelly. Marna Le wore a garment like the young girls had. Hers included thigh-length shorts, though, under a simple pullover. The outer garment was roomy in the shoulders with too much sleeve material, called dolman. The skirt had a separate vanity panel in the front so both knees were visible, and the skirt's back was less than knee length. This practical garment could be shed for the wetsuit in a single gesture without loss of modesty.

"I assume you approve," Henry whispered.

I must have been staring with my mouth open. "A better diet and daily exercise have increased her strength," I said in even tones.

Kyros pushed his chair back and stood. "Hiki, Kyros rabbe Sudl," Dulcinea said holding one palm high. "Hiki, Hershel Henry and Captain Chandliss. May we join you?"

We said our melingas and secured chairs for them at the end of the table, more than a foot from where we sat.

"I have asked my cousin to share some of her story," Dulcinea said in honeyed tones. "Not so much for pity, or to confess. She has information you should know. She was among the Abydian when decisions were made."

The cousins sat facing each other and barely looked our way.

"I was held through two seasons of netta by Abydian soldiers," Marna Le began, rubbing her wrists absently. I could see her profile only in the gathering dark, backlit by our campfire. "The daughters of Deborah seldom lasted so long in the brothel. One of the sons of Ananke led the camp. He liked to abuse me. In his own culture he could chase no women, just handed from mother to wife without experience in the world. His options were few unless he wanted a circus performer, or to follow the path of Patrick Hartley."

She glanced at Kyros for a moment. "His name is Analli, the youngest of the ten sons. He knew little about, um, what to do. His intent was to punish. I tell you this not to make you sad, just to show I was in that place when the men talked.

"Analli had a set of rooms at the end of the barracks," Marna Le continued. "A front room where the men gathered to receive orders, a kitchen and eating area, and his sleeping area where he liked to keep me tied up. Why me, you would ask? I think hurting me was the same as hurting his mother. He would beat me senseless sometimes, after he got news from Urbyd about his extended deployment or the successes of his brothers.

"Over time I learned much about Abydian. They were not trained with weapons, you know, the sons. Rather they learned poetry and foreign languages such as Cochin, and talked endlessly about the city-states, especially Utica, like a mythical city that glows in the dark. They called Urbyd a backwater outpost, their own city where his father was khalif. All the officers hungered for reassignment in one of the urban centers in Cochin."

She sighed and looked to Dulcinea for support. "Analli wore jackets made in Cochin," Marna Le added, "and his jewelry was a strange style. He drank wine from there and spoke about the size of their seaports. He had many antiques, even a flute made of chime coral. He couldn't play it, of course, but I once saw Aeolis troubling the individual pipes using a small tuning fork, not for a melody but, um . . . just for curiosity. There was also a scrying bowl, and Analli tried his hand at pouring hot wax to, um, discern the future. He only tried that a couple times before he gave up.

"Anyhow, two things you should know." Marna Le glanced again at Kyros, swallowing her shame. "Aristides visited during the conflict with Goras. That's right. Aristides ran the show in Urbyd, and still does most likely. Khalif Ananke wants palace life and doesn't care who is sacrificed to keep his place. It's said that Ananke invited a Cochin circus to live in the palace, and his favorite minister is a contortionist who also serves his, um, his needs in bed.

"So Aristides played Analli for a fool and promised him riches and travel in exchange for learning the maneuvers of Goras. They had a captured officer there; I never knew his name. Aristides had him beaten and strangled near to death and broke the bones in his hands. The poor man told them everything he knew before he died. Analli stood on the side biting his own hand and trying not to watch."

She coughed slightly, turning her head away. "Then Aristides left and nothing happened. Troops were not called up and the assault was not mounted. It's hard to know from the absence of action, but Analli became limp and uncaring, drinking all night and muttering about his brothers. So, the Abydian rulers could have captured Anaxagoras, could have carried out the execution without more raids from Madquii or Arrivi. Why not? Why did they wait when a quick end was possible?"

Marna Le paused and glanced again at Kyros, but he was providing no answers. "The other thing you should know is that Aeolis visited with several of his men." Marna Le looked down at her hands. Dulcinea glanced at Kyros and this time he spoke.

"Aeolis made the armistice," Kyros said. "Maybe he was traveling to make connections."

"I'm certain you're right," Marna Le said in barely a whisper. "Except he and Analli acted like they were close, maybe school friends. Aeolis admired his treasures and wine and asked about other friends he knew. They left together. I was released into the women's camp. Nobody wanted me, maybe fearing that Analli would return and start up with me again. I was still among the daughters of Deborah in the brothel when the armistice was made and Abydian fell back to Urbyd."

"Maybe you're lying," Kyros said. "Maybe you agreed to serve your Abydian master to survive. Maybe he told you to spread lies."

Marna Le hung her head. Dulcinea spoke for her. "Cleo says no. Cleo says this one speaks true."

"Cleo says?" I asked. "The test for truth in war reports is the gypsy girl?"

"We can call Cleo out here," Dulcinea said. She didn't look at Kyros or anybody.

"What did you see among the Madquii, Dulcinea?" Kyros asked.

Dulcinea hung her head as though her pregnancy was as shameful as Marna Le's imprisonment. "I was there only for my last trimester. The women were jealous and kept me separated. They liked to display their foreign goods, though, from Cochin. Silks and metal objects I didn't recognize, with fine tooling and inlaid gems. I can confirm that the women spoke about circus performers living at the Urbyd palace. I saw no Cochin men, but we don't show our secrets to Madquii either."

There was a long pause while Kyros considered this new information, rubbing his chin and jawline with one hand. Finally, he shrugged as though to close the discussion. "We thank our cousin Marna Le for her confession that I know was difficult, especially in the presence of these Softcheeks. Rufus and Kelly will remain here with Marna Le's clutch. Rufus can learn the new gadgets from Captain Chandliss, and Kelly can help Cleo sort out the daughters of Deborah. Perhaps others among them can reinforce this tale of abuse by Abydian."

Kyros turned to me. "Mark will remain as your interpreter so you aren't mixing with the women. We'll find other work for Aensilus so he no longer comes to this camp. The Madquii will think we're hiding something valuable when we turn away our friend. Henry will come to Cylay with Dulcinea and me. And we'll bring Millie home."

The two women murmured their melingas and walked back to the women's camp with arms around each other's waist.

Kyros pointed one finger toward Henry. "I have a new task for you. This season of kari shows strong growth that will bear much fruit. We must make new plans."

And that was how all Arrivi workers were scattered from the butterfly pool and our settlement named Chrysalis. Each was given marching orders for concerns that were beyond my bailiwick.

TWELVE

 at first light. She swam to the silicide beds and indicated the progress, but I had other needs today. I only nodded and gestured left so she followed me to the aperture that led to the larger chamber. In the solitude of the scuba gear, I was puzzling out my role for this season of kari. Diminished warriors and rescued sex slaves, guided by expendable Softcheeks consultants, were assembled for this new garrison and with an untested leader. Were we bait for the Borabean? Come get us; come see what we hold dear.

If the stinger could be disabled, or if Rufus was flying past the dunes, our position could be overrun within twenty minutes from any direction. Six scouts and two squads of regulars were no challenge, especially with the lure of silicide to exploit. Every person here was part of window dressing—second-string workers easily sacrificed without damage to a larger plan. I didn't like the feel of that at all.

I reached the opening that was now high and dry. Rains came seldom these days, and the savannah billabongs were receding. Marna Le surfaced next to me and handed me her light bar. She removed her flippers and mask and attached them to the double tank before she slipped it off her shoulders. She secured the tank to her waist with a sturdy rope, and looked at me with humor in her eyes. She swam to the wall and used dugout footholds to climb to the opening. She swung a leg over and dropped to the other side with a grunt. She reached around and pulled the tanks toward her to hoist them over the rim. This maneuver had been developed in my absence while I had struggled with the new gadgets, as Kyros had named them. Marna Le showed her face at the opening for just a moment, an obvious challenge. I saw lights flash on the other side. The divers had secured some equipment there, a prudent addition.

On my utility belt, I carried a big spool of nylon thread that had been twisted into rope, sturdy as silk and less likely to rot when immersed for long periods. I balanced both light bars against the wall and secured the rope end to the high wall. I removed flippers and mask and performed the same sequence Marna Le had used, switching off the lights, which we could retrieve on our return. I was careful not to tangle the nylon rope and dropped blindly to the other side. I landed on a narrow ledge and looked about. Along the ledge was a sturdy shelf with a wide net that held needed supplies for a diver in distress, but no full tanks. On my left side was an unexplored passageway that had been a swift river days before. We would explore in that direction tomorrow. First, I wanted to retrace Kristos's journey.

To the right, Marna Le treaded water in readiness by a long cause-way and a smooth concave wall where the current had hollowed out a turning place before it crashed into a lower flow. I got into the gear and got wet again. Marna Le was already stroking toward the smooth wall. We had not discussed my intent for today, but she must have made this trip before. Once we reached the wall, finding a catch hold was a struggle. Marna Le indicated several iron rings bored into the rock but too high for us to reach today. This part of the journey was obvious, so I didn't need to secure the nylon rope here for guidance.

I held my hands horizontal and parallel, palm facing back, then at different heights to ask how deep the lower pool was. She only tossed her chin twice and pushed her mask tight. She scooted into the rush of water and dropped, with arms crossed, into the dark expanse below. Cheeky wench, wasn't she? Of course I had to follow. I felt the tug of the nylon rope playing out until I hit the oxygenated water under the falls, deep water judging by the muted reverbera-tion of my fall. Marna Le was below me, stroking her long legs and fins. She flashed the light bar across my form and turned to dive deeper. I followed, curious about what she had found even though this was a detour from my real goal.

The water here was still and cold. When I came alongside, Marna Le did a complete sweep of the walls and floor with the light bar. I saw twisted rock formations carved by centuries of fluctuating water volume, and even some sluggish fish drifting without fear, but no rock crystals identified as silicide. I nodded and we swam up, stroking slowly to follow the bubble stream.

We swam back to the waterfall and pulled off our masks. I labored too long under the falling volume to secure a metal ring with a loop of nylon rope. We swam out from under the pounding spray, treading water.

"Did you find the acacia stand where Kristos escaped?" I asked.

She paused before nodding briskly. She was probably thinking I was an old fool for wanting to recapture the glory of a fireside chant.

We secured masks again, and she led me underwater—easier with the tanks buoyant—across the pool and along the tunnel wall. She surfaced where she found a marker, and I came up behind her. I saw daylight flicker briefly overhead and knew that was our wombat hole. I slipped out of my tank, diving for a moment to secure the nylon rope to the marker she had already provided. When I came up, she was climbing without mask or tanks to dry ground, using toeholds previously chiseled by her divers, no doubt. I decided I liked Marna Le, not waiting to be instructed but contributing to the day's adventure with insight and real help. It was only when she was out of the water that her fire blazed uncontrolled. We sat without tanks on a spat of dry ground under untidy acacia roots.

"What's down that way?" I asked.

She used gestures to indicate a wall with only small openings for the water.

"The overhead escape hole," I instructed, "will have to be reinforced, made wide enough for a man's body and concealed above ground." I still used big gestures to express ideas, even though we understood each other well enough now. "We need a bolt secured high and run the nylon rope back to the aperture so there are two guidelines, high and low." She only nodded like she would have underwater.

I dropped my hands, feeling silly for the big gestures. "Tomorrow we'll explore in the other direction at the aperture," I added more quietly. "We'll find an egress under the barracks so soldiers can also drop underground when attacked. Got it?"

She splayed her fingers as though grasping a basketball before she pointed with index fingers in two directions. "A wombat's burrow with two openings," she said evenly. "Escape from the killing."

"That's right. I'll tell Rufus to instruct the soldiers. You talk to the women."

She looked ahead without question. She had accepted, as I had, that only the quickest among us would survive an attack at Chrysalis, and defenders would surely lose our lives. Marna Le and I were bonded not by ritual or blood, but by the indefensible station others had chosen for us.

When we arrived back in camp, I didn't recognize the place. We had been invaded, but not by Gora. Two transport choppers had landed near the barracks. In our camp a metal feast table was laden with food and gifts in brightly colored wrappings. Guests milled about, families dressed for celebrating. I saw Karlyhi with two toddlers on his lap and squinted; maybe I was going mad. A wrong mix of oxygen in my tanks and the world was inverted.

Millie came to me wearing her new clothes that Kelly had designed and a laurel twist in her hair. "Hurry! We waited for you, but they're getting started now."

"What is this?"

"The wedding of Rufus and Kelly. Quick! I have a part to play."

Marna Le joined her clutch with questions and chatter. I went to change and found clothes laid out for me on the cot. Millie's work, I was certain. I joined Mica and Yuri who stood with Hershel Henry on the outskirts of the group.

"Have you met Dr. Spinelli?" he asked. "Working at the Uburu digs." He was dressed in camp fatigues much like Henry and my soldiers. Spinelli had bushy eyebrows and held an unlit pipe, lending an old world flavor to our gathering.

We shook hands. "A pleasure." I said.

"And this is Ned Sumuki." Spinelli said. "A cousin to Martina." Sumuki was a big man and barrel-chested. His blue-black face was too active with eagerness.

"Ned was trained at the clinic school," Spinelli explained, "from their very first classroom in Cylay. He's a doctor now. A medical doctor, and just completed his internship on Cicero."

"Melinga, Dr. Sumuki," I said.

Mark was officiating. Karlyhi and Colonel Sector stood in a row with Rufus. Omiibuk and Millie stood for Kelly who wore the new-style clothes, much like what Millie and Marna Le and now several others were wearing. The choice of dress gave this event held in our dune encampment a modern feeling; impromptu and responding to impulses for the season of kari. Dulcinea and the newborn lingered with Marna Le; they were cousins, after all. The gypsy and wood owl hovered nearby, also dressed modern, watching but not touching. Dulcinea must have banned pickpocketing from the wedding party.

Kyros stood near Colonel Sector, also with his wife Hakulupe Le and a younger daughter, along with the two dark-skinned toddlers who were Karlyhi's sons. Seated next to them and not far from us was Brianna Miller, the only guest who sat during the ceremony. Standing behind her were a Putuki woman who I didn't recognize, maybe a servant, and three Softcheeks who whispered together.

Rufus held a length of blue ribbon that he played out while Kelly, holding the other end, walked in a wide circle around the center fire. Kelly stepped in tight loops, walking toward Rufus so that the ribbon wound around her torso. In this way Arrivi showed that the man chooses the woman, but she binds herself to him. Rufus did no kissing or hugging in the presence of the gathering. He took Kelly's hand on his arm and turned our way amid polite applause and clucking from the women's group. Kelly would have to be content with that.

Many rushed forward with congratulations and to admire the wedding necklace of gold acacia leaves that Kelly wore with a much more valuable peridot necklace.

I stepped to Brianna's side. Surprisingly, Brianna wore the new style clothes, the same fabric and color as Kelly's, except the trousers were loose-fitting and came to her ankles.

"This is Ali Abrar Ebnli, the biologist," she said without getting up from her seat.

The man reached to shake hands. Although clean-shaven, he had the hairy look and cunning eyes of a Saudi.

"And Victor and Chantara Putivoc from Croatia, who are botanists," Brianna added.

He was broad and blue-collar. She was diminutive and with a weak chin, not an impressive couple at all. We endured several minutes of greetings all around, even including Martina who was visiting from Two Forks where she served Mrs. Shaw as a nanny, and who seemed inordinately attached to the newly minted doctor, Ned Sumuki.

"No Lynus and Alaise?" I asked when the melingas were complete.

Brianna was grey from her recent pregnancy. "On Borabean land." She shrugged. "Harder to work out the logistics for travel."

"And no Edwina?"

"She wasn't told about Kecouroo's act of self-torching. Not told in advance, I mean. Edwina's own fault, really, since she put the ban on remote viewing. She can hold a grudge."

"Millie's too young for the wedding party," I whispered. "Why not you?"

"Kelly saved Millie's life once. Did you know?" I shook my head. "Millie asked for the duty," she added, "and Kelly wanted it."

Kelly made her way among the well-wishers to Brianna Miller who stood on unsteady legs and provided a hug. "Mrs. Shaw is still at Stargate Junction," Brianna said. "And Sarah was sent to Mayschool on convent business. Cymarta sends her best. Kecouroo would have been proud."

A shadow passed over Kelly's bright face with a laurel twist and loose coppery hair framing her features, but her spirits were too high for worry on this day.

"And you remember Martina, who serves Mrs. Shaw?" Brianna said. "This is Dr. Ned Sumuki, her nephew who was a student at the clinic school."

"A medical doctor?" Kelly said. "Will you work at Beecham Place?"

"For now," he said, his features too bright with eagerness. "But I want field work. I want to work among the people."

"So, Martina, our first home-grown doctor, huh?" Kelly said very host-like. "Dolviets serving Dolviets." Martina turned completely around, about to melt into a puddle from pride. They went as a group to greet Hakulupe Le and Dulcinea.

I noticed that Brianna avoided Dulcinea and the newborn, while Omiibuk and Hakulupe Le cooed at the squished-faced thing with orange hair. Brianna was seated again, maybe considering a nap. She signaled me, and I stepped to her side.

"Are you well?" I asked.

"Working too hard, I guess." Brianna saw me glance at Dulcinea and back at her. "We're still business partners," she whispered. "She understands my . . . distance."

"Doesn't your body ache for . . . for—"

"I took a hypo so my milk dries up, Jessup, if that's any of your business."

"I don't mean to pry."

Brianna pulled herself out of the chair. "Walk with me awhile." She held onto my arm as we moved into the shadow of the tents. "We will find no peace with Aeolis and the Madquii," she started.

I only blinked and stared.

She didn't seem to notice my surprise, looking out as though ruminating on a present concern. "It's a different religion, after all. Even if our ideal leader ruled in Urbyd, the Borabean clans are not our allies. They will seek to make converts of us all."

"No export route for industry?"

"Now you see . . . You understand me. Why don't the others understand me?"

"Did you talk with Mrs. Shaw?"

She threw up one hand. "Don't even start about her." She saw me trying to hide my grin and smiled, returning to her worries. "At best, we can expect parity in Urbyd, and a structure of tariffs. The Siibabean, though, have been our allies for nearly a generation."

"What's on the other side of the forest?"

"More forest," she said. "But leading to a narrow landing below high cliffs. Some fishing families are there, mostly exiled Striiduc."

"The Siibabean have no cities," I postulated. "No central government, no offworld trade agreements. Less competition for grabbing the mineral wealth."

"I intend no exploitation of our neighbors," she said. "I'm simply seeking a back door." I understood the desire for a second entrance, a life-saving escape route. Brianna had a similar problem as my own, only on a larger scale. Her appraising eyes watched me closely. "You know about earth-moving equipment, right?"

"Yuri knows surveying. Mica was a mechanic."

"We can secure road-building machinery from Cochin and avoid Company channels. Most of it was retro-engineered from Soft-cheeks designs, and I can get translations for the operator manuals."

A gaggle of kids who were cousins and wedding guests ran past us, led by the wood owl, of course, playing tag-and-run among the tents. One toddler lagged behind, his face anxious. Brianna grinned and waved him along their path.

"How soon?" I asked.

"We have the surveying, um, apparatus now. So hand the sili-cide recovery to the teams you trained here and find me in Cylay."

"Chrysalis. This settlement is called Chrysalis after the cocoons the caterpillars make. And what's this new task for Henry in Cylay?"

We continued our stroll among the tents. "Blancom will make the record when Ely steps down," Brianna said. "We cannot trust the offworld journalists to get it right."

"And who will you back for rabbenu?"

"Perhaps I should run for office." She showed me a smirk.

"And risk another assassination attempt?" I asked. "Besides, rabbenu is small potatoes to you now. How soon will you travel to the cities of Cochin?"

She chuckled softly. "I like you, Jessup Chandliss. You did well with the kenoma boys. It's good to see you on the right side of events for once. Walk back with me now."

We turned toward the noise of the celebration. "You're leaving the party?" I asked.

"It's best to keep moving so we're not an easy target. The wedding is a good mercy seat, though, to mark the season of kari. Poor Kelly, huh, and the lifetime of heartache she'll know with Rufus."

"I was thinking Rufus was the loser today, mated to the viper."

"I heard you had nicknames for them; fire-eyes and wood owl. And for me too?"

"Don't you have enough names, Rularim?"

"That's not really mine, just a hand-me-down."

Millie rushed toward us and skidded to a stop. "Hurry! They're opening presents now. Hurry, hurry! You're missing the feast."

Brianna soon left in one of the transport choppers accompanied by Dr. Spinelli, Martina, and the new scientists. The others began performing goodbyes and moving toward the choppers. Arrivi could waste as much time with goodbye as hello.

I sat at my regular table and was stowing tools to move the sonar work to the hangar, when Hershel Henry joined me suddenly. He was packed and waiting for a ride to Cylay and better work there. "I need a token, something metallic and shiny," he said as he fingered my stuff. "A diving valve or a tool you never use."

"The only useless tool in this camp is you."

He grinned. "Something from the new gadgets."

"Ask the wood owl. She probably has a pocketful of stolen objects."

"It has to come from you."

"You mean like an exchange of talismans?"

"We can do that, but this is for my doorjamb in Cylay to discourage theft. I have blue parrot feathers that say I'm known to Brianna Miller to whom Dolvia whispers each morning before dawn. So I need neighbors to know I'm associated with Jessup Chandliss who will smother them with his foreign chi like an octopus on a starfish."

I looked overhead and twisted in my seat. "The chopper is leaving without you?" I reached into my pocket and showed him a glide ring for a breathing hose. "Broke it this morning."

"Thanks," he grinned. "You're a good man, Jessup. I don't care what people are saying about you. Come on." I walked with him to the gathering by the choppers. We stood with Cleo and Camille as the women hugged and cried and exchanged more gifts.

Dulcinea came forward with her treasured smile. "If you're ready, Blancom?"

He shouldered his small pack and casually saluted, brushing the top of Cleo's head when he passed. She and Camille giggled. "See you down the road," he called over his shoulder. Henry helped Millie with the babe in arms into the chopper, shooing away several yellow butterflies, and climbed in after.

Kyros and Colonel Sector waved for an honorable farewell while Dulcinea held a palm high for melinga. We hunched against the turbulence. The chopper had barely lifted off, with the two girls running forward waving wildly, when divers and soldiers turned back to camp.

I looked around at the parched land. Nettom was just rising, less than half full but amber while traversing Nettki's domain. The girls and I walked left. "I suspect this is the beginning of a marvelous friendship," I intoned grandly and they grinned, accepting the warmth of Softcheeks wide-flung chi if not understanding the sentiment.

PART FOUR

Four are sacrificed and two are rescued
Two more barely born.
Harmony gained by fecund women
Warriors in service, the fabric whole
In kari, Dolvia populates the future.

Karisma, last son of Dacupitte
Weaned on Dulcinea's milk
Will grow fat and lazy
Unless put to play with Karlyhi's sons
Teaching him to play, anon, leaders are grown.

THIRTEEN

from Herschel Henry

IT WAS A NIGHT OF HALF-MOONS, SO THE SHADOWS WERE BROWN. The transport chopper approached the illuminated pad in the Consortium barracks yard in Cylay. General Sector's girls were asleep, and the baby was cradled in the arms of Dulcinea.

The engine noise comforts them, I was thinking, after the excitement of the wedding day. I found it unusual to travel with so many kids, but I was glad to hitch this ride and leave behind the dry dunes of Chrysalis.

The chopper sat down with a crunch, and the kids woke with blurry eyes. Millie tumbled out first and took the newborn from Dulcinea's arms.

After she released the shoulder strap, Hakulupe Le turned to me. "We have a curfew in Cylay, Blancom. You will stay the night. With so many from the tribes staying in the city to witness, um, certain changes, we are doubling up for sleeping arrangements. I hope you don't mind."

Several people waited on the ground for our group to disembark. The officers brought messages for General Sector while soldiers managed our freight. Their footsteps made crunching noises on the dry grass. Millie and Anna walked away with Dulcinea. Lupe led me past the unloading, across the yard, and along a wooden porch to a single room, one of many. Before I entered, I looked down the way where Millie was just coming out of another room, maybe where Dulcinea had settled in with Karisma.

The assigned room was stuffy and smelled of kari root.

"Kelly and her mother were staying in here," Hakulupe Le explained as she picked up some clothes left by the former occupant. "I'm afraid we didn't stow her personal items."

"I just need a pillow and some quiet." It was a fitting punishment, I was thinking, that I should have to sleep on Kelly's cot.

Lupe grinned, flashing those arresting green eyes. "Would you come to the suite when you're settled? The general has something you should see."

I dropped my pack on the bed. "We can go now."

We passed Millie carrying fresh linens toward Dulcinea's room. We entered a larger suite of three rooms, standard in most garrisons. A kitchen and eating area were behind the front room, and a place to sleep was separate.

The general and two men were bent over an old-style DVD player and turning over the cartridge to insert into a slot. General Sector shook my hand, an unusual gesture among them, but they saw me as Softcheeks and a civilian. "Henry, glad you're back. How was the hunting for rock lizard?"

"Rufus and Karlyhi were enthralled with the laser scanner." I handed him a memory stick that Rufus had entrusted to me. "He said you may like this, although too much data for easy compilation."

"The EAMs are too public for this data storage," the general said. "It's a problem we'll need to resolve."

I glanced at the officers who referred to a manual and inserted plugs where the diagrams indicated. "The videotape player is your solution?"

Sector chuckled, his salt-and-pepper mustache moving over full lips. "Please meet my officers. Captain Mason Compavel from Cochin and Colonel Nick Shananinni from Cicero." They stood to shake hands as he spoke. "Nick is a cousin to General Shaw, in fact, although he tries not to trade on the name."

"Shananinni?" I asked. He had broad shoulders and a firm handshake.

"The practice to, um . . . refine our names for Company acceptance has been trashed. We use our real names now, and the Company be damned."

I turned to Compavel who wore his dark hair as long as regulation allowed. "That hair can be a liability in a fight with a warrior," I said.

He nodded, appraising me darkly, and turned back to his task.

"Once Cochin allowed Softcheeks colonists," Sector said, "at the same time as Somule. Did you know that? For a couple of seasons of netta. On the transports, long hair showed they weren't conscripts.

In cities along the coast of Cochin, any sailor has a long braid and any dockworker has, shall we say . . . windblown hair."

Compavel didn't even look up.

"So what do we have here?" I asked.

"We need your advice," the general said. "We have some old footage, but how do we add the images to a news segment? May we?"

He and I sat on some folding chairs gathered in a semicircle, and Hakulupe Le joined us. Captain Compavel struggled with the screen on a tripod, and then lowered the lights. Shananinni switched on the player and projector for a taped newsreel of a Consortium event from another season of om. In the flickering lights, I saw a Hardhand ambassador sitting with a transport officer, a lieutenant.

"That's Hamish Nordhagen," Lupe said. "He disembarked three times to work with the tribes. A good man."

The flickering images showed Ely as a young man, trim and muscled, with burning eyes and round-rimmed glasses. He sat across the table from the ambassador and flanked by two warriors with shields, who gave no room to the crowd of photo-journalists.

"That's Ely when he first became rabbenu," Lupe said in a dreamy tone. "He carried much honor in those days. That's the Putuki healer Quentin, now lost to us, and Cara who was companion to Cyrus. Look at those shields," she said with pleasure. "They make a good showing, huh?"

The suite door opened and closed. The officers turned tensely, a move that made me uneasy, but it was only Millie returning. Was all this a secret, and secret from whom? The edited footage continued; the same event viewed from more than one camera, a serious archival treasure for this Arrivi teacher to timely produce. On the tape the ambassador spoke to the camera, before young Ely demanded that uranium called sufferstone be left in the ground. The ambassador claimed that demand was impractical.

"Impractical for whom?" Ely asked, his focus piercing from where he sat between the tall warriors.

"While he is made ready to step down, Blancom," Lupe said, "Ely must receive honor for his former acts. He was not a usurper like Ananke, and not a butcher like Anaxagoras. We seek a peaceful transfer for an honorable leader who has lost his way."

On the DVD, the ambassador stood to leave and the event ended, but the camera focused on a crowd member, an older and blond Softcheeks who stood in the back. Journalists shook his hand with questions. "Who is that?" I asked.

"Brianna's father," Lupe said. "I had forgotten he was on the tape." We watched in rapt silence for a moment while Brian Miller refused to comment for the record.

"Well," Lupe said finally. "Something for your reporting. We know how much journalists value rare images."

"I can get this to the Press Club, or maybe to Doug Endicott in Cochin, if he's still there. But I'm not on staff anymore."

"Yes, well," the general said, "we were thinking . . . an independent reporter working for the best interest of the tribes. Maybe post reports to social media on the transport to avoid, um, lost ideas."

"Where's John Milan? Where's Regan Villines?"

"Milan's in Cochin trying to sell his skills. His video of the execution of Anaxagoras was rejected in all quarters. We were surprised he didn't petition to jump back. Villines was on Stargate Junction, but is expected in Cylay soon to report on regime change. We were hoping to, um, set you on a different path."

"It's all one package." I shrugged. "My work won't be aired on the Company comtechs unless I'm part of the press corps."

"General Hartley thinks he can enlist some self-styled newsmakers on Cicero who aren't part of the mainstream. For syn-di-ca-tion, is that the word? You can talk with him in the morning. You should know that tribespeople call him Hamilcar from the days of venom collection at the bush clinic."

"Chanted in the Cylay plaza," I said. "Death to Hamilcar."

Sector nodded absently. "Anyhow, Hartley thinks these news hounds may embrace the minority report to show they can out-maneuver the powers-that-be. The general says changeover events in Cylay should proceed slowly so people have time to digest, um, developments and find a new attitude."

Hakulupe Le made a snorting noise and looked away.

I wasn't sure about their family strife, so I kept my big mouth shut. I remembered there had been some tension after Michael Peter was afflicted with autism.

General Sector showed his best smile under the big mustache. "We want to establish a station across from the governor's house to broadcast events at all hours. To force the press corps to focus on the end of Ely's tenure."

"You've been chewing on this awhile," I said. "And you just now called me in from lizard hunting?"

The general glanced at his wife. "Residents here believe they have waited a long time. We will need an interim leader while free elections are organized."

Lupe inspected her cuticles on one hand, fairly pulsating with a different answer.

"We can provide a salary," Sector continued. "Your voice remains objective for talking to all sides, and you will have protection and special access to the players. What say you?"

"Do I have to live in the barracks?" I asked the general.

"The Consortium maintains several watch stations in the city, like police stations, except we don't hold detainees there. One is located on the same street as your studio, and soldiers have orders for protection. You will appear independent, living among the people. You can take the DVD player too."

"You have thought of everything."

"Just be warned. Emotions run high among the unblessed ones. With the change-over mob rule is a real possibility. There has been some, um, retribution already and several kidnappings for revenge. What needs have we neglected? You have EAM codes and—"

"I'm all set for now, assuming my gear is still intact. Who did you talk to in the press corps?" The officers were dismantling the DVD equipment, and Compavel handed me the cassette.

"The one guy, uh, Paul Spurlin," Sector said. "That's his name? He seems balanced, but says his hands are tied for providing equal time on the news."

The captain placed the DVD player in its carrier on the table. "Melinga," he said to Lupe before they left.

General Sector glanced at the closing door before he leaned forward confidentially. "You need a cover story for where you were during this cycle of Nettom. Don't mention the butterfly pool. We cannot say you were lizard hunting, either. That's too close to killing gualareps, which is a real sore spot here. We can't say you were with Aensilus and the Madquii because reporters will want a story on that, a follow-up to the execution. Say that you had malaria and stayed with the Uburu. That's neutral, and nobody challenges Dulcinea. You're certainly gaunt enough for it. But don't give too much detail."

I stared at him, sucking my teeth. "I suppose warriors are assigned to shadow me?"

"Not so you'd see them on camera. Siize and Siiloba are sacrificed, sadly, and were too recognizable. We have a couple Cylahi in place since they blend easily with unblessed ones. Unless there's someone you prefer?"

"No harm can come to my neighbors, Genki and Blanc and the others."

General Sector thought about that for a moment. "We cannot move them out; that's too obvious. Our Cylahi men can warn them on the quiet, but residents are free to choose."

We talked around and around about winners and losers, while Lupe went to check on the sleeping kids before she turned in. Putuki bazaari in Cylay were under pressure, and kidnappings were targeted on them. Some disappearances had ended with a mutilated body rather than ransom. I wondered about Voki Manuki with his four remaining daughters, but I had no power to ease his situation.

General Sector seemed to think the next rabbenu would be Orin rabbe Murd, although several candidates were mentioned as favorite sons.

"Not Brianna Miller?" I said.

Sector blinked three times in surprise.

"You are allowing the women to vote in free elections?" I added.

"These are not my decisions to make," the general hedged. "But, um, a woman governor with surrounding tribes that allow their women nothing is, um, awkward. Could she command the militia?"

"Ha! My money's on Brianna Miller. She's the equal to Karlyhi, and she gets her way with everything."

He nodded, suppressing a yawn. "Brianna speaks well of Orin rabbe Murd, maybe bringing him along for this post while she pursues, um, other interests."

Our talk had run down. I realized we were the only two left in the room, a generous gift of the general's time. "You were assigned a place to sleep tonight?" he asked.

I said my melingas and wandered down the platform to my space. Nettom showed the fat side of a half-moon as though his belly was exposed, while all corners of the barracks were shadowed in brown and tan.

During the wee hours, I sat at Kelly's writing table and jotted a few impressions. I wanted to develop a background segment about the history of Rabbenu Ely's time as governor, using the archival footage, so I was prepared when I spoke with Spurlin and with General Hartley. I thought about my photo archive and noted that I should search for the images of Brianna Miller when she had emerged from the killing fields at the massacred village. I also thought about my photos of Kyros Kenoma and Dulcinea together. They would be players in this passion play. It felt righteous to exercise my writing skills again, like I was in my correct place.

I stretched, ready for sleep, and stepped out onto the long porch to light a kari root stem. The barracks yard was sparse with clumps of razor grass maintained along the clapboard buildings. I raised a match to strike it, but paused at the sound of voices. I stepped back into the shadows. A man and a woman whispered, and her voice was peppered with Softcheeks accents.

"Don't do this again, Eugene," Brianna said. "I won't come to you."

Eugene Hartley? Sector had said I could talk to him in the morning, but I had not realized he meant in person.

"Just consider what I am saying here," Hartley said in a pleading voice. "You'd have a louder voice from the transport."

"That's your pipe dream. You cannot save me from myself."

"Come away with me," he said. "You can serve like Mrs. Shaw from Cicero. Her voice has volume."

"You want me to be more like her?"

There was a pause followed by their quiet laughter. I suspected an embrace was involved. "My body is an empty cavern after the pregnancy," she whispered. "How can you want me now?"

"Just come to the transport. I can protect you there."

"You think I would desert them when so much is—"

"For me."

Another lengthy pause, so I turned to go inside.

"I'm sorry, Eugene," she choked. "I don't feel the same as before."

He sighed heavily. "I can make you."

"But you won't. That would empty my soul as much as my body suffers now."

"It doesn't have to be—"

She caught her breath, and I heard slurping sounds. Hard to break away, was it?

Brianna came around the side of the yard. I put my back against the wall, but caught a glimpse of her face as tears clung to her cheeks. The odor of kari root smoke told me the general lingered. I ducked inside, unwilling to expose my eavesdropping.

I woke to the smell of food, so I hurried through a morning routine. I strode down the wooden platform and saw Millie peeking from the screen door of her father's suite at the end. She motioned I should come to her, and I entered. The family sat at breakfast with General Hartley as their guest, looking fresh as a daisy. His body clock was tuned to a different rhythm, though, so he could be in the middle of his day.

"Join us," General Sector said.

Both generals were in uniforms and sipped tea from big mugs. As soon as I was seated, Hakulupe Le placed a heaping plate of breakfast in front of me.

"Are those real eggs?" I asked to be polite.

"He was briefed?" one general said to the other. Sector nodded.

"I have a few questions," I said between bites. "These independent reporters that Sector mentioned; why do they care about events on the savannah?"

"They don't," Sector said. "You have to make them care."

"The online audience," Hamilcar informed me, "is suddenly larger. People have turned to social networks and many have cellphones, although not on the savannah."

I talked between bites. "I can research the kidnappings—what factions, what frequency? But distributing printed news is time consuming. I cannot do both."

Hartley's brow wrinkled. "Hence the syndication."

"My reports should be part of a larger package so the user returns, a competing platform to Company-sanctioned news like a Cylay Gazette."

"The security exchange has a business page," Sector said, his mustache wet with tea. "I'm told Arrivi women log on daily to buy two shares of gum arabic."

I sat back, my stomach pleasantly full. Millie took the plate and refilled my tea mug. She wore the new style clothes, new to Cylay and the convent schools. "We can raise the volume of the minority report to Company news. We can strike a bell for home rule."

Hartley squinted. "We want a neutral voice. Balanced but informative."

"You'll get more traffic with the emotional appeal. Is there a writer who—"

"There's Kelly Osborn," General Sector said with humor in his voice. Millie giggled on the side, ever-present, and he winked at her.

"What about Mark?" I asked. "He seems to turn a phrase well. He knows all the players and speaks several dialects."

"His face on the Gazette in competition with those China-doll announcers?" Sector asked.

"As a ghost writer, then, or an archivist of chants."

"Women in Somule have idle hands, I'm told," General Hartley said. "Translating and reformatting could become a sideline for them."

General Sector sat back. "So, the birth of a newspaper. What funding?"

General Hartley considered the ceiling beams for a long moment, and I shrugged. "If the gazette is online," I said, "the only real cost is staff and equipment, at least for now. Printing could be later and with its own cost center. Is there a crusader for home rule who can put his name on the masthead?"

"Well, there's Kelly Osborn," Sector repeated.

"Aren't she and Rufus stuck in Chrysalis for a good long while?"

"Kelly's brother and cousins were Junction Boys," Hartley said, "so she has a natural connection. And the business news is already in place, just in need of expansion."

"So the money comes from where?" I asked.

The general was counting ceiling beams again. "I have a couple ideas," he said. "Just, um, go forward as though this issue of capital is resolved."

General Sector stood. "A good breakfast, Lupe. We should do this more often."

Hakulupe Le in the Arrivi gown and Millie dressed for school stood by the door, waiting for a ride. Anna hovered behind her mother's skirts, still too shy. The table was clear and the dishes were drying. I could get accustomed to being served so well.

I said my goodbyes there, tugging on Millie's braid to elicit a giggle. Later a lieutenant in a Consortium bobcat provided a ride to the Cylay apartment where I had been absent for several cycles of Nettom. The city streets were dry but not overheated. One Putuki business was blackened and empty from a Gora pipe bomb. Birds chattered from rooftops and fence posts, mostly parrots seeking a likely treat snatched from a garbage pile; whole flocks of healthy birds with flashes of red under the grey wings and a long tail, but scavengers at heart.

The debris was smelly and piled high, a result of Cylay's non-functioning municipal government. Since Ely wasn't running for office, he had no reason to make a show of pleasing the voters. The Consortium didn't do garbage pickup, and Karlyhi's militia groups certainly didn't. Some enterprising owner of trucks should open a new business. The despair and laziness of residents of Cylay seemed in opposition to the self-reliance I had seen on the savannah, as if they were from different cultures. I should write a byline about this social disgrace and the value of nascent capitalism.

When I got out, the bobcat pulled away spewing clumps of dried mud onto my trousers. I saw Genki standing in her accustomed doorway under the filthy burka. She performed the Arrivi greeting with palm held high and crossed to touch my shoulder. "Blancom, you're so thin. Were you tortured too?" she asked in Arrivi.

"Ah, no."

She nodded knowingly. "So, just starved in the Consortium prison?" The last she had seen, I rode away in a Consortium jeep with a couple of junior officers. These people needed a newspaper, one in print.

"I have been, um, sick with the malaria chills, but not in prison."

She nodded. "Some beans on a patty for you?" When I tried to object, she added, "For free. No charge for Blancom who was sick."

I couldn't refuse, so I waited until the beans were heated and the patty toasted. I saw a flash of something from the rooftop, maybe a glint of sunlight off the barrel of a weapon. I accepted the treat from her hand.

Genki watched closely, so I bit into the meal and chewed with big gestures as I nodded my thanks. I turned toward my entryway and glanced up to see another reflective flash. That must be my shadow, one of them. He needed to cake some mud on the karkar barrel.

In the corridor, well, the passage to my rooms, another man peered around a corner, rather like a dingo that sits out of sight and looks left, showing only his snout. My second shadow. So. . . Dingo and Flash. Somehow, I didn't feel safer.

The door to my rooms was ajar, and the blue macaw feathers were missing. I sighed and pushed the door open. The bed was made and the closet set right. The EAM coolant unit was dusted and a bowl of orchids rested on top, maybe a signal from my shadows. I unlocked a metal case that I kept for photo archives, and all seemed to be in order there too. I looked closely at the door, trying to determine how recently it had been abused.

I sat on the cot, but jerked up immediately when I heard the hiss of a snake. Its strike fell short. I grabbed a tripod leg and pinned the head, then used my beltknife for a more permanent solution. I searched thoroughly for a second intruder, including the ceiling. They seldom nested alone. No nest and no cohort, so a recent addition to my room. I looked over the body, sleek and well fed. Somebody's pet. What a fine welcome home gift, and the relative cleanliness meant to mislead. The snakeskin soon decorated my doorjamb along with the hose glide from Jessup Chandliss.

My next stop was the Press Club where all was in disarray. Several young reporters had just arrived on the shuttle and now filled the hotel lobby with their camera packs and duffel bags for clothes. Untanned, bright-eyed, smelling of shampoo and hand sanitizer . . . Ah, I remembered the days.

John Milan was in Cochin, so I didn't look for him. Regan Villines was traveling, or so I had been told. I made my way to Endicott's office that Spurlin occupied but found a different news dog there—a sweating, oily man whose cunning eyes told me he wasn't long for backward Dolvia.

"Hershel Henry," he said and shook hands. "Here to get your job back?"

"Is that an offer?"

"You saw the parcel of eager-beavers out there. What do you bring?"

I grinned. "Well, I speak the dialects for openers. And I can tolerate the climate."

He wiped his face with a big handkerchief that he forced into his trousers pocket.

I glanced around, noting the photo of this man with a Company executive named Wan Su. And he thought to hang that image on the wall?

"I'm Steny Morse and I served at New Shanghai, so don't get any ideas that I'm behind the eight ball here."

I nodded. "Earth idiom. Interesting."

He squinted. The sweat had reappeared on his face.

"In a few days," I added, "you'll sweat out the toxins from a Consortium diet. Stick to vegetables like okiioc and taro."

"Can you get an interview with Brianna Miller or Orin rabbe Murd?"

I shook my head no.

"What about this other one, uh, Simon Sumuki?"

"Never heard of him."

"Yeah, well. The Putuki won't gain seats in free elections. There's too much resentment. Can you get a quote from General Sector?"

"About the kidnappings?"

Morse stared sharply before his eyes were hooded. He didn't know about the kidnappings, I was thinking. "What do you want?" he asked.

"Looking for Paul Spurlin."

"I'm in that seat now. State your proposal."

I turned my mouth down, acting innocent. "Just the honorable goodbye."

Morse waved a hand dismissively. "He's cleaning out his locker. Don't linger overlong."

I found Spurlin in the locker room adjacent to the hotel pool. He was studiously inspecting each item before he dropped it into his pack on the bench. "Henry," he said, "you were told to move along too? When events spill over, the heavyweights move in to grab the glory. That's the Company way."

"Are you slated to jump back?" I asked.

He shrugged and brushed his hand over a pate of thinning hair. "On to Cicero. Tell me: what do you know about this man Otieno and his fleet of ships in space? How many? A network? How funded?"

I sat on the edge of the bench. "I have an idea that may interest you. Drop out of the system, independent agent, shoestring enterprise. We need an editor who can bring along writers and researchers. There's a salary. Not Company standards, but—"

"I couldn't jump back later."

I liked Paul's quick mind and knew he was our man. "Not through the Company, but others have those privileges."

"I need a guaranteed jump back number at tour's end and bonuses for investigations that produce results. And exclusive decisions for hiring staff."

I was grinning. "Done."

He squinted, probably thinking he had sold himself cheap. "And I want an interview with Brianna Miller."

"We can go there now," I said.

He zipped his gym bag, unbelieving. "Sure we can," he chortled.

On the way out, we requisitioned three handheld video cameras and a carton of memory chips, whatever we could grab. Spurlin eyed a lighting array for a reporter station, lanky and heavy, but I shook my head no. "We can buy one using treasure funds," I said.

He frowned. "The treasure of Rularim?"

I only chuckled and moved to guide him across the plaza.

We passed EAM cafes where women sat to log in and purchase two shares of gum arabic, some of them unveiled and sporting the mark of Rularim. I noticed many women had shed the burka—an interesting development. I recognized Len rabbe Murd, the trader on the upstart exchange, who watched us pass an outdoor café where he sipped tea from a big mug. We passed the shrine to Kyle Rula where the torchings had taken place, now gleaming under harsh sunlight.

Putuki protestors watched us with hungry eyes, milling about near a couple of stations like kiosks at the native bazaar. We paused as a jeep and two lorries passed our corner to enter the gates of the governor's mansion. The lorries were filled in the back with soldiers who looked Putuki and cradled karkars just alike. We approached the academy and I pulled on the cord, shooing away the female beggars who bared their arms from under ragged burkas, holding grimy and bony hands forward. Three kids huddled in the shade.

"Brianna Miller hangs out here?" Spurlin asked with sweat beading in his thinning hair. "This whole time? How did you get close to them?"

One academy resident glanced at my beltknife but allowed us to enter, while another distributed yesterday's bread from a shallow basket through the bars of the fence, drawing the beggars away from the gate. The kids quickly joined the begging women, gobbling the offered morsels and looking left and right as if someone would snatch the crusts from them.

"Hakulupe Le, please," I said. Her eyes wandered from me to Spurlin who was glancing around with wonder. Unimpressed with me, her hard face barely moving, she led the way into the school.

As we walked I answered Spurlin's main question. "To survive on the savannah, you must give yourself to it. There's no foot-in-each-world method. That was Milan's mistake, trying to be both."

The resident stopped at an administrative office and stood by the door. I peeked in and choose to knock lightly on the doorjamb. The room was filled with workstations and filing cabinets, with teaching modules in brightly colored covers lining the windowsills. It even smelled like a principal's office, dusty and over-sweet. Lupe handed a file to another and came forward with question in those green-green eyes.

"Hakulupe Le," I said, "I hope we're not intruding. The newspaper idea . . . I brought, um—"

Lupe touched the sleeve of the resident who still waited in the hall with us. "Thank you, Jenna Le, for your service." The hard-faced woman jerked her chin in a brief nod and left.

Hakulupe Le held a hand high with the palm turned up. "Without Edwina's gift of remote viewing," she said to Paul Spurlin, "we hardly know who will show up next. I'm Hakulupe Le."

Spurlin stared. "Four women burned themselves to spare you? You're the one?"

Lupe lowered those eyes, like turning off a camp light. "So goes the story. Blancom, why so rude?"

I realized that I was fidgeting, shifting my weight from foot to foot and shouldering cases for the cameras we had pilfered. I knew I had ruined the greeting, Spurlin's introduction to native protocol. "You wanted a permanent news station to watch the governor's mansion, but that's more than a one-man job. Spurlin's your news editor now."

She showed me a face of surprise before she turned to him. "You would sacrifice the right to jump back?"

"Ah, no," he hedged. "We'll start with a three-year contract."

"He means a full season of netta," I corrected for her benefit.

He squinted. "Is translating my phrases part of giving yourself to savannah?"

Hakulupe Le grinned and took his arm. "We'll just have some tea," she said drawing him into the busy room. I sighed, blowing the air from my nostrils. I followed them into the principal's office with extra bounce in my step.

I had done a good day's work today. This was a good day.

FOURTEEN

THE CYLAY GAZETTE BENEFITTED FROM THE STUBBORNNESS OF Rabbenu Ely. We had a daily front page story while he resisted tribal demands. We took over the masthead of the online financial news, adding our bylines and repeated images from the footage of Ely as a young leader. That story went viral and remained our most popular archived issue for a full cycle of Nettom. I immediately heard from Steny Morse, the news dog at the Press Club, about exclusive franchise and honing in on his territory—how dare I?

I asked him what was legal in Cylay and who was empowered to settle corporate law suits, and then I shrugged him off.

We established offices on the seventh floor of the municipal building, otherwise vacant, with big windows in the hall facing the plaza and the governor's house. We had just four rooms and several EAM stations, and desk phones attached to landlines, all gained through Paul Spurlin's requisitioning. I tried not to ask too many questions about his sources. We did a printed version of the gazette as a trial using the history of rabbenu and bios of leaders, thereby securing a welcome when we returned for quotes on new events. Steny Morse called again when our second printed issue was distributed, complaining that I had an extensive interview with General Hartley who had always refused his reporters. I mentioned the Company's shabby treatment of John Milan and how Hartley didn't want to be responsible for the sacking of another veteran reporter.

"You know you sacrificed the right to jump back," Morse sneered.

"News from Perth or Paris or New York City no longer interests me."

He hung up with a slam. The Press Club was located across the plaza, but this news dog chose the landline for his tirades, like he was sitting at his news desk reading the gazette and couldn't resist a call to my news desk.

The following day a comtech interview with Rabbenu Ely, carefully staged in an opulent mansion room, refuted each of General Hartley's ideas from our interview. Responding to scripted questions, Ely asserted the strength of the stock exchange, the ended conflict with the Borabean, foreign funds for Consortium troops, and the minister system for collecting taxes—all benefits gained during Ely's rule. I watched the segment several times, since Ely had made no public appearances. I was tempted to call Steny Morse at his news desk, a return of professional courtesy, but never got around to it.

We had a barrage of landline calls and EAM messages, followed by visits from Arrivi leaders who competed for the opportunity to answer Ely's claims. Kyros Kenoma towered over my desk claiming, "These advances are in spite of Ely's rule, from the leadership of Karlyhi and Dacupitte." I sat down for a taped interview with Kyros who I knew from our time spent at Chrysalis.

The controversy lasted several days, and online traffic for the gazette jumped markedly. Spurlin solicited op-ed pieces from Kyros and Orin rabbe Murd, and fresh chants from Mark and Kelly, both still stationed at Chrysalis.

Spurlin established the print version of our gazette in Cylay with runners tied to the kam-man system. Always in negotiations with Hakulupe Le, he soon had a printing press in a warehouse building on the flats of Arim, and secured two sigpywa for distribution of the printed weeklies. That was a sight for a misty morning on the flats; the loaded armor-plated centipedes lumbering toward Somule or Mayschool, guided by their Arrivi handlers.

For a cycle or so, we printed four versions of the same paper, one in each dialect. Since it was four pages only, with the financial news inserted as a slick flyer, this was no trouble for typesetters— one woman from each tribe who checked the translations while she did setup. Spurlin rode roughshod over their habits for coming to work when farm chores were done and the natural secretiveness that Arrivi women harbored.

Spurlin redesigned the pages so a story ran in three dialects in the same printing, rather like a Rosetta stone, dropping Cylahi because he claimed the ones from that tribe who could read cared little about the news and mostly read Arrivi anyhow. His proof was that no chants were printed in Cylahi and nobody seemed to complain.

I tried to insist the printed issues should include Borabean, or maybe a shorter version in that dialect only, but Spurlin saw no profit there. "Get me a couple of stringers in Urbyd," he said, "who have real access to Ananke or Aristides, and we'll jump on it." He knew I couldn't be in all places at one time.

We solicited ideas for stories from everywhere, but especially from Putuki businessmen who still ran the Cylay bazaar. Simon Sumuki was a frequent contributor, and Hakulupe Le mentioned that he was related to Martin Sumuki, her favorite figure from two generations ago, so we ran a history of that man and the human interest story about the growth of Somule after the Company left with the failure of uranium mining. Hakulupe Le refused a bio of her or direct quotes, although we often quoted General Sector's words. Lupe held many influences in secret and, I suspected, had the typesetters report to her so she could delete possible mention of those tribal secrets she held dear.

That was the easy part. Working in Cylay, I had six stringers who visited my four-room space with man-on-the-street quotes and daily updates of the burgeoning stock exchange. One worker was lazy and only brought in the police blotter news, which I suspected he collected while he was running a kam lottery at the stations. One reporter was a radical and submitted articles studded with inflamed rhetoric from the Putuki about how the tribes had cheated them and Brianna Miller was a witch who could fly over the savannah on murmurey wings. I was afraid to let him go, however, worried that he would soon be writing pamphlets and chapbooks with the same claptrap.

Regan Villines dropped by twice, once for congratulations and one more time seeking confirmation on a story about the deaths from the vaccine poison. Did I have more details?

"You're a little late on that story," I said. "The kids are all dead, and Dr. Richardson was reassigned."

She blinked, and I could fairly see the gears turning in her head for how much she wanted to share. "Richardson's at Urbyd," she said, "and we heard complaints from the souks who were his patients. Not sexual abuse, but his attitude and treatments that don't work. The hospital there is a pit, with poor hygiene and the nurses quitting all the time."

"So you want background on Richardson?"

She rubbed her chin. I began to suspect she was fishing for a job offer. Her name wasn't on my short list, though.

"There's a protest group in Urbyd called the daughters of Deborah," she said, "that has lodged many complaints. Apparently, this group is like a Sisters of Mercy who help the dying."

"I have heard of them."

"Well, Aristides arrested a leader called, um . . ." She glanced at her notes. "Called Imogene. She's Uburu and never married, so there's no outcry from the tribes of the savannah. But it's all connected, right?"

"The daughters of Deborah are—how is it said?—without cover from the tribes."

"But the real story is about Richardson," Regan insisted quickly. "The protesters lodged complaints about his efficiency as a doctor." She waited two beats, but I had nothing more to add. "The Company wants to keep this story under wraps."

She looked around our cramped space, already dusty and stacked with files. "I'm just saying here: if we can link Richardson to medical malpractice in Cylay, that's a pattern, making my story a public health issue. Ely has to respond to a public health issue, surely."

I laughed out loud. "You mean like garbage pickup?" I jotted a note on my desk blotter to complete my byline story about nascent capitalism. "Steny Morse will kill your story on Richardson, sure enough."

Regan shot me a dark look and ripped three pages from her notebook. "This information is confirmed, but I won't get far with publishing it. And don't mention my name." She smiled sadly and turned toward the door. "Housekeeping doesn't cost that much, you know," she added over her shoulder. "Get a Putuki woman in service here."

One Putuki reporter named George Luluki offered business news from the local bazaar and from the trading stations along the Iamida river. He asked about advertising and could he mention new shipments of bolts of silks from Striiduc or canned delicacies from Ninleau? We set ad rates and the paper blossomed to eight pages seemingly overnight. I moved George to sales and provided a staff of three. He also edited the financial news we gained from Len rabbe Murd. The two became great friends and often took lunch together.

That was when I heard from Doug Endicott by EAM. He was in Ninleau, running an operation similar to mine except funded by the cellphone corporation there and with a flashy broadcast station for comtech news segments.

"So, you got the gazette up on its legs, huh?" he said on the EAM80 screen.

I saw the retro-neon lights behind him that showed so well when he served as anchorman to the six o'clock news. I swallowed to manage my jealousy, tasting marjoram. I chose to consider Endicott a colleague more than a competitor.

"Any new cases of influenza there in Cochin?" I asked.

Endicott's eyes were red-rimmed and world-weary under the buzzcut. "The Oloo don't import conscript labor."

"It was never shown the conscripts were the source of the influenza."

"Except it followed them."

"From the Company freighters. Conscripts were victims."

"Never lost your sense of righteous indignation, huh, Henry? Well, you'll burn out soon enough. I give you one year; eighteen months on the outside."

"What is a year?" I shrugged. "Besides, you said something similar about my living in that Cylay neighborhood."

Endicott laughed, healthy and rosy and probably a private drinker. "And I was right, wasn't I? Don't be a stranger, Henry. A courtesy call before a big story goes online, and I'll do the same. Endicott endit."

He was right about the burnout, though. We all wore several hats, although George Luluki didn't get the Earth phrase when I said that. Eighteen-hour days were telling after a time. I closed my apartment in the Cylay neighborhood, a deathtrap for snakes anyhow, waving goodbye to Genki who just stared as we drove away. I moved into the back room of the office where the ventilation was cut off each night. I had extra electricity installed for the EAM coolant units and a personal fan, and I paid for a shower installation in the communal bathroom down the hall. Soon enough, my reporters and Len rabbe Murd had lockers there, and we just moved in. I rented the extra office spaces along the corridor complete with a 'Press Club' sign over one door, for napping and drinking. I did get a Putuki woman to visit each day; otherwise, the shower area would have been too grim to face.

We anticipated that Rabbenu Ely would leave the mansion in the middle of the night and with considerable luggage, so we established camera outposts at the shuttle launch pad and at our offices that overlooked the plaza. We just set up at the end of the corridor, with long distance lenses on a stationary camera focused on the mansion gates and a cubicle wall for the equipment. Kyros had stationed Siibabean guards there, although they were mostly new warriors who'd taken the detail as punishment for some infraction. I replaced them with Dingo and Flash, the Cylahi who General Sector had assigned to me and who couldn't manage to hide from a toddler. Len and George soon had those two running errands and delivering messages. I paid their wages, and they were always loitering in our press club.

Funding came from the transport that orbited Dolvia: infrequent packets that were mostly peridot or slender gold discs with Striiduc words stamped on them, as well as quarter-kilo bundles of gum arabic, like pirate treasure. There was even an old instrument, a three-pipe flute in an acrylic pouch. I blew into one of the pipes, but only caused a shrieking noise. I put the flute on a shelf in the press club. Maybe another person knew how to make it work.

Paper money with Ely's image was sometimes included in the package, but only for payments for local equipment. The paper money was so devalued that the bulk needed to meet expenses was not practical, and employees didn't want it for wages. We supplemented that capital with income from ads and a regular bonus for printing the financial page, and from Spurlin's other interests that I tried with all my heart to ignore. I knew a newspaperman must be sanguine, accepting of the many sources for news, but I resisted complicity.

Spurlin secured a secondhand bobcat, like a dune buggy with reinforced roll bars. Working in the back alley, he mounted a stiletto tripod in the bobcat so a camera could be raised above the heads of protesters. He used a laptop while seated in the bobcat to rotate the camera and focus on the faces or placards carried in the crowd, as the Putuki shouted hatred for Hamilcar and the sor'shum and burned an endless supply of Consortium blue tams.

Protestors soon figured out the use of the bobcat and watched for its arrival. They didn't bother to raise their voices in the plaza until they saw Spurlin coming their way. They played to the camera, looking outraged, and they gathered in a tight group that filled the lens space. Occasionally, they burned a Consortium flag they had scrounged, the powder blue backward C tangent to a P on a dark blue background, as if loyalty to that flag was a sticking point for Arrivi.

Across from that entrenched group a different set of protestors gathered, mostly Arrivi women, but reinforced by Cylahi and Putuki beggars who they daily fed. The brutish street gangs seemed to provide security in exchange for food, easily facing off the Putuki protestors camped across the plaza. The female protestors displayed placards with a grainy image of Brianna Miller, younger and with her long hair coiled in traditional fashion, maybe enlarged from a bad photo. When I saw those placards, I was certain Brianna had her eye on the governor's mansion as its next resident. The women who sported the forehead mark chanted "Arisen Rularim" in competition with Putuki chants of "death to the sor'shum." Stacks of political pamphlets and chapbooks of chants were on display along with printed copies of our gazette. I even saw Genki among them, serving at the food tables and approached often by the feral kids. She had sacrificed her prime doorway spot for solidarity with home rule.

At the office while I edited some footage taken from the bobcat camera, Len rabbe Murd watched over my shoulder. "Why don't protestors burn the Company logo with the panda?"

Dingo spoke up immediately. "Hamilcar is to blame for the order of impunity and for the vaccine that kills Cylahi. Why are sor'shum officers free, when trusting Cylahi kids all died? Hamilcar protects his own." It was the longest piece of conversation I ever heard from Dingo.

I glanced up at Len. "A better question is why do they use that image of Brianna Miller when I posted so many that are in focus?"

"She's wearing native earbobs there, more traditional," Len said. "Besides, they used their own sources, not the EAM."

I developed relations with leaders and other strong voices for defining the political narrative for the tribes. I talked often with Mrs. Shaw who complained about recruiting through the wormhole. "Softcheeks applicants resist learning several languages," she said. "The scientists who just disembarked don't even have medical degrees."

"New diseases in the forest, are there?" I asked.

Her image came over the EAM80 from her research station in Two Forks that was her kitchen with Martina washing dishes in the background. "I sent Ali Abrar Ebnli to Urbyd for a rotation with Dr. Richardson," Mrs. Shaw said. "What a disaster. He was just coming out with Dr. Gutierrez; you know, expressing his preferences. But Richardson wanted to play. Old games, like with Hartley's son. Too liberal for a repressed Saudi, I guess." She rolled her eyes. "Why can't they just focus on the problem at hand?"

"What did the new guy say about conditions at the hospital in Urbyd?"

"They get cases of mutilation from sectarian violence, even kids. Pipe bombings are a weekly occurrence. And now they have the bird flu." She shook her head. "Too busy with killing each other to clean the apiary, I guess. Bird flu will spread from that fishing village where the Goras are crowded together and cover the whole savannah. Mark my words."

"Is Richardson taking precautions?"

"Ha! What a waste of skin, that one." Her image blurred as she moved suddenly. "Brianna was correct on that point. We have no friends in Urbyd. Better to find a trade route through the forest."

I sat back when she ended the call, wondering how she was so astute about Cylay politics from her station on Cicero. She was the wife of General Shaw, so there was that.

We spent the season of kari mostly concerned about increased pipe bombings in Urbyd and a few in Cylay. Where were the Gora leaders and why didn't they take defeat gracefully? I was pondering the question of armed resistance one day when Kyros Kenoma entered the Gazette offices accompanied by Akana of Urbyd. Kyros wore a double-breasted blue suit that covered his increasing girth. Akana wore a finely made galabia under his silk kaffiyeh. I stood quickly, nearly knocking over my chair, feeling blue-collar in my worn khakis limp with sweat, and reached to shake hands with the Abydian son of Ananke. Maybe it was Kyros's suit that prompted the Softcheeks gesture. Akana looked at my hand before he stretched his arm to reciprocate.

The siege of Urbyd by Goras had ended while I was at Chrysalis. The Royal Square at the Urbyd palace where I had attended Akana's wedding was repaired. Only the daughters of Deborah remained as protestors there. The local bazaar was thriving again.

Akana's crafty eyes glanced at the pile of work on my desk and around at my employees. Kyros spoke quickly to fill the awkward moment. "Akana is considering a gazette for Urbyd to circulate stock market news and health warnings. He's wondering about the cost."

"There's a certain start-up investment, to be sure, mostly for the printing press. Have you been out to the flats of Arim where we do typesetting?"

Behind Akana's shoulder, Kyros made a face at me.

Dumb question, I was thinking.

"So many people," Akana said. "How do you keep them busy?"

"I wish we had more qualified people," I said. "Four dialects are used in Cylay, you know, so clear communication was our first hurdle."

"And you employ the women?"

"Yes, at all levels." A tone of pride had invaded my voice.

"But not as reporters?"

"We print editorials from Kelly Osborn and Mrs. Shaw. The streets of Cylay are too dangerous to send a woman reporter with a cameraman. Perhaps if the Gora were—"

His look was sharp and cold. Here was a man who knew his authority, maybe a protégé of Aristides. I knew little about him except that Akana was married and spoke against the use of stri-isnia that had diminished his father. The ten sons were like parts of one son. Apetu was the oldest, but none had distinguished himself in business or the military. None had evicted Ananke's favorite circus performers from the palace, for example.

George Luluki came forward eagerly and shook hands with the Abydian. Akana looked at his own palm for a moment. I was impressed that George towered over the other two men. His bald head often reflected the overhead lights when he sat at his desk; I had noted that before, but not his size.

Akana chatted briefly about George's duties and how well the gazette was received by Arrivi. Where did the stock market quotes originate and verified by what method? Technical stuff.

Kyros stepped to my side as the other two talked shop.

"Did Akana also visit Rabbenu Ely?" I asked him.

Kyros shook his head no. "He wants no photo op either. No interview. Opaque about his purpose here."

"Did you take him out on the savannah?"

Again he slightly shook his head no. "Just the day trip to Cylay."

"What's going on?"

"When I find out, I'll let you know."

We shook hands again before they left together. Akana was getting comfortable with that gesture. Welcome anytime: please alert us to developing news in Urbyd. As Akana and Kyros walked to the elevator, George joined me with a big shrug.

"How do you know Akana?" I asked.

"As a kid I traveled with my uncle to Cochin sometimes. Akana was with Aristides as part of the treaty to end dhimma with Khalif Olpul, some seasons ago." He crossed his arms and hunched his shoulders as though he felt too big for the space. "You know that Olpul was rigveda over all the city-states?" he asked. "Before Otieno moved operations to Stargate Junction."

"You'll have to tell me the story one night over a bottle of Kiam gin. Just now, I have deadlines."

George took the cue and went back to the staff room.

Over the passing weeks, there were some odd developments. One unveiled Cylahi woman burned her ely certificate in the plaza gathering a crowd who maybe sought to witness another immolation, but no police bothered to arrest her for the double violation. Veils were soon discarded by all but beggars and married Arrivi women. The kidnappings increased, often ending in mutilation of Putuki captives who were cronies of Ely, but the police didn't pursue the culprits. Retribution and lawlessness were twins, while fear of the street gangs full of boys with rust-colored hair reinforced the curfew.

The news came to us that Jessup Chandliss had found a strain of emeralds under the dunes at Chrysalis, not enough to spark a mining rush but big enough to start chatter about his jump back number. I contacted him via Kelly's EAM codes. An image of his tanned face loomed on the EAM80 screen. "Got time for prospecting, do you?" I said.

"Better than sitting on my hands waiting for Ely to make a move."

"I bet you miss lizard flank for dinner."

"Won't miss it when I jump back with Striiduc gold discs jingling in my pockets."

"Your find, your profits?" I asked.

His image squinted. "Off the record, right? Brianna Miller says I was working on her dime, so the treasure is hers. I should get the same cut as for bushels of clearstone."

"You mean the silicide? And you're going along with that?"

Chandliss grinned easily over the EAM. "We were tunneling under the barracks to provide an escape route for soldiers. We were several days digging past the aquifer passages, and Marna Le's clutch had not noticed the colored wall, like buckshot peppering the rough sandstone. A pouchful of emeralds, no more. Rufus claims that emeralds are found all over the savannah, provided by Dolvia when the need is there."

"So . . . he thinks the emeralds are his to build community?"

Jessup's image shook its head no. "He says Mekucoo need only the land. It's Brianna Miller I must negotiate with, and none other."

"Well, stop by on your way out of town. We can share a bottle of Kiam gin."

"Just don't assume that I'm buying. Chandliss endit."

That same week, I covered several street-level stories, but the one I remember as indicative was the warehouse kidnapping. Karlyhi's militia still ruled in Somule and Mayschool, his authority reaching to Beecham Place even. We had heard that Karlyhi tended to be heavy handed with kidnappers who were often betrayed by their neighbors. He simply stormed the location from his stinger and killed everybody. The hostage was probably a criminal anyhow, was his reasoning. Welfare ministers lodged a complaint about side-stepping the judicial system, but Karlyhi had the backing of the Mekucoo and Siibabean and pretty much did whatever he wanted.

So in this one situation in Cylay that I covered, a Cylahi man and his brothers held a Putuki police captain in an abandoned warehouse by the river. They had demanded ransom from the family, but the Putuki police acted on a tip and surrounded the ramshackle building with a squad of ten. The police stood pat and called on the Consortium to intervene. I found Captain Compavel near his men who had established a perimeter to hold back curious bystanders. He also had called in patrol boats, which now bobbed in the churned water of their own wakes, watching for an escape attempt using the river.

In the hot afternoon, Compavel stood with two police officers who I didn't know, and with Voki Manuki who had styled himself as a mediator for tribal tensions. Compavel saw me at the barricade and left his companions to walk my way.

"What's the plan? I asked.

"The police want to starve them out." Compavel shook his head, and I noticed his longish hair was caught in a thin tail below his blue tam. "Kidnappers could live for weeks on rats and river water and abuse the hostage the whole time. Meanwhile, street agitators will gather here demanding a rescue."

"What's the alternative?"

"One gang leader offered to burn the warehouse." He chuckled softly.

"Was it Stuben?"

"Ah, yes, actually. You know Stuben?"

I only shrugged.

"We trained the local police here. Did you know?" the captain said. "But they have no heart. Putuki were promoted for nepotism, and some for a taste to jostle starving women in the slums. The uniform means nothing to them: just a paycheck and access to Ely."

"Do you have sharpshooters?"

He moved his tongue over his gums and looked away.

"Off the record," I added.

Compavel's face pulled back in a tight smile. "Nothing we do here is off the record."

Voki Manuki joined us suddenly and without invitation, holding out a hand in supplication. "I know them. I can talk to them."

Compavel could barely contain his dislike of Manuki. For my benefit, in front of a reporter as it were, the captain said, "The kidnappers have no reason to surrender. They see no future."

I knew Voki Manuki from when he had visited my place in the slum asking for work for his daughters. Two had died from the flu or the vaccine for the flu. I wondered if the other daughters were farmed out as domestic servants on Cicero. I didn't ask him, though.

We lingered several hours in the heat. I was considering returning to my news desk and assigning this story to a stringer, when we were approached by Mark and Stuben. I performed the honorable greeting for Captain Compavel while Stuben gave me the reckless eyeball. Maybe Mark had told him about Chrysalis and how they ate lizard flank for dinner.

"What do you think, Henry?" Compavel said. "They want to go in, just the two of them."

I rubbed my chin with one hand while I considered the issue. Mark controlled his grin, and Stuben rolled his eyes. "The kidnappers are Cylahi," I said. "These two are Cylahi. Each tribe resolves its own issues."

Captain Compavel sighed shortly. "Go around by the water."

Mark nodded my way before they left, and Stuben frowned. What honor did I deserve, he was thinking. Forty minutes later, Mark and Stuben walked out of the building with the bruised and bleeding hostage between them. Amid the useless police, Voki Manuki rushed to help him while the rescuers joined Compavel and me.

"And the kidnappers?" the captain asked.

Stuben stood tall with his shoulders back. "They have robbed the desert of some."

The rescuers left, and I immediately said, "You should recruit Stuben and his gang as local police when Ely steps down."

Captain Compavel showed a face of surprise, but I could see that he was impressed.

I returned to the offices to find Paul Spurlin and George Luluki in a heated argument about relative guilt. George's cousin had lost an arm in a recent pipe bombing in the Cylay bazaar. His position was that the Goras must be punished; caught and brought to trial for each offense.

"All the tribes do kidnappings for ransom," Paul countered. "So many kidnappings that we don't barely report them anymore."

"Goras are different," George said. "They use terror tactics to weaken the economy and discourage offworld companies. No investment in education, in medical care, in roads. Goras build nothing; only destroy."

"The medical advances came from Mrs. Shaw," Paul said with a shrug. "Education was started by Hakulupe Le, with grants from Mrs. Shaw. And the roads are built by General Shaw with Consortium money."

"And Arrivi didn't murder either of them," George insisted. "Goras only feel strong when the other tribes are made weak."

I groaned and went to my private space in the back. The unventilated room smelled of dirty socks. I threw myself on the cot with a forearm over my eyes. I was snoring within two minutes.

FIFTEEN

THE WAITING SEEMED TO GO ON FOREVER. OUR DAILY NARRATIVE was about how Rabbenu Ely must step down, except no action was taken. People organized their lives around the idea that Ely's rule was ending and new commerce beginning, except Ely took credit for each advance. He remained entrenched in the Cylay mansion with a mostly Putuki guard.

Paul Spurlin oversaw responses to the unrest in the Cylay plaza and was out of the office most days until late afternoon. Residents in Cylay had more freedom now. Expressions of that liberation were everywhere, but especially among the women who discarded the burkas and chose to show some leg under brightly colored calf-length skirts. Spurlin took up with a Putuki woman who had two kids, while George Luluki sidestepped a claim of broken promises from her cousin.

I admit that I gave into temptation more than once to help a young woman discover more about her new feelings of liberation.

Even Captain Compavel had a native girl, a Cylahi who was related to Stuben. I didn't see that one coming. But . . . what do soldiers do when told to stand and wait?

I accompanied George Luluki to Urbyd to cover a conference with General Hartley about inland trade. The usual players were there and talked about the usual tensions without resolution. Hartley seemed more interested in spending the time with Brianna Miller. She made more than one inflammatory speech about what she saw in the future, even in the presence of Aristides. "The tribes should skip Urbyd," she said while friends and competitors kept their faces neutral, "and enter into maritime treaties called dhimmas directly with trading families in the Cochin cities of Ninleau and Utica. Arrivi have the erriv meat and trade goods. Arrivi have the market for gum arabic and precious gems. We are seeking new channels for trade."

Brianna Miller reasoned that the Arrivi tribes could develop paper money in competition with Striiduc gold discs and set the agenda for trade, instead of looking to Khalif Ananke and his ministers for justice. Aristides stood behind Brianna as she spoke, his face blank while his eyes looked inward.

Interestingly, Brianna Miller was not embraced by the daughters of Deborah who often protested in the plaza. Brianna had worked with Kenru in the Gora conflict but was not close to any of these women related to him. There was no photo-op with public embraces or calls for shared fundraising. The daughters saw Brianna as negotiating for the men, while the daughters of Deborah demanded domestic rights for mothers and widows.

Reporting on economic growth was George's wheelhouse anyhow. I was more of an investigative reporter, seeking outrages for inequality and new initiatives to build community. Growing bored with the posturing, I visited Agora, the fishing village packed with Gora survivors. On the other side of Urbyd than the busy port, the village clung to a rocky inlet below the cliffs of a deep fjord with a wicked rip tide. The fissure was the first of many ridges of a flysch that formed a barrier to the rolling hills of Striiduc. On a topographical map, the narrow ridges and deep gorges were south and west past the Madquii dunes, looking like claw marks left by some deep-water kraken.

The Gora men were absent each day, leaving early in three-man boats with the tide and returning with the incoming tide. Except when it rained, of course. Daily life was a struggle, especially during the rainy season when even the birds knew to migrate to the savannah. The Gora triskelion was displayed at many Agora shops, and Gora women worked on the docks for portage and fish packing. Guinea hens were kept in cages behind most wooden homes, and some women wore a chador or medical facemask against the bird flu contagion.

I stowed the camera in the misty day and walked to the end of the wharf where the air was fresher and young people gathered during a break in the work. One student was organizing her school notes, and the breeze caught the loose papers and blew them toward the water. She chased some pages but couldn't secure them all before three laid flat on the salty waves. I picked up two pages I had caught with my foot and returned them to her.

"Goshan," she said, their word for melinga.

"You could use a binder," I suggested.

She looked down at her bare feet and tattered skirt hem.

"What are you studying?" I asked to be polite.

She stared out to choppy sea before she grabbed a glance at my face. "I must know accounting to work in my mother's shop."

"In Agora?"

She ducked her head and turned a cold shoulder to me. "In the bazaar at Urbyd," she barely whispered.

"Gora workers are allowed there?"

"We pay the usury fee," she claimed with bitterness. "Putuki make us pay."

"Not the Abydian?"

"Abydian make Putuki pay."

I chuckled. "Come. I'll walk you home."

She followed easily but avoided my touch on her arm. Others glanced at us and whispered together. Goras were clannish that way.

"What does your mother sell in the Urbyd shop?" I asked to have something to say.

She kept her head down and shrugged one shoulder. "Jewelry and trinkets. Blue macaw feathers."

"I have bought those feathers before, but in Cylay."

She looked up eagerly, flashing green eyes with brown flecks in the irises. "You know Cylay? You have been there?"

"I live in Cylay and have a business there. I'm just visiting Urbyd with friends."

She looked around with jerky movements as if expecting an attack.

"They're in a meeting, my friends, in the palace."

She squinted suspiciously. I could not make out what she was thinking. "What is your name?" I asked.

"Anagella. You want to make the fickyfik?"

"I don't know what that is. I have to get back soon." I brushed my chin with one hand, feeling the two-day growth of beard.

She smirked and led me to a small home on a wooden platform with planks for walls. The front room was the kitchen and the back room was where everybody slept. Flattened cigarette cartons lined the planks. To block the draft, I was thinking.

I sat outside on the platform's porch area with my feet dangling toward the muddy hillside, as my new friend brewed tea that I was hoping was called fickyfik. Three more houses were in the row set back from the wharf foot traffic. An ancient woman was sitting like me on the end porch smoking kari root in a pipe. She ignored me. Maybe she was blind.

Anagella handed me a mug of tea. "I will wash myself for you," she whispered.

"Really, I have to be going." I sipped the tea to be polite. It was really delicious. "When do your parents get home?"

She entered the kitchen area, slipping two straps off her shoulder. "With the tide."

I caught up with George Luluki at the Rendezvous Bar across from the Urbyd palace. We both wore khaki slacks and pullovers, the preferred dress of field reporters. We carried our cameras and gear in shoulder packs. I gladly set the weighted pack on the bar. George's head and chin were shaved, giving him a turtle-head look.

"Where did you get off to?" George asked.

I grinned. "Just, um, investigating." The bartender brought our drinks. The gin fizz was not nearly as tasty as fickyfik tea.

"Richardson is here," George said, indicating a booth along the wall. "He's with Aeolis and Analli."

"Yeah?" I strained my neck to see them. "I know Aeolis. I interviewed him before."

Aeolis had gained a reputation of keeping the Gora remnant contained while he ruled over those villages tangent to Madquii lands.

"He went to the Urbyd school with my uncle," George said. "A real suck-up to the royal brothers, who used him for pranks. He made inroads with them by protecting Analli."

"Aeolis protected Analli?"

I looked their way again; two bearded men in desert garb with kaffiyehs, and Dr. Richardson in a cream-colored business suit. They were seated in a half-round booth with a quilted backing, the kind where everybody has to scoot left for the middle person to get out. A Softcheeks style considered elegant, no doubt.

"I'm scheduled to visit the hospital tomorrow," I added.

George wrinkled his nose and sniffed twice in my direction. "Are you sure you'll have the time?"

We carried our drinks and went to the booth for salutations. Dr. Richardson was on the end, so he stood for handshakes and slapped George's back. I thought Luluki might punch him, but he only grinned. Chairs were brought up, and a second round of drinks was ordered by Richardson.

"I'm to visit the hospital tomorrow," I mentioned to Richardson. "Maybe an article about ending the bird flu."

"Ah, I'm in the field tomorrow," Richardson lied. "We fly out with Kenru for nurse's training in the Uburu mesas."

"Just watch out for the flash floods in the gulches," Analli called. "Wash you away."

Analli was a soft man, appearing small next to the muscled and tanned Aeolis, who sat with both elbows on the table. Analli had a nervous tic, where he pulled on the edge of his kaffiyeh before he spoke, like signaling his turn.

"Flash floods?" I asked.

"Happens every rainy season." Analli laughed, pulling on the kaffiyeh edge. "Bright sunlight and some unsuspecting fool is trailing among the mesas. Doesn't realize the Iamida has overflowed her banks. A bore tide from the ocean can channel into a sudden wave, and he gets picked up and washed away."

Dr. Richardson smirked at him. "Tomorrow the chopper will rest on the mesa top. We're just spending the afternoon to demonstrate the hygiene packets." He turned to me, showing his palm. "Against the bird flu, in fact."

That was the thing about a good lie; it was close to real events.

"Should I show them?" Analli asked Aeolis, sitting behind his shoulder like a new wife. Aeolis looked back at him with disdain, a look that Analli misread. He leaned forward. "It's from Utica. You know Utica? A city-state directly across from Urbyd. Not a sister state, more a competitor." Analli placed a wooden box with an ornately inlaid top on the table, more than a foot long and eight inches high. It looked heavy. "You're going to love this."

He opened the box lid, which settled parallel to the padded interior, doubling the display area. With an eager look of anticipation, he rubbed a finger along one edge. The silicide etchings on the box walls seemed to glow and expand. What emerged was a battle scene that grew in stages along lines of blue silicide, as if the viewer watched an advancing force with warriors in leather, armed sigpywa, and trained birds of prey. Just when I was wondering who they ambushed, the moving display froze, filling the space on both box and lid, and maybe twenty centimeters high. Several figures were frozen in military action; the kind of image I associated with carvings in ivory, like you'd see in a museum.

George crossed his arms as though hugging himself. "That's all it does?"

Analli smirked at him.

I reached to touch the action figures. "It's silicide, right?"

Analli quickly tapped the box, and the image folded flat in the interior, like a pop-up book. "I saw many of these in Utica. A beautiful city of cadres, all aglow after dark, like they were decorated by the same builder."

Aeolis watched me with no expression, his elbows still on the table and his demeanor the opposite of Analli's need to please. He wanted Analli to shut up before he gave away their secrets, I was thinking.

I felt a draft when the saloon doors opened and five men entered. Four of them took up bodyguard positions, as Apetu stalked toward our table. George stood, so I did too. Dr. Richardson stood and Analli slid out of the booth. Aeolis remained seated with a sly smile.

I reached to shake Apetu's hand. "The talks finished early today?" I asked.

I knew him from Stargate Junction, where he was often invited to dinner at the table of General Hartley. A well-proportioned bearded man wearing a fine galabia and silk kaffiyeh, Apetu was shorter than George Luluki. I liked that George was the tallest of our group, an unreasonable response since he was only my employee.

"The khalif was asking for you," Apetu told Analli.

"Like he can tell when I'm gone," the youngest brother complained. "Which acrobat tattled on me?"

Standing between them, George crossed his arms and looked at the floor. Apetu nodded briskly at Aeolis before he turned on his heel and left. Analli trailed behind him and the four bodyguards also left.

"Well," George said to Dr. Richardson. "We should be going too. Big day tomorrow."

"Thanks for the drinks," I said to Richardson, shouldering my pack and nodding to Aeolis with a false grin.

We slipped outside into the moist night in a bigger rush than I wanted. Apetu and his personal guard were nowhere to be seen. We were around the corner before I spoke again, my legs pumping to keep up with George's long strides.

"What was that about?" I asked.

George grinned, and the tension seemed to flow away. We walked into a street of shops that were closed with many metal grates on the storefronts. The sidewalk bazaar stands were locked tight. I wondered which kiosk sold jewelry and blue macaw feathers.

"You know that Ananke has a resident circus at the palace?" George said. "He barely has time for Apetu, let alone the eight brothers in line ahead of Analli. I think that's why Analli acts out so much. Trying to gain some attention. Analli is Apetu's favorite whipping boy."

"And Aeolis?"

"Who knows? I don't see respect there either."

"Traveling companions to Utica apparently."

"That trick box?" George asked. "You can buy those at the Urbyd bazaar or at Stargate Junction, if you know the right people. A hidden commerce, though. Ananke embraces the Striiduc circus performers but hates hedge magic."

"Hedge magic? I thought that was banned from the Urbyd port."

"Utica is a city of wards. They use hedge magic in harvest festivals and the like. It was Otieno who spoke against allowing the talents. Ananke's dhimma with Otieno carries a restriction on hedge magic in the port, a condition of trading using Otieno's ships."

"He hates the talents that much?"

"Otieno blames serpent magic for the death of his second son."

I nodded absently, looking around. The street was deserted and the lights were low. "Which one of these shops is your uncle's?"

"Do you mean Simon Sumuki? I have several uncles who are bazaari," he said neutrally. "Simon has an interest in four shops here, I think. Four at my last count. The souks who run them are my cousins."

"Did you ever work in the shops?"

He squinted, as if wondering why I asked that. "It's women's work. At least Putuki keep our widows busy. Not like Kenru, who pushes them out to protest on the streets."

I glanced around but could not tell one closed kiosk from another. Oh, well.

In the afternoon of the next day, I was in Agora again. I skipped the hospital visit, since Dr. Richardson was not available for the interview. I found the small platform house, but it was unoccupied. I waited a short time, but the smoking crone down the way gave me a prurient look. I left gifts inside the door—some sugar and tea and a bundle of erriv meat. Anagella must be tired of eating fish every day. I also left some material for making a dress. My urge was to buy her a dress, but I didn't know her size and the gesture felt wrong somehow.

I returned to the conference that was winding down and hopped onto a chopper for the ride back to Cylay. General Hartley sat across from me. Brianna Miller had taken a different chopper to Ninleau to spread her message about bypassing Urbyd for trade. I didn't see George at the landing pad. Maybe he stayed to visit family in Urbyd.

That same workweek Hakulupe Le visited the Cylay Gazette offices, flanked by hard-faced Jenna Le and a Putuki girl who was about Millie's age. The two girls wore the new clothes style, while Lupe wore an Arrivi long skirt and a decorated burka as a shawl, along with well-made peridot jewelry. Paul Spurlin played host to her, disgruntled with me for not delivering the interview with Richardson. Len rabbe Murd honored Hakulupe Le with bows, and Dingo and Flash fairly fawned on her offering refreshments.

When all the greetings were accomplished, finally Lupe had a few moments for me. "Hiki, Blancom," she said. "You know Jenna Le already, I believe. May I present Bybiis, who is visiting from Stargate Junction where she works with Bernice Datong from Somule Gems?"

"Melinga," I said, wondering what trouble Lupe was cooking up today. "I heard about the emerald find at Chrysalis."

Lupe waved a dismissive hand. "Softcheeks are so easily impressed. Is there a place we can talk privately?"

We shared everything at the offices, needing to spread information quickly, often shouting over each other when facts were verified. Privacy was not a concern. I couldn't take her into the room where I slept, so we went to our press club, freshly cleaned by the Putuki maid, thankfully. Jenna Le stood at the door, while Hakulupe Le sat with me.

Bybiis took the lute from a shelf and removed it from the pouch, turning it over in her hands. "Where did you get this?"

I shrugged. "Ah, it came with a shipment of capital used to pay our bills."

"The jongleur's lute," Bybiis told Hakulupe Le, like that should mean something. "More valuable than a shard of Uwar that brings war and strife." She grinned and added, "From the old stories of origin of the tribes."

"I wonder what happened to the jongleur," Lupe asked.

"His graphite mimic must have stuck its tongue out at the wrong person." Bybiis joined us at the table. She placed the lute in its pouch next to my hand. "Keep this close, Blancom. Rare and valuable. It will bring you luck."

"Not so lucky for its former owner," I said.

Bybiis smiled briefly with sad eyes.

"We need your advice," Lupe said. "Show him."

Bybiis drew an old book from a leather satchel that she carried, maybe a rare book with thick binding and crinkled pages that had been wet at some point. She placed it on the table, like an artifact from another world.

"What do you see here?" Lupe asked.

"Is this a test?" I asked.

"Indulge me."

Bybiis only stared, so I picked up the book for inspection. "In Softcheeks libraries old books contained lead in the colored ink added for decoration. Monks would go insane from lead poisoning after following the script with a wet finger. This book was probably made in Cochin with eel skin for binding. The paper has a good weight."

I held the book high to look at a page under the lights. "Some kind of fiber or papyrus, I'm thinking, maybe an old skill lost to printers these days."

I looked at Lupe for confirmation, but she only gestured that I should continue. I splayed the book that was stiff and the binding seemed to creak. With it spread wide, I held up the butt end to examine the state of the glue. I caught a musky odor maybe from dried mold, underscored by something acrid like cat piss. My eyes watered, and I lowered the book, blinking several times and wiggling my nose against the odor.

"Nu delaya," Lupe said.

Bybiis snatched the book closed and inserted it into her satchel.

I was dizzy like from breathing toxic fumes, and I sat back resisting visions of flying women with long loose hair and a dragon on a distant cliff belching fire. "Wha' . . . what is this?" I managed to say while the back of my tongue swelled and I wavered in the seat.

I woke on the floor. Hakulupe Le was splashing water on my face. She pinched my arm and I pulled away. "I'm here," I said to avoid more punishment.

"Don't try to get up," she said.

"I'm good." I stifled a big yawn, and my vision cleared enough to see three faces, two wondering and one as hard as ever, staring down at me. I looked at my hands and flexed my fingers to gain a sense of my condition.

"Better?" Lupe asked.

I moved to rest on one elbow, not trusting my legs to get up. Jenna Le smirked and returned to her station by the door.

"You just love to play tricks on Softcheeks, huh?" I said.

Lupe looked at Bybiis and back to me. "Softcheeks, that's right. It's because you're Softcheeks. Can you get up now?"

"No more tricks." I looked hard at Bybiis. She helped me back to the chair, and I rubbed my face all over with one hand. I forced my eyes wider open and rolled my shoulders as I gulped air.

"You can nap soon," Lupe said, "but tell us what you saw."

"Witches flying in the air. A dragon on a cliff."

She nodded several times. "Good. That is good."

Bybiis spoke sharply. "The same as Bernice, maybe for any Softcheeks. This proves nothing."

Lupe raised her eyebrows. "But now she knows that we know." She focused on me with bright eyes. "What did you smell?"

"You knew the binding was toxic? And who is this phantom she?"

"The binding? Not the pages?"

"Old glue," I said with a shrug. "Dried musk, vanilla, and then cat piss."

Bybiis nodded in agreement.

Lupe asked quickly, "You didn't see fumes rise? A vapor maybe?"

"Maybe something green before the vision. What was it? A truth serum?" I was suddenly listless and sat back, squinting at the bright lights. I looked at the women looking at me, but didn't really care what they wanted.

"You should rest now," Lupe said. She and Jenna Le helped me to the couch while Bybiis stepped to take Jenna Le's place by the door. "You will have vivid dreams," Lupe murmured. "Tell me later about your dreams."

"I'll get you for this," I slurred. "I'll get you back."

And then all went blank.

SIXTEEN

I KNEW I WAS DREAMING; MY HEAD PUSHED LEFT AT A PAINFUL angle. I smelled burning grass, mixed with burning fur. Sunlight was blotted out by rolling smoke; the fire line's veneer consumed prairie grass moving my way. I was alone, with a shovel in hand. Got to save the goats! Here! Here is the place I cleared for you.

The billy came. Yah, sure, he came through the break I had forced in the fire line. Singed back, wisps of flames following his rush. Tackle and smother him on the crisp field. I saw raw flesh, blistered and red.

More goats made the jump, following the leader. Running toward the fire line, herd instinct was strongest. Two more, just two. Come on; stay with the group.

Juniper pops. Oh no. Dry wood, heated sap, crackling branches. It's bursting! Get away! Get away! Percussion and a heat wave . . . then I'm spitting out singed dirt. Through tears and tasting my blood, I saw the leap and felt the scream. Have you ever seen a leaping goat on fire? She ran ten feet, trailing flames as the others scattered. Da was sure to dock my wages.

A wall of flames; a looming face. Wavering thermals turn to blue water. What is this face in the water? Medusa? Water-seeker?

I woke when I rolled off the couch, aware that I had been snoring with my mouth open and dry. Angry voices sounded in the hallway, but they meant nothing to me. I had to reconstruct where I was and who I was, and establish that I had a body with two arms, two hands, two legs. I breathed in cool dusty air, my face too close to the floor. My knee throbbed from the impact of landing. I sat up, my back against the couch and my legs stretched out. They were my legs; move one up, move it down. Yah, my legs.

I heard more angry voices and a door slammed. At least they weren't robbing the place; they would have been quiet for that. Presently, I was at the sink and splashed water on my face, trying to sort out fading dream images of Da and brothers shouting and slamming doors. I felt stubble on my chin and realized I had been asleep for a good long while, but I didn't feel rested.

I saw the lute in its acrylic pouch, still on the table. I returned it to the shelf as a test of my balance and depth perception. Got that done. I wandered down the hall, glancing down from the big windows there. It was late at night, and the plaza was lit with torches where a few in the sleepy crowd milled aimlessly, like they had been waiting for too long.

I turned into the offices and found two generals at the EAM80 watching the same scene they could see through the corridor windows. Along the other wall sat two Putuki girls, one of them

Bybiis. I leaned away as if she would strike me, and walked wide of her to join the men.

"You're wobbly on your feet, there, Blancom," General Sector said. "You drunk?"

"Ask your wife," I muttered and sat in a chair. "No, wait. That sounded wrong." I discerned a noise in my back room with the cot. "Are you rifling through my stuff?"

General Hartley showed me appraising eyes. "We're just waiting."

I put my elbow on the desk and my chin in my palm. At least I no longer had to remember to breathe. "You spend more time in Cylay than on Stargate Junction," I said idly to General Hartley. "What's the errand today?"

The door to my room opened and closed as Paul Spurlin entered all businesslike and busy. I glimpsed Carl and Patrick, though, seated on my cot like they were mad at each other.

"Back in this world?" Spurlin asked while he went to the other EAM station.

"Ely released Carl," I guessed watching the general. "Care to make a statement?"

"Already captured," Spurlin said with his back to me. "My job keeps me busy. I don't need your job too."

I realized my chin was still in my palm, so I rolled my shoulders and sat up straight. "And I take it she's one of Ely's mistresses," I said to the general. "You're waiting for the shuttle launch time."

General Sector grinned under his mustache that showed some gray. "You're sharp, Blancom. My wife always said that about you. You're really sharp."

"I'm going with you."

"That's why we were waiting."

"Not likely. Some neutral place to park Carl who doesn't want to leave."

The generals exchanged glances. Spurlin spoke with his back still turned to me. "You could get cleaned up. Somebody may want to take your picture later."

Sector moved his head left. "Go on, we have some time here."

With a big yawn I left for a shower and shave.

It was barely dawn when Dingo showed his face at the office door, signaling that we should come. The two girls left first—the second one was named Khloe, as it turned out—followed by a subdued Carl Hartley and sullen Patrick Osborn. Spurlin waved shortly from his seat at the EAM, barely looking up, as I carried a camcorder in my camera bag and served as caboose to the traveling group. We took the freight elevator and were greeted in the alley by Colonel Shananinni who hustled us into the back of a lorry, one of Ely's. Two Putuki men, dressed as Ely's soldiers, took the seats closest to the tailgate. The colonel guided the two girls to a second lorry driven by a Putuki in uniform.

I spoke to Sector. "We're not going to the mansion?"

"We learned the art of disguise from Mike Shaw," General Sector said, "who got around on the savannah pretty good while the Company had a warrant out for his arrest. He was even known to travel under the burka."

"I bet that was a sight to see," I whispered to Patrick, who was seated next to me. He only frowned with his sullen face.

We turned a corner to approach the shuttle launch pad, and I noticed a smallish rocket situated piggyback on the upright shuttle that was already spewing fumes in readiness. "You're going directly to the Junction," I guessed. "The mail route."

"These Junction Boys need to catch the jump-back yacht," Hartley managed through clenched teeth.

"Both of them?"

Hartley fingered his neck and jawline. "I know it's only news to you, Blancom—"

"Better than what Karlyhi plans for us," Carl said, the only time he spoke.

He meant ritual death on the desert, I was thinking.

The lorry made an abrupt halt. The general looked out and I strained to see who was in the crowd at the quanza hut that served as a waiting area—families of travelers, maybe, and a couple of idle Softcheeks reporters. Several Consortium soldiers were present but apparently not on duty. I didn't see anyone I could identify as a protestor from the plaza. Daylight was coming up; the shuttle launch was soon.

"You first, Blancom," General Sector said. "Boot the camera station in the waiting area, like a dry run for when Ely makes an exit."

I stood and made my way past several sets of knees to the tailgate. "Yah, sure, boss. Shakin' it, boss."

When I jumped down, I banged into a bandy-legged pilot who showed his face to the generals, maybe the rocket pilot giving a readiness signal. He entered the waiting area with me and scurried to an employee-only door.

The small and overlit area was rather full, with a couple Bora-beans wearing kaffiyehs over their desert caftans, and students who waited with rich parents. I saw traveling businessmen with small cases and two Company men, accompanied by four Blackshirts with guns. This collection of travelers spoke volumes for how channels for offworld travel had lately constricted. The out-of-uniform Consortium soldiers seemed to gather themselves by the camera station that I unlocked and booted. They showed bored faces to the crowd, a show of force to discourage pipe bombs.

Two reporters who worked for Steny Morse—a man who was too fat for field reporting and a young woman with short hair and big teeth—positioned themselves to best focus on the Company men, as though the Han-Chinese travelers were the VIPs. I set my camcorder on the ledge. I had learned some time ago that a backup was essential to good reporting. I slowly panned the crowd using the stationary camera, thinking I might later want to show who was present at this launch.

The call for boarding came, and the students moved forward. They passed onto the tarmac, and the generals entered with Carl and Patrick. Colonel Shananinni was behind them with the two Putuki girls. Bybiis and Khloe fairly marched past the thinning crowd to the boarding chute where General Hartley flashed a Consortium badge, as though the attendant couldn't tell by his uniform who he was. The Softcheeks reporters turned their cameras toward the short discussion about the number of people in Hartley's party.

General Sector shifted his weight from foot to foot and glanced my way. I focused on a motion in the crowd; my move was more from training than from understanding.

Voki Manuki stepped forward, holding a karkar, his face twisted in anger and despair. "Death to Hamilcar!" Two flashes from his gun, and General Sector went down. Sector had shifted just in time to block the assassination of his superior.

People in the crowd ducked and crouched. The Blackshirts stepped in front of the Company men for defense.

"Death to the sor'shum!" shouted Manuki turning the gun on himself. The soldiers around me rushed forward to capture Manuki, but the karkar fired and his brains were splattered on the metal ceiling.

Colonel Shananinni and two more soldiers shielded General Hartley, pulling him away from the sight of his friend crumpled in a pool of blood, and rushed him through the boarding exit, followed by Carl and Patrick and the two girls.

I left the stationary camera that would capture the soldiers' activity around Sector, who I knew was already dead. I grabbed the camcorder and rushed to the exit, pushing my way past an attendant on his knees behind a desk. In the crisp morning air, I saw the general's group hesitate at the shuttle hatch, though the two girls were guided into the lighted interior. More passengers poured through the doorway, including the Company men and their Blackshirts, hurrying to make this most precious connection.

Colonel Shananinni held Carl by the shoulder, and the general closely watched the stream of passengers. He saw that I was making a record using the camcorder. He sighed shortly, his mouth in a deep frown. After my camcorder had captured their positions, the soldiers allowed Carl and Patrick to enter the shuttle hatch.

I approached the general. "Do you have a statement for me?"

"I'm staying," he pronounced.

"You cannot stay," Shananinni countered. "Protocol demands—"

"Sector was my friend! He was a better man than . . . than all these." He gestured widely. "The funeral, the transfer—"

"Hamilcar was the target," the colonel countered. "My duty dictates that you enter the shuttle and leave safely."

"Damn your duty, and damn protocol. Just once, I want to act for myself."

"Sir, the reporter is, um—"

General Hartley took a moment to compose himself, turning a cold shoulder to my camcorder. He stood at his full height and turned back, each muscle of his face becoming chiseled granite in the light from the shuttle opening. "We know General Sector's family and will think of them often over the coming days," he articulated slowly. "This incident only points to the chaos that surrounds the end of rabbenu's tenure. Ely must step down in favor of home rule."

Colonel Shananinni stood near the hatch and saluted smartly. "Sir, the passengers are all aboard."

I saw the hatch of the piggyback rocket close and realized what he was saying.

Hartley returned his salute and nodded to me. "Blancom, we appreciate your service here. More eventful than we wanted." With heavy steps Hartley boarded the shuttle and the colonel stood next to me.

I lowered the camcorder and looked left and right before I hurried with Shananinni back to the waiting area. "I need a lift to my office," I whispered. "Don't leave without me."

I resisted the urge to kneel over the body, as many had already, while people in the crowd wept and the women clucked loudly. I went to the stationary camera to check the focus and was glad to find that it was recording all movement, clear and bright.

The assassin's body had already been removed. The well-trained Consortium soldiers had worked fast. The two Softcheeks reporters crouched by the kneeling soldiers capturing images of each face.

I let the camera run while soldiers pushed the crowd away and lifted General Sector's body. I got a clear image of Shananinni's features streaming with tears before I focused on stunned faces in the crowd who were parents of departing students, mostly Arrivi and Putuki. I shut down the station and pocketed the footage, careful to move deliberately through each gesture and to secure the locks.

A soldier waited at my shoulder while I grabbed the camcorder and left the building into the bright day. One lorry had left, probably carrying the general's body and the assassin. I climbed into the back of the second lorry and sat in silence with the stunned guards. I held the camcorder just so to capture his movements as one guard began to strip the uniform used for disguise as one of Ely's troops. He dropped each piece out the back, until he sat in shorts and socks only. The second soldier discarded his jacket but no other garment. The nearly naked guard raised the karkar to pitch it past the tailgate too, except his buddy stopped him. They sat in silence and didn't bother with me until the lorry stopped behind the municipal building and I got out.

I handed the camcorder and memory stick to Paul Spurlin, who went to the relative privacy of our press club to post an online video and develop pages of commentary for a special issue of the gazette.

I sent Dingo and Flash to stop everybody at the stairs and lobby elevator, saying the offices were too crowded for more visitors. I sent Len rabbe Murd to the freight elevator to allow a select group of his choosing to ride to the seventh floor.

My first EAM call was to Hakulupe Le although Millie answered and said little. That call was followed by one to Brianna Miller, asking her to look in on the widow. I contacted Doug Endicott in Cochin saying I was sending exclusive footage he could use on his broadcasts, as well as the statement from General Hartley who had been correct to board the shuttle that waited for no man.

George Luluki sent the stringers out with camcorders to get man-on-the-street footage in the crowded plaza, before he put his staff to manning the landlines in the other rooms where the overhead comtechs had been muted.

"Get information from callers," he told them. "Don't give information."

Kyros Kenoma was the first in tribal leadership to arrive. His face was bloated and his eyes rimmed in red. I asked quiet questions, using a tape recorder because I believed he wasn't presentable for the viewing audience. Orin rabbe Murd was hard on his heels, looking polished and camera-ready. I shrugged, and Spurlin drew him into the hallway for a video interview with the busy plaza in the background.

Later I was seated at my desk watching the footage posted by the Softcheeks reporters who worked for Morse. The two newbies assigned to cover the shuttle launch had just made their reputations in Westend by capturing images of the assassination. They placed blame squarely on General Hartley, asking why he had boarded the shuttle when his officer was down. Wasn't that an act of cowardice? Wasn't Hamilcar more interested in securing the safety of his own son than the officer who had sacrificed his life?

George Luluki rested his bum on my desk and crossed his arms. "We have to speak against that narrative," he said.

The strong lights created a reflected pattern on his bald head. I wondered why he shaved his head, making him look strangely vulnerable. Didn't he know that only conscripts had shaved heads?

"Hartley was right to leave and to take those Junction Boys," he added as a prompt into my silence.

"Kyros said that in his interview," I agreed. "Orin also talked about Manuki and the misplaced blame."

"But we aren't saying it yet."

"I'd rather Dolviet voices were loudest."

"But you do think the general was right to leave?" His eyes searched my face.

I shrugged slightly. "Staying would have pitted Hartley in a screaming match with Ely as though they were equals. That's what Ely wants, even though Manuki wasn't one of his. I mean, not acting directly on Ely's orders."

Luluki uncrossed his arms and pressed the heels of his hands against the desktop. "Ely will linger now. Sector was the point man for security during his exit. Ely will want more concessions. I knew him, you know."

"You know Rabbenu Ely?"

"My father worked with him, seasons ago." George ran a palm over his bald pate. "At first, Ely invited tribal leaders to meetings at the mansion and listened to many before deciding. Later, though, if one crony asked a question about new taxes, he got a beating with sticks. So only Putuki attended since they were in business with Ely. He often opened those meetings with 'Today I have decided so-and-so,' rather than asking for ideas.

"My father disagreed with some edict," George continued, "so his business suddenly had violations for every civil law, and he had to re-open under his wife's name. Now bazaari applaud whenever Ely speaks. Silence follows when Ely asks for questions because nobody wants a beating.

"One brave soul complained that his income was down, so he couldn't afford taxes or to attend meetings. Ely shouted, 'I'm done with you then! I'm done with all of you!' So you see how he made his own prison. He built the walls with his own hands. Then he began taking hostages. His mistresses were all daughters of police captains or bazaari, to keep them in line, except he abuses the girls and gets them pregnant."

"Your sister maybe?"

"I have six sisters. Ely has not noticed them. Thanks to the lashes of Cyrus for that."

Later the Putuki maid whose name I could never remember set a plate of sliced fruit at my elbow and a drink. "Melinga," I said, and looked around at the noisy and busy room.

George Luluki ran operations, and Paul Spurlin managed the postings. I had completed several interviews with tribal leaders whose opinions counted; I couldn't remember how many. I leaned back and saw an amber sunset through the hallway windows. We had worked through the day.

There was so much to unpack from these events, mixed in my mind with irritation at Hakulupe Le for the knockout trick. My vivid dreams of chaos and guilt, populated by those lost to me, amplified my anxiety. Except Hakulupe Le was suddenly a widow with two small children and most likely made to move from the Consortium barracks soon, so my anger at her was useless.

I watched a replayed online segment with Mrs. Shaw on Cicero while the Cicero interviewer filled the time waiting to broadcast a public statement from Rabbenu Ely.

Mrs. Shaw didn't mince words. "Nine women endured death by fire to call attention to the need for regime change in Cylay. They couldn't capture Westend attention for begging. Then one Consortium officer dies." She held up an index finger in accusation, her acerbic outrage playing well to the native audience. "Dolviets are counted as cheap by the Company and by the Consortium. Only conscripts are cheaper. But the tribes count each individual as unique in the world. Each tribal person, all the unblessed ones suffering in Cylay; every Dolviet counts!"

The clip ended abruptly, and I chuckled softly wondering what sedition Mrs. Shaw must have expounded next.

"Henry, you'll want to see this," Luluki said from the other room, where his staff talked on the landlines and the overhead comtech blared.

We crowded together without consideration of rank, to watch the images of Rabbenu Ely walking up an ornate corridor in the governor's mansion to step before a bundle of microphones mounted on a podium. He was dressed in a uniform tailored to his considerable girth and slowly removed his military cover with a polished bill, showing a sad but determined face to the cameras.

"Puts on a good show, doesn't he?" George asked with humor. The lights in this room made patterns on his chocolate brown pate.

"We are greatly saddened today," Ely said as the camera lights glinted on the lenses of his glasses, "to learn of the assassination of General Sector by a deranged and lone gunman who sadly had lost two daughters to the fever that followed the vaccine distribution by the Consortium. I am speaking today to his widow and daughters, not as rabbenu, but as a father who knows what it feels like to lose loved ones during this struggle for safety and security in Cylay and across the savannah. Our hearts go out to Hakulupe Le, a teacher in our schools who is revered by the tribes for her many works of charity and guidance."

He said more, but I couldn't hear any of it. Many angry voices were raised around me, including the Putuki maid who clucked loudly and spat on the floor by my shoe. She did cleanup, so I guess that gesture was allowed.

We heard a din in the other room and moved toward the hallway windows. The crowd in the plaza below was suddenly animated with slogans shouted in unison from opposing organized groups. They heard Ely's words in real time on the company comtechs and as videos on the few cellphones in the crowd.

I glanced at the stationary camera. "We're getting all this, right?"

George Luluki nodded. "From here and from the stringers. Spurlin went out with the bobcat a couple of hours ago."

"I hope Spurlin doesn't get himself killed," was all I could manage.

George and I stepped back to the comtech where the newly famous reporters seated in the mansion press group asked scripted questions of Rabbenu Ely, still standing at the podium.

"Their names are Robert and Bobbie," George said with humor. "Bobbie's the girl."

I shook my head. "Oriika's eyes."

On the comtech, Ely was graciously answering Bobbie's question. Ely who had set aside Marcy for a string of young mistresses and had tried to give Brianna Miller welts from a switch any time that he saw her. "It's true that Carl Hartley and Patrick Osborn," Ely slowly articulated, "were on the shuttle with the general, an opportunity they couldn't sacrifice for these events. They could have left while the general stayed, however, to . . . to attend services for a fallen comrade."

We heard more voices of outrage rising from the plaza. "Ely had better watch his words," Luluki said. "Soon, it's his turn to make a dash for the shuttle."

"These claims of sympathy," I agreed, "are just another nail in the coffin."

George crossed his arms again, maybe to make himself appear smaller, more in keeping with the size of others in the room. "Of course, we don't use coffins," he said. "That's a slag term."

"Slag term?"

"My word for Softcheeks, just a nickname." He smiled sheepishly and then brightened with a new idea. "We could say death by a thousand cuts. That implies ritual death on the savannah. Yeah, I'll tell Spurlin when he gets back. Ely is enduring death by a thousand cuts."

On the comtech, Ely was retreating down the long corridor, and the reporters stood to repeat his words with commentary.

I put my hand on George Luluki's shoulder and turned toward my desk.

"Spurlin wanted to ride with the generals to the shuttle, you know," George added, "if you had slept until dawn. He was jealous that they preferred you."

"I didn't even think about it." I shrugged. "It was always me. I mean, I was—"

"He knows, but you need to let Spurlin lead sometimes."

"Yah, sure. I'll speak to him about it, um, later."

Kyros Kenoma was there again, dressed in a blue suit with a red tie, asking for a video interview where he refuted each claim from Ely's press conference. I led him into our press club to develop pertinent questions and scripted some tailored answers before we turned on the cameras.

"Be sure to say death by a thousand cuts," George said behind us.

I expected Orin rabbe Murd would soon show his face in competition with Kyros for voice among the tribes. I was looking at a long night.

The next day George Luluki and Len rabbe Murd stood over my shoulder, just in from lunch together, as I explored the myriad news segments. We saw Steve Swanweil on a Junction talk show, seated next to a Consortium general I didn't recognize, articulating the idea that Arrivi tribes weren't ready for self-government and were especially not ready to lead the Siibabean and Borabean.

"The savannah tribes don't have a common currency, a structured judicial system, or even the same gods," he asserted. "How can the

Arrivi claim the unction to rule? Doesn't that cast them just as the same as rulers they are trying to discard?"

"Unc-shun?" Len rabbe Murd asked.

"Uh, confident in claiming rights over others," George said.

Swanweil was talking again, his oiled hair glistening under the lights. His image seemed to double like he moved faster than the cameras could record. "Hamilcar boarded the shuttle, leaving his dead officer behind," he said in crisp tones. "Where is Hamilcar now? Why hasn't he come forward to answer our questions?"

"What a useless tool," George said while we were all riveted to the video.

The male interviewer asked a general named Demali about Hartley's silence. "There are questions," the general said in whole tones, "about uneven application of the law of impunity. Captain Manenowski was sacrificed, also Joey Osborn, without an investigation. The officers for the vaccine incident were reassigned offworld and not subject to tribal logic. General Hartley has lost his sense of balance for what is best for the Consortium."

"Hartley boarded the shuttle," Swanweil repeated. "He cannot get past that." The segment ended and the China-doll announcer started repeating the timeline events. I turned down the volume.

"I told you we needed a stronger narrative," George said to me. "They'll repeat those questions every hour leading up to the funeral."

"Who is this officer? Why does he speak against a superior?"

"Demali is stationed in New Shanghai," Len rabbe Murd said. "He provided security for the opening of the stock exchange there." He walked to the doorway, on his way to his trading duties after the lunch hour. "He's married to Swanweil's sister," Len added over his shoulder. "Two kids, I think, a boy and a girl."

After Len was gone, I looked at George. "Get your staff to develop profiles on Consortium officers and staff, three levels deep. I don't want to get caught with our pants down."

He squinted. "I'm sure that phrase has meaning for slags."

"Sector's funeral pyre may become a moment of karsci," I said. "I want to know who the new players are."

He nodded and went to roust his workers in the other room. I realized suddenly how limited a reach we had for real news. Once offworld, Hartley was surrounded by Company reporters and armchair experts. None of us could interview him directly. We at the gazette were so focused on how events in Cylay impacted the tribes; we couldn't capture unfolding events on the transport or at the Junction.

Meanwhile, Paul Spurlin negotiated with Dulcinea rather than Hakulupe Le for rights to film the funeral pyre of General Sector to be held in the Consortium barracks yard. It had been delayed three days so attendees could trek here from savannah towns. Spurlin was everywhere, sometimes on two phones at once, wrangling the parties into agreement.

The hours were long and studded with making decisions. Cylay seemed to fill with idle warriors and erriv herders and women under the veil who managed gaggles of kids. Streets were lined with makeshift sleeping areas, and many tribesmen stated in front of the cameras that they intended to remain in Cylay to witness historic events of regime change. The Putuki police were absent for preventing thefts and rapes, busy guarding the mansion, but the street gangs seemed to impose order well enough.

I developed a eulogy on General Sector and his good works since his time as a lieutenant in the days that General Shaw had led, using stock images and some that Dulcinea provided. We ran segment along with continuous feed from the stationary camera still focused on the governor mansion gate. Rabbenu Ely spoke on the comtechs against the spectacle of a public pyre. He had no intention of attending, and the tribes were divided on the issue. "Why broadcast the funeral to a Westend audience," Putuki men asked in front of Spurlin's camera? "Milo-pilo was Softcheeks, so why should he receive this honor?"

Dulcinea was in our office twice, accompanied by Millie and two others, always holding a toddler in arms. Spurlin's interest in Dulcinea's looks faded when he realized her commitment to family. She wore an engagement bracelet from Kyros Kenoma, but their plans had been set back by the funeral events. I asked her for a statement from the widow Hakulupe Le, but Dulcinea only shook her head no.

As we assembled the event, I saw on Endicott's news channel that two more bombings had happened in the Urbyd bazaar. I ran the segments in slow motion to identify people in the crowd, even a glimpse of the dress material I had purchased, but found no hint of Anagella or her risk level.

The day of the funeral was bright and cool, and the pyre was set for noon instead of sunset. Spurlin had talked with Captain Compavel about the freshly constructed bleachers facing the pyre and had ordered a raised booth across the way, from where we could record each tear and whisper. Metal crowd-control barriers were added and extra security precautions were taken to prevent a pipe bomb. Network reporters were denied passes for the Consortium compound, and soon enough I heard from Steny Morse on that development. The newly promoted reporters, Robert and Bobbie, were relegated to the barracks gate where they appeared to accost each tribesman who walked around them with resistant gestures. Regan Villines finally pulled the junior reporters to the side with whispers about native protocol.

Endicott had sent John Milan as a stringer, and all we got from him was grief. So bitter. Finally, we provided a personal camera-man and a station for Milan where Dolviets in leadership would enter and exit, and we agreed that Endicott could edit the feed. That move at least deflected Milan's arrogance.

Spurlin was adamant to me. "Don't hire Milan, not even for oblu. Tribeswomen believe that when Milan opens his mouth, spiders and beetles fall out."

At the funeral event Hakulupe Le, under a blue burka, was seated forward so the Consortium officers who managed the services could honor her. The two girls were there as well as Sarah and Jenna Le, without veils and sitting like stone bookends. Karlyhi was absent, of course, but Omiibuk sat next to Dulcinea, both surrounded by children. Brianna Miller sat with Orin rabbe Murd, Len, and extended family. Rufus and Kelly were in that group, wrapped in an aura of honeymooners. Brianna looked around and twiddled her thumbs, even rising to step to Dulcinea's side for whispered comments.

I looked over the common crowd and realized that Hakulupe Le and many in the gathering wore burkas, although some only sported the mark of Rularim. Kyros Kenoma was prominent in the men's group, and George Luluki sat at his side. Several bazaari bent to whisper into George's ear in turn, including Simon Sumuki. I realized George and Kyros were both big men, young and coming into their own for leadership.

No Dolviet including George Luluki gave a public statement on the day of the event, so Paul Spurlin and I sat in a booth and chatted together. We noted early that General Mike Shaw and his wife, who was the Sheeks-Cylom, were not in attendance. I knew most of the players and had crib sheets for the Putuki bazaari I had not met. Spurlin took the lead and we kept our voices low, allowing many moments of silence between infrequent gestures in the crowd that needed commentary. The live broadcast of long silences lent solemnity to the afternoon's events.

During the proceedings, Mark offered a chant, standing among the gathered Cylahi. Colonel Shananinni put on a good show for the Consortium to honor the body, even folding a blue-on-blue flag to present to the widow. The pyre burned hot for forty minutes while women swayed and clucked loudly and a few men slashed themselves with beltknives.

When the fire was smoldering and the widow was led away, we packed up the equipment ourselves since I trusted nobody with the cameras. We were escorted by a Consortium detachment back to the municipal building, and I sent Dingo and Flash ahead to sweep the offices thoroughly for snakes. I entered the newsroom, undoing my tie and wrinkling my nose at the scent of furniture polish. Perhaps the maid could come once a week when events settled instead of every day. I was hoping Rabbenu Ely missed a couple more shuttle launches and lingered in Cylay, because I needed a break from unfolding events.

John Milan showed up at my desk with a bitter smirk. Who had allowed him in the elevator? I felt too tired to parry his demands and looked around for Paul Spurlin. Guilt grabbed my senses, though, since Paul had worked tirelessly in the past days.

"You're an ungrateful pup," Milan said, with his lip curled. "Even Endicott says that. I remember when you first disembarked with your vest and light meter and surfboard. Now you have your own enterprise here, huh, Henry? You decide what's important for the tribes and what to ignore."

I scratched a temple where the insect repellent had made my hair stiff. "What do you need, John? Your feed is already with Endicott."

"You think I'm washed up, huh? My past with the Company ruined my voice with the tribes, huh?" He was trim and sporting a two-day growth of beard on his tanned face.

"I never said—"

"Well, I'll show you," he said too loudly. "I'll get the biggest story Westend has ever seen, and I'll break this system wide open."

"The only story is Ely stepping—"

"You think you're the center of Westend?" Milan asked with a bitter smirk. "This story of pipe bombings and regime change is easy to capture. When was the last time you were out on the streets, huh, Henry? When was the last time you pursued a story they were trying to hide?"

"We're just trying—"

"I'll get the conscript story. That's real news." He showed his teeth but not from smiling. "I'll travel with Otieno to the asteroid mines and get the real story of Westend, how the system operates on the back of orphans grabbed up from Earth. You haven't heard the last of me yet. Old John Milan still has in-ves-ti-ga-tive reporting in him. You just wait."

I walked toward the room where my cot called to me. "I hope it works out for you."

"You just wait," he called behind me. "I'll blow this whole can of worms wide open."

I waved him to George Luluki and closed the backroom door, where I fell onto the cot for a delicious nap.

Dreaming again. I stand near the cliff's edge in shorts only, shivering with goose bumps from swimming in the gravel pit. Three brothers, older and jeering, taunting but never teaching—jump, jump. "Are you scared? Lily-livered? Need a push?" I look over the ledge, but I know already it's a long fall, and the water is clear with the cold. Unseen rocks to break my fall. "Go ahead. Dive in, lily-liver."

But wait . . . in the water, I see two girls circling, swimming easily, buoyant, with long fish tails. "Here, here! Safe to land here." Who are they? Who would . . . it's Cleo and Camille. What are they doing in the water? How did they grow tails?

"Safe here, safe to land here."

A punch on my shoulder. "Jump, jump, or we'll throw you over. Let's get him." I run four paces and throw myself off the ledge with limbs splayed. Behind me their hard jeers fill the air. Where are the mermaids? I cannot see the girls who called safe landing. Falling, falling . . .

SEVENTEEN

I ROLLED OFF THE COT BUT BROKE MY FALL BEFORE I BANGED MY head. I decided that I needed a real bed in this room. After a shower and cursory refreshment, I joined Paul Spurlin in our press club.

"You can really saw some logs, huh?" he said.

"What'd I miss?"

"Brianna Miller was here. She said Jessup Chandliss will remain in Westend. That woman he calls fire-eyes will start silicide recovery at Mayschool. Chandliss is joining General Shaw in the Siibabean forest, along with his two Russian buddies."

"So they found the northeast passage. We should send someone for an interview."

"I'm busy with free elections after Ely steps down." He showed me a cold shoulder. "Shananinni said that election officials from the Consortium—for fairness?—are not the best idea, but maybe some from Cicero. Carline Bryant wants to be included in that group. She's already planning to live in Somule."

"She grew up there," I said, "along with Dacupitte and rabbenu's first wife, Marcy. We should do a story on Carline, as one of the colonists' kids, and maybe one on Mark as the last of Lucy's kids."

"I finally made a chart for myself with family ties," Spurlin said. "Did you know that Omiibuk is a cousin to Dulcinea? Anyhow, Mrs. Shaw is in residence now at the Uburu digs. Carvings there connect Uburu to the Siibabean, and she wants to test DNA to confirm."

"Geez, how long was I asleep?"

"Mrs. Shaw said you should visit the digs."

"You can go instead, if that's what you want."

He gave me a sidelong glance full of smoldering resentment. Beads of sweat stood in his thinning hair. "Your angle can be forging a new nation from former enemies. We can attract Uburu and the Siibabean readers with a story about the ruins."

I blinked several times. Spurlin was really dug into tribal affairs. "So, you are forging this nation?"

"All the players changed with Sector's death."

"A moment of karsci."

"Good, good. You can say that in your story."

"I thought we reported the news, not generated it."

"Well, then . . . Get Mrs. Shaw to say that, or Dulcinea."

"Don't get ahead of the tribes, Paul, else there will be toads and frogs falling from your mouth when you face the cameras."

George joined us and wanted me to edit his article about how Putuki bazaari were pursuing opportunities in Urbyd and port cities in Cochin and Striiduc.

I added my chicken scratches to his pages, but was distracted by low murmuring. I glanced out the big windows in the hallway.

The Cylay plaza had filled with Arrivi drawn from herding duties and idle warriors from the militia, expectant of changeover events.

"They have a couple of oversized machines stationed in the plaza," George said. "They're bringing in that statue of the sisters of Arim, that big one that's out on the flats. It's weighs several tons. Shananinni agreed to use a transport chopper and just lift it, so it swings in the air for 37 kilometers. I want to see that!"

Paul barely looked away from the EAM screen. "Relocating the statue is an excuse to prepare for storming the gates." He was certainly sour today, but maybe he hadn't slept.

I was reading the last paragraphs George had penned. Mark silently appeared at the door. "You will come."

I looked at Spurlin. "Ely won't show his face," Paul said, "until he can make a dash for the shuttle. You have a couple of days."

I grabbed my small pack and my camera case and followed Mark down to a Consortium jeep where two lieutenants who I didn't know waited to escort us to the barracks. Mark and I clambered into a transport chopper that was taking supplies to the Uburu digs. Once airborne, I looked down at the few straight streets and a warehouse district along the sluggish river surrounded by misaligned slums in all directions; a speck on a small planet in a nondescript system. I sat back and sighed.

Mark offered me a bit of kari root to chew.

The Uburu digs were situated on a bald hump of mesa on the other side of the Iamida river, nestled among wadis filled with tamarind and mida trees. The uneven terrain ensured that only the most tenacious foot traveler visited. The escarpment wall rose high above but at some distance, illuminated by glaring sunlight. Along the side of the mound, a couple wooden structures were built in round Mekucoo style and also several tents. A long table and mess area enjoyed the shade of a twisted thorn tree, its branches rising above the mound on one side only. The camp was smaller than I had imagined since it was long established, but I remembered that the scientists abandoned the area during the rainy season.

General Shaw waited with his wife as the chopper set down. He was a big man but trim from his work and with gray showing in his mass of hair. I was impressed that he showed himself, seemingly relaxed at this remote station and wearing a uniform of the clutch of Murd even though he was retired from militia work. Mrs. Shaw appeared tiny next to him; funny to me, since I had seen her so often on the comtech, her face looming off the screen. They were in residence here but had not attended the funeral? And how had she disembarked when the shuttle had not returned since Sector's assassination?

I stepped down with Mark, and he took charge of the unloading as I was led forward to greet Dr. Spinelli and Dr. Gutierrez, researchers who also treated wounded warriors when needed. "We'll talk at dinner," Mrs. Shaw said and walked left with the doctors.

General Mike Shaw led me to the shaded table and offered warm beer in a bottle. "You mustn't drink the water here," he cautioned, "and stay out of the ravines. The cenzea will kill you within fifteen minutes." He meant the toxic mist that rose from the thin mantle plates.

A large map was spread on the table and anchored with mugs and plates. "Is this the northeast passage?" I asked.

Smile lines appeared on his weathered face. "We call the forest route the backdoor, except that title maybe insults the Siibabean. This map, though, is the interior of the cavern with carvings and tombs and ancient stores of grain and wine. My wife wants to use a laser scanner to map the tunnels."

"How did she wrestle the laser from Rufus?"

"Rufus has, um, another purpose for it. She ordered one for this location."

I slowly nodded. "Unlimited funds must feel great."

"The rainy season is the real obstacle for research. And shipping channels. We get some work done, though."

"River blindness, poisonous spiders, cenzea in the cavern."

"We use caged parrots," Mike said, "like the canary in the coal mine trick? Just stay out of the side tombs, and you won't rob the desert of one. We have some images on the EAM but when you're in the cave, the maps are more useful. We can walk down there later, if you want."

The detailed map indicated a raised platform in the center of an open cavern, probably used for sacrifice. The carved and decorated walls had many alcoves for the bodies of ancestors. Some additional loose pages held sketches of carved plump figures all in a crowd, wearing jewelry and little else and posed as if dancing.

"How do you figure the Uburu are related to the Siibabean?" I asked.

"Ah, my wife can tell you about that. She'll bend your ear until Nettom sets. Let's get you situated." We walked down to the tents where I was allowed to drop my pack on a cot next to Yuri and Mica who murmured their melingas.

"Are your twins here?" I asked Mike Shaw, but he shook his head no.

"Still at school in Two Forks, staying with an aunt. My wife says they can disembark in the season of cylay, after a battery of inoculations. The boys are not headed for the forest, though. My wife didn't relent even after tears were shed."

We headed back in the direction of the camp's center table. "Is the forest as grand as the stories we hear?"

"Awe-inspiring," Mike Shaw grinned. "We ran out of names for all the lemur types. The ketiwhelp are huge, with long teeth like a monster in a dream. The new scientists are stationed here at the digs for now, though. They will travel with me for forest service where they can catalogue the plants and creatures."

"I met them: guests of Brianna at Kelly's wedding. A biologist and a couple who are botanists."

He only pointed at an exposed root on our path. "Watch your step there."

"So tell me about—" I stopped short when I glimpsed a veiled Arrivi woman seated in a large tent with the flap pulled up. I knew it was Hakulupe Le because Millie and Anna played on the side. Marna Le was there, as well as Mrs. Shaw. They were focused on several files and stacks of binders.

Marna Le immediately came forward, and Mrs. Shaw closed the tent flaps behind her.

"Hiki, Blancom," Marna Le said holding her palm high.

I knew her from Chrysalis where she had trained as a silicide diver. She was cousin to Dulcinea.

"You must excuse our good friend Lupe," Marna Le added into my silence. "The first days of widowhood."

"Is Brianna Miller here too?"

They both chuckled. "You won't often find Brianna in the same camp as my wife," Mike said. "She's in Cochin making new friends."

"And you're planning a new government for Cylay," I said quickly, "for when Ely is gone."

Marna Le raised her eyebrows and shrugged to the former general. "Karsci had caused a shift," she told me. "Some have claimed the season of cylay is already here, maybe since the death of Milo-pilo. The holy woman says the season of cylay starts when Ely leaves."

"Maybe a new season starts at different times for different groups."

Marna Le blinked as she thought about that. "In karsci, we hold onto the words of the holy woman."

"Yah, sure," I said. "The holy woman who never shows herself to the men or to Softcheeks women even—she gets the last word?"

"Good, good. You understand. Melinga, Blancom." She moved back to the tent, and I pushed on with Mike Shaw.

"Have you ever seen this holy woman?" I asked as we picked our way through the camp.

"Where I grew up near Two Forks," Mike said, "we had a story about a woman in white who collected the souls of the dying. When you saw her on a misty night, you weren't long for this world."

"But that's a spirit, right?" I asked. "The holy woman is real, right? A real person. Is she here at the digs? Are Cleo and Camille here?"

Smile lines appeared again on his face. "So many questions. All in good time, Blancom."

Mike Shaw led me down to the entrance of the cavern where Dr. Spinelli waved from inside for me to enter. The general left, and I waited a moment for my eyes to adjust to the deep shadows. The air was pungent with the odors of dirt and decay. At my hesitation, Spinelli wrinkled his brow so his bushy eyebrows seemed to touch. The new scientists lingered on the side, the botanist couple talking with heads together focused on some ancient latrine detritus. The biologist, a Middle Eastern man who needed a shave, stood alone as if bored and unwilling to get dirty. I wondered at that since Dr. Spinelli jumped to serve in any crisis and Dr. Gutierrez regularly did doctor's rounds at Beecham Place.

Dr. Gutierrez came up behind me carrying a wire mesh frame with fragments sifted from some ancient grave. "Mr. Henry, I heard you were coming to visit." He walked with me to Spinelli's table that was banked by clay jars and a couple of tarps covering more jars.

Ali Abrar Ebnli joined us, expecting the honorable greeting. We shook hands while his cunning eyes flitted from face to face.

"How are you adjusting to the climate?" I asked to be polite.

"I spent my boyhood on the edge of a desert."

"Blancom too," Spinelli cheerfully added. "Australian, you know."

Dr. Ali only nodded. When Spinelli launched into an excited explanation about the treasures he had identified, Ali stepped back and within a few minutes he left the cave. He was waiting, I was guessing, for a helicopter ride into the Siibabean forest where his work could begin. The botanists, though, kept rooting through more piles of old dung several feet from us, holding each fragment under handheld lights before discarding it for the next one.

Spinelli and Gutierrez eagerly showed me dozens of patterned shards that they seemed to treasure, along with drawings that connected the ancient culture with Uburu and Siibabean patterns in homemade clothing. "We need a wide sampling of DNA," Spinelli said, "to confirm tribal genealogy. Your news article could include a call to action for the tribes."

"After the poison vaccine, will the tribes will agree to more injections?"

"Welfare ministers can run the show, and we take a skin scraping. No injections."

"You should ask Karlyhi first. He decides about cooperation."

Later we walked back to the communal table for a meal. Sunlight lingered on the distant wall of the escarpment, creating a rosy glow for more than an hour after the heat of the day.

Kenru came up from the caverns with Captain Chandliss. "Blancom!" Chandliss said. "How goes the ragsheet in Cylay?"

"Jessup Chandliss. Well met."

"He's called Marnahand now," Kenru said. Chandliss pushed his shoulder with a forearm, but Kenru chuckled. "Since he works instead of just giving orders," Kenru explained, "the clutch of Marna Le thought he was Hardhand like Mike Shaw. And he trained only Marna Le."

"I was told to!"

"Marnahand," I said. "It suits you."

He held his arms wide, a gesture I had seen often at Chrysalis. "What? Based on two mistakes. Even Blancom could find a better nickname."

Kenru said his melingas and went to join Yuri and Mica at the workmen's fire. Chandliss and I walked back to the center table. "Mike Shaw is called mida-Mike now," he said, "mostly by the Siib-abean who don't want him to cut their trees."

"I thought you were too rich from the emerald find to continue with pioneer work."

"Ah, it's true," Chandliss said. "I thought of myself as old and rich and tempered by the savannah. But next to General Shaw, I'm viewed as young and poor and slag. That's their word for Soft-cheeks. My little pouch of emeralds, among this crowd, barely gets me a seat at the table."

"So you were living on the mesas for a while, huh?" I said. "What do you know about flash floods there?"

"When the Iamida overflows? Or the bore tide?"

"Uh, both, I guess."

"It's mostly this one gorge, very famous," he said with a shrug. "It's angled just right at a bend in the river. The story goes that it fills suddenly on a sunny day, like the water just appears. The mesa walls there are marked with water damage, so it can't be too much of a surprise. A coincidence from when a bore tide moves inland."

"Yah, sure."

Marna Le and Hakulupe Le did not join us for dinner; perhaps they were managing the many kids who had free run of the place. The new Softcheeks scientists must have eaten during an earlier shift and were also absent. The women, except Mrs. Shaw, waited as the men filled plates from a long serving table and grabbed another warm beer from the stacked supplies. We sat at the rough-hewn staff table and picked over the steamed vegetables and dried fish flavored with cumin. A big bowl of Uburu corn chips was placed in the center, and each person grabbed a fistful in lieu of bread. We stood abruptly when Mrs. Shaw joined us—the former general, the two veteran doctors, Chandliss and me—and then sat and dug into the food.

I realized that here was the epicenter for offworld support for the savannah tribes. When Ely stepped down, when Hakulupe Le and Dulcinea moved into administration at Cylay, the need to gather at bush stations would vanish.

"So," I said, as an opener, "when will the announcement come that Hartley is stepping down?"

Mike Shaw was guzzling beer and spat a big spray to one side. The doctors laughed together. "You will do well in your profession," Dr. Gutierrez said.

"I'm thinking the Consortium threatened to expose his liaison with Brianna Miller," I said, "to force a quiet exit. He has his reputation, and hers, to protect."

"When did you know?" Mike Shaw asked.

"When he collected his son to jump back." I shrugged. "The other general, Demali? He's angling for the job, right?"

Mike exchanged glances with his wife who only rolled her eyes. "The nations of the Consortium of Planets will vote later," he reported, "but Swanweil has been taking Demali around to meet the different players. Otieno, you know him. He started the new freighter traffic that Rularim invested in."

His wife smirked at the mention of Brianna Miller's native handle.

"Anyhow," Mike Shaw continued. "Otieno agreed to back him after Demali promised to lower Westend mining tariffs and to end the conscript traffic."

"And the Company has agreed to stop trafficking?" I asked between bites.

In the waning light Mike Shaw's weathered face showed more lines. "The Company is mostly relieved to sell off the mining rights and the aging ships. Work in the asteroid belt can be treacherous."

"A spinning rock of iron and nickel," Chandliss said with irony, "with uneven gravity and unpredictable gas jets. No planet to establish a colony and the ship under constant threat of bombardment. What could be the problem?"

"Stinking group quarters, punctured EVM suits," Dr. Gutierrez added. "Jailers more interested in moving the ore than saving a wounded worker. I'm surprised the conscript practice lasted this long."

"And Otieno will do better?" Dr. Spinelli asked.

"Otieno knows what it feels like to suffer under the lash," Gutierrez returned.

"He finds work for his tribe only," Spinelli said, "and promotes them for loyalty over talent. More exclusive than any Chinese."

Chandliss and I watched the two doctors who probably argued like this each night. I thought about our many talks at the butterfly pool and wondered if we had sounded the same.

"How long can you stay with us, Henry?" Mrs. Shaw asked.

"Until the chopper leaves, I guess. I'll never hear the end of it, if Spurlin is left high and dry when Ely makes an exit."

"At least there's no shooting war," Dr. Gutierrez said. "Regime change in my country only came after a bloody civil war where the capital city was bombed into ruins."

"We think an interim leader is needed," Mrs. Shaw said, "to establish elected positions for police and village councils. And appoint judges."

"But rabbenu is an Arrivi office," Chandliss said. "What leader can dictate to the tribes for civil service?"

"Too bad the new Rularim is a woman," I said without caution. "Brianna could—"

"Ha!" Mrs. Shaw interrupted.

Mike Shaw leaned back with big eyes and shook his head 'no,' like I had stepped into her favorite topic for a tirade.

"Arisen Rularim, that's a laugh," his wife said. "She's not able to work on committee. She barely knows how the treasure is used, always pushing duties onto others. Did you know she wants Sarah to move to Cochin? To serve her there, without thought of how hard Sarah has worked at the—"

Mike Shaw placed a hand on her forearm, but she jerked it away.

"Don't shush me," she said. "I know what I'm saying here, and I'm right. Any person can see that 'Arisen Rularim' is unsuited for rabbenu. It's actual work, you know."

"You want Hakulupe Le for the interim," I guessed.

They all stared at me, a disconcerting face-off.

"The would-be leaders," I slowly added, "were her students over time, and she has the sympathy vote since the funeral was broadcast. Consortium officers ate at her table. You're grooming her now in that tent, under the burka as a cover story. The grieving widow."

They reacted by relaxing. Both doctors crossed their arms on their chests. Mrs. Shaw pushed her forearm against her husband again, demanding her own space.

"Isn't Hakulupe Le a goulep from way back?" I asked. "Something about her birth and the Company prison."

"Yes, well," Mrs. Shaw said, "we can turn that unfortunate beginning into a badge of honor with the tribes. We have some paragraphs of biography for your gazette. Lupe was raised with the holy woman, Kat. Did you know?"

Our meal broke up soon after that. The women who were servers occupied our seats at the staff table for their shared meal. Dr. Spinelli argued purposefully with Dr. Gutierrez about lost souls in space; what happened to the souls of conscripts? I spoke quietly to Jessup Chandliss as he packed some bottles of beer into a satchel.

"Maybe the holy woman is made up," I said. "I mean, like a fantasy used to raise the volume of the women's voices. Did you ever wonder about that?"

"Careful now, or they'll make you visit her," Chandliss said. "Maybe she reads people better than that gypsy girl Cleo."

He headed down to the native fire, where Kenru sat with Yuri, Mica, and Mark. Chandliss passed the bottles around, settling in to tell lies about the Softcheek ocean and hear chants about the deeds of dead warriors. Their next station was the leafbed under the canopy of the Siibabean forest, I was thinking. They were the Dolviet and Softcheeks specialists following mida-Mike.

Near the women's tents, Marna Le stood with Jenna Le, both tall and big boned, with little animation in their faces. Maybe cousins? Marna Le gestured that I should join them. "You'll want to speak with Hakulupe Le now. Jenna Le will show you where."

"No tricks," I said as I followed her. "I can sleep just fine without being gassed."

I was led not to a tent—perhaps the girls were asleep already—but to a specimen building where the lights were bald and glaring. Hakulupe Le sat alone and without veil at a long table where the two doctors often catalogued their unearthed treasures.

We entered, and Hakulupe Le stood and held a palm high in greeting. "Hiki, Blancom."

"Melinga, Lupe, the next rabbenu in Cylay."

She looked at Jenna Le who shrugged and sat on the side, rather like a chaperone for this unveiled widow. I sat across the table from Lupe.

"Of course," Lupe began, "the women who are deserving of this honor all embraced death-by-fire in protest to Ely's rule."

"Practicing your public statements already?" I said. "Good humility. It aligns you with Kecouroo and Kyle Rula."

"When did you get so cynical?" I saw those green eyes flashing with humor. "You have some questions for me?"

"May I use a recorder?" I pulled a small one from my pocket and worked the buttons. "How will the free elections be managed? Will the women vote in their villages? The Uburu are included, I'm guessing. Can the Siibabean vote too? Who will you promote as a candidate for rabbenu?"

"These are good questions," she said. "You know that I only agreed to serve for the interim because of the great need among the tribes following my husband's death. We have identified a few who may be called to serve as ministers. Orin rabbe Murd may manage the slate of judgeships, for example. Sarah will speak to certain savannah ministers about civil positions. Kenru will solicit Uburu for some offices, especially village elders for trade, and Karlyhi will begin recruiting for police, except in Cylay where Mark will oversee the question of police who are not Putuki. How am I doing so far?"

"You cannot push out the Putuki tribe. You'll only sow the seeds of resentment."

"We like Simon Sumuki for the justice minister, and maybe George Luluki as commerce minister, if you can spare him. We're seeking balance and inclusion, allowing each to serve where he was valuable during the strife with Borabean."

"And Aensilus?"

"Well . . . Madquii are not the Gora, so he is a friend and brother to Aeolis. But, um, Urbyd has a government already and a different tradition of law. We must table these issues until there's a constitution for home rule and a statement of individual rights."

"You don't want Borabean input for relative civil rights?" I asked while I made notes. "They would exclude the women?"

Lupe paused, maybe seeking the right words to use. "Let's stay positive. One chunk of civil law at a time."

"And who provides security for you and the girls? This job can no longer go to the Consortium. Siize and Siiloba were sacrificed. Dingo and Flash are useless in that job."

"Do you have a suggestion for me?"

"Do you know a gang leader named Stuben? A friend of Mark's, and he knows everybody in Cylay."

She nodded slowly to show that she considered my suggestion. "You bring fresh ideas to us, Blancom, as you always have. The agent of karsci."

"That's only because the gazette seems to be in the middle of events."

"Did you consider that the gazette is because of karsci? But, um, I wanted to apologize for the problem when I visited your office with Bybiis. We really didn't—"

"Where did she get that book with the toxic binding, anyhow?"

"It was Cochin made, but a gift from Striiduc."

"Bybiis is a threat to them?"

"Ah, no," Lupe said while question rode her features. "The book was a wedding gift to Bernice Datong, wife to Ambassador Otieno. Bybiis recognized the trick and snatched it from her hands. But Otieno went into a rage, spoiling the wedding reception and demanding that Bernice be sequestered with Bybiis as her only servant."

"Bernice is just a kid, an orphan from beyond the wormhole. What threat?"

"And now she carries Otieno's son." Lupe showed me those lambent eyes with a twinkle of glee. "But, closer to home . . . We see a danger for you. At the gazette, I mean. We may have a precaution that serves."

"What danger?"

"The carromancist. You have vivid dreams, and maybe you can become easily enraged for no reason."

I snorted derisively, briefly blowing air from my nostrils. "Because of your trick with that musky book."

She allowed a long moment to pass. "You seem to shimmer, Blancom. A person's view of you is doubled, like a reflection in water. We first noticed this effect on Steve Swanweil from many seasons past. Also on Carl Hartley, but maybe because he was hiding personal secrets. Only when more of our friends were affected did we see the patterns."

I sat back, feeling the effects of my long day. I had seen a shimmering effect around Carl, and maybe glimpsed one on Swanweil during the infrequent times we had met. So that was the reason, or assumed to be the reason within tribal prophecy. Time was truly a loop.

"What do you want me to do?" I asked quietly.

"Be careful only," Lupe smiled. "When you feel enraged, or are tempted to an act that you otherwise would not consider, take a step back. Are these your motives or something extra?"

"And that's it?"

"Like I say, we have a possible counter-balance in mind."

"Not Cleo and Camille? Not Bybiis with her tricks?" I had been irritated recently, and for no reason but exhaustion and unwillingness to sleep for fear of dreams. "What a gaggle of kids all of a sudden," I said after a long moment. "And Ely's pregnant mistress too?"

"Khloe will have a daughter; Elle we think is a good name." Jenna Le shifted in her seat, but Lupe didn't seem to mind the silent comment.

"These recounted souls," Lupe said, "born from the call to fertility, find a new beginning in the season of cylay and will prosper only if Elle prospers. By this method, we honor the benefits of Ely's tenure and the contributions of the Putuki tribe."

I rolled my eyes. "A polished statement from a committee of women. You know I won't report what I cannot verify."

"The tribes will see. That is enough."

"When will you return to Cylay?"

She blinked as if surprised that I didn't know the answer. "Tomorrow, with you. All that we have discussed at this mercy seat will soon be made public."

"Do you have a statement for me about General Hartley?"

"As the widow of his good friend General Sector, I'm confident that Hamilcar made the right choice to board the shuttle that night, following Consortium protocol concerning a attempt on his life. The new Consortium leader will have big shoes to fill. The correct Softcheeks phrase, huh? Big shoes."

"Oh, you're good at this. You're really good."

"I've had many seasons of netta to practice."

I glanced down at my notes. "And can I get a statement about the conscripts who the Company will discard? How will the Company mine clearstone from the asteroids? You know the Borabean call it clearstone?"

"Three questions," she grinned. "The Softcheeks rhythm of considering issues as separate."

"Regime change and asteroid mining are not—"

Hakulupe Le shrugged slightly. "The tribes have no opinion on the conscript issue just yet. Exposing the abuses now may rile responses from many factions."

I squinted wondering at this oblique response. "But trafficking will stop? A place will be found for conscripts already in Westend?"

She sadly shook her head. "Not by the tribes. This issue is a wedge used by some to justify their actions."

"You mean that new general Demali made an empty promise to Otieno? The conscript trade will not end."

She shrugged slightly. "We don't know. We're willing to wait and see."

I grinned. "When rabbenu is elected, you should become ambassador. You know when not to speak. That's a great talent."

"You are too kind," she said, glancing at Jenna Le who had watchful eyes but her stone face had not changed.

"Hamilcar will settle on the savannah now," I guessed, "maybe working with mida-Mike?"

"Mida-Mike; you heard," she grinned. "Brianna likes her freedom, though, whereas Mrs. Shaw works within communities, even causing them to overlap. And Brianna can turn any friend into an enemy. Like with Edwina. Did you wonder why Edwina didn't come down from the forest for Kelly's wedding?"

I only shrugged. "It was said that Edwina was resentful that she wasn't told about Kecouroo's intentions before the torching."

"Ah, that's how Brianna tells the story," Lupe said with her lambent eyes glistening in the poor light. "When Mrs. Shaw disembarked the last time, she and Brianna went together in a chopper to General Shaw's camp in the Siibabean forest. He operates wholly low-tech, you know, not wanting to impact the clans there. These pa-tri-cian women hovered and landed and called Edwina onto the carpet, so to speak, lecturing her like a truant schoolgirl. Get yourself down to the savannah, so on and so on. Brianna always judged Mrs. Shaw for her high-handed manner, but joined in to make this scene." She shook her head but was smiling. "I think it's the distance from the savannah that blinds them."

"Edwina refused," I guessed.

"She hissed and dropped a pile right there before she scurried into the bush." Lupe laughed heartily and even Jenna Le's face moved, her eyes actually showing expression. "Edwina always preferred the company of men. They should have known."

I thought about the forest and how often Mrs. Shaw must have visited there without venturing to Cylay. That was why she was so well-informed about Dolviet politics whenever she spoke on the talk shows. My life seemed constricted, focused too much on plaza protests.

"Edwina prefers mida-Mike and hunting fresh lemur every night?" I asked.

"And now, one more person would speak with you," Lupe said, ignoring my intrusive question. "Go with Jenna Le. But no recorder, please."

I clicked the instrument off before I pocketed it, offering my melingas. I was led along a tricky path filled with tree roots to the entrance of the digs, where Jenna Le took a torch from a wall mount. She handed it to me and gestured that I should enter.

"Who's in there?" I asked. "Shouldn't you show the way?"

She only repeated her hand gesture, so I entered alone with the torch.

I walked to the center altar and turned full circle. I imagined that whoever waited would show herself. I peered down the main tunnel and a couple side tunnels before I saw a candle flame in one alcove. I stepped closer to find a woman dressed in a blue Arrivi gown and seated on a camp chair with her back to me. She was moving the candle to study the figures carved in the wall. "The figures seem to dance when you move the light, did you notice?" she said.

"Are you the woman who troubles my dreams?" I asked.

"You know that I'm not. Put the torch in a wall mount over there."

I stepped to the side, feeling cool air swirl as the torch sputtered. I reached high to secure it in the stone cup before I returned to the alcove, now only candlelit. "You must be the holy woman," I whispered, "the one they call Kat. Can you ride my dreams?"

Kat lowered the candle and turned to me. Her eyes were blue, or at least blue in the poor light. "Mostly, the dreams of Softcheeks are closed to us, except you broadcast your fear. Swimming at the flooded gravel pit and brothers who want you to jump."

"I used to dream along with Edwina. I miss the volume of her song."

The flame fluttered, casting moving shadows on her face. "We all do."

I cleared my throat trying to think of something to say. "Lately, the dreams are confused. A woman's face looms in water with torches behind her. And voices. Do you dream the same?"

She pursed her lips and rolled her eyes left. Maybe I was staring again. I stepped back a fraction and crossed my arms to contain my eagerness.

"Let me ask you," she said. "If you wanted to weaken a group who value dreams, what would you do? Destroy the dreamer? Destroy the interpreter of dreams? Or make the dreams change so they are no longer true?"

"Muddy the waters," I agreed. "To weaken a strong argument, bring in unrelated trends to confuse people. It's a political trick called muddy the waters."

She barely moved, her appraising eyes steady on my face. "You have asked about me, more than once. But can you see now why the holy woman is held close? Our actions are not to insult you or exclude you."

"And Cleo too?"

"Cleo's confidence in her gift compromises her discretion. Doubts are better."

"And you have doubts?"

She nodded her head three times, slowly and deliberately, but I noticed her comments matched few of my questions. "This woman you see in the water," Kat said. "She plays on our doubts." She looked down at her feet just as though she had dropped something. "We seek consensus; we always have. One person's voice does not rule."

"Can this water woman confuse anyone?"

"Her range is limited, Bybiis says. Her time is consumed with four or five people who she follows. And she sacrifices her life to serve her master." Kat reached forward to pick up what she must have dropped.

"Maybe she has no master," I said hoping to prolong the talk. "Only ambition."

"I have something for you." She lifted a smallish birdcage the held an infant gualarep.

"I live in the city. I cannot—"

"Just while he grows, keep him close." She passed the cage to me, and the creature raised its shoulders, alert and cooing. It was a hatchling, cream-colored and too young for weaning.

"A male? What does he eat?" I asked.

Kat stood and smoothed her skirts. "Dingo and Flash will bring his meals, but he must be fed by your hand. As his first steward, you have naming rights."

"A precaution, then, so Edwina can watch over me?" I guessed. "This woman in water, can she see us now? Is she watching us now?"

Kat looked around the chamber. "Hold onto your doubts, Blancom. Doubts are a powerful motivator. And now, you must leave ahead of me. Take the torch."

"But I have questions. What about—"

She put two fingers on her lips and gestured that I should go, much like Jenna Le had gestured.

I sighed heavily wondering how she viewed me, what she saw in my future. I had no courage to seek a personal word from her. I was alone when I struggled out of the entrance of the digs carrying the torch and the birdcage. Jenna Le waited there and handed me a small tin like a sardine container. Food for the gualarep so he didn't wander off, I was thinking. She took the torch and led the way back to camp.

As we picked safe footing along the trail, I stopped short at a noise in the bush, even hoping to encounter Edwina. My response was silly. Edna was gone, of course, and Edwina preferred the forest.

I was about to focus again on the path when I recognized Chandliss standing with a woman, his hand on her arm. Marna Le turned her face away, but Jessup directed a cynical look at me. I knew I was interrupting and quickly looked forward, only to see an identical cynical look from Jenna Le.

I held my hands wide, balancing the birdcage in one. "None of my business."

We reached the musky tent that I shared with Mica and Yuri, and Jenna Le left. I placed the cage on the nightstand. Yuri turned over on the narrow cot but didn't wake with questions. I opened the tin and fingered a dead beetle to offer the gualarep through the wires of the cage. He sniffed my fingers and the food but then he jerked around, mounting the cage walls and tilting his head.

"Cenzea in the ravine," I whispered. "I cannot risk freeing you. How can I face Lupe again if you're gone missing?"

I lay back on the cot, fully dressed, hoping for a few hours of rest before boarding the chopper. I listened to Mica's snoring and Yuri's regular breathing, except there was a cricket in the tent or just outside. The cage rattled each time the insect chirped, and I knew I wouldn't sleep with that irritation.

I sat up and opened the tin, and he grabbed the dead insects. I thought about it for a moment, most likely a mistake, before I released the cage door. "You're free now, Edwin. Do you mind if I call you Edwin? Food here, or go chase the cricket. Just a little quiet, that's all I ask. A few moments of quiet."

He was stock still as I spoke, just as though we were in conversation. He scurried down the table leg, quick as you please, and under the tent wall. That didn't take long. I flopped back onto the cot and was soon snoring in unison with my tent mates.

I dreamed of swimming and choking, breaking the water surface in the gravel pit where I went swimming with my brothers. I dreamed of diving deep, while moving my hips with feet together like a mermaid. Two large fish swim around me, singing maybe, except they have the faces of Cleo and Camille. They draw me deeper and I feel pressure in my lungs. Breathe. I need to draw a breath.

The dream shifts to the cavern at the digs. My footsteps reverberate, as I hurry in a tunnel toward the light. I'm here! Don't leave me in the dark! I stumble and go to one knee, gasping and tasting the moist air stale with decay. Where are they? Why am I deserted?

I move up a tunnel that gets more narrow, so I have to bend at the knees and shoulders. I find a tiny alcove with a wooden box and the lid ajar. I open the box and see two bodies, desiccated and twisted to fit into the tight container. They seem to shrink to bones only, wearing tatters and beaded bracelets. I know they are Cleo and Camille. I know they were just swimming with me. My face wet with sobs. Can't catch my breath.

I hear a soft cooing. I feel the infant gualarep climb up my pant leg. He's on my chest, rocking on one front and one back leg. He switches legs, almost prancing on my chest. Click, click, click— he's telling me something. He nestles at my side, with his tiny back against my ribs. Breathing okay now. Breathing is good.

The dreams vanished.

EIGHTEEN

THE BIRDCAGE WAS USELESS. EDWIN CLUNG TO MY SHIRT UNDER my vest, or added himself to my pack under the flap. He walked onto the palm of my hand when offered that perch, cream and celery-colored with sharp teeth and a long snout for his size. The tin of dead insects was empty, and crickets didn't sing in the daytime, so I decided he was fed for now.

At the mess area, a Putuki woman offered dried fish on a native patty, but I shook my head. The chopper was slated to leave that same hour, so I could eat in Cylay.

As we grabbed hot tea, Dr. Gutierrez noticed Edwin peeking out of my collar. "Visit us at Beecham Place, Blancom, during the rainy season," Gutierrez said with his usual balance. "We'll open a bottle of Kiam gin."

I walked to the mound top where my exit was pending. Mrs. Shaw was at the helipad talking quietly with Hakulupe Le. She spoke to me in turn. "Brianna visits Cochin for now, but she plans to be in Cylay for the free elections. We'll let you know."

"Melinga, Mrs. Shaw."

In the transport chopper, I strapped in next to Hakulupe Le who was traveling with her daughters and Jenna Le who sat without expression across the aisle. Mark looked small seated next to Jenna Le and staring out the hatch window. Edwin was clicking softly, and I noticed he was focused on another tiny creature that peeked out from the folds of Lupe's Arrivi veil/shawl. She was covered the same as me by the song.

"His name is Edwin," I said. "What did you name that one?"

Shards of early sunlight made her bright eyes glimmer. "Is Milo a good name? The males wander off at a certain age to live a solitary life. But that's many cycles of Nettom from now. What you really need, Blancom, is a woman of your own."

"Don't start."

"You have a life here now," she grinned. "Not an adventurer who will jump back when his fortune is made. What do you hear from Jesse Hartley?"

"What? The general's daughter? I met her one time in passing." Actually, it was nine times over seven days; thirty-one smiles, and twelve giggles. But who was counting?

"You danced with her at the Consortium ball. Kelly told us."

"I danced with Kelly too. That didn't make us great friends." I returned Lupe's all-knowing smile and sat back, only to see the stone face of Jenna Le.

Jesse. Jesse Hartley in a yellow ball gown with her hair piled up to expose the neckline. White gloves to the elbow and beaded slippers. Classy Jesse Hartley, the general's daughter against whom all other women were judged and found wanting.

We reached the barracks yard. Many helpers were present. Probably to manage Lupe's daughters and the considerable luggage that was the paperwork for new civil law, I was thinking. Mark greeted each helper and gave instructions.

I was rude enough to solicit a final quote. Hakulupe Le kept her voice low. "Ely signed many treaties over the seasons that are at risk now. Some in the tribes will call for a public trial to showcase his corruption. His cronies will be slapped with civil suits. The people must see, though. Ely is allowed to live."

"Allowed to serve tribal logic?" I asked.

She lifted her chin, nailing me with lambent eyes. "Today I'm glad that Marcy has robbed the desert of one and need not endure this spectacle." She left in the center of a sizeable Arrivi escort. Jenna Le walked with them, taller than most, and turned to show me that immobile face again.

I made my way by catching rides from officers in bobcats and reached the gazette offices. I waved to Luluki, who was manning the stationary camera at the end of the hall, before I turned sharply toward the showers.

Edwin sneezed at the smell of disinfectant and waited in the locker, nestled in my dirty clothes, until I dressed. I chose a lightweight, roomy jacket so Edwin had some room for play.

As I padded along the hallway to our press club, through the tall windows I surveyed the sunlit plaza. Many Arrivi lingered in Cylay since the funeral of General Sector. The wide square was packed with tents and established lanes for foot traffic. Women sat in organized groups, and gaggles of children chased around. Consortium vehicles waited in alleyways where soldiers smoked kari stems and bantered with young people. A couple of big tractors with yellow fenders waited near the limestone wall, along with a bulldozer with a backhoe attachment. Inside the mansion gate, Putuki soldiers stood in line for breakfast service, apparently bored with monitoring the growing crowd.

I stopped near George Luluki who also watched the activity below. "Anything new?"

"The statue will be delivered today, we think. Academy residents removed the shrine to Kyle Rula with an elaborate ritual. The segment I captured is already online."

"Kyle Rula is also part of the bigger sculpture, right?"

He nodded, not asking questions about my adventures. "With her three sisters."

In our press club, I scrounged some corn chips and hot tea and switched on an EAM. Edwin seemed focused on the pouch that contained the chime coral lute, so I pulled it down for him. He hopped about in different postures, like a dance, while he sniffed the lute and bumped it with his nose.

"If you knock that off the table and it breaks, then um . . . no insects for a day," I warned. How did one punish an infant gualarep?

I saw an EAM segment, where Bobbie with her big teeth flashing interviewed George Luluki, except her questions made no sense. George wore dry makeup so his bald pate didn't reflect the lights. Bobbie wanted to know if he was a socialist and if he thought the work of the people had been exploited by Rularim.

George entered the press club as I was chuckling over his discomfort with the absurd questions. He poured a mug of hot tea from the urn and joined me. "Bobbie asked if I thought Ely was a fascist. How do you answer a question like that?"

"Turn the question on its head. Just assert that Ely runs the government like an oligarchy. Only Ely and his cronies hold power."

"O-li-gar-chy," George repeated slowly.

"Your turn to talk into the camera," I added, "doesn't have to match the question. Speak to home rule and free elections." I thought of my questions to the holy woman Kat and wondered if my words seemed posed from a discordant worldview. "Your first interview as a politician?" I asked him. "When were you going to tell me?"

He grinned and relaxed. Maybe he was seeking an opportunity to mention the new job offer. "A minister position may be a false start, Simon tells me, depending on who is elected as rabbenu."

"Your uncle, the Putuki bazaari?"

George nodded. "For now, I have more credibility working at the gazette."

"Yes, well," I tasted sage and shrugged to manage my irritation. "Be sure to train someone for this job before you make the jump into politics."

"What's with that?" George asked as he took the flute away from Edwin's grasp. The infant let out a bark that sounded like a squeak, and jumped twice with his tail raised. "Not yours," George told him teasingly.

"I call him Edwin. We'll have to set Dingo and Flash to insect hunting."

"A duty they may actually be good at." He handed the flute and pouch to me. "Better put those out of sight."

I stowed the pouch and flute in a desk drawer. Edwin scurried down the table leg and up my pant leg to nestle in my shirt. To cover the tickling sensation, I asked, "What did I miss here?"

"You were gone for one day," George said. "The shuttle leaves at dawn tomorrow. Ely and his, um, crowd bought out the seats. Colonel Shananinni plans a security net through the streets. They don't want a repeat of Sector's death."

The early shuttle arrival was prompted by the need to complete this final task before General Hartley retired, I was thinking. Hartley and Rabbenu Ely would leave office in tangent.

Paul Spurlin joined us, and we began a strategy session for how to cover pending events. My stories about the findings at the digs were considered filler articles and were set aside in favor of Cylay news. I decided to keep mum about General Hartley stepping down, since we had no route for verification. Paul Spurlin called dibs on the shuttle camera station at dawn. I said the place would be deserted except for Ely's group and the Consortium soldiers, the least interesting station, but Paul smirked. He soon left with two others.

"What's with him?" I asked George.

"You spent the day with Hakulupe Le. He was left to negotiate with Dulcinea."

"It's Dulcinea!"

George nodded with a big grin. "She's so tight with oblu, she straightens the twist. And she can't manage a conversation of three sentences without wiping some kid's nose."

"That's a way for her to—"

"I know what it is, and so does Spurlin. They all ask 'Where is Blancom?' as the first thing out of their mouths. Spurlin's native handle is Bobcat, did you know? Like he named the vehicle after himself."

"Oriika's eyes." I grabbed the camcorder and two cameras, leaving to work the plaza crowd before the heat of the day. My method was to chat with the people until the novelty of my presence wore off and candid shots could be captured. The plaza was flooded by unrelieved sunlight, and Edwin scurried into my shirt, settling along my back above the belt.

Several political parties had sprung up, not tagged as liberal or conservative but each claiming the ideal of home rule. Slates of candidates were published and revised, and pamphlets with candidate photos were stacked on all tables. The placards with Brianna Miller's image were missing. Instead, I saw Orin rabbe Murd's face touted by the Independent People's Party. Posters with Kyros Kenoma's face were everywhere, put forth as the next rabbenu by the Coalition Party. Images of many women candidates, all Arrivi, were prominent in the swirling crowd carrying placards. I just wished we had bid on the printing franchise for this free election, a windfall in the making.

I went first to the Press Club station and shook hands with Robert and Bobbie. "I saw the piece you did with George Luluki," I said to be friendly. "Is he your choice for the new rabbenu?"

She shook her head with a turned down mouth. "Luluki had no answers. He doesn't even know what buzzwords to use."

"Well, I thought I'd circulate a bit. Get a feel for the man on the street."

"What are you expecting?" Robert asked. He was sweating pro-fusely, and his shirt was wet along his back too. He needed to lose the girth if he wanted savannah duty.

"The shuttle doesn't leave until dawn," I said with a shrug. They both stared. I was certain they knew the shuttle had arrived earlier than scheduled. I was certain they knew Ely had bought all the pas-senger seats for the next launch. So why was my statement a sur-prise?

Cunning flickered across Bobbie's face. "How will the Consor-tium manage to move Ely's group past these demonstrators?"

She was fishing for sure, but I could play her off. "Maybe they'll make him walk," I suggested with a big grin before I melted into the native crowd.

I went to the café and used a landline to contact George Luluki in our offices. "Turn the camera," I said. "Can you see a back gate? Can you see a different exit?"

"We had people stationed there for days," George said. "There's no movement."

"Ely must be using a tunnel. I'm thinking the Putuki soldiers in the compound know that Ely left already. That's why the alert is relaxed. Did Spurlin know?"

"He said nothing to me."

"Weasel," I complained. "What a weasel."

George snorted, an unbecoming response. "And you visiting the Uburu digs and all."

"Henry endit."

By the lashes of Cyrus! Colonel Shananinni must be keeping secrets, allowing the tribes to wait in the heat as he maneuvered a gopher jump. And those junior reporters knew already.

I walked briskly toward the Coalition Party tent. Irritation must have radiated from me, because Edwin poked his head out from my shirt collar, tilting it left and right as if asking a question. "Yah, yah," I muttered.

I saw Genki without a burka at one of the tents and made a beeline in that direction. Unblessed kids ran across my path calling "Blancom, Blancom!" and begging for a photo. My steps slowed and I tried to manage my outrage. So what if Dolviets didn't follow my plan for their fates? So what if the Consortium got ahead of events to prevent assassination? If I was Colonel Shananinni, wouldn't I do the same? A shuttle launch was covered for the gazette since Spurlin was in place at the launch pad. What was lost?

Mark signified on me for melingas. He and Genki pointed to their station, as if to involve me in their good work. Genki was a handsome woman, now that I could see her face, but big-boned like Jenna Le and with a jutting jaw. I snapped images of Mark in front of Genki, smiling together and showing election pamphlets with rosters of party candidates.

Dulcinea was in the tent. Before she came forward, she pulled her bodice closed and handed an infant with orange fuzz on his head to Genki. "Hiki, Blancom," Dulcinea said, holding a palm high. "How was your visit at the Uburu digs?"

"Does this machine belong to Orin rabbe Murd?" I demanded, skipping the response that showed respect.

She looked over the heads of several to spy the big tractor near the gate. "Is there a problem?"

"Ely is no longer in the mansion," I told her bitterly.

Dulcinea only returned my hard stare.

"You knew already," I guessed. "What are you waiting for now?"

"Rabbenu Ely leaves in disgrace if we don't force him," she said in even tones. "He deserts the office of rabbenu." Her looks that relaxed the eyes were incongruous with her words, like she repeated a lesson learned at school. "We may occupy the mansion in our own time. As a public building that belongs to the people. Not as a scene for riots."

I made a snorting sound. "The plaza is filled with protestors."

"You see protestors?"

I felt an itch along my back and moved my shoulder irritably. "Then why are these people here?" I asked.

Dulcinea gestured widely, opening our conversation to any who wanted to join. "As witnesses to history. Jour-na-lists like to use words that are con-fron-ta-tion-al, gained from your Softcheeks history but used here to define Arrivi events."

"What do you see here?" I finally thought to ask.

Dulcinea's eyebrows shot up, shaping an inquisitive look. "Our governor deserts us, so we must reinforce tribal law and rewrite treaties with our neighbors."

Kyros Kenoma came up behind me, flanked by Stuben and two of his gang members with rust-colored hair. "Blancom, did you come to endorse me as candidate for rabbenu?"

"Ah, the policy of the gazette is to remain impartial," I faltered. "I can post a chart for political parties and lists of candidates."

Kyros put an arm around my shoulder. "Good! That is good, Blancom. Stuben will stay with you today. He's im-par-tial too."

"I don't need an escort."

Kyros leaned in close. "Today you do," he whispered, and he broke into a public smile. "We are honored that Blancom visited our campaign headquarters first," he said aloud for all to hear. "We know an entire day can be spent reaching each party, so we encourage these im-par-tial campaign workers to guide you through the crowd."

I was defined as Softcheeks attending native events. I accepted the offered campaign material from Genki's hand and moved down the line with Stuben at my back. Liberation maybe led to many impulsive acts. The people could easily turn for freedom or for riot, or against an intruding Softcheeks.

The hour was spent accepting pamphlets, taking photos of party workers, and chatting with the many women who served food and murmured my name; "Blancom, Blancom!" The repetition only reinforced my strangeness among them. When I lingered at a party table, my presence lowered its popularity.

Stuben and his redheaded friends waited several paces distant like Siize and Siiloba would have. I was covered by them but not brought forward by them for the honored greetings. Candidates for the smaller parties stepped into my path and solicited my attention; otherwise, I was on my own.

Arrivi belonged here. I knew that. They were rooted on the savannah and accustomed to the cycles of om. If Hamilcar resigned or if he lingered; what was that to them? They were languid and fatalistic, expecting no savior and no advancement, the same tomorrow as today. Friendly to a bench mate just because he was sharing that hour in the heat, they would trek home tomorrow or the next day because chores were waiting. Tales in the villages would be applauded, no matter if Ely showed his face or Kyros Kenoma was elected. "We are back now from Cylay," they would tell waiting family members. "What a time we had there in the season of kari."

Shadows were long by the time I was circling back toward Bobbie's position where she reported into the comtech cameras with her big teeth flashing under stage lights. I felt a twinge of jealousy that Bobbie was supported by a structured organization where she was part of a larger narrative, part of a whole industry. Except I despised the narrative she touted.

I was suddenly tired and murderously depressed. Thermals rose from the hot pavement impacting my vision and slowing my steps. Within the shimmering heat radiating from the biscuit-colored wall decorated with graffiti, I thought I saw vapors of a woman's face, also in a bitter smirk, maybe sorry she had devoted the scrying time to follow me and not some other player.

With a loud roar, the shuttle rose overhead spewing a stream of white vapor. It rolled and pushed into the sunlit sky with diminishing noise. The crowd cheered, animated and celebrating. The big cameras swiveled to pan the crowd while Bobbie showed me a look of disdain.

I decided that today I had worked enough hours. I turned toward the municipal building, longing for a nap. I needed to recharge the camcorder anyway.

Dkar was suddenly before me, blocking my steps. "You're still here, Blancom, among us unblessed ones? Ely just left, and Hamilcar has left; but you linger here with us. Why is that?" His grin was sinister, showing the missing teeth on one side of his mouth. "The rooms are unclean," he added in a slimy tone, "and the women smell bad. Genki's food is not worthy. Why do you linger with these unblessed ones?"

I focused on him: my landlord and friend who had helped me buy blue macaw feathers to secure my room. "Dkar, I have joined the tribes. I have—"

He stepped back a fraction showing apparent surprise. "Joined us? Join the Putuki? Did you offer help to Voki Manuki and his daughters? Did you wonder what happened to them, the girls? No? It didn't cross your mind what happens to the smelly women unworthy of your touch."

"But . . . we're friends," I complained. "I counted you as a friend." I stepped back, probably a mistake, opening the space between us.

Dkar leaned in to crowd me, and he wasn't the only one. "Looking down on us, the gaze of Softcheeks." He spoke to faces in the crowd, nobody I knew; maybe nobody he knew. "Learn to help yourselves, he wrote. Pick up your own garbage, he wrote. Lazy, thoughtless, unworthy." The murmuring crowd repeated his words. "Unworthy, unworthy."

I saw the butt end of a karkar flash before my eyes and braced myself for the jolt. The show of weapons was from Stuben and his gang, though. I heard the crunch of bone when the gunstock connected with Dkar's cheekbone. Stuben's gang quickly surrounded me and faced off the few tribesmen who stood behind Dkar, stooped and holding his palm against his face.

I saw pamphlets fly out of Dulcinea's tent before the percussion sounded. I knew instantly that a pipe bomb had exploded—and where. I rushed forward in a crowd that scurried away, Stuben and his friend on my heels.

Dulcinea and the babe were not present, spared from the explosion. Two bodies only were marked and bleeding, lying twisted on the lane. Dolviets started throwing buckets of dirt onto the burning tent while the alarm sounded an emergency call. I knelt next to Genki who stared up with sightless eyes. Her arm was missing and the crisscross of her Arrivi gown was stained red. Genki who had offered me what services she could muster from friendship. The other victim was Mark, lying on his stomach with shards of wood and metal embedded in his back. I snapped images of them bleeding together and thought of the early photos of their smiles as they embraced the political work.

"You must leave," Stuben said while he pulled on my upper arm.

"I know her!"

"No place for slags."

"I can use the camera. I can capture—"

"Save your heartstone for the funeral pyre," Stuben said in hard tones. "You must go now. Back to the glass building for slag safety."

My escort rushed me across the square while the crowd milled in all directions. Individuals seemed to step aside for the armed gang members. At the municipal building, I noticed that several Putuki men followed us. I was pushed into the polished lobby that had an escalator and felt the chill of recycled air. Stuben's gang jimmied the revolving doors from outside and blocked the other exit. Men in the crowd pounded on the floor-to-ceiling windows, though, shouting "Death to the sor'shum! The sor'shum must die!"

I took the moving steps two at a time, and turned to look only after I was on the mezzanine. The Putuki men in the crowd quieted and lost focus when the noisy engine of a big chopper was heard. Over the roof of the mansion, we saw a heavy statue swinging slightly and held horizontally by hefty cords extended from a Consortium transport chopper.

I breathed out, blowing air though my dry lips, glad for new events that captured the attention of liberated tribesmen. The disturbance from chopper blades blew debris and slapped pamphlets against the windows while the protestors hunched and covered their eyes. The statue depicting four women and a ketiwhelp was slowly lowered onto a cement pad where the fountain and shrine were once located.

As the chopper hovered and the bindings were removed—first the base, so the weight was situated upright—I got on the elevator. When I exited the elevator on the seventh floor, Dingo and Flash rushed my way. I stepped back fearful of a betrayal here too. Dingo took the elevator going down, and Flash secured the stairwell doors.

George Luluki stood in the hall with question on his face, just as some projectile bounced off the big window. There was no force behind it because we were so high up from the streets. George pressed his back against the wall as more rocks and pebbles sounded on the panes. He waved for me to come to him, and we ducked into the office. I saw Flash rush into the press club.

"Mark is dead," I reported. "And Genki. From a pipe bomb. We have to find the cowards and bring them to justice."

"Feels different when the chaos is directed at you, huh?"

"Sorry," I murmured. "I mean, sorry for not caring when the bazaari were, um . . . But who's doing this? Who is setting off bombs on the day of liberation?"

George sighed heavily. "Liberation is intoxicating. A tribal event and not for you."

"Me? Why me?"

"Today you are slag and nothing more."

We craned our necks forward, still hugging the wall, as the chopper finished its delivery. The ropes pulled up to a wince, and the helicopter banked left. The air settled and the crowd swarmed the plaza center. Below us, dancing and clucking broke out just as though two Dolviets were not lost; just as though Mark and Genki didn't count.

"A good choice to bring in the statue today," George said. "Not tribal anger at Ely's retreat. A good marker for a new beginning."

"And that's it?"

"We can post a eulogy for Mark. Many will mourn him at the funeral pyre. But not just now. Ely and his ministers and his mistresses are gone. The season of cylay is upon us. We have regime change with no bloodshed."

"No bloodshed?"

"No civil war. No chaos leading to home rule."

"Are you writing an editorial?" My voice carried a sour note I had not intended.

George looked at me and blinked. "My words and those of Orin and Kyros should fill the gazette today, not slag words."

"Stop calling me that. I was working for—"

"We know."

"Paul, too. He never took a break, always working for—"

"We know, but today you can take a back seat. Just for today."

"Yah, sure. I was thinking about a nap, but with all this commotion . . ."

George Luluki's shoulders were hunched and one hand covered his mouth and chin. He was biding his time until a new rabbenu was in place and he could join the administration. His service at our ragsheet was a steppingstone.

I sighed and turned toward my room, already composing in my head ads for new personnel.

Help wanted: Dolviets who write in three dialects and don't judge me.

NINETEEN

I DIDN'T SLEEP, TROUBLED BY IMAGES OF GENKI'S STAINED BODICE and empty eyes. Paul was back in the office an hour later, and he scowled when he caught me apparently napping. I showed him an open palm. "Hey, I was told to stand down. Anti-climactic, anyhow. Ely slinked away using a tunnel or something."

"We got the video."

Paul led me to our press club where he uploaded the feed from when Colonel Shananinni escorted Ely into the shuttle hanger. We saw soldiers in uniforms and blue tams who shaped a barrier to onlookers and would-be assassins. Ely carried a satchel and dragged a suitcase, looking Old World and harried in his blue suit. The women huddled together with no understanding and certainly no presence before the camera. Other Putuki who had clung to Ely's rule were sour-faced and anxious.

"And he was rabbenu for almost thirty years," Paul said as we watched them file through the chute. Paul looked at me and shook his head. "We'll put this online with no editing so the tribes can see.

John Milan boarded the shuttle too, but not in front of the cameras. He jabbered at me about a story-of-the-decade he was working on, and how you're an ungrateful pup."

"Yah, sure," I said with a shrug.

As he worked, Dingo and Flash hovered in the doorway. Flash stepped forward and handed me a bell jar with live insects: beetles and damselflies mostly.

"Melinga," I said.

I screwed off the lid and set the bell jar on the floor on its side. Edwin needed no more encouragement than that. He was off me in a second and pounced on each victim as it tested the container opening. The beetles were bigger than Edwin's head, but he used those sharp teeth and forced the parts down his throat. Dingo and Flash squatted and watched with laughter.

"What have you got there?" Paul asked as he worked.

"Sleep therapy. I named him Edwin."

"Just keep him out—"

Edwin had made short work of the provisions. He scurried across the floor, swinging his body and tail. He was up the table leg and on Paul's arm before we could reach out. He stood on Paul's head, nuzzling the thin hair with his long snout and with a long series of clicks.

Paul waved one hand over his head. "Hey, get down!" In a flash, Edwin was on the keyboard, barely covering it and too light to press the keys but breaking Paul's focus.

"What the hell?"

George Luluki was laughing heartily, and Dingo and Flash hid their humor as Flash collected the jar and lid. "He likes you," George said.

"Just keep him out of my stuff," Paul complained. "I don't need him pissing all over the cameras."

I made a chucking noise like I had with my favorite palomino at the station. Edwin came down the table leg, across the floor, and up my pant leg in a single motion. He got into my shirt, tickling my side, and settled where he had before in the small of my back above the belt.

Paul rolled his eyes and went back to work.

Nettom and Nettki hovered overhead as night closed in, both full like uneven headlights, as if they wanted to join the celebration. We watched from the seventh story windows. Blue moonlight competed with the yellow bonfire situated in front of the big statue in the plaza. The crowd also had cooking fires all around. The young people gathered in tight groups before the statue and started a native dance with girls in one line and the boys facing them. Family groups were chanting and dancing, seemingly intimate and relaxed.

"Aren't those fires illegal?" Paul asked.

George shrugged. "We should call out the police to ensure that each family has the ely certificate. Do you think the Putuki officers will respond?"

Established tents below also had EAM screens, flashing blue lines from our angle of view where Dolviets gathered to watch Paul's segment about the exit of Ely on the shuttle launch. Some cheered and pointed. Some joined the dancing. Some sat alone, staring ahead to savor this change of seasons that the tribes shared as one people.

I talked briefly with Dulcinea on the EAM. She claimed that Genki was remembered and Mark's funeral pyre was tomorrow, if I wanted to attend.

"My heartstone is crippling," I complained.

"Genki was a friend to you. She valued you."

"Who did this? Who will investigate?"

"We don't look to Gora today. We look to—"

"Gora? But that was your publicity tent." I felt an itch along my back. I wanted to know for certain that I played no part, was not responsible for the death of my friends. Not revealing the location to a carromancist through my carelessness. "The target was maybe you and Karisma," I said. "Just a misfire."

Dulcinea waited two beats. "I appreciate your concern. You should get some rest now, Blancom. Edwin is there with you, no?"

"Yah. Uh, yah, he's here in the offices. Somewhere."

I looked toward the windows at a bright flash. My stomach twisted from fear of another pipe bomb. On a timer, the lights to the mansion had flared to illuminate the broad deserted yard inside the gates.

"I must go now, Blancom," Dulcinea said on our comtech call. "We'll talk again."

"Thanks. Henry endit."

I joined Paul and George at the windows. "Aren't they afraid of the pipe bombs going off?" I asked.

"Today's explosion is past," George said. "Seldom two on the same day."

"This is no ordinary day."

Below us, people moved toward the mansion entrance in curious groups. Most had never been in the main rooms, always channeled to a back entrance to pay fines and purchase the ely. Two tractors were in the square from earlier, one much larger and managed by Arrivi ranchers. The bulldozer was primed; the engine roared with gears grinding. The air must taste of diesel fuel, I was thinking. Drivers jumped onto the other two machines with big yellow fenders, and kids from the street gangs also found seats on the fenders and running boards. The behemoth machines hesitated for a tense moment, waiting for some signal.

"We had better get down there," Paul said starting to gather his cameras.

"I'll go," said George. "You should stay. This one night, let the tribes take the lead."

Paul looked at me, and I nodded. He smirked and stomped to the big stationary camera in the hall, ready to assume the controls.

"Stay safe," I said to George. "The stringers are out too, so don't risk yourself to capture all moments."

George headed for the elevators, Dingo and Flash trailing his steps carrying loose equipment and materials. I need to get backpacks for them, I thought.

I poured tea into two mugs and noticed that Edwin was free in the press club, so I closed the door. I carried the second mug to Paul where he sat, and we settled back with this bird's-eye view. Below us, the bulldozer slowly took action, pressuring not the gate but the biscuit-colored limestone wall. People hung back in clutches. After a couple of false starts, the bulldozer driver was able to mount an angle and dislodge top stones. A tractor approached. The long backhoe arm, drawn forward from its resting place above rear wheels, was activated with complaining gears to scoop the heavy stones, stacking them against a different section of the wall. It was slow and methodical work, but nobody went home.

The second tractor was a big-wheeler with polished yellow rim covers. Towering over the other equipment, it climbed the pile of angled debris the backhoe had constructed. The weight of the wheels against the wall pressured limestone blocks. With roaring engines and grinding gears, the other equipment was positioned so strong headlights illuminated the work. The tractor operator made a second attempt to breach the wall. There was a breathless waiting in the humid air tasting of fuel oil.

Stones toppled into the landscaped yard of the governor's house. A cheer went up. Unblessed ones pressed against the big machines, waving arms and chanting.

"They're just begging disaster," Paul muttered, as he panned across tribal faces engaged with in chanting and dancing. The police were absent, and Consortium soldiers hung back near their lorries in the alleyways.

The big wheeler backed down from the debris pile. The smaller tractor took a position within the breach and assaulted the wall shortways, knocking stones left and right with the backhoe arm. The bulldozer entered the widened breach and ran treads over the adjacent side, crumbling the wall like week-old biscuits. Bulldozer destruction pressured the wrought-iron main gate. The drivers knew their work; a committee-reasoned exercise wherein each completed an agreed role.

Supporting stones were dislodged, and the gate twisted like licorice, then clanked and clattered onto the street pavement. People cheered and chanted, pressing forward and pulsating in an excited dance. The driver brought his backhoe arm to rest, balanced on rear wheels behind his head like grasshopper legs. He slowly motored over to the gate, his headlights demanding the center of attention while tribesmen stepped back to let him pass.

Arrivi ranchers dressed like Orin rabbe Murd lashed ropes to the mutilated gate. The tractor dragged the fallen symbol toward the crowd. The driver shifted gears. A phalanx of unblessed ones backed away while he pulled the gate around the center of the square, around the big sculpture of the sisters of Arim.

The crowd was suddenly exhilarated. The tractor's relative speed; the impromptu act of defacing Rabbenu Ely's most prominent symbol; engine noise and wrought iron scraping against stone. Sparks flying. The tractor driver took a second turn around the big statue like a victory lap.

Safely seated high above the action, Paul Spurlin shook his head. "Begging disaster."

The tractor stopped so headlights fell on the opening where the gate had been, and the engine switched off. The driver stood in his seat, arms raised and fists shaking in triumph. It was Orin rabbe Murd, his face unevenly lit by the mansion lights. His men who had secured the gate, dressed the same as him, pushed aside the street kids and climbed onto the tractor with Orin. Together they turned to the unblessed ones, arms raised in triumph.

Victory suddenly had a new face. Orin rabbe Murd could run for office.

The crowd was jubilant. People surged against the piled stones of the breach and broke through, forming a long stream into the dry yard of the governor's house. Others rushed the tractor to carry Orin on their shoulders through the gate opening, carrying the campaign placards and calling for friends to hurry so they entered together, shoulder-to-shoulder. They swarmed the manicured yard and passed the fountain and up the steps to assault the big double doors. Young people frolicked in the fountain, climbed trees, and threw paint-filled bladders against the mansion windows and walls.

An open jeep carrying four Arrivi men and a woman in a sky-blue burka edged through the crowd in the square. On the side, Consortium officers signaled that soldiers should stand pat. The crowd slowly parted while the jeep made its way past the wall and through the gateway and into the mansion's circular drive.

Hakulupe Le stood in the jeep, protected by the others. With one jerk she removed the burka, throwing it down.

Lupe's hair was long in the traditional fashion and coiled at her neck. She was rested and glowing with health. She wore lots of peridot jewelry, as well as the amulet of honor on her upper arm for a recently lost husband. The crowd went delirious as she stood with arms spread wide and lifted her face to the lights from the illuminated entrance.

I saw George and two stringers in the front of the crowd. I was certain he got a great close-up of Lupe receiving their adulation.

"She's not Rularim," Paul said to me. "What honor?"

"The widow of a respected officer," I said with a shrug, "The academy founder. A symbol of resistance to the Company because of the manner of her birth."

"A target while Rularim and Dulcinea are not at risk."

"That too," I said. "Hakulupe Le deserves the honor, though."

"She was my first introduction to the leadership circle. You took me straight to her."

Hakulupe Le and her escort mounted the steps to the main door that was opened for them from the inside. She turned and said a few words, but the long-distance camera was not useful to capture her meaning.

She walked into the governor's mansion. Others followed in an orderly fashion, hesitant and wondering, as though they entered without invitation into the sanctuary of a strange religion. She asked them to respect of the office of rabbenu, I was thinking.

People quieted their chanting and dancing. They filed through the yard and the double doors with wonder. Maybe the Consortium officers were inside, ready to channel these guests walking between velour ropes linked stand-to-stand to gaze at the wonders of architecture and decoration, to later file out the rear like a White House tour. Their dusty footprints from worn sandals would dirty the polished tile.

And that was it, the peaceful deposing of Rabbenu Ely in favor of home rule.

"Not a shot was fired," Paul said quietly.

I shrugged. "Except the private assassinations of Ely's cronies, we mustn't forget. Sectarian deaths in every tribe. The attempted assassination of General Hartley, the sacrifice of Sector. The loss of Mark and Genki just today. But . . . why spoil the moment?"

"Not a shot fired in the plaza." Paul reached up from his seat behind the big camera, and we slapped high-five. "Worth every minute," he dryly added.

The elevators opened, and George Luluki returned with two stringers. We sat at our desks and started the editing and uploading of commentary for this most native event. People came and went, and I saw Stuben and his followers with rust-colored hair among the revelers who had exited the elevator. Our chatter had reached a peak, like an office party, when Kyros and Dulcinea arrived.

My table phone started ringing, and Stuben nearly jumped out of his skin, his first experience with a landline.

"That will be Steny Morse from the Press Club and ready to gloat about getting the scoop on Ely's exit," I told George and reached to pick up the receiver.

It was Doug Endicott on the line, calling from Ninleau. "Have you heard?" he asked.

"Yah, Ely was deposed and has left the planet."

"I've been watching your online news site," Endicott shouted into the phone, maybe because he could hear the chatter that surrounded me. "I mean the other news. Brianna Miller is taken."

"Taken where?"

"Listen up, Henry," Endicott said over the line. "Aristides detained your Rularim when she was returning from Cochin. The Abydian have her, and you know how they treat prisoners."

I turned my back to the revelers. I stuck a finger in my other ear and tried to keep my voice calm. "But Brianna traveled with an escort."

"She did. I have their names here . . . um, Lynus and Aensilus. Both dead."

"What? They're dead?" Lynus the brother to Rufus, and Aensilus the Madquii; they had served as my escort when I had first disembarked and trekked across the Madquii dunes.

"We know about the kidnapping," Endicott said on the phone, measuring his words, "because the bodies were returned to Aeolis for the honorable pyre. Aristides is working both sides of the fence."

"But why take Brianna Miller? Why now?"

"Sector is dead. Ely is out of office. Hartley will step down tomorrow. Who are her champions who can mount a rescue?"

"But why do the Abydian care? Ananke is so insular."

"In Urbyd, Brianna was talking alliance and bypassing the port for trade. She was seeking dhimma with kels in Ninleau to consolidate the silicide enterprise." Endicott's voice was silent for a moment before he chuckled softly. "You didn't invite Abydian to your little experiment with home rule. So like the wicked queen in Sleeping Beauty, Aristides has crashed your party and taken the heir."

I sank into my chair ignoring the revelers. Today's pipe bomb event made more sense to me now. "Where is she held?"

"In the Urbyd palace," Endicott said. "Aristides will keep her alive to manipulate the next rabbenu, but it won't be pretty."

"Hartley will show up and throttle him red-handed."

"Not with the Consortium behind him," Endicott said over the landline. "Timing is everything. Your Rularim was not covered while Ely stepped down."

"I see what you mean. Thanks for the call. I'll spread the news here."

"Wish I had something more cheerful to report. Endicott endit."

I hung up the phone and sighed. Should I tell Kyros now, or allow them one night of joy and new confidence? I wanted to consult with Paul Spurlin first, but I knew what he would say. Bad news was best reported immediately. I stood to face the crowd.

Dulcinea was talking with Spurlin. She saw my face and her smile faded. She came to my side. "Blancom, you look pale."

"Brianna Miller is kidnapped by Aristides. Lynus and Aensilus are dead."

Several expressions passed over her features as she digested the news. She touched my arm lightly. "They were your friends."

I noted through the buzz in my ears that Dulcinea's first concern was for others, for the loss. She would manage the news deftly, but her gesture grew my esteem for her to fill this room and all the rooms in the municipal building. I wanted Dulcinea to succeed, to set an example for all tribal kids.

"Stuben," she said quietly, "bring Kyros and Bobcat. We have much to discuss."

Dulcinea guided me into the backroom where I sat on the cot. Edwin was in my shirt. I didn't realize when he had mounted my pant leg, but maybe when the others had opened our press club door. Edwin peeked out with a quiet series of clicks like asking a question, and his miniature head tilted.

Dulcinea noticed Edwin and smiled sadly. "You are truly the agent of karsci, Blancom. It is good that you have come to Dolvia to serve the tribes."

And so the season of cylay began.

Explore how the saga begins. In *Brittany Mill: A Dolvia Origins Story*, Brian Miller sets events into motion for Kyle Le and the Arrivi tribe when he establishes Brittany Mill and hires tribal women as textile workers, conflicting with the needs of Mekucoo warrior Cyrus.

When she finds work at Brittany Mill, Kyle Le stops sharing her gift of second sight with Cyrus who leads the resistance to the offworld mining company. She must choose between tribal logic and the offer from Brian Miller for more financial and political freedom. Will she lead her sisters and the Arrivi tribe into a modern future?

BRITTANY MILL

A DOLVIA ORIGINS STORY

EXCERPT

On the third day, I decided I could tolerate exposure long enough to get through my appointment with Martin Sumuki. The high-ceiling lobby of the Tri-City BankCorp was a pleasant surprise. Martin came out of his office and bowed, aping Company manners. He wore a rumpled, cream-colored linen suit and looked like his dossier photo, only heavier. He spoke English, Westend's universal language for business, and was pleased with my appreciation of the cool bank building. "It's native adobe, and we imported the ceiling fans. We keep air-conditioned rooms for visitors who don't care to acclimate. My office is similar to this room, if you're comfortable with that."

Martin's office was painted gray and apricot, furnished with cane chairs and a ceiling fan. Sunlight filtered through the slats of interior shutters. He switched off the single lamp on his small desk, which was really a plank over two sets of drawers. The luminous dial of a dehumidifier glowed from inside acrylic doors of a low cabinet, the only expensive piece of furniture in the room.

"Do you smoke, Mr. Miller?" Martin asked. I shook my head no.

He lit a thin aromatic cigarette, an act that classed him as ground-born. "So," he began, "we secured the buildings and off-loaded the equipment. I studied the delivery schedules, but they are not your real problem. Your labor force statistics are outdated."

"I saw conscript gangs at the hotel."

"A dirty business."

"Ricardo mentioned the possibility of employing the women at Brittany Mill."

"For the Cylahi perhaps, but few live in Somule."

"And Arrivi women?"

"There's a harem mentality among them. You will see, Mr. Miller. There's a wedding tomorrow for Haku rabbe Murd, who owns land and works at the rabbenu's limestone quarries. His bride is Karima Le of Arim. The event is out-of-doors and will last maybe three hours. How are your land legs?"

"I'll do fine. Thanks for your concern."

Back at the hotel, I ate several patties of the salty native bread. I switched off the air-conditioner in my room and opened the doors to the small balcony, determined to spend the remainder of the hot afternoon in the open air.

Sweating and light-headed, I managed to set up my briefcase monitor with a coolant unit. I locked in the EAM and waited for my codes to clear.

Presently the screen read, "Brian Miller, good day."

I indicated that I wanted to communicate in Arrivi. The screen blinked and read, "Rabbenu Miller, hiki." The program used a title of high honor. Rightfully, I should have been addressed as Brian rabbe Miller. At least the gender was correct. Had the program assumed I was a woman, I would have seen the diminutive form, Brian Le.

The EAM signed off for forty minutes every six hours while the transport's orbit dropped below my location's horizon. With an open-ended dialogue, the call automatically rebooted with my geographic time of day and the accumulated cost of the trunk call.

During the break, I looked over the balcony rail and realized it was night. Dolvia's two moons had not yet risen. Except for the well-lit hotel entrance and restaurant, the yawning blackness was deep. I heard the humming hotel generator and workmen hammering in the rail station where an engine was being repaired overnight.

The screen came up, showing "25:367 amk, 3418.420. Rabbenu Miller, hiki. Parle hai Rabbenu Menenous?" A cold chill ran down my back. I'd felt safe from surface peeping toms but had forgotten that the transport was wire heaven. Ricardo could have tracked the wanderings of my mind for hours and have been on a trunk call with Martin Sumuki the whole time. I knew instantly that I wouldn't depend on the EAM again. I typed in "Rabbenu Menenous, hiki."

A facsimile of his round and balding head came onscreen. He moved a dial. "I cannot see you, Brian," said his electronic voice.

I typed in "This is an EAM-12."

His image nodded. "Order an EAM-50 from the transport. Did you contact Martin?"

"Today at the bank," I typed. "A good man, Martin."

But Ricardo was on to business. "There was a puncture in the cargo hold. The loom was frozen clean through. Under gravity, it will crumble like peanut brittle. Occupy the buildings and set up everything else. I have a line on a local replacement. How are your land legs?"

"About the labor situation—" I typed.

"Yeah, yeah. We must talk again. Keep in touch."

I exited the screen and powered down the EAM. I lay on the bed in the humid night to get what little rest I could with a salted stomach and thought about the need to go bald.

During my tour in the asteroid belt, there was a news story about a paranoid personality who insisted his head had been wired—that he was the same as the machinery, just another piece of equipment. He refused services and ranted about his need to go bald. He was terminated as a recalcitrant. Going bald became freightate for traveling without technical support.

For field men, going bald was a very real possibility. Survival training was basic second level. My only bald assignment had been on Earth and before I'd known space travel. In those days we were sent out in groups and monitored.

I got up very late and went to the balcony. The air was cooler but dry. The two moons hung low in the quarter phase. A night bird called from the rustling bush beyond the hotel's light. Where was the balance on Dolvia? How did the savannah test one's mettle? How much the mettle of a bald administrator?

GLOSSARY

of character names in Home Rule.
*A second glossary of locations and terms
is also provided.*

NOTE: *Characters are listed by last name (where available)
and designated by status when first introduced.*

Aegiv—leader of Borabean Madquii clan, father to Aeolis and Aensilus

Aeocin—third on of Aeolis by Dulcinea the Uburu, raised Borabean by
   Aeolis's sister who lost her husband to the Goras

Aeolis—middle son and successor to Aegiv, brother to Aensilus

Aensilus—youngest of Aegiv's sons, friend to Lynus

Alaise—Borabean wife to Lynus

Anagella—Gora villager in Agora

Analli—tenth son of Ananke, abuser of Marna Le

Ananke—Borabean ruler in days of Brianna Miller, with ten sons

Anaxagoras—leader of Borabean Goras clan

Aristides—Abydian minister in Urbyd

Asmach—Borabean hero

Dr. Henry Beecham—hospital administrator after Dr. Abercrombie

Bibi Le—Southeast Arrivi married to Kyros rabbe Sudl, mother to Kristos and Karry and two daughters

Blanc—kam-man in Cylay who ran the street corner lottery

Blancom—"the last blonde", a nickname for Hershel Henry in Cylay

Bobcat—nickname for Paul Spurlin at the Cylay Gazette

Brian—second adult male Gualarep imported from Cicero

Carline Bryant—sister to Joey Osborn and half-sister to Dacupitte, married to Sean Bryant of the Cylay Bryant cartel

Sean Bryant—a cartel founder and sweatshop operator, husband to Carline Bryant, brothers Daniel and Patrick

Bybiis—half Borabean resident of savannah convent, staff member to Bernice Datong on Stargate Junction

Cara—Mekucoo prince and companion to Cyrus

Captain Jessup Chandliss—accompanied Brianna Miller to the jump back yacht on Earth with his detachment of 12 soldiers, later called Marnahand on Dolvia

Daniel Chin—Company executive, boss to Tuang Cho and Wan Su

Tuang Cho—Company executive and friend to Daniel Chin

Cochin—seafaring tribe beyond the Borabean who sought contracts with the Company for work as miners on asteroids

Colonel Mason Compavel—Consortium officer originally from Cochin, a descendant of Company colonists

Cyrus—1) Mekucoo warrior scarred from Company torture, 2) wild Gualarep on Siibabean land

Dacupitte—(pronounced dac-you-pit-tea) Mekucoo for "he who waits with angry eyes", their name for Hamish (Pete), the illegitimate son of Hamish Nordhagen and Heather Osborn, raised by Kecouroo

Ahmed Datong—member of clutch who remained on earth and worked with Somule Gems in China

Ankos Datong—male Earth orphan and member of the clutch of Cleo

Bernice Datong—oldest of the clutch of Cleo, agent for Somule Gems at Stargate Junction

Camille Datong—pickpocket from the clutch of Cleo brought from Earth to Dolvia, companion to Cleo

Claire Datong—middle girl of the clutch of Cleo

Cleo Datong—rescued member of clutch of Cleo Datong, touched by om

Dominic Datong—member of the clutch of Cleo

Leah Datong—leader of the clutch of Cleo

Rosalyn Datong– quartermaster of the clutch of Cleo

Saed Datong—male Earth orphan and member of the clutch of Cleo

Deborah—first wife to Kenru who organized the clutch of Deborah, later known as the daughters of Deborah

General Demali—Consortium replacement for General Hartley

Dingo—nickname for Cylahi employee of Cylay Gazette

Dkar—landlord to Hershel Henry in Cylay

Dulcinea—Uburu woman and friend to Brianna, later wife of Kyros rabbe Sudl

Frank Duerr—Cicero-born civil authority in Somule and Cylay

Ali Abrar Ebnli—biologist from Saudi Arabia helping Mike Shaw on Siibabean land

Edna—one of two female Gualareps submitted to Dr. Greensoro, later to Hakulupe Le

Edwina—one of two female Gualareps submitted to Dr. Greensboro, later to Kecouroo

Rabbenu Ely—Arrivi leader, a former revolutionary follower of Mula

Doug Endicott—manager for Company news in Cylay, left for upstart news organization in Cochin

Flash—nickname for Cylahi employee of Cylay Gazette

Genki—street vendor in Cylay who sold beans outside Hershel Henry's studio flat

Dr. Edna Edwina Greensboro—bush clinic research doctor, also known as Sheeks-Cylom, later wife to General Shaw, sons Eugene and Larry (You-Gene)

Dr. Gutierrez—researcher at Uburu digs, later at Beecham Place

Hakulupe Le—wife to Colonel Sector, mother to Millie, Anna, and Michael Peter

Hamilcar—common tribal name for Colonel Hartley, taken from Hanthudilciage which means talking-head

Billie Hartley—General Hartley's wife, mother to Carl, Heather and Jesse

Carl Hartley—son to General Hartley, one of Junction boys

Heather Hartley—General oldest daughter, named after Heather Osborn

Jesse Hartley—youngest child of Colonel and Mrs. Hartley

General Eugene Hartley—Consortium officer stationed on the orbiting transport, wife Billie

Hershel Henry—Australian born photo-journalist, also called Blancom

Imogene—member of the daughters of Deborah and arrested by Aristides in Urbyd

Jenna Le—resident of the Cylay convent and school, serving Hakulupe Le

Judell—pilot for the mail run from Stargate Junction

Karima Le—oldest sister of Arim, sometimes called May, married to Haku rabbe Murd

Karlyhi—Cylahi refugee picked up by Dr. Greensboro

Karry—older son of Kyros rabbe Sudl held captive by Borabean Goras, later called Huck Finn

Karisma—last son of Dacupitte (Pete) by Brianna Miller, raised by Dulcinea

Kat—youngest of Haku rabbe Murd and Karima Le's four children, named for her dead aunt, later a holy woman

Katelupe Le—second oldest sister of Arim, sometimes called Terry, later known as Terry the martyr and unfortunate mother to Hakulupe Le

Kecouroo—daughter to Cyrus by his first wife, raised Dacupitte, niece to Cara, a bush clinic school teacher

Kenru—Uburu leader, son to Kecouroo and uncle to Dulcinea

Klistina Le—third-born sister of Arim, sometimes called Tina, Brianna Miller's mother

Kristos—younger son of Kyros rabbe Sudl held captive by Borabean Goras, later called Tom Finn

Kyle Le—youngest sister of Arim, sometimes called Kyle Rula or Rularim, also as a businessperson called Kyle rabbe Arim, a goulep blessed with second sight. Wife of Cyrus and mother to Lynus and Rufus

Kyros—mother to Cyrus

Kyros Kenoma—later name for Kyros rabbe Sudl

George Luluki—Putuki reporter, later manager, for the Cylay Gazette

Lynus—son of Cyrus and Kyle Rula, brother to Rufus, married to Borabean Alaise

Lt. Billie Manenowski—Consortium officer, married to Vera, daughter Marsha

Voki Manuki—Putuki bazaari with six daughters

Marcy—Cylahi mulatto and one of Lucy's kids, wife to Rabbenu Ely

Mark—last of Lucy's kids, hamstrung by Siibabean, composer of chants

Marnahand—Arrivi handle for Jessup Chandliss

Marna Le—rescued cousin to Dulcinea, a diver for deep pool silicide

Martina—Martin Sumuki's oldest daughter, scarred on her eye by a former fungus growth, also known as Lula

Mica—Softcheeks soldier and companion to Captain Chandliss

John Milan—Softcheeks journalist in the days of the Uburu refugee crisis

Mildred—longtime secretary to General Hartley

Brian Miller—hero of the Company refinery battle, father to Brianna Miller by Klistina Le, a sister of Arim

Brianna Miller—daughter to Brian Miller and Klistina Le of Arim, the second Rularim

Dr. Pierre Mitterand—French research doctor completing his residency on Dolvia

Petra Mitterand—niece of Pierre Mitterand who inherited his estate

Moab—Uburu hero and short-time husband to Kecouroo in the days of Cyrus the Ketiwhelp killer

Steny Morse—third news network manager at Cylay

Haku rabbe Murd—Arrivi cattle rancher, blind and obese with old napalm burns on his face and neck, husband to Karima Le of Arim, father to Orin

Len rabbe Murd—younger son of Orin and brother to Hakki, a securities exchange clerk and newspaper printer

Orin rabbe Murd—oldest son of Haku rabbe Murd and Karima Le of Arim, father of Hakki and Len, Minister of Finance under Kyros Kenoma's rule

Spindel rabbe Murd—brother to Haku, killed on the road in the days of Martin Sumuki

Hamish Nordhagen—transport crewmember, father of Dacupitte by Heather Osborn

Ohero—Oloo hero of legend with many adventures, friend of Oria and Ohunt

Ohunt—Oloo hero of legend and architect of Utica's cadres with builder's wards

Omiibuk—wife of Karlyhi, brothers Siize and Siiloba

Onela—daughter to Onetel and friend to Bernice Datong

Onetel—Engineer on Stargate Junction working for Ambassador Otieno to refurbish freighters

Oria—mythological Arrivi warrior present in many tribal chants

Oriika—Dolviet holy woman in the seasons of Martin Sumuki

Oroc—mythological Uburu warrior present in many tribal chants

Heather Osborn—wife to colonist Carl Osborn, mother to Joey and Carline Osborn and Dacupitte (called Pete), later wife to Brian Miller

Joey Osborn—oldest child of Carl and Heather Osborn, brother to Carline, half-brother to Dacupitte (called Pete)

Karen Osborn—Joey's wife and mother to Kelly and Patrick

Kelly Osborn—chapbook poet, later wife to Rufus

Patrick Osborn—Company junior executive, one of the Junction Boys

Onela—daughter of Onetel and friend to Bernice Datong

Onetel—Striiduc engineer serving at Stargate Junction

Otieno—Striiduc ambassador seeking mining contracts from the Company

Pete—nickname for Dacupitte, illegitimate son of Heather Osborn and Hamish Nordhagen

Chantara Putivoc—Croatian botanist working on Siibabean road building project

Victor Putivoc—botanist working with Mike Shaw and husband to Chantara Putivoc

Ralph—Cicero-born male Gualarep, Mike Shaw's pet

Dr. Richardson—Softcheeks doctor at New Shanghai hospital, later at Urbyd

Rufus—younger son of Cyrus and Kyle Rula, brother to Lynus

Rularim—latter-day name for Kyle Le

Sallmus Le—staff member to Bernice Datong on Stargate Junction

Sarah—goulep and welfare minister, friend to Vera and Karen

Colonel Milo Sector—Consortium officer married to Hakulupe Le, children Millicent (Millie), Anna, and Michael Peter

General Michael Peter Shaw—Cicero born Consortium officer, married to Dr. Greensboro, sons Eugene and Larry (You-Gene)

Colonel Nick Shananinni—Consortium officer and confidant to General Sector, originally Hardhand and cousin to General Shaw

Sheek-Cylom—native name for Dr. Greensboro first given her by Karlyhi, ghostly Softcheeks

Siize—Siibabean brother to Omiibuk and Siiloba

Siiloba—Siibabean brother to Omiibuk and Siize

Dr. Spinelli—archeologist at Uburu digs

Paul Spurlin—former network dog who manages upstart gazette with Hershel Henry

Stuben—Cylahi leader of Cylay street gang, later recruit for local police

Wan Su—Company executive with Tuang Cho

Karry rabbe Sudl—a captive of Goras, later a silicide diver

Kristos rabbe Sudl—older brother to Karry and captive of Goras, later a silicide diver

Kyros rabbe Sudl—Southeast Arrivi, married to Bibi Le, sons Kristos and Karry, later known as Kyros Kenoma

Martin Sumuki—Putuki officer at Tri-City Bank Corp in the days of Brian Miller

Dr. Ned Sumuki—Putuki general practitioner at Beecham Place, nephew to Martina

Simon Sumuki—uncle to George Luluki, Minister of Justice in Cylay gov't under Kyros Kenoma

Steve Swanweil—Bryant cartel employee with connections to the Company

Terry the martyr—Katelupe Le, second oldest sister of Arim

Bobbie Ventura—Company network reporter stationed in Cylay

Vera—wife to Captain Manenowski, mother to Marsha

Regan Villines—Softcheeks journalist and friend to John Milan

Yuri– Softcheeks soldier and companion to Captain Chandliss

GLOSSARY

Terms used in Home Rule

Abydian—Borabean ruling clan, includes Ananke and Aristides

Acclimation pill—Company-issue stimulant for newly disembarking executives who experience difficulty with Dolvia's climate

Aequii—ancient Borabean god and brother to ocean god Bydquii

Agora—fishing village where remnants of the Gora clan are exiled

Airbus—an imported Consortium bus in three sections, the driver's cab, the patient section and a truckbed

Alousha—recent Borabean god in competition with Aequii and Bydquii

Arrivi—Dolviet tribe who own land and herd erriv. Their women wear full body veils with facial panels

Baktu—male Uburu garment consisting of a colorful wrap-around from waist to knees

Bald—freightate term for a person who live among the tribes without technical support

Beecham Place—later name for savannah hospital started by Dr. Abercrombie

Blackshirts—Company enforcers, some Han-Chinese and some former conscripts

Biosphere—Company built station on Cicero

Borabean—tribe living next tot he ocean north of Uburu land

Burka—required Arrivi body veil with facial panel

Bydquii—ancient Borabean god and brother to Aequii

Canyon of Buttes—Dolviet cluster of buttes within a canyon west of the savannah, a sacred area for Arrivi

Carromancy—reads the future by pouring how wax into cold water to interpret the future from the shapes

Cenzea—air laden with carbon monoxide on Uburu land near the digs

Chador—Softcheeks term for the Arrivi burka with facial panel

Chikiocahi—the middle Softcheeks plane, within Dolviet spiritual viewing, which embodies the social self, also called the chi

Chi cylay—Mekucoo phrase that translates to "pay attention".

Chrysalis—name of village that grew near the butterfly pool

Cicero—Westend planet nearest Dolvia, a member of the Consortium

Company—Han-Chinese Earth corporation with mining interests in Westend

Company logo—an off-black and eggshell white image of the long extinct Chinese giant panda roundly sitting with one paw on its knee, superimposed over a circle of mandarin yellow rimmed with royal purple

Comtech—linked screens that broadcast Company sanctioned news in public areas throughout the transport system plus at Stargate Junction

Consortium—loosely formed federation of domestic governments on the four inhabitable planets of the tri-star system in Westend which includes Dolvia and Cicero

Cylay—1) the capital city of Dolvia's savannah region, 2) one of four Mekucoo seasons when forces spread out from the source

Cylahi—poor Dolviet tribe who wear few clothes and fashion gold jewelry for a trade

Digit cohort—tribal children fitted with artificial arms after mutilated by Borabean

Dkar—landlord of Hershel Henry in Cylay

Dolvia—small planet with two moons, a ring of rain forests at its equator, plus an arid savannah region that includes the cities of Cylay and Somule

EAM—extra-atmosphere modem, a tabletop computer screen for communicating via satellite or directly with the transport. EAM-12 is text only, EAM-50 has video-conferencing

ECCAV—enclosed cross-country air-conditioned vehicle, the Consortium car

Ely—a house-and-hearth certificate demanded by ordinance of Rabbenu Ely in Cylay.

Erriv—Arrivi cattle with row of horns along the crest of the skull and neck

Eve of the Hunt—night before the ketiwhelp hunt

Feast of Oria—Arrivi high holiday that takes place after the rains

Flats of Arim—geo-thermal section of the savannah that includes geysers, bubbling mud pools and mineral springs, originally owned by Len rabbe Arim, Kyle Le's father

Fortress of Arim—manmade cave dug into the caldera wall above the flats and used as a hiding place by Kyle Le and Heather Osborn

Freightate—transport slang

Galabia—loose clothing of Borabean, typically a tunic and roomy trousers

Goulep—persona non grata ostracized by her own tribe

Gualarep—marble-hide reptile originally from Cicero that can regulate its colors, identify by scent, and throw its thoughts

Hai—Arrivi word for yes

Hamstrung—Siibabean war tactic wherein the warrior's ankle tendons are slashed crippling him for life

Han-Chinese—Earth minority group who comprise the elite pool of Company executives

Hardhand—Dolviet term for disembarking colonists who set up small trade businesses in Cylay and Somule

Heartstone—Edna's word for empathetic pain for another's suffering

HGEAM—holographic extra-atmosphere modem that projected a deep-view image of the speaker

Hiki—an Arrivi greeting

Jump back—freightate for the return to Earth through the worm hole

Junction Boys—Westend educated economists including Carl Blakesley and Patrick Osborn

Kaffiyeh—headdress of Borabean with a binding agal

Kam—Mekucoo penny, a copper twist

Kant—a lack of kari, no growth or reinforcement from Dolvia

Kari—one of four Mekucoo seasons when new growth presents itself

Kari root—medicinal herb that Dolviet men smoke as a cigarette

Kariom—Dolviet gray lungfish that hibernates in the riverbank until the ran comes, once worshipped as a god

Karkar—tribal automatic weapon, literally "stuck in kari"

Karsci—sudden shift of events with a season

Ketiwhelp—four-legged furry omnivores that plague Arrivi cattle

Kiam gin—imported alcoholic drink

Low-fic—short wave communications apparatus

Lucy's kids—eighteen mulatto Cylahi children, including Tommy and Marcy, sired by transport conscripts who Lucy Kempler takes in after their mothers die of dysentery

Maser—medicinal laser used for sealing cleansed wounds

Mayschool—common name for the Karima Le of Arim and Murd Memorial College

Mekucoo—Dolviet tribe renown as Ketiwhelp killers

Melinga—Dolviet greeting, literally "may Dolvia embrace you"

Mercy seat—Mekucoo ideal taken from Earth culture, a peaceful gathering where all parties gain something

Mida—tribal name for gum trees, a form of eucalyptus

Muezzins—orators in the temple for Borabean factions

Murmurey bird—large flesh eater that nests year-round on the savannah

Netta—1) a symbiotic balance of sulfur over silica, superheated for decades by subterranean geysers and spewed out the vents before the cooling rains to be captured on natural burlap, most often harvested by Arrivi women, 2) the longest of four Mekucoo seasons when the savannah is dormant, 3) a dry balance

Nettki—female Dolviet moon that never rises to a zenith but hovers continually at the horizon

Nettom—male Dolviet moon that passes overhead before sinking into Nettki's sky

Nu delaya—Mekucoo command to wait

Oblu—Mekucoo quarter, a silver twist

Okiioc—fibrous stalk, a staple in Siibabean diet that helps prevent cataracts and build strong teeth

Oleastra—wild olive shrubs on the savannah

Om—shortest of four Mekucoo seasons when all is made known

Onchocerciasis—river blindness caused when an internal colony of mites breeds and clouds the eyes with larvae

Putuki—Dolviet tribe who are mostly businessmen or domestic workers

Rabbenu—(pronounced ray-ben-you) a title of high honor reserved for the elected Arrivi leader

Regent—Company leader

Rigveda—Overlord to several city-states

"Rob the desert of one"—to attempt a foolish act that will kill you before the desert can

Romark—Cicero equivalent to the dollar

Second sight—the ability to discern more than is apparent

Sigpywa—oversized imported centipedes used as beast of burden by Borabean

Silicide—a form of silicone created in the absence of oxygen (as part of a meteor shower) and found in deposits on Madquii land and the flats of Arim

Siibabean—traditional Mekucoo enemies, tall and lean with perfect teeth, who wear a halo headdress of Murmurey feathers

Smogen—Striiduc for companion or colleague

Softcheeks—a Dolviet term for Earthlings including Company executives

Somule—the Dolvia savannah city closest to the flats of Arim

Somule Gems—major Westend company to grow out of the treasure of Kyle Rula

Sor'shum—native word for Consortium, used especially during street protests

Stargate Junction—the space station at Westend's wormhole entrance

Stroenuk—(strew-knock) outcasts of a Striiduc tribe, some with spiritual powers.

Tektite—meteor stone found all over the savannah and said to enhance native skills of telepathy or skills of second sight

Travel number—permission to jump back to Earth by way of Company shipping routes through the worm hole

Treasure of Kyle Rula—a chest containing peridot and topaz gems and Cylahi gold jewelry plus some natural netta that had been offered over time as bribes to Captain Ellis to ensure Katelupe Le's relative health in the Company prison

"Three planes of Softcheeks"—within second sight, how Softcheeks but not Hardhands appear to Dolviets

Tunanin—dust columns on the savannah, ancestral spirit who survey the land before the rains

Two Forks—a Cicero city where Mike Shaw's parents had a farm

Tzu—Company-made laser gun

Uburu—a southern mesa tribe

Uburu digs—archeologist site visited by Softcheeks scientists

Unblessed ones—residents of Cylay slums who lived in conditions so grim, they were unblessed by Dolvia

Urbyd—Borabean capital city

Westend—a space quadrant beyond the wormhole and loosely ruled by the Consortium

Wormhole—the connecting time-compressed space anomaly between Earth's solar system and Westend

ABOUT
THE AUTHOR

STELLA ATRIUM IS A CYNICAL SEPTUAGENARIAN. SHE HAS SPENT a lifetime exploring female characters for real world reactions to obstacles. Often pushed into submissive and non-verbal roles, women really live in a world of networking among aunties, cousins, wives of husbands, convenient friends and neighbors. This rich world is largely unexplored.

"I grew up with all brothers, so I knew about women from stories and from school. What I found at school wasn't anything like in the stories, so I set out to learn why."

If you enjoyed *Home Rule*, leave a reader review on Amazon or Goodreads. Visit Stella's website to order the prequel, *Brittany Mill: A Dolvia Origins Story,* at stellaatrium.com.